CANNI

DANIEL O'CONNOR

ISBN:978-1-940250-38-0

This book is a work of fiction. Names, characters, business organizations, places, events and incidents either are the product of the author's imagination or are used fictitiously. Any resemblance to actual persons, living or dead, events or locales is entirely coincidental.

Artwork by Andrej Bartulovic

Interior Layout by Lori Michelle
     www.theauthorsalley.com

Printed in the United States of America

First Edition

Visit us on the web at:
www.bloodboundbooks.net

ALSO FROM
BLOOD BOUND BOOKS:

This book is dedicated to you.

FOR A HEART DRAINED OF LOVE,
ONLY BLOOD REMAINS.

Owatonna, Minnesota

Sterile.

It was all Wilk could think of as he captained the roaring Freightliner snow plow through the white-blanketed streets. People often asked him why he never got sick. They thought he'd be a prime candidate for pneumonia—up at 3:00 AM, out in constant sub-zero temperatures, clearing the roads while the commuters were still snug in their beds.

Yet, he couldn't remember the last time he'd even had the sniffles.

He thought it was an old wives' tale that *the* cold could give one *a* cold. The common cold was caused by viruses. That much he knew. He also refused to believe that viruses could flourish in this barren snow globe, where snot turned to icicle before the hanky left the pocket. It all just looked and felt so virginal. There weren't even any smells.

Wilk thought back to when, as a child in winter, he'd held little wood frogs in his hand. They were frozen solid, like some unearthed Himalayan cavemen. He and his friends would return to their swampy habitat as spring approached, to watch the amphibians "come back to life".

That is how cold his world was.

How sterile.

He bundled in layers. Serious layers. Thermal underwear, sweatshirt, sweater, hoodie, insulated jacket with high collar, three-hole balaclava over his face, hood on top of that.

Sticking out of all of that was the green and gold of a well-worn Minnesota North Stars cap. The NHL team had relocated to Dallas decades before, but they had seized his heart when he was young, and that is where they endured, like a first love.

He motored past the frozen skeleton of a structure called River Springs Water Park. He liked to recall bustling summer days when he'd taken his son and daughter for some fun in the sun. The park would live again come June.

But it was winter that paid his bills.

The plow fought its way through nearly three feet of fresh, white powder. The sound of the enormous scraper, combined with the rumbling of his 450 HP turbocharged engine, provided the bass and drum to some melody only in Wilk's head. While his subconscious mind composed a song of the various sounds, he was lamenting the fact, as always, that his North Stars never got to hoist a Stanley Cup, when he hit it.

Thump.

"Okey-dokey," he mumbled.

He could have blasted through, but he stopped the plow. The snow still came. Sideways. But, he was the type to do the right thing. He preached it to his kids, so he had to do it himself. He'd once hit a Siberian Husky, but he determined that the animal had previously died in the street and was covered over by the storm. He knew this because he dug it out and it was frozen as solid as those wood frogs. Usually, a *thump* was from some buried trash bags or other junk that had found its way into the path of his rig. He'd come across an old air conditioner, and even a broken office chair with a naked mannequin taped to the seat. Pranksters would sometimes bury things in the high snow just to fuck with the plow operators. He didn't understand the pleasure of screwing with the working folk, but he couldn't come to terms with a lot of things people did. He had once struck a hefty, snow-buried, Igloo cooler, still packed with cans of Surly Furious beer. He and his fellow plowmen divvied up the crimson-hued ale, but Wilk kept the cooler. Months later, he got stopped trying to lug the cooler, packed with sandwiches, snacks, and fruit drinks, into River Springs Water Park.

The sight of the bulky, clothing-layered Wilk descending from the truck cab might bring to mind an image of Neil Armstrong departing the lunar module. His first boot print in the snow was the only such impression for as far as the eye could see. He carried, not Armstrong's Stars and Stripes, but a long-handled, steel snow shovel.

He trudged around to the front of the plow, vapor blasting through his mouth like a steam locomotive. With no idea what was buried in the snow, he employed his shovel with prudence.

No reason to damage the blade.

He cautiously lifted a few inches of snow and tossed it aside. Flakes attacked his eyes, circling in the wind like frantic gnats. Another couple of shovel scrapes and he hit it.

It was reasonably hard, yet felt moderately pliable. This was no air conditioner.

Time for some hand-digging. He knelt. His thick gloves brushed the powder aside, increasing in speed until he uncovered something. He could, initially, only see about a two-inch window of it.

Black. Maybe leather. He thought it might be a purse, or even a small suitcase. Further digging proved otherwise. It was a boot. Fancy women's kind.

Worst of all, it was still on a foot.

Wilk dug like a hungry badger. Once he saw her leg, he quickly scurried over to uncover her head, in the faint hope that he might revive her.

That was before his digging revealed the frozen blood. Looked like someone had dropped a case of cherry snow cones. He furrowed past the first layer of red. There was her face. Seemed like she took pride in her manicured eyebrows, but the green eyes below them were wide as the Minnesota Plains, and her mouth was agape, filled with snow, and frozen in her final horror. Her left cheek was gone.

He removed one of his gloves. The frosty air bit at his skin. He felt her crimson-caked neck for a pulse, but only grasped the chafe of ice. He pressed harder, and his fingers penetrated a wound he hadn't detected. It had been camouflaged by the frigid blanket of blood.

He mumbled the phrase he would utter to himself no matter if he had just been handed two nickels in change or, apparently, discovered an eviscerated corpse.

"Okey-dokey."

Bill Smith's plow had come from the other end of St. Paul Road. The two rigs faced each other, framing the body of the exhumed woman between their scrapers. Smith was so tall and lean that he didn't appear to be the bulky Sasquatch that was Wilk, even with his own layers keeping him warm. Smith was Wilk's most trusted ally. He was like an older brother.

"Oh ya, she's a goner," Smith said, as he knelt beside the body. Wilk stood behind him.

"You betcha," replied his friend. "The police are on the way."

"Ya think maybe it was a bear or something?" asked Smith.

"Crossed my mind, don'tcha know. Didn't see no tracks of any kind. Everything was all snowed over and such."

Bill Smith had retired from a career in public relations, and just loved operating the plow. He had the oddball trait of being the only Boston Bruins fan that anyone around Owatonna knew. No one held it against him. Worse was probably the fact that he had the exact name of a New York Islanders goalie who had been instrumental in denying the North Stars a Stanley Cup. The boys never let him live that down.

Smith stared down at the woman. Wilk coughed behind him.

Whatever, or whoever, did this, thought Smith, *wanted her neck exposed.*

There was no sign of a scarf, which she almost surely would have worn. It was probably covered over nearby. He couldn't help but stare into her eyes. He pondered what image she may have taken to her grave. He didn't want to contaminate the crime scene any further, so he decided to stand up and back away, but he couldn't turn away from her green eyes. Something inside him, inexplicably, half-expected her to awaken. Pure nonsense, but it did cross his mind.

Bill Smith, as a child, had also played with the wood frogs. He'd seen things return from the "dead". He was contemplating the frogs, most of which were brown, or tan, and how he had occasionally uncovered a green one. They were green as the gaze from this dead woman's irises.

That was the final reflection he had before his lifelong buddy, Wilk, killed him.

DANIEL O'CONNOR

Lake Elsinore, California

The vibrant green of the dress was what struck her. That, and the fact that the alternating vertical lines of the painted garment did appear to be true black. But the green lines were much wider, and the color leaped from the lower half of the photograph.

Still, she had read that Claude Monet avoided true black in his work, preferring to create a similar color through the blending of others.

The crash course in Monet, and the painters of Impressionism in general, was undertaken because she was about to meet the nineteen-year-old daughter of her new beau for the first time. The girl was almost fanatical about art—and Monet in particular. Knowing a bit about him could be an ice-breaker for Anita Chuang.

She didn't want to screw this relationship up the way she did her marriage. Twenty-five years down the drain. She was well-off enough; her relocated medical practice was doing fine. She could afford the finer things in life.

But there was a hole in her heart.

It felt like Edgar might be the one to fill it. It was important to make a positive impression on his daughter, Verde. She was the greatest joy in Edgar's life, and Anita desperately wanted to connect with her.

The month of March in Lake Elsinore rarely prohibits leisurely outdoor activities, so the barbeque was fired up in the lush backyard. It was a perfect seventy-three degrees.

As the briquettes changed color on the rear patio, Anita put down the book on Claude Monet. It was the third one she'd read that week.

Her plan was to gently introduce Verde to some delicious vegan burgers, and to also share her love of classical music. Appreciating its joys was not much different than enjoying art-on-canvas. There was color in music, too. The attractive doctor removed her 180-gram vinyl edition of Wolfgang Amadeus Mozart's *Symphony No. 41 in C Major* from its rice paper sleeve, and placed it on her Rega P8 turntable, running a soft brush across its grooves. This particular version, by Herbert Von Karajan and the Berlin Philharmonic Orchestra, had always been her favorite. She loved that it was recorded in 1970, the year of her birth. This particular piece had a strength about it, almost a finality, that felt reassuring.

Doorbell.

Mozart filled the room, the barbeque grew hotter, and the burgers— painstakingly crafted from chickpeas, sweetcorn, and a host of seasonings—chilled in the fridge. The oven was still warm from her homemade buns—whisked together from flax egg, non-dairy milk, coconut oil, and pink

Himalayan salt. Dr. Chuang carefully arranged the three art books on her table, hurriedly fixed her black hair for the umpteenth time, and scampered to greet her visitors.

"You can't tell me this is not flesh. This is insane!" smiled Verde, as she swallowed Anita's meatless creation.

"Told you," laughed Edgar.

"Thank you, Verde. I'm glad you enjoy it. No meat at all. Promise," replied Anita.

The music played softly from small B&W patio speakers wired to the main system. They were no match for the majesty of the Magnepan Tympani flat-panels that delivered the classics in the doctor's living room, but they got the job done.

Anita noticed Verde's head nodding a bit to the symphony.

"Rocking out to my Mozart, are you?" she chuckled.

"A little, yeah. It's not the Foo Fighters, but I can see why you dig it."

"Well, that's nice to hear from someone your age."

"She's quite open-minded," added Edgar.

"There aren't too many teenagers with such a love for Claude Monet," said Anita, as she poured more Cabernet Sauvignon for herself and Edgar. Verde's glass was still full of Coke Zero.

"I'm almost twenty," answered Verde.

"Still a teenager," smiled her father.

"Well, Claude is the man," said Verde. "I saw your books inside, Ms. Chuang—or should I call you Doctor?"

"Please call me Anita. When you come for an office visit, you can call me Doctor," she smiled.

"Cool. Dad says you're gonna give me my HPV shots."

"If that's what he wants—well, if that's what _you_ want."

"Sweet." She took another bite of her burger. After chewing, she added, "Yeah, keep all those viruses away from me, please. Freaking bird flu, ebola, all of that stuff."

"You don't have to be concerned with any of that," said Anita.

"They said on the internet that all kinds of people in Africa have died from Ebola and then, like, came back from the dead. There's some ABC News footage of it, too."

"Oh, Verde," said Edgar.

"Dad, I'll show you the video on my phone."

"It's likely they were all near death, and presumed dead by non-professionals," said Anita. "I promise you, none of them were dead. There may have been clinical death in some, but we have that every day, where we can sometimes revive people, if caught in time."

"Some dude was being *buried* when he popped his butt up again."

Anita laughed, "That was someone's mistake. I wouldn't want to be that doctor!"

"Right?" said Verde.

"The internet," said Edgar, "is as terrible as it is wonderful."

"Dad . . ."

"It's packed with bullies," he said, "You should only know the things they have written to, and about, my daughter, Anita."

"I'd say that's more the fault of humanity, and a likely lack of parenting, than of the internet itself," replied the doctor.

"Nailed it," said Verde. "People are rude."

"In those art books," said Anita, switching topics to lighten the mood, "I found myself drawn to that painting of the lady in the green and black dress."

Verde's eyes darted up.

"Oh, for sure. *The Woman in the Green Dress* is what it's called. That's Camille!"

"Camille?"

"Monet's wife. You haven't read *all* of those books, have you?" she laughed, sipping her soda.

"You know, I think I spent most of the time looking at the photos of his paintings."

"Then, they achieved his goal. They drew you in. Text be damned, Anita Chuang is gonna enjoy the art!"

They all laughed. The Berlin Philharmonic were kicking ass.

"In all honesty, and I do try to be honest, I'm not such a fan of all the water lilies. Seems a bit much for me . . ."

"But . . ."

"Wait a second," laughed Anita, "I really loved a lot of his work, but I can't tell you how many water lily paintings of his I've looked at this week, and I never saw even one frog. Have you?"

Verde sat still for a moment.

"I . . . I never thought of that. He has hundreds of lily paintings. There must be a frog in there. Could appear to be just a smudge of paint, but surely there is one somewhere. Unless the presence of a frog might deter from the peacefulness of the work . . ."

"The absence of frogs," said Edgar, as he gulped his wine.

"What does it all mean?" giggled Anita, discerning the initial effects of her alcohol. "Who is up for the next round of veggie burgers?"

"It's not about the meaning," said Verde. "Monet said it was not necessary to understand, only to love. He wanted people to feel something from his work, not to read into it."

"Wow. That's nice," said Anita. "I did feel things from a lot of it. Oh, I put some titles in my phone—hang on."

She slid the screen door aside and entered the house. Edgar looked at his daughter.

"Do you like her?" he whispered.

"Yeah. She's cool."

"Did you want another round of burgers?" he asked.

"Oh, no. Can't get fat. Internet bullies, you know."

"*The Parc Monceau Paris,*" came the shout from inside. "That's one of the better ones, to me."

Anita appeared again as the sliding door squeaked. "I also liked—let me see . . . " She looked down at her phone, "*The Garden at Argenteuil.*"

"Yes, the dahlias," answered Verde. "So beautiful."

"And I already mentioned the green dress."

"A favorite of mine too," said Verde, "She seems ready to go out and have a wonderful time—I mean Camille, in the painting. I often wonder where she was going, and what it was like to live then. I mean, in this country, that was the world of Abraham Lincoln. What was life like in Monet's France?"

"American Civil War," said her father. "Not a great time to be alive. As for France, weren't they invading Mexico around that time? Talk about HPV shots—the list of deadly diseases back then was enormous. Am I right, Anita?"

"Yes, *Debbie Downer,* medicine has come a long way."

"Camille died at thirty-two," said Verde. "Monet painted her on her death bed. Compare the lack of color in that painting to the earlier ones. He felt guilty because as she lay dying, he found interest in the colors that death brought to her face."

"I saw that painting in one of the books. How sad."

"I don't recall seeing that one," said Edgar.

"I've showed it to you, Dad. How could you forget that one?"

Thip . . . thip . . . thip . . .

"End of the record," said Anita. "The better the turntable, the fewer convenience features. The mysteries of high-end audio. I have to lift the tonearm myself and put on another record. I'll bring the Monet books out so you can show your father the painting."

"I can type *Camille on Her Death Bed* on my phone and get an image up," said Verde.

"The picture in the book is much larger," replied Anita.

Thip . . . thip . . . thip . . .

"True. Monet deserves better than a phone screen."

"Also, the sound of that record stylus is making me bonkers," said Anita. "I'll be right back."

The squeak of the screen door.

Thip . . . thip . . . thip . . .

With Anita inside the house, Edgar touched his daughter's hand.

"I can tell she likes you a whole lot," he said. "That makes your old dad happy."

He inhaled the pleasant, arid air, and decided he might just want another burger. He thought about getting up and tossing one on the barbeque himself, but Anita had such a way with cooking, that he'd surely fall short in some manner—even with a task as simple as pseudo-meat on a hot grill. The setting sun flickered through the fluttering leaves of the California Ash tree behind him. Its warm rays danced on the back wall of Anita's home. She'd told him it reminded her of glittering diamonds. He thought more of the flaring bare light bulb that hung above his childhood bed.

"We should bring her to the Getty Museum to see some legit Monet. She'd like that, Dad."

He leaned in and whispered, "But we always grab hot dogs there. She wouldn't be too keen on that."

"You're funny. They have veggie meals. I almost got one last time."

Thip . . . thip . . . thip . . .

"I wonder what album she'll put on next? Maybe Nirvana," he joked.

"I wish. Or the Pixies."

Edgar marveled at how his little girl wasn't even born when most of her favorite bands broke through. He recalled taking her to see Weezer in Anaheim around the time of her eighteenth birthday.

Thip . . . thip . . . thip . . .

He reached down for his glass to finish that last smidgen of wine.

That was when Dr. Anita Chuang came crashing through the screen door to kill him.

She ended Verde's life beside the toppled barbeque and the next round of burgers.

CANNI

Mohave County, Arizona

"They aren't fucking zombies," she said. "They're alive and breathing just as you are, asshole."

Not the lovely nothings one might expect to float from the mouth of a bride-to-be in the days before her wedding.

Well, it's not like she agreed to be married in Vegas, but *he* was hoping for it.

"I'm sorry, Cash" he replied. "I wasn't referring to your uncle—but some of those people around him . . . "

The uncle in question is the one who may have given her the nickname, "Cash". She also doesn't agree that ever happened, but *he* swears he heard it. *He* is her boyfriend—sometimes barely—and he was behind the wheel of a 1983 Malibu sedan, with Cash beside him, and her best friend, Teresa, in the back seat. They were all considerably younger than the Chevy, but old enough for a vacation in Vegas, with the possibility of nuptials slightly more likely than three 7s on the slot reels. Nearing the end of a week-long trek from New York to Nevada, they hurtled through the bleak night on a black strip of highway that, from far enough above, looked like a piece of thread dropped randomly in an enormous, mountainous desert. Almost two hours till a warm sunrise, and there had been no other cars for miles, not since some clowns in a dirty red pickup tossed a bag of Taco Bell refuse out their truck window and onto the road.

Cash was still pissed about the callous zombie remark as they entered a little sliver of Arizona, on I-15, between Utah and Nevada. Her boyfriend's given name was Winthrop, in tribute to a great-grandfather who was a tobacconist of some note. He learned early on that it was much too fancy and regal a name for a kid bumming around Brooklyn, so he took to calling himself Rob. It was his middle name—Robert. Cash's real name, and the one most people other than Rob called her, was Caroline. Winthrop and Caroline. Could be a king and queen. But in the then and there, and for as long as the world would permit them to grace each other, they were Rob and Cash.

"Calling them zombies? That's probably the worst thing I've ever heard out of your mouth, Rob. And that's saying a lot. They are heavily medicated."

Teresa remained quiet in the back seat, staring out the side window, taking in the dancing moon shadows of the desert and tweeting on her iPhone. Cash pulled up on the door lock button beside her, then, pushed it down again. She repeated the action a second time. Rob had seen her do this repeatedly during the road trip, had occasionally promised her that the door was indeed locked, but knew better than to offer any reassurances this time.

He knew his foot was already ankle deep in his mouth, and he was formulating a meaningful apology in his mind. He'd tried to be funny with his "zombie" comment, but knew it sounded wrong even as it rode out upon his truck stop burrito breath. Cash's Uncle Reg had been a New York City cop for 25 years. He was always kind to his niece, and the joker of what remained of her broken family. A steady buildup of plaque in his brain had changed him from a vibrant soul into a shell of his former self. So much so that he had difficulty remembering and identifying even those closest to him, and he found himself, though only sixty years old, in an assisted living facility. Rob had referred to some of the older patients as "zombies" for how they ambled through the corridors the last time he and Cash had visited—just before they left on their cross-country journey. Rob and Cash had been talking recently about how she earned that nickname. He said that Uncle Reg called her that the first time Rob met him, but she swore that no one had ever used that name before Rob.

He tried to lighten the mood with a running gag that he usually enjoyed a lot more than Cash

"Wanna start a band?" he asked with a grin.

"What would we call it?" she answered robotically, with an obvious lack of gusto.

"Rick Wakeman's Cape."

"I don't even get it," she sighed.

He was pondering an explanation, or an apology, when he saw the lights in his mirror.

Cops.

The red and blue illuminated the night sky and coated the mountains with color. The car approached quickly, but sans siren.

"Damn it," sighed Rob. "I wasn't going *that* fast."

Teresa surfaced from her boredom in the back seat, mumbling about a pimple and closing her hand mirror. She turned her head to peer out the rear window. The interior of Rob's Chevrolet had the look of a night club, or maybe, in this particularly old vehicle, a disco, as the lights streamed in from behind. The sedan got right on their bumper, and just as Rob began to pull over, it quickly crossed into the left lane to pass them.

Relief.

Rob looked over at the police car as it passed. They all did.

Male officer driving, female cop in the passenger seat, facing backwards. A third figure was caged in the rear of the marked sedan, behind the steel-framed partition.

Some type of bag over its head.

The hooded rider was thrashing wildly, arms cuffed behind the back. The covered head smashed against the side window of the police vehicle just as it passed Rob's car, fracturing the thick glass.

"What the hell?" was all Rob could muster. "Did you guys see that?"

"Creepy," said Cash.

CANNI

"Wonder what the one in back is trippin' on?" asked Teresa, as she leaned forward.

"But did you *really* see the one in back?" asked Rob. "Did you see the *uniform?*"

"Huh?"

"He was a cop too."

DANIEL O'CONNOR

East Islip, New York

The plumber had arrived promptly, just after the kids headed out for school. He was friendly and professional, and he promised to get Joyce McDougald's kitchen drain clear.

Stereotype, she thought, holding back a chuckle. *This chubby fella is gonna fix what neither my coat hanger snake, plunger, or three containers of ultra-heavy duty, foaming, sizzling, industrial strength liquid gel acid rain unclogger could do—and here I am thinking of plumber butt jokes.*

His rump divider protruded from the top of his pants as his lower half protruded from the cabinet beneath her sink.

"I'll have this done in no time," came his muffled promise. Joyce could see his arms moving and hear wrench-versus-pipe percussion. Sweat began to bead on his exposed back, like grease on an undercooked bacon slab. The thought of a droplet sliding down his cheeky crevice was too much, and caused her to turn, coffee in hand, to admire the refrigerator artwork of her twins.

"Take your time," she replied. "Just happy that you're here!"

The Long Island sun steamed in her kitchen window as *Good Morning America* could be heard from the living room plasma. She was a bit concerned that this workman would do what so many others had, and charge her more than the agreed-upon estimate, after discovering some "complications" during the repair.

While studying her son's Crayola portraits of various X-Men, she thought she heard the plumber sneeze.

"Bless you."

No reply.

She gazed down at all of the bottles and cans on the tiles surrounding the repairman's feet; the stuff that would normally occupy the space under the sink; floor cleaner, furniture polish, a clear, label-less, bottle of smoky, topaz brown, mystery liquid.

I really need to go through all this junk before I put it back in the cabinet, she thought, as coffee aroma filled her nostrils.

Sounded like his wrench dropped.

He was still for a moment; exposed back sweat droplets evolving into tiny puddles.

Then his leg twitched.

"You okay, sir?"

Expecting to hear something like, "Yep, be done in a jiffy," Joyce jumped when his legs began kicking about like a bullfrog on ice. The bottles and cans went flying in all directions, smashing and rattling throughout the sunny kitchen. She feared the worst, as grunts and growls came from beneath the sink.

CANNI

Oh God, my drain-cleaning acid spilled out of the pipes onto his face!

She reasonably envisioned that particular scenario to be "The Worst".

It wasn't.

Good Morning America had gone to commercial. The early spring birds could be heard singing outside of Joyce's quaint ranch home. They danced on the hedge that sat just below her bow window. A former NFL great blared from the television about how his aging prostate no longer kept him awake at night.

In the kitchen, Joyce McDougald was already dead on the floor.

Her blood snaked across the beveled tiles, gravity filling in the crevices like some grand design. It mixed with the spilled floor cleaner and smoky topaz liquid, and pooled up at the bottom of the refrigerator, below the X-Men drawings.

DANIEL O'CONNOR

Mojave County, Arizona

Fifteen minutes had elapsed since the speeding police car had passed Rob's old Chevy. They weren't getting much reception on the car radio, so Cash and Teresa knew Rob would resort to the dreaded 8-track player. The decades old car, including the ancient tape deck, and the assortment of music cartridges, were all that the young man received after his drunken father fell asleep with a Camel in his hand and turned everything, himself included, to ash. Seems the only thing Rob's dad cared about was that car and its V-8 engine, so it was in great shape, and like vinyl records—and maybe even 8-tracks—it was slowly transforming from a funny oddity in most people's minds, to being rather *cool*.

So Cash and Teresa couldn't get Lady Gaga or Rihanna on the radio, but they did get the first album by Bachman-Turner Overdrive, and the pounding anthem "Stayed Awake All Night", which was quite appropriate. Rob sang along with every word, as he could to most any song in his late father's collection. Scary thought for the two female riders: after several days in the Malibu, they were learning some of the songs too. They'd made a bit of a pact to distance themselves from the real world during this journey, avoiding radio news and not checking websites that could ruin their escape. Still, some news was just too big to avoid entirely.

"I am so tired," yawned Cash.

"We'll be in Vegas in like an hour!" replied Rob. "The home of the coolest weddings on the planet!"

"Hmmm."

"Come on, you've even got your maid of honor in the back seat!"

He turned back to Teresa, who flashed a sympathetic, heartfelt, and groggy smile.

"I need to sleep, baby," said Cash.

"Well, our Vegas hotel will definitely be a lot nicer than the shitholes we've stayed in along the way," he replied, as they approached a curve in the road.

"That'll be pretty sweet," said Cash as her eyelids slid down. The 8-track was between songs, and brief seconds of nothing but soothing tape hiss blanketed the car as Cash rested her head against the window. Sleep called.

The freeway sign read: VALLEY OF FIRE.

"Holy shit!" yelled Rob, trashing the tranquility.

Cash came back to life. Teresa leaned forward, her head coming between her friends.

"Wha . . . ", she whispered as she saw it. Rob shut down the tape deck.

There, again, was the police car.

It was off the road, twenty yards into the dark desert landscape. It had crashed into, and nearly uprooted, a Joshua tree. Smoke escaped from beneath the crushed front end that consumed the yucca palm. The overhead lights still flickered red and blue. A tractor-trailer was stopped at the side of the freeway, flashers on. Rob and the girls could see the truck driver sprinting toward the police car.

"We've gotta help," said Rob, as he slowed and pulled over in front of the semi. He looked at Teresa, "T, call 911."

She fumbled with her phone, "Where the hell are we, exactly?"

Rob was out the door, Cash just behind him. They darted across the brush. The trucker was on the far side of the car, where both passenger side windows had been smashed. The air bags had deployed. As they were almost at the vehicle, they could see the truck driver opening the back door.

The handcuffed rear seat passenger, with a hood over his head, and a cop uniform on his large body, jumped from the smoky vehicle, nearly knocking the burly trucker to the ground. His yells were muffled by the head-cover. There was no gun belt around his waist.

"Settle down," said the semi driver, in a southern drawl. "I'm takin' that hood off, but them cuffs is stayin' on, big fella."

Just as Rob, then Cash, reached the accident scene, the hood was pulled off. Rob ignored that, as he ran to the front seats. The officer behind the wheel was obviously dead—his head down at a difficult angle. What remained of his face was bathed in syrupy blood. His neck had been torn apart. The female cop, who had been in the passenger seat, was nowhere to be found.

Cash hadn't seen any of that, but she trembled nonetheless, as she saw the big cop's hood come off. He was pale and sweaty, snot stringing from nose to lips, eyes bloodshot, with rusty caking around his mouth.

Dried blood. Parched vomit.

The stench of his breath smothered Cash's nostrils from five feet away, but it was his eyes that commanded her stare. Sure, they were red, but Cash had seen swollen eye vessels and discolored sclerae before, though never accompanied by such ghostly white pupils. Yet it was the brilliance of the red that kept her transfixed.

More red than blood, she thought. *Redder than fire or rubies.* Her mind raced in search of a comparable color. Nothing seemed appropriate.

Back in the Malibu, Teresa gripped her phone. A single car passed her window but continued into the early morning darkness. The bright lights from the idling tractor-trailer cut through the misty black and into the rear window of the Chevy.

"I . . . I know we're on Interstate 15 . . . not sure if it's Utah, Arizona or Nevada. Wait, not Utah. We left Utah. I think it's Arizona . . . "

Cash took another step back from the handcuffed cop as the trucker tried to settle him down, yet she still focused on those eyes. Rob emerged from the front seat and tried to scan his surroundings for the missing female officer. It was all red and blue from the police lights, but beyond that immediate area, only pitch-black desert.

The big, sweaty officer finally formulated a sentence.

"God, what have I done?"

Cash felt wobbly. Her most recent meal wanted out.

"Tell me exactly what happened, partner," drawled the trucker.

Teresa's frustration grew in the Chevy.

"I'm doing the best I can. Maybe I can use my phone's GPS . . . "

Behind her, outside, by the trunk of the Malibu, silhouetted by the harsh lights of the empty truck, moved a figure.

"You did all this here?" asked the trucker of the ranting cop.

No answer. Moist, crimson eyes. Maybe a slight head shake.

Rob grabbed the arm of the inquisitive driver as Cash looked on. He whispered in his ruddy ear, "Did you see the dead cop behind the wheel?"

"Uh-huh."

"Looks like his throat is basically gone."

"Yeah."

"Well," continued Rob, "I'm no detective, but I can't see how this guy did any of this, while handcuffed, hooded, and locked behind a cage in the back of the car."

Cash was dizzy from the horror and the whirling police lights. She tore herself away from those eyes, leaned her backside on the crushed passenger side fender, and gazed out into the cobalt and crimson darkness.

She muttered something for Rob to hear, but he was too engaged with the rig operator to notice.

"Red," she said. "More red than blood or fire."

Her head turned one more time toward the big, handcuffed cop. One more look at the eyes.

"Red, like a devil."

Back in the old Chevy, Teresa had some words for the 911 operator.

"This is insane. I'm gonna get out and look for a highway marker. Do you at least have someone headed in this direction?"

She slid over toward the door, bathed in the light from behind.

"Don't you hang up on me now."

She opened the door and it hit something. A leg. He was standing right there.

"Fuck me!" she yelled, almost involuntarily.

"I'll definitely file that request," he replied. "But for now, I'm just checking to see if you're okay."

CANNI

He was tall, smiling, Asian, and clutching a motorcycle helmet. Teresa's heart returned to its designated position.

"Can you tell this operator exactly where we are?"

Rob continued whispering with the trucker as the shackled cop whimpered and cried. Cash was feeling a bit stronger since leaning on the wrecked police car. She once again forced her focus on the oddly comforting darkness of cactus and brush.

Something, in the distance, moved.

Just a shadow from all these damned dancing lights, she thought.

Then, out of the black it came, into the red and blue wash.

"Rob . . . "

He was deep into his discussion with the big rigger.

The figure zig-zagged just a bit as it approached.

"Babe . . . "

Both men turned toward Cash. She just lazily raised her arm to point behind them.

Apparently not an animal, it was indeed a human form that approached from the dry wild.

"Who's out there?" yelled the trucker. The fettered cop slowly raised his head to observe.

"Uncuff me," was all he mumbled.

"Hello? Who is that?" hollered the rig driver, even more loudly.

Rob stepped over to get between Cash and the approaching roamer. There was no response to the trucker's calls as it trudged closer.

"Fuck this," declared Cash as she suddenly bolted into the front seat of the police car. She tried not to notice the soaking warm blood or bits of torn flesh that adorned the uniform of the dead officer behind the wheel. She held her breath to avoid the powdery chemical stench of the air bags. Cash just wanted a gun. She could hear Rob and the truck driver continue to call out to the desert walker. Her fingers managed to pop open the plasma-soaked button strap, but she couldn't get the weapon out of the belt holster.

She thought she could now hear the approaching footsteps in the brush. Her palms were covered with blood as she finally thought to tilt the gun forward before trying to pull it out.

That worked. She had the pistol.

Cash crawled backwards out of the car and spun to face the advancing visitant.

It was clear now. This was the missing female cop. Cash initially had the gun raised but began to lower it. Then she saw the face of the diminutive woman. Pale, wide-eyed, and with that caked vomit/blood composite around her mouth. Same as the big cop. Blood all over the front of her uniform too.

Cash brought the gun back up. She flashed back to when her Uncle Reg had taken her to the NYPD range to shoot, and then on to the Statue of Liberty. She couldn't, however, dismiss the nagging fact that blood covered her hands. Felt like it was gluing the weapon to her palms. All Cash wanted was to scrub herself from the elbows down. But that would have to wait.

The approaching officer said nothing. Her arms were to her side. A gun dangled from her right hand.

"What's this all about?" yelled Rob.

The cop didn't even look his way. Her white pupils seemed trained on the interior of the police car.

"D-Don't come any closer!" yelled Cash, not even sure if she could ever pull the trigger. She could feel the cold steel adhering to her skin. Felt like drying mucus. She needed to scour her hands.

But the catatonic cop kept coming.

"I told you to *stop*!" demanded Cash.

"Please uncuff me," repeated the big male officer, to no avail.

Just then, the bloody female cop stopped. Cash's hands trembled.

"You want me to take that gun from you, baby?" whispered Rob.

"No."

The uniformed woman stared into the vehicle at the murdered policeman behind the wheel. From the opposite direction came Teresa, her new biker friend—who was recording the scene with his phone—and a couple of other travelers who had just stopped to help. Teresa saw her best friend aiming a gun at one ghoulish-looking cop, while another stood handcuffed beside an old trucker.

The female officer's eyes never moved from the sight of her slaughtered partner. She slowly raised her handgun. Cash almost pulled the trigger, especially when she got a good look at the eyes—red like a devil—but something stopped her. The impassive cop put the gun to her own right temple and blew off the top of her head.

Screams and gasps.

Cash dropped the weapon she'd been holding and fell to her knees. Rob engulfed her. Instinctively, she scraped her hands against the sandy ground below her, trying to get rid of the blood, but it only stuck the dirt to her, like breading.

The burly officer, arms still shackled behind him, redness fading from his eyes, had some words for Cash that cut right through the night air.

"Fuck it. Keep that gun. Take hers too. You'll need them."

CANNI

Evans City, Pennsylvania

Father and daughter. They relished sunny days because they could make shadow hand puppets. Their silhouettes were strong and deep against the concrete. His shadow was much larger, of course. It was crouched, and he was just forward of his daughter. Her shadow showed her pigtails quite clearly, as well as the spokes of her wheelchair. There was a big blue chalk-drawn heart containing the words "Daddy loves Bug" on their cement screen.

"A bird is an easy one, Daddy!" she laughed.

Her hands formed the wings as she easily outdid her father's attempt.

They looked, not at each other, but directly down as each of their creations appeared.

"You're too good for me, sweetheart."

"I get a lot of practice."

"I really need to work on my shadow puppets," he laughed.

"Here's my goat," she said. "Yes, his name is Billy."

"I love that one," he replied, as she used both hands to form a great looking creature including horns and dangling chin hair.

"You can make Billy, too. Just keep at it," she told him.

The shadow of her head titled just a bit as her arms formed something of a long neck.

"Make your hands into a big tree," she told her father.

He opened his five fingers widely. The best he could come up with. Her hands formed a head.

"A brontosaurus!"

They both chuckled as her handiwork moved over to her father's "tree" and began to munch.

"Does it tickle, Daddy? I'm eating you!"

The wheelchair shadow moved slightly, and the wind kicked up a bit.

"Go on, make the goat now," she said with a slight cough.

The silhouette of her pigtailed head remained still as her father tried his hands in different combinations, almost getting the goat puppet, but not quite.

"Nearly had it, Bug," he said.

She didn't reply as he tried varying combinations of fingers to make the horns. The sun was hot on his neck, but the shadows were brilliantly strong against the concrete. The blue heart was bright in the backdrop of the emerging goat.

He didn't notice as the black shadow of Bug's head twitched just a bit.

"It's a bit of a sad animal," he said. "Looks more like Christian Bale at an AC/DC concert."

DANIEL O'CONNOR

As he tweaked the goatee a bit by shifting his pinky to different angles, Bug's pigtailed shadow slowly stood from that of her wheelchair. He didn't see it as it turned to face him. Her silhouette was in dark profile and a black depiction of liquid streamed from her mouth to the ground. He heard the gurgle and turned to face his baby.

His hands were still in goat mode when she was on him.

They became a single umbra between the earth and the sun.

Blood splattered onto the chalk heart.

CANNI

Las Vegas, Nevada

"**Having fun in Vegas?**" asked the scaly-skinned waitress.

The four of them sat at the table, their minds somewhere between lethargy and slumber. Rob managed to reply, as he hoped this was just some continuation of the lucid dream that was surely nearing conclusion.

"Just got in," he said, as he collected the menus and handed them over.

Rob, Cash, and Teresa were about to have their version of breakfast with the Asian motorcyclist. He had told them his name was Sum Yung Cum, but couldn't keep a straight face and soon admitted to being Paul Bhong, though he'd often use the surname, Smith. He had claimed Chinese, Japanese, and *OnMeKnees* ancestry before fessing up as a Korean-American. They hadn't even believed his drug-bubbling surname until he produced his license for the cops at the precinct.

They were at the station for over eight hours—maybe two hours of individual interviews and six of waiting around in separate offices. Still, they got off easy for seeing two dead cops and a third—babbling and possibly freshly insane.

There were several suits at the precinct house. Took them hours to arrive, and they sure weren't local cops or detectives. They did most of the interviewing, without ever saying exactly who they were. *Government* was the catch phrase. Cash was sure that most of the questions would revolve around a certain missing police gun, which had found its way, on the advice of the handcuffed officer, to a spot below the front seat of Rob's Chevy. When the questioners almost completely avoided that subject, Cash knew that some hardcore shit was brewing in the desert. When cops don't care about a missing service weapon, there must be some humongous fish to fry.

It was late afternoon now, but Paul Bhong had led them to this little place on Fremont Street in downtown Las Vegas that had won a *Best Pancakes in America* title, and damned if they weren't going to try them. Despite the cooking accolades, the joint was nearly empty. Other than brief police station chair and bench catnaps, the three cross-country travelers hadn't been to sleep for two days.

"Hope y'all have lots o' luck here," said the waitress as she left their table.

"Can't get any worse," mumbled Teresa. The others offered tired laughs. She caught Paul smiling at her, and it felt nice. He gave her a gentle tap on the hand. That felt nicer.

"You look as exhausted as I feel, Carrie," said Teresa.

"I'm shot," she replied, rubbing hand sanitizer all the way up to her elbows.

"*Carrie?*" asked Paul. "I thought you were Cash?"

"Only to him," she smiled, tossing a thumb at Rob.

"And her favorite uncle," answered Rob, as Cash shook her head.

"Never happened," she said.

"So I should call you Carrie?" asked the biker.

"Carrie, Ca, Caroline . . . all good."

"Hmmm," pondered Paul, "How 'bout . . . Khaki?"

"What?"

"Yeah," replied Paul. "That lovely skin tone you have. Almost like khaki."

Her skin did have compelling color but was obviously dry from over-cleansing. She was flattered by Paul's compliment, but unsure of how to respond.

Rob wasn't. "*Caroline* would be a good name to call her."

He shot his best *Keep Your Distance* look at Paul. Teresa slid her hand away from their new pal.

"Caroline it is," he said. "Sorry, I like to have fun with names n' shit. Didn't mean to sound creepy."

Trying to dump the awkward, Cash pointed that thumb at Rob again.

"Paul, I bet you'd never guess what name that 'Rob' here signed on all that police paperwork today."

"I'm not ashamed of it," said Rob, not missing a beat. "My name is Winthrop. Winthrop Robert Van Morrison-CrosbyStillsNash, and I am damned proud of it."

Silence.

"Okay Paul, I lied about the last name. But my name is Winthrop."

"That's one sweet name, bro. Why don't you use it? Sounds important."

"I like Rob," he replied.

"If you go by Winthrop, you're allowed to wear a monocle and junk."

The waitress returned with four water glasses.

"Thank you" said Rob. "So, did we catch you between lunch and dinner?" he asked her, just trying to make small talk.

"What's that?"

"I mean, it's kind of empty. My friend here told me this was a popular restaurant."

Rob and the server both looked over at Paul.

"It is popular," she answered. "But lots less people have been coming since *the flyover*."

The waitress turned a bit to the side and her right hand made a quick and sloppy sign of the cross.

"Ah" replied Rob, while peering at Cash.

"Guess folks are just scared," added the woman, as just a hint of apprehension came over her worn face. Paul could sense the change in her. He spoke up.

"Me change mind!" he bellowed, with machine gun speed, and a completely new accent. "No want pancake no more. You got Korean noodle, mung bean, and ddukbokkie?"

"Oh . . . I . . . uh . . . "

"What 'bout dog? You roast Boston Terrier for customer?"

"Sir, I . . . I . . . "

He smiled at the confused woman. "Just kidding, ma'am. Having a bit of fun with you," he said in his normal voice.

"Oh," she grinned. "You had me there. Very funny!"

She was smiling broadly as she headed back to the front counter. Mission accomplished.

Paul looked at his new friends. "I do like fucking with people and Asian stereotypes, but, also, she looked like she needed a laugh."

They all appeared a bit cheerier after his ridiculous impression. Teresa slid her hand back closer to his, almost touching. He made her happy. She also loved the fact that he was of ample height. Teresa was endowed with the slim, sturdy frame of a fashion model, but finding a boyfriend over whom she didn't tower was always a consideration.

"You keep that Chevy looking and running so sweet," said Paul to Rob.

"Thanks, man. I try."

"Can't believe you took it cross country, though. Five thousand mile round trip. Lots of sand n' shit. Ballsy way to treat that ride."

"Well, it's supposed to be a sweet vacation, and I'm hoping . . . " began Rob, before Cash cut him off.

"I can't fly," she said. "I've tried, but I had to leave the plane before it ever took off."

"Ahh," replied Paul, as he watched Cash run her unused cutlery through her table napkin. "Well, we all have our *things*, I suppose. I hate the sound of Styrofoam. You know, like when the top of a cooler rubs against the base. Makes me wanna beer dick my own goddamn ears. But, for this guy to put that awesome car through this kind of trip . . . damn, he must love you, sista."

Changing the subject, Cash asked, "Why didn't you give the cops the video you shot back there?"

"Hell, no," replied Paul. "They'd keep my phone. I keep trying to shoot something that will go viral. Bring subscribers to my YouTube channel. No luck yet."

"You won't post that horror, will you?"

"No. Not fair to the victims. Paul Smith-Bhong loses out again."

In the United States of America, a flyover was usually thought of as a coordinated, respectful event where an aircraft, or group of aircrafts, would pay homage to an occasion or anniversary with a majestic pass under the sun, ideally against a clear blue sky. Some countries would refer to these ceremonies as *flypasts*.

The flyover to which the waitress referred was coordinated indeed. Took a decade of planning. Involved hundreds of small aircraft. Covered each and every one of the forty-eight contiguous states. Occurred on the fifteenth of March—a day infamous for another historical conspiracy—and was less than a fortnight gone.

However, it was anything but respectful.

Most of the planes, and all of the pilots, were no more. A handful were shot down, but most completed their integrated mission by intentionally crashing into the most inviting and catastrophic targets in their vicinity.

It was unanimous. The pancakes were indeed the best they'd ever had. But now they sat like lead weights in the stomachs of three exhausted travelers. The group had parted ways with Paul, promising to hook up again during the trip. The hog-riding jokester had proven to them, via his driver's license, that he was indeed a Vegas local, but he had told them he was both a software developer and a dishwasher for *Hot Phat Dung Noodle Bar*. They tended to believe the former.

The Malibu headed south down Las Vegas Boulevard. Wedding chapels, great and small, lined both sides of the street.

"That's the one!" shouted Rob. "Everyone from Frank Sinatra to Bruce Willis got married there. Michael Jordan. Britney Spears, too."

"What about Angelina Jolie and Billy Bob?" asked Teresa, as Cash gazed in the other direction.

"Don't know. That might be another chapel. There are loads of 'em!"

"Rob," said Cash, without looking, "are any of these people *still* married?"

"Technically, yes."

"But to *other* people."

"Correct."

They drove on. Radio stations were plentiful in the city, so they listened to Adele as they motored along. Rob lifted his 8-track copy of *Some Girls* by the Rolling Stones and waved it around slowly.

"No." replied the girls in unison.

"This tape," said Rob, "has versions of some songs that never appeared on either vinyl or CD!"

"What about downloads?" asked Cash.

"I don't even say that word," he answered.

"Can you stream it?"

"Shut it."

"I don't even know how those tape things still play," offered Teresa.

"Don't get him started," sighed Cash.

Too late.

"There are two things I really know how to do; fix cars and 8-tracks. They'll both last a lifetime if you treat them right. With tapes, it's all about repairing or replacing foil tabs and fuzzy pads. I can show you someday, if you like. Cash has seen me do it."

The girls exchanged glances. Teresa gave her friend a *he's cute* pout. Cash smiled in agreement.

"Would love to see it when we get back home," smiled Teresa.

Then it was before them. The Las Vegas Strip. It was daylight, yet somehow things still got a whole lot shinier as they passed the landmarks one-by-one: Stratosphere, Encore, Wynn, Venetian, Mirage, and more, almost too many to grasp. Fewer tourists than they'd expected, though.

"Which one are we staying at?" asked Cash. "I can't take the suspense!"

"I told you—it's a surprise," answered Rob.

"Caesar's! *The Hangover!*" chuckled Cash.

"Aaaand the Ides of March," added Teresa, gazing out the passenger side window as they approached the Bellagio and its legendary fountains.

They motored on.

City Center, Paris, MGM Grand, New York, New York, Luxor and others.

A huge jet lumbered over them as it descended on McCarran airport. It felt reassuring to the trio, after several days of no aircraft, save for the occasional military fighter.

"Well, I guess it's Mandalay Bay," offered Cash, pointing at the last of the big beautiful casino resorts at the south end of the strip. "Cool!"

Mandalay came and went. Rob drove on. The Killers were on the radio now.

DRIVE CAREFULLY. COME BACK SOON, said the backside of the famous WELCOME TO FABULOUS LAS VEGAS sign.

About ten wordless minutes after that, Rob pulled into a motel parking lot. Three young men in hoodies huddled together in a handicapped parking space, blowing smoke rings toward the sky.

IN-ROOM HBO bragged the weathered sign.

"I'm borderline certain that said 'In-room hobo'," sighed Cash.

In the modest motel lobby, Rob checked in while the girls did their best to recline on a tattered sofa.

"I bet this couch was the bomb in the days before this guy took it out of the Caesars Palace dumpster," said Cash.

"*This* is our 'surprise hotel'? O-M-G," Teresa said.

"Yeah. Rob said he thought since the address was on Las Vegas Boulevard, it had to be part of the strip. He said we can't afford those nice ones because they quadruple their prices for the weekend."

"How 'bout we stay weeknights in a nice hotel, then spend the weekend in a cardboard box behind the Palazzo?" They both laughed as Rob dealt with the clerk behind the desk.

"One room, two hotties. Well played, my friend, okaaaay," coughed the middle-aged turtle, with an unlit cigar hanging beneath his thatchy mustache.

"It's not like that," answered Rob.

"Sure you don't want the room with one king bed?" he replied, sounding like a garbage disposal on the fritz.

"I'm sure, bro."

"Mackey. Call me Mackey. We had a cancellation. I can slide you twenty percent off. Okaaaay?"

"I'm marrying one of them. The other one is her best friend."

"Sweeeeeet," replied the clerk, transforming the explanation into one of his fantasies. "Which one is the bride-to-be?" he asked, more loudly than his previous mumblings.

"We're both brides-to-be," replied Cash as she sauntered up to the desk, " . . . eventually."

The clerk studied her carefully enough for Rob to want it to stop. He smiled broadly, revealing the teeth he had retained to date.

"I was telling your groom about a Honeymoon Suite we have . . . "

"I wanted to ask you something," interrupted Cash. "Is the name of this place actually 'In-room HBO'? Because that's the only sign we could see out front."

"Cash . . . " said Rob.

"No, there's a small temp sign. We're having the main one redone," answered the clerk. "We're in the middle of renovations, but you'll like your room. All three of you . . . Cash."

The name suddenly sounded dirty.

"More importantly," he continued, "unlike them big casino hotels, we ain't had even one *incident* yet, okaaaay?"

They understood, especially after the conversations they'd had with Paul Bhong upon leaving the police station, but it was not something they wanted to think about until some official facts came out from an ominously silent presidential administration. Quite likely, the current situation did not lend itself to immediate transparency.

The clerk handed over the keys while studying the registration form that Rob had filled out.

"1983 Chevy? Really?" asked the clerk as he eyeballed the card.

"Really."

"I gave you all a room on the penthouse level. Best views of beautiful and romantic Las Vegas."

They all knew the place consisted of two floors.

The tired trio gathered their luggage and headed for the door. The desk man caught Teresa's eye.

"Hey slim," came the words from his gravel pit of a throat, "if those two ever need their *alone time*, you can always bump by and chill with me. I got some Four Loko bouncing 'round the mini-fridge, okaaaay . . . ?"

The door closed.

The sound of a running shower echoed in the distance as Cash and Teresa lounged in separate beds.

"Can't believe we are finally clean and in bed," said Teresa.

"Feels nice," answered Cash. "I don't think I can even raise my arms."

"Not surprised. I'd be shot too if I disinfected the place inch by inch. You could perform an appendectomy in here now," smiled Teresa. She craned her neck to be sure Rob was still in the bathroom.

"Well," replied Cash, "it seems this place has two room types; smoking and chain-smoking."

"So, have you been thinking much about a wedding?" whispered Teresa.

"Been thinking maybe I should go for it, but I don't know."

"He loves you so much."

"That's not it. Weddings . . . I mean his mom left him. Left his whole family. His father turned to drink and then there was the fire. He hasn't seen or heard from his own mother in years. My parents split up. When do I hear from them? Sometimes marriage is like the kiss of death."

"That's all true, and what do I know?" responded Teresa. "But that guy in there would never leave you. Never."

Cash smiled, "Cars, old music, and me."

"You're ahead of the cars and the 8-tracks," said Teresa. "I'd trade places with you. Have you kept score of the losers I've dated?"

"Well, Rob keeps mentioning that guy John G from California. Swears you'd hit it off."

"Not a fan of blind dates."

"If we do get married here, he's coming in as best man, so it might not be too awkward in that situation."

"But you've never even met this John G guy, Carrie, and Rob never answers my question about how tall this mystery man is."

"They were best friends till they were twelve, but John moved to Cali before I ever met Rob."

"Tall Paul is pretty cute," offered Teresa.

"If you like the *you-can't-believe-anything-I-say* type, then maybe, T."

"He's just a joker. Seems pretty smart, too. Sounds like he knows a lot about everything," whispered Teresa, as she stared at the peeling motel ceiling. The shower water stopped. Sounded like the little shampoo bottle, or something, fell to the floor. Teresa continued, "Some of the stuff Paul said about whatever the hell is going on lately is pretty scary. I don't know if it's true, but if it is, you might want to think about getting married before this world goes completely ass up."

No response.

"Carrie, you hear me?"

A bit of heavy breathing. Teresa lifted her head to peer over at her best friend. Rob rattled around in the bathroom.

"Ca?"

The strong breaths turned into something of a mild snore. Teresa laughed to herself and tried to snuggle into her thin, hard pillow.

The three of them were torn from their dreams by the same tumultuous boom. The room was much darker than it had been when they'd drifted off. Teresa checked her phone. 3:15 AM. Sounded like a wrecking ball was battering the motel. As heads cleared, they realized it was the room next door.

Bangs, crashes, muffled voices.

"What the hell?" moaned Rob.

"Rough sex," sighed Cash.

They shared a brief chuckle till they heard the growl.

Is an Alaskan Grizzly getting laid in room 29?

"Quiet please!" yelled Rob, as he pounded the wall.

Seemed to stop for a few seconds, then it resumed, like *two* wrecking balls.

Was that a scream? And a shattering table lamp?

"I'm calling the cops," groaned Teresa, as she grabbed her phone.

"I'm gonna knock on their door," said Rob.

"No, you are not," replied Cash. "First, I think we are hearing some 3AM, Sin City, in-room hobo sex. But either way, you are not getting murdered, Sam Cooke style, in a shitty motel."

"Sam who?" asked Teresa.

Ignoring the question, Rob declared, "Then I'm going to the manager's office. Maybe they have a security guard or something. What if a woman is being hurt in there? Or if someone flipped out in one of those . . . *schitzo* . . . or whatever those episodes are . . . "

"I got a recording," said Teresa. "Now I'm on hold. I think I've called the cops once in my entire life and now it's becoming routine. Just great."

Boom! The wall thumped.

Rob was barefoot as he reached the motel office. There was no one behind the desk, but it sounded like a TV on in the back office. He pounded the bell so hard it stuck to his palm.

"Coming," came the voice from the back. Rob hoped the verb was being used in the traditional sense.

The office manager appeared. Looked like the same guy from the day shift.

"Hey, uh . . . Mackey," said Rob, "do you have any security at the motel?"

"One, I ain't Mackey. Two, yes I do."

He bent down for a second, then stood and dropped a thirty-one-ounce Rawlings aluminum bat on the desktop.

"You're not Mackey?"

"Nope," replied the clerk. "He's my brother. Works days here."

"Really?"

"Yep. I got more choppers than him. See?"

He proudly displayed a mouth that was almost full of teeth. Rob preferred to look at the baseball bat.

"This here bat is signed by both Derek Jeter and Mariano Rivera," he said.

"There's something going on in room 29."

"I'm sure there is."

"No. Not that. Sounds like a fight or even . . . "

"Okay, let me ring the room."

The clerk picked up his phone and dialed. Rob felt a bit of relief.

"So you and Mackey are twins, I'm guessing."

"Nope," he replied as the phone rang in room 29.

"What? You look . . . "

"Triplets."

The phone continued to ring.

"Yeah," the manager continued, tapping two fingers on the bat handle, "I'm Jackie. Then there's Mackey—who you met—and then there's . . . "

Rob found his mind zipping through the alphabet searching for a third rhyming name.

" . . . Galileo," said the clerk.

No answer from room 29.

"Papa liked the stars," he concluded, as he grabbed the bat. His voice did sound less like drywall than Mackey's.

Rob and Jackie inched up to the door marked 29. Rob noticed that beyond the railing behind him, one floor below, the three hooded teens he'd spotted over twelve hours earlier were still in the parking lot, still smoking. Unless they had gone home and then returned—or were three entirely different hooded teens.

"Galileo works at a fancy joint out in Lake Las Vegas," whispered the clerk. "He don't make no time for his brothers."

"Let's listen," mouthed Rob. He shot a glance at the door a few feet down, hoping it remained locked the way he told Cash and T to keep it.

Jackie leaned in toward the closed egress. Rob tried to find a crevice in the dark curtains behind the rectangular motel window glass. He wondered why there were no moths or flying insects bouncing off the unwashed pane, as there had been in all their previous cross-country stopovers. Then he remembered they were now in the desert.

Silence.

The motel manager shot a look at Rob. Their bodies relaxed a bit.

Then it sounded like room 29 exploded. There was a short, sharp scream. Jackie plunked the aluminum bat to his shoulder and pounded on the door. Rob moved next to him and turned a bit to the side, preparing himself for what might come.

Footsteps. Loud ones.

Jackie stood with his Rawlings slugger as if his last name was Robinson.

The latch clacked. The doorknob turned. Then another clack, but from behind the door to Cash and Teresa's room.

Both doors began to open simultaneously.

"What . . . the . . . fuck . . . do . . . y'all . . . want?" the man jawed as he came into view in the partially-opened entryway.

He was at least six and a half feet tall. Maybe that wide, too. Bald, black, and buff, he stood completely naked, save for the towel that was not wrapped around his waist, but hung like a sheet on a clothesline from his obviously blessed and fully erect penis. The phallus came through the doorway, followed by the rest of him.

"Put that bat down before you eat it, girlfriend."

Jackie complied. Quickly. The heads of Cash and Teresa popped out from their room next door.

"Go inside," said Rob to the girls, to keep them from any possible danger, and to prevent Cash from seeing a stark-naked Adonis with a dick like a five-dollar-footlong. They obliged, or pretended to. Rob wasn't sure because his attention was back on the giant before him.

"Excuse us, but we wanted to be sure everything was okay," offered Rob, while Jackie was already turning to leave.

The large man huffed as the breeze fluttered the towel that draped his manhood. "Come here," he yelled to someone in the dark room behind him. A slight and pretty Hispanic girl appeared with a sheet half-draped around her. A detailed tattoo of the face of Jesus Christ covered the area between her neck and breasts.

"Hi," she smiled. She was about five-foot-three, and looked like a preschooler next to the behemoth.

"These superheroes are worried about you, baby," said the man. "You need help or anything?"

"No. All good," she replied, staring into Rob's eyes.

"Let's go," said Jackie to Rob, reaching for his shoulder. "Sorry to disturb you," he apologized to the couple.

"*I'm* the one who needs help!" yelled a different female voice from somewhere within the room.

Rob and Jackie eyed each other.

Oh, shit, was all Rob's brain could muster.

"Sir, would you open the door, please?" asked Rob, hoping he wouldn't soon be swallowing teeth.

The muscled fellow just laughed as he pushed the door wide. Light from the street lamps flooded the room. There she was. Another slight woman. Caucasian. Completely naked and bent over a steep-angled, red microfiber sex wedge that sat atop the disordered bed.

CANNI

"I need the help of my big man, honey," she slurred.

"Mother . . . fucker," sighed the ebony-toned weightlifter.

His lone towel had fallen to the concrete as his softened shaft could no longer tent-pole it.

DANIEL O'CONNOR

Las Vegas Boulevard

Captain Jack Sparrow stood there in the afternoon heat, right beside Spongebob Squarepants. Their costumes were slightly tattered, and a bit soiled. They stood proudly on the sidewalk, near the curb, not far from something resembling Minnie Mouse. But her character head was off and tucked under the arm of the role-player—a bearded, greasy-haired phlegm machine with a brown Tiparillo dangling from a bottom lip as parched as the hot air that engulfed him. Cigar smoke danced around his red and white polka-dotted skirt. They all wanted the same thing: your photograph with them in exchange for a decent deposit in their tip jars. Several feet from these urban entrepreneurs stood Rob, Cash, and Teresa. They leaned against the railing of the beautiful, eight-acre manmade lake that housed the famous Fountains of Bellagio. Though best viewed after dark, Cash was impatient and wanted a daytime experience as well. The next musical presentation was due to start momentarily. A family of ducks floated by, all in a row. The water was just a couple of feet deep by the edge, and the bottom was lined with coins from those hoping for a granted wish. The crowd was a bit sparse for the midday viewing, but there were still enough tourists to make it difficult to grab a prime center-railing spot.

"This is amazing," said Cash.

"I hope I can keep my eyes open for it," replied Rob, raising his sunglasses to reveal a slight redness.

"We're not destined for sleep during this trip," added Teresa from behind her Starbucks cup. "Did that shit really happen last night at *In-room Hobo*?"

"We def need to learn more about sex," laughed Cash.

"Speak for yourself," replied Rob with a grin.

"Huh?" said his girlfriend. "Buddy, you're one to talk. I think your favorite position is the ten and two." Her hands were gripping an imaginary steering wheel. She gave him a light kick to his shin.

"Too much info," added Teresa between coffee sips.

A man paraded behind them holding a sign warning people that Jesus would disapprove of anything they decided to do in the city of sins. Spongebob hurried after a couple who neglected to fill his tip jar. Cash's driving jab had caused Rob's thoughts turn to his old Chevy. He was happy he chose to park in the Bellagio garage because it seemed safe. Not that the one older security guard who waved them up the ramp was much of a deterrent to thieves, but it was better than nothing.

Fountain pipes began to ascend, jutting ever so slightly out of the Bellagio lake. Most didn't notice.

"Did our new friend Paul call you yet, T?" asked Rob.

"Don't think so. Have to check my voicemail just in case," she answered.

"He's cool, but I really want you to meet John G . . . "

"I know. I know."

Spongebob almost crashed into the religious zealot just as he was howling anti-gambling rants at passersby. Teresa was digging out her phone to check for messages when the brisk sound of a string section filled the air.

"Luck Be a Lady", the Frank Sinatra version.

She put the phone away as the fountains exploded, in time with the recording.

Howls and applause came from the crowd that encircled the huge display.

"So beautiful," sighed Cash.

Rob was thinking the same thing, but he was canvassing Cash, as she enjoyed the water dance. The gigantic bursts of spray were timed perfectly with the music. A gentle mist teased most of the onlookers. Rob hoped that the romance of the fountains might turn Cash's thoughts to marriage. He gently caressed her neck as the spray tickled her smiling face. Unbeknownst to the others, his surreptitiously slung cent was coming to rest at the bottom of the lake.

There came heavy-footed running behind them.

Those freaking costumed con men, thought Rob, *ruining the moment for everyone.*

He ignored it all until he heard the screams. Louder than the excited shrieks that came with the start of the fountain show.

The fast-paced steps belonged to a trio of helmeted Las Vegas Metro police officers. The screams belonged to most everyone else who was closer to the commotion. Something halfway up the street to the north, maybe a fight. Many were scampering from the activity.

Sinatra still sang about luck.

Cash, meanwhile, tried to ignore the incident. She didn't feel particularly threatened. Whatever the problem was, it was pretty far up the street, and there seemed to be plenty of cops. She wanted to be lost in the song and the moment.

Unlike his girlfriend, Rob tried to get a peek at the scuffle by craning his neck. He was still gently stroking Cash's. All he could see was the movement of the crowd, police uniforms mixed within. His study quickly focused not on the disturbance in the distance, but on the fountain spray droplets resting on Cash's soft, caramel-tinged cheek. He hungered to remain in that world.

Though she tried to ignore it, it was Cash who first saw the result. She took in the dancing waters while smiling at Frank Sinatra's use of the word "dame" in the classic song. That first millisecond, from the far corner of her eye, she thought it was the duck family returning to her view, atop the lake.

She turned just a bit toward it.

A man. Face down. Dead, or dying. Camera still strapped around his crimson neck. A circle of his own blood traced him like a marine spotlight. He'd float there until either his lungs filled, or someone came and got him. Cash squeezed Rob's hand. Then he saw it. Teresa too. The fountains continued to blow, as did the music. One cop landed in the water, followed by another, and a couple of civilians. They trudged through the knee-deep section, trampling the lucky coins, toward the man in the bloody circle.

Looking into Rob's eyes, Cash said nothing. If her gaze conveyed anything, it might be described as helplessness.

Or hopelessness.

The fountains, and the accompanying music, were abruptly halted.

They wanted a quiet place to just sit and chill. It was now too much, this trip that began with such promise for the three of them. *Quiet* was not going to be possible on the strip. To be more specific, *quiet* and *affordable* were a match that wouldn't be found in the immediate area. They had headed back to the parking garage and took a fifteen-minute drive looking for a place to make sense of things. No music was played during the ride. Occasionally, they would hear the sound of Cash locking and unlocking the car door.

They found a place on Spring Mountain Road, Pat & Alice's.

It had the feel of a diner but was a small storefront in a strip mall. The three of them sat in a faded booth in the barren eatery. A television hung from a corner, right near a photo of, apparently, Pat and Alice, with some well-dressed Vegas celebrity who looked vaguely familiar to Rob. As some talking head rambled on the TV, Rob couldn't help but ponder how he was surprised that Pat and Alice were actually two older women. He thought they'd be a couple.

Oh, wait. They probably are a couple.

He shook his head, realizing that even a man as young as he still had some old-fashioned preconceptions set as defaults in his mind.

"I'm not hungry at all," said Cash, as Teresa agreed.

"We can split an appetizer or something," said Rob, as his brain abandoned his odd crusade into the sexuality of the restaurant owners.

"How can you eat anything?" asked Cash.

"Well, we can't sit here without buying something. I'll down it all if nobody wants any. I haven't eaten anything all day."

Cash gave him a light kick to the shin. Teresa had her phone out, checking for messages from Paul.

"Anything?" smiled Cash.

"Um . . . no . . . but a bunch of missed calls from my mom. Let me go call her. Be right back."

As Teresa left for some privacy, her friends' attention turned to the television as the counterman aimed a remote to raise the volume.

"We're expecting the president at any moment," stated the announcer. A camera was fixed on an empty podium with the presidential seal on it.

"Maybe some answers," mumbled the workers to each other.

Sounded like some dishware fell and crashed back in the kitchen.

Cash flinched, then thought back to a time, maybe two weeks earlier, when the sound of breaking plates usually meant no more than broken plates. The counterman rushed through the swinging doors into the back kitchen along with a waiter. Rob and Cash kept their eyes on those doors, not noticing that the President of the United States had reached the podium. He began to address the American people, but despite the anticipation of this moment, and the possibility of some intensely important—and quite dire—information being disseminated, Rob and Cash were fixed on those swinging doors.

"You, the American people, have heard very little from me, or my administration, over the past couple of weeks," said the president. "I sincerely apologize for that. But frankly, we didn't have much that we could share with you. Nothing of substance. The last thing we want to do is spread fear and hysteria without any concrete information. We do now have somewhat more that we can pass along. I ask that you might consider asking younger children to leave the room so that you might explain this to them later in a manner more fitting."

Rob and Cash stayed fixed on the swinging doors. They said nothing.

There was a sound like running water. A sink. Surely no one would be using the sink if there was a life-and-death struggle occurring in Pat and Alice's kitchen . . .

"Our enemies continue to believe that they can intimidate and deter the American spirit through terror," said the commander-in-chief. "On March fifteenth there was a coordinated attack on our homeland. You know by now that there was a well-planned and well-funded air assault on our country. After exhaustive and incessant research by several government agencies, along with the help of many private institutions who have responded to our call for assistance, it has been determined that we have been subjected to what appears to be a biochemical super-agent of sorts. We are still at work trying to pinpoint the complete effects of this chemical, along with its origin and any possible antidotes. At this time, it is not clear exactly how many of us have been affected by this, and what, if any, symptoms might occur, other than one significant behavioral change, that appears to be temporary, yet may reoccur."

A muffled commotion drew the attention of the president. He glanced to his right, toward the back of the room. A dog barked. The camera began a 180-degree turn, to record whatever was transpiring. A meaty grasp blocked the lens, forcing the hand-held to return to the president. In the movement, several blurry figures in black-visored helmets were glimpsed running toward the disruption. More barks. As the camera was returned by force to the president at the podium, he was flanked by two of those battle-dressed guards, who looked more like Navy SEALs about to raid a compound than the nattily dressed, well-manicured agents who normally flanked POTUS.

DANIEL O'CONNOR

At Pat and Alice's, the swinging kitchen doors were pushed open. The counterman came through. Rob thought he saw blood all over the man's apron, but quickly chalked that up to paranoia.

Ketchup. Maybe tomato sauce.

All seemed fine as the waiter trailed behind, laughing.

False alarm.

Cash exhaled. Rob gave her a smile.

She shouldn't have to live in a world like this. She deserves better.

The president was relatively young when he won the election. Though still in his first term, his dark hair had grayed considerably, and lines had formed around his eyes and forehead.

And that was before all of *this* happened.

"The major effect of this chemical agent seems to be that it causes something of a convulsive state that may cause the victim to become extremely aggressive toward anyone they may come incontact with. I need to emphasize that I mean literally *anyone*. There have been instances of parents murdering their own children, and vice-versa. A person in this altered state will have their strength drastically increased, and they cannot be reasoned with."

Teresa returned to the table. A basket of chicken tenders sat in the middle of it. Three different sauces. Rob had two pieces on his plate already. Cash stared at the television. She was aware that her best friend had sat down across from her, but she was still getting her head around the words she was hearing. Her thoughts turned to Teresa, and she half-expected to hear that she had spoken to Paul.

"So," began Cash.

"Carrie," interrupted Teresa, her eyes welling, "my cousin Joy-Joy is dead."

"What?"

Rob laid his chicken down as Teresa continued, "My mom just told me. She was killed. Murdered by one of those *things*."

"People suffering from one of these episodes can be dispatched by traditional methods, if self-defense becomes a primary factor," declared the president. "This is not some cheap horror film about the undead. We're not talking ghosts or zombies here. However, it is imperative that we all understand that if we kill one of these infected people, there is no bringing them back. These incidents are generally lasting from ten to fifteen minutes, after which the afflicted return to relative normalcy, with little or no memory of what occurred. We must do all that we can to avoid these situations and shield ourselves from them as best as we can. We don't want to kill family and friends because they're in the midst of a ten-minute episode. Remember, *your* convulsive state might be next. We can't go around eradicating each other. That's what our enemies want."

Teresa's head was in her hands. Cash slipped over to her side of the booth.

"Mom was going to buy a plane ticket for me to go home," cried T. "She was trying to get enough money to pay for all of us—not that you would fly, Carrie—but she thought it over and wants me to stay with you out here. She said Rob will keep us safe. She's convinced things are worse back east. Said a second-grade teacher grabbed a little girl and . . . "

"Safe Zones," said the president. "We are working with local agencies to create safe zones to accommodate as many folks as possible. Mainly for getting some restful sleep. Perhaps on some type of rotating basis. We're still not sure exactly how these would operate, as those who would protect us are not immune to violent episodes themselves, but our goal is to protect children first, and to help stabilize our infrastructure. This is obviously something no nation has ever had to deal with before, but together, we will all get through it."

Teresa's phone rang. She hesitated, fearing more tragic news, but then saw who was calling. She wiped her eyes.

"It's Paul," she said.

Cash caressed her best friend's shoulder and looked over at Rob.

This will cheer her up some, thought Cash.

Cash and I, thought Rob, *Why do we even have phones? No one ever calls us.*

On TV, the president went on trying to reassure the American people. Rob began to think about how he might be able to protect the most important person in his life, and her dearest friend. He felt a chill crawl up his legs as he realized that he probably couldn't.

"We'll take turns sleeping," offered Cash, almost reading his mind. "One of us will always be awake . . . "

"Won't work, baby," he answered, as Teresa managed to smile at whatever Paul said on the phone. "What if the person watching the sleepers is the one who *turns?*"

Cash just stared at him as Teresa left the booth to continue her chat in private. Cash looked up at the television, down at the plate of chicken tenders, and then out the window into the sunny Nevada afternoon. An armored truck was double-parked, its guards picking up some cash from a neighboring business. Life appeared to be going on, but what kind of life would this be?

Rob saw the vacant look in his girlfriend's eyes.

"Hey," he said, "give me another kick, baby. I don't feel right when my leg isn't hurting."

DANIEL O'CONNOR

Loudoun County, Virginia

The good people of Loudoun County are usually listed as having the highest median household income of any county in the United States. Often, when one of these well-to-do families had a dog or cat in need of medical care, they'd head out past the historic grist mills and battlefields and through the renowned horse country, to the charming old office and home of Dr. Robert. Most didn't know if that was the actual name of the area's favorite veterinarian, or if he'd been tagged with that moniker from the old Beatles' song. Most also didn't care. Some said his real name was Roman or Romeo. Those who bothered to read his dusty framed degrees, or glanced at his prescription pad could've found the answer, but legend had it that the name, over the decades, had changed. Regardless, he did great work, and had for over forty years, right from that same old house with the big ol' barn in the back. 'Twas a bit out-of-the-way, but his homey approach and astonishing success rate at healing animals made it worth the trip.

But there was that big ol' barn in the back.

What none of the visitors had ever seen during all those years, was the inside of that old barn. There was a well-worn dirt road that led 'round the back of it, but Dr. Robert always had that towering, heavy-duty, chain link fence around it.

Never seemed to rust.

If one were to slink into that barn, they'd be greeted by a couple of big, smiling rancher types, straight out of Dorothy's Kansas bedroom, who'd ask if the visitor was, perhaps, lost.

If one happened to pay particular attention to the number of cars parked in the barn, asked a question too many, or somehow noticed the heavy-duty vehicle elevators that disappeared below the strewn hay to somewhere deep below the ol' doc's property, the following would likely occur:

1) You'd think, *Holy shit. Places like this do exist.*

2) The big smiling "ranchers" would immediately neutralize you and your body would never be found.

Rooted far down below the barn rested the end of this particular rainbow: a large, climate- controlled, U.S. government research facility. Dr. Robert had known about it of course, since his days of caring for President Gerald Ford's golden retriever, Liberty. He agreed to have his practice front the research station, because he liked and admired Ford, and he loved his country. However, Dr. Robert—nor President Ford or any subsequent POTUS—had ever actually been inside the facility.

Naturally, there was a direct video monitoring connection to the White House and the Pentagon.

The "volunteers" spent most of their time strapped to their beds, wired to various devices, awaiting any possible behavioral change.

They were technically volunteers, as nobody had been forced to participate. Some were non-violent prisoners looking to have their sentences commuted. Others were caught up in the recent financial recession, looking to save their underwater homes from foreclosure. Some just wanted a cash payment or other government favor, all in exchange for monitoring, and perhaps some mild tests.

The scientists in charge were brother and sister geniuses, both in their mid-forties. Though not ideal in the eyes of the Big Brother powers that be, the government decided to not deprive themselves of the brilliance of this gene pool despite the familial ties, and any possible complications that might arise from it.

V. Anderson was the woman, R. Anderson, her brother.

There had never been any sibling squabbles at the center, never a hint of anything less than professional. They referred to each other as "Doctor".

Outside of the office, the fair-skinned duo enjoyed their own lifestyles. V was usually transported to work by a military driver, with, only recently, a second man in the front passenger seat, as she intently devoured medical journals in the back of a town car. R always blasted in on his Harley. For relaxation, V would grab a water bottle and run forever through the back roads of Virginia. R would eat those roads on his denim black, Screamin' Eagle Fat Boy.

This day, they sat together and studied the monitors. Two black-helmeted men, dark visors down, stood several feet behind the doctors, and a greater distance apart from each other.

"Anything new this morning?" asked R of his sister, tapping his Diet Mountain Dew can—his version of coffee.

"So the tardy scientist has questions for the punctual one?" smiled V.

"C'mon. I wasn't that late. My garage door opener shit the bed."

"You used that one 'bout two months ago."

"That was a *different* garage door, Dr. Anderson. Different garage."

"Right. Nothing happened this morning, but Dr. Martinez told me that number nine flipped during the night. Lasted eleven minutes."

"How did she smell?"

"Well, you know the stench can be especially strong if they exhibit the mouth foam . . ."

"I was talking about Dr. Martinez."

"Focus, my brother."

"But that bouquet she has. Is it her shampoo?"

"You can go over number nine's vitals from before, during, and after the episode, once we watch the video. This is the first of our subjects to turn during apparent sleep. You do know that, right?"

As the recording began, number nine—an unremarkable-looking Caucasian woman of thirty-eight years; interchangeable with anyone who might be seen pushing a cart in Target—slept peacefully. A monitor showed her heart rate at sixty-eight. Her arms and legs were strapped to the bed and she was wired like a 1960s switchboard. Her mouth was slightly ajar, head turned to the side on her pillow. The room was dim, but a light shone through a small square window on the door to the corridor.

R. Anderson sipped his Dew as he studied the recording beside his sister. Several feet behind them, one of the guards titled his head, presumably to glimpse the activity on the monitor. The other remained motionless.

On the video, monitors beeped and whirred, but number nine had sent herself off to sleep imagining them as crickets and breeze.

She sighed.

The tail-end of her hushed breath featured a drop of white foam.

Number nine tensed up. Her head turned from its resting position and faced straight up at the ceiling. The beeping monitor sounds came more quickly.

Her eyes opened hot and red just as a volcano of foam blasted from her mouth.

Gurgle turned to growl.

The bed shook and rattled as she pulled against the restraints. Dripping teeth clacked as her neck craned to reach the straps with her mouth.

Her room lit up as a pair of attendants burst through the door and hit the lights. When she saw them, she went berserk. The growl intensified, as did the heart rate. It was nearing two hundred already. The heavy bed bounced as she tried to get at the aides. She spat at them, eyes devil red, teeth clattering.

R took another sip of his diet soda, as V typed into a laptop. Behind them, the one guard still had his head tilted, his face not visible behind his darkened shield. The other guard—the motionless one—had an issue behind his black visor.

From the bottom of it, by his chin, fell a single drop of foam.

On the screen, number nine railed so violently to escape her restraints that, in quick succession, both of her shoulders dislocated. She didn't notice.

Her one and only goal, her sole reason for existence, was to sink her dripping teeth into the warm flesh of another human being.

Behind the Andersons, before a second drop of foam had hit the floor, the helmeted guard's right hand appeared to make a cursory wave at a small controller on his left wrist, but he never touched it, as his knees buckled for just an instant.

The cold Diet Mountain Dew refreshingly gushed down R's throat. The replay of number nine's episode had dried his mouth. It was during his cold, caffeine-laced swallow that it crashed into the back of his skull. R lurched forward. The soda can flew from his grip. It landed on his sister's laptop, spilling onto the keyboard. The twitching guard's dark facemask had slammed into R. Anderson's head. Warm white froth poured onto his neck and back. He could hear the convulsing protector's teeth clattering behind the mask.

CANNI

The second helmeted man already had a long prod in his hands, rushing to neutralize his afflicted partner. V grabbed the right arm of her brother's attacker. It felt like a steel beam. She couldn't pry it away from R's neck.

"Move away, Doctor!" yelled the agent with the prod.

V released her grip and stepped away. R thrust his feet up against the edge of the desk and pushed back against the man who was choking him and trying to bite through his own visor.

The helpful guard thrusted the prod into the attacker's back and hit the switch. A loud *zap* was heard as the foaming man jerked. R went limp from a brief transference of electricity. The violent guard froze for an instant, then released R and turned toward his partner. The afflicted one's visor had cracked a bit against R's skull, and a thin view of his chomping teeth could be seen. The rescuer sent a second wave through the prod, but it was ripped from his grip and tossed aside. The helmets smashed into each other, damaging both visors.

More teeth were seen.

V wanted to attend to her brother, but she knew she first had to retrieve that prod. The infected guard slammed his helmet against his victim's. Over and over he smashed, trying to get at some face and neck. He took him to the floor and straddled from atop. Frustrated, the violent attacker had the presence of mind, or instinctive ability, to wrap his hands around his prey's neck and begin choking.

If he couldn't bite, he would still kill.

The guard on the bottom tried desperately to press the button on his raging partner's left wrist, but soon stopped struggling, and went limp.

V had the long prod in her hands. She fumbled briefly for the trigger mechanism, as she had never touched it before. She glanced at the recently installed panic button on the far side of the room. If she could push it, more help would come through the doors. But maybe the fallen guard didn't have that much time, with super-human strength crushing his esophagus.

She charged him from behind and got the electrodes on the shock end right up below the assailant's helmet, close to his spinal cord.

Zap.

He stopped for a second, then quickly resumed choking his victim.

Fuck this, thought V. She squeezed the trigger again and held it long and hard.

She hoped it wouldn't kill him. He was, after all, just infected, as she surely was, and would soon return to normal.

It didn't kill him.

It just pissed him off.

She could smell the burn on the back of his neck as he turned his cracked visor toward her. The split in his face shield allowed the stench of vomit to overpower the scent of burnt flesh.

He was on her.

His teeth clenched and clacked as his drippings fell onto V's face below him.

He felt like a horse on top of her. She managed to get a finger on his wrist button. Just as she pressed it, there came a click, but then, nothing. She was defenseless against him.

I should've pressed that fucking panic button instead.

His hands went to her throat. She was sure his thumbs would tunnel through her in some brutal tracheotomy.

She couldn't suck a wisp of air. Through his visor, she saw a shaded glimpse of his distended sockets. The blackness of the mask dulled it, but she knew just how glaringly red they were. V was about to close her eyes and imagine something pastoral as she died.

Then her brother leaped onto the back of her attacker.

The grip loosened just enough to let a rush of air into her lungs. R pulled back on the attacker's neck, just under the helmet. He was no match for the powerful adversary, but was just enough of a thorn-in-the-side to take his attention away from V. She called out to her brother, as he pulled the man back with all of his might:

"Just don't let that . . . helmet . . . come . . . off!"

Too late.

The entire headgear came off in R's hands as he tumbled backward.

Now, the complete head was exposed. Inflamed, watery eyes, redder than the fire extinguisher on the far wall. Mouth wide like a croc's. Stinking and dripping.

He came at V again, this time with a teeth-rattling growl. Tearing her lab coat aside, he went for her neck, but got too much shoulder. He bit through anyway. He was in deep, and it burned like hell.

He chawed out a chunk and swallowed it down.

V grew dizzy, yet briefly flashed back to the T. Rex swallowing the goat in *Jurassic Park*. She knew to try and tuck her head down to keep him from her jugular. She feared he might tear out part of her face as he came in for more.

It sounded like the slamming of a car trunk. Like when, as a child, she'd finished helping Mom unload the last of the groceries.

The twenty-pound Badger fire extinguisher.

R had slammed it into the maniac's head, with everything he could muster. The assailant went down in a heap, blood pouring from his fresh wound. V scrambled out from beneath him, her own bloody issues dripping from her shoulder to the floor. R dropped his new weapon and grabbed some towels for his sister's bite.

"No", grumbled the other guard, as he removed his own helmet. "You might've killed him."

He grabbed the remaining towels for his unconscious partner's skull.

"I had no choice," said R, gasping for air as he knelt beside his sister.

Foam overflowed from the fallen attacker's mouth, as he lay motionless. He was turning blue.

"Fuck," blared his partner. "He's drowning in that shit. We've got to clear his airway."

He put one hand on the man's forehead and another under his chin, tilting his head back.

Gurgling. Now a darker blue.

R got to his feet in order to dash over and help.

"Got to clear the airway," said the guard again. He extended two fingers and plunged them into his partner's volcanic mouth.

"No!" yelled R.

Not a second passed before the afflicted officer slammed his teeth closed, tearing off both of his partner's submerged digits.

"Aaarrrgh" screamed the victim.

The attacker, still blue, with eyes closed, shut his lips over the ingested fingers. R ran for the panic button and slammed it down.

He heard running. They were heading toward the room.

R staggered over to the door and opened it. Here came five or six attendants in lab coats.

The cavalry, he thought, with the slightest sigh of relief.

Then he looked beyond the stampeding herd.

Another attendant, lab coat covered in blood, eyes wide and red, pupils white, teeth hammering, charged after them. Behind him, on the floor, was another of the helmeted guards in a thick pool of blood.

They all blasted into the room, one of them tripping over V.

Their attacker came, growling and hungry, through the doorway.

Thud.

Down he went, to the sound of the slamming trunk.

Dr. R had swung the extinguisher again.

He looked down at his second manic conquest.

"Insert catch phrase here, motherfucker."

DANIEL O'CONNOR

Las Vegas

The Love Chapel. The Forever Chapel. Chapel in the Clouds. The TCB Chapel.

The brochures were scattered across the dashboard. Rob had another in his hands as he sat behind the wheel of his car. Cash was beside him, as the sun set behind the motel. While Rob studied the pamphlet, his girlfriend gazed out the window at Teresa, who stood with Paul, beside his bike, in the motel parking lot.

Cash was sure she was about to witness their first kiss. She had also already become accustomed to the sound of passenger jets floating down over the motel on their way to McCarran Airport. A majestic Southwest Boeing 737 appeared, landing gear down. Despite her fear of airplanes, it felt comforting. She had heard about how, before the flyover, there'd be an almost non-stop lineup of planes in that flight path. At night, one could see their lights, one behind the other, all perfectly spaced, as far as vision would permit, ready to land in Las Vegas. Now, it was just the occasional descent, carrying those brave enough to fly. Some passengers were returning to their families—yes, people do live in and around Vegas. Others were coming for what they believed to be a final fling, tossing their fears and money to the wind before—as they saw it—the end of the world.

"These are cheesy," grumbled Rob, tossing the brochure aside. "Not good enough."

The Southwest jet was directly overhead, engines roaring, when Cash watched her best friend receive her first kiss from Paul.

"Aww," she sighed, not realizing that she'd verbalized her thought.

Rob peered through the window to witness the end of the kiss.

"Well, John G is still the best man," he said. "Even if T is now with this guy."

At the far side of the parking lot, behind Teresa and Paul, Rob spotted the hooded teens. There were only two of them this time. They were staring, either at the kissing couple or at Paul's red Harley. Rob knew a lot about cars but was no expert on motorcycles. He did know, however, that the CVO Road Glide Ultra that Paul Bhong rode was not cheap. The guy had a bohemian attitude but owned a pricey ride. It was one of the reasons why Rob wasn't ready to trust him.

The kissing couple began to walk toward the old Malibu sedan. Cash gave her lifelong friend a smile through the open car window. Teresa knew what that meant.

"Room service is on me," said Paul, as his fingers intertwined with T's. "I've been invited to dinner in your room . . . if that's okay."

"Of course," grinned Cash. "But not sure if room service . . . "

"Busting chops," replied Paul. "There's a bad ass chicken joint nearby, and they deliver!"

Cash turned to Rob, "Dipping sauces!" she yelled with a smile, as she tapped a hand on the dashboard. Some of the brochures slid off and fell to the floor of the Chevy. Rob began to retrieve them, more quickly than what might be expected.

"Hey, Paul," he said loudly, without looking up from his retrieval mission, "not sure I'd leave that nice bike of yours unattended here."

"Oh, it'll be fine. You've parked that classic car here without incident, right?"

"I guess, but those kids over there have been eyeballin' your Harley."

"Hmmm," said Paul, as he let go of Teresa's hand and headed slowly toward the hoodies.

"Crap," sighed Teresa. "I am so tired of drama. Why did you have to say that, Rob?"

"I just didn't want the guy's bike stolen or vandalized."

"Those kids are just chillin'," said Cash. "They haven't done anything."

"They're always watching," replied Rob. "Why the hell are they always in this parking lot?"

Paul reached the kids. They stood defiantly; arms folded. Rob half-expected a fight, so he opened his car door out of a sense of obligation. Paul's back was to the Chevy, his arms to his side. He raised one arm and pointed, half-heartedly, toward his motorcycle. When he lowered his arm, both kids bolted from the parking lot, full speed. They never looked back.

Paul took a moment before he turned around. Cash grabbed onto Rob's forearm, as the worst of thoughts overtook her.

Was Paul changing into . . . ?

"T," she whispered to her friend, who remained outside, "get in the car."

As Teresa took a step toward the Chevy, Paul turned to face them.

He smiled.

"South Korea up in this bitch."

Three collective exhales.

Bird shit covered the railing, so Rob kept his hand off of it as the group headed toward their second-floor room. He still couldn't figure what Paul may have said to send those kids running, and the biker had brushed off each question with a one liner. Still, it was comforting to gaze down at the lot and feel a little better about the safety of his vintage Malibu. Further comfort was provided by the stolen police gun stuffed down the back of his pants.

"Does that place have any grilled chicken, or is it just fried?" asked Cash.

"Hmmm," answered Paul, "I'd consume Rob's ball sack if it came from a deep fryer, so you're asking the wrong dude. I'll ask when we call."

"Wait. Shhhh," whispered Teresa. "We're coming up to room 29. This is the one we told you about, Paul."

"Ah, where Rob almost had a cage match with Flagpole Dick."

"Shhhh, let's listen," hushed T.

Rob wanted no part of the fun. Plus, the room was dead quiet.

"They're probably out. We're the only losers in Vegas who'll be in our rooms this early," he said. He checked the railing behind him for droppings, and seeing almost none, leaned back against it while the others listened for raucous sex.

There they were, the four of them. Rob against the metal rail, Teresa and Paul just to the right of the door to room 29, and Cash over to the left, beside the long horizontal window—all three of them desperately hoping to hear a grunt, moan, or salacious exclamation.

Let them have a laugh, thought Rob. *They've seen enough hell already.*

He allowed his attention to take him to the sky. He'd heard that engine sound again and assumed a big passenger jet would be coming into view any second, from over the roof of the motel. He thought of the people on the plane, as he watched his girlfriend smiling from beside the long window.

Keep on living.

The engine sound was especially loud now, more thunderous than any he'd heard before. It was enough to draw the attention of his friends away from room 29.

This jet came in from a slightly different angle, at a much higher altitude, and there was another beside it. F-35 military fighters. Rob knew Nellis Air Force Base was nearby, but rather than the comfort brought by the passenger planes, this sight alarmed him.

He wondered what use they might be against an enemy that we are not intent on killing. That's when the first piece of glass hit him.

It all came at once. The glass, the noise, and the horror.

A naked body had flown through the window of room 29. The large, chiseled, black man landed at Rob's feet. His eyes were wide, mouth agape. His neck had been torn apart. The legendary penis—the topic of many a recent tale— was gone. Looked like some novice attempt at sausage-making: blood, skin, and bits of dangling meat.

Rob's first thought was to check for signs of life, but he quickly abandoned that and went straight for Cash. She was frozen, as were Teresa and Paul.

He had his arms around his girl when he saw the leg step through the shattered window. It was sliced open by a shard of glass that remained in the frame. The limb was slight and tanned.

Rob pushed Cash behind him, pressed her up against the wall. He shot a hand in his pocket for the room key.

The rest of the figure emerged from the window. He saw the tattoo of Jesus. It was the small Hispanic girl. She turned to face Rob and Cash. Her eyes were devil red, her stare blank. By a combination of hair and the remnants of a sexy nightie, she dragged the Caucasian girl behind her. Not being sure if the female victim was dead or unconscious, Rob shot a look at Paul.

Should they act? Would that only serve to endanger Cash and T? He had that gun, but he wasn't sure if he could kill anyone that wasn't an immediate threat to him or his friends.

Before Rob could weigh the options, the infected girl leaped over the bird shit railing, hauling her victim with her by one tiny yet Hulkian arm. The white girl's back slammed against the rail before they both fell quickly onto the hood of a parked Hyundai below.

It didn't slow her down. She bolted across the lot like a sprinter, her prey's skin tearing against the pavement as she dragged. When she reached the sidewalk of Las Vegas Boulevard, another runner appeared in the distance, and went right for her. It was a man in an iconic brown UPS uniform. Rob and his friends first thought the racer to be an intervening hero.

Then the UPS man and the Hispanic girl fought for the right to tear her victim apart.

They sat in their room, door locked, chain on, chair wedged under the doorknob; stolen police handgun under Rob's side of the bed. He had made an attempt to call 911—even to just alert them to the dead bodies—but he got a recording and hung up. Decided he'd rather smoke Paul's pot. They passed two fatties around in the dim light of the fuzzy, and muted, television. The four of them sat at the edges of the beds, facing each other. The TV news flashed images of crime scenes at Coronado High School, Hoover Dam, and the MGM Grand.

"My version of a stiff drink," Rob said to Cash. She had politely refused the marijuana and wasn't thrilled with his smoking. He rarely smoked—to her knowledge, anyway—but she didn't want him becoming addicted to anything, given his late father's demons.

"If there was a bottle of anything in here, I'd need it after that crap," he said. "Don't give me that look, Cash. Please."

"Is ordering that chicken out of the question?" asked Paul, "Shit should be calm by the time the delivery guy gets here."

"Are you serious?" asked Cash.

"Well, wait—these bitches gonna be hungry soon," he replied, thumbs pointing at both himself and Rob. Teresa had cordially rebuffed the cannabis as well.

"Those two fighter jets," said Rob. "What do you figure?"

"Scary," said Teresa, as she thumbed through the Twitter feed on her phone.

"The scariest part," inhaled Paul, "is that they are single-pilot cockpits."

"That thought is more dangerous than these freaking . . . whatever the hell they are."

Cash repositioned herself in the bed, picking her legs up and stretching out. "They're *us*," she sighed. "Nothing more, nothing less."

That line floated in the air, with the pot smoke, for at least sixty seconds.

"Shouldn't they only fly two-pilot planes, in case one of them becomes . . . ?" asked Teresa.

"Probably not less than three pilots," said Rob, "and give everyone stun guns or something. Same thing with police cars . . . "

"Trains too," said Teresa.

"Operating rooms?" asked Cash.

"Classrooms," offered Rob.

"We are so completely fucked," whispered Paul, then he looked at Cash. "To think, you were afraid to fly when the biggest threat was wind shear."

"At least I feel safer in here with that door locked," said Cash.

"I dunno." Paul inhaled. "We have to be real, dude. We are no safer in here."

They all just studied each other, knowing that any one of them could become a raging killer within seconds.

"Give me that shit," Cash said, taking a joint from her boyfriend's fingers. Though she thought she could almost see the germs crawling over it, she rushed it to her lips and sucked.

"That chair under the door will keep us safe," chided Teresa. "Being all together will keep us safe. Smoking pot will keep us safe," she said, not hiding her sarcasm.

On the muted television broadcast, someone, identified as a school nurse, broke down as she addressed her interviewer. Paul's motorcycle helmet sat on the dresser beside the TV, its visor projecting a mirrored, distorted image of the entire scene.

Rob watched his girl eyeing the television as she inhaled her marijuana.

"You want me to turn up the sound, babe?"

"No," she replied. "I'm too scared to hear any more right now."

He grabbed the remote and attempted to flip to the next channel. Nothing happened. He tried a couple of more times as he pondered about cheap motels and rarely-changed batteries. Finally, he squeezed so hard that the tip of his thumb turned red, and the TV flickered to a different channel. This time, the scene was of a commuter train, somewhere in a snowy landscape. It was derailed and on its side amid billowing smoke and flickering emergency vehicles. Next came a shot of two photos, side-by-side. Beneath them were the words *Motorman K. Ledger*. The image on the left was of his official employment snapshot—it depicted a rugged sort, middle-aged, with a scruffy black beard, peppered gray. A beaming smile partially concealed below the brush. The second photo contained no such grin. Appeared to be a blurry phone shot. There was Mr. Ledger on the snow, a gash across his forehead. Eyes red. Scruffy beard now peppered with blood and caked vomit. An oxygen tank sat in the wet snow beside him.

Teresa, not watching television, handed her phone to Paul and nodded her head as if to say *look*. He stared at it and gave it back without expression.

"What is it?" asked Cash.

"Just Twitter," answered Teresa. "Can't believe that stuff."

"No, show it to me, T. This weed is already making me paranoid. I need to see it."

CANNI

Teresa tossed the phone across to Cash's bedside. The first tweet she saw was:

Some ppl r flipping 2 #cannibal mode n stay that way 4 good

"Oh, balls."

Cash scanned the list of nation-wide trending topics:

cannibals
#zombies
walkers
#apocalypse
biters
bieber
#flippers

It was an hour later when Paul ended his phone conversation. All but Teresa had continued smoking the cannabis. They had also gone through a myriad of television channels, each one an unsettling harbinger, until they finally found a broadcast that offered an alternative to doom: a Nickelodeon rerun of *Kenan & Kel*. The four of them managed to laugh at a show that had brought them innocent joy as children. Seemed like such a different world, yet it wasn't that long ago. Now, all but Teresa also wanted that damned chicken.

As Paul lowered the phone, he looked at Rob. "They no longer deliver. Apparently, no one does. Not even from those third-party apps. If we want it, we have to go get it."

They all looked at each other.

"There's the question," said Rob, through a hazy, stoned grin. "Who goes for the chicken?"

Nervous laughter.

"I'll go," offered Paul, as he stood.

"Not alone, you won't," said Teresa.

"I'll be fine. I always travel alone," he pulled his in-ear headphones from his pocket and quickly flashed them before stuffing them back in. "As long as I have my phones in."

"I'm the only one with a clear head right now," she responded. "I'll go with you. Can you drive your bike in that condition?"

"Sure. But I'm not putting you on the back with me in this condition," he smiled.

"Do you trust me driving your car, Rob?" asked T. "I can go with Paul."

Rob thought for a moment.

"Honestly," he replied, "the safest way would be for all of us to go together."

Cash was stretched out on the bed, enjoying the television.

"I'm shot, people," she sighed. "I really don't feel like going anywhere. Screw the chicken. I'm hungry, but not enough to move."

"The next best option would be to have three of us go, and lock the remaining person in the room alone," said Paul.

"Remaining person says that's fine," answered Cash.

"Welcome to the new world. Need to employ military strategies in order to get a chicken leg," said Teresa. "How 'bout you big, strong manly types take Rob's car and I'll stay here and babysit my stoned best friend?"

"I don't know . . . " began Rob.

"You cool with that, Carrie?" asked T.

"Sure. Just be careful, you guys. That was some creepy shit that happened out there."

"But it didn't start *out there*, it began in the room," answered Rob.

"She'll be fine, Rob. There will only be two possible cannibals in this room when you leave. Outside, there are millions. You boys need to look after each other out there. We're relatively safe in here, right Carrie?"

"Fo' sho. Oh, and Paul, were those actually Hello Kitty headphones, or am I totally wasted?"

"Yes," he answered, sheepishly. "But they're just temps. My real ones shit the bed and I . . . "

Cash put her hand up with a grin.

"Don't," she said.

Rob pulled the chair out from under the door handle. Paul stood behind him, and the girls were on the beds watching Kenan and Kel chase a large rat around their store for an entire episode. A gush of wind blew in as the door was opened to the dark balcony. Rob poked his head out and looked both ways. All quiet. Nobody around. As he and Paul stepped into the night, Teresa came behind to lock the door behind them.

"Do you want to take that gun with you?" she whispered.

"No," answered Rob. "I'd rather you guys have it. Cash knows it's under our bed. Anyone tries to get in, you use it."

Teresa nodded as Cash yelled, "See if they have some orange soda."

The door closed. Rob waited to hear it lock, then he and Paul walked softly along the balcony, avoiding the bird shit railing, the pool of blood, the shattered glass, and the body of the dickless Casanova from room 29. Seemed in this new world, a corpse on a motel balcony drew neither a crowd, nor the police. No people anywhere to be seen. Only occasional traffic sounds could be heard as Rob and Paul made their way down the steps, and toward his Chevy. Neither of them uttered a word. Rob took one last glance up at their room as they got in the car. All quiet.

Inside the room, Cash allowed her dazed mind to wander from the television.

"T, if the world is about to end, maybe I should get married, right?"

Teresa laughed, "Let's not get ahead of ourselves. Nobody said it was the apocalypse."

"Well, there *was* everybody on Twitter", answered Cash, speaking slowly.

"Then it must be true!"

They both giggled.

"You should get married if you love Rob and you're sure he's the one."

Cash played with the remote as she thought. Kenan chased a rat on the TV screen.

"Can't argue with that . . . "

"I can be sure of a couple of things," said Teresa. "He loves you to death. He'll never mistreat you or cheat on you. He'll sure as shit never leave you. He is a bit overbearing at times, but he thinks he's protecting you, and he would never, ever hurt you, Carrie."

Cash ran her fingers along the remote as Teresa went on. "Now, how you feel is a different matter. I once heard my mom say something to my cousin Joy-Joy, R.I.P. Mom said, 'If you hear a love song, and it always brings the same person to mind, that's the person you love'. Sounds pretty simple, right?"

"It does."

"I can't tell you if he's the one, Carrie, but there's a whole world full of shitty dudes you can sift through to replace him. Think hard before you let Rob get away."

The remote slid through Cash's fingers and fell off the bed. It landed on the worn carpet, beside the pistol that rested beneath her thin mattress. Kenan and Kel were now trying to save the rat before an exterminator could kill it. As Cash retrieved the controller, Teresa had one final comment. "I think the only thing that comes near you on Rob's affection scale is that old car of his."

Paul Bhong was now in love with the Chevy.

"This ride is killer, buddy," he said, as he studied the Malibu's interior.

"Thanks," said Rob, as he drove down Las Vegas Boulevard. The streets were quiet and almost empty. He thought there'd be more traffic, maybe even some accident scenes or police activity. He wasn't sure if the dark emptiness was reassuring or distressing. He also wasn't thrilled with Paul being plopped down in Cash's seat. He glanced over at the lock button on the passenger side door.

Stopped at a red light, Paul found a case of 8-tracks that had partially slid from under the seat.

"Whoa. These are really sweet. Can I look?"

"Yeah, just use some care. They were my father's."

"Def bro, these look almost new! How do you keep 'em this way?"

"It's just about caring for things that are important to you."

Rob took another look at the door lock.

"You must have that old jam, 'Born to Be Wild'. Did you see when Adam Lambert did that one on *American Idol*?"

"No. It's a Steppenwolf song."

"I mean, I know it's not an Adam Lambert song, but that was like the first time I heard of it."

"What? It's in like one out of every four movies; every time someone gets on a bike or in a fucking car."

"Great biker song, bro."

"Try this one. Grab that Doors tape. No, the other Doors tape."

As Rob hit the gas, he loaded the cartridge in. Some words floated from the speakers,

A cold girl'll kill you in a darkened room . . .

"That's not the one. Wait."

He tapped a button twice to reach program four.

"Here it is; "Riders on the Storm". It might be more about hitchhikers, or killers, than bikers, but it's really about all of us, I think. Try it on your ride someday."

Girl, you gotta love your man . . .

"Last thing that Jim Morrison recorded before he died."

"Man," said Paul, "I mean, I've seen his picture on shirts and all, but I . . . "

Bhong seemed a bit embarrassed at his lack of knowledge in that area. Rob sensed it.

"Listen Paul, you know a whole lot about a wide variety of things. That's obvious. My knowledge is pretty much streamlined toward cars and classic rock. I'll hit you with some Emerson, Lake & Palmer if you teach me about everything else in this world."

Paul grinned, "What lake? Never mind. Sounds like a sweet plan. In the meantime, I'm about to school you on some bad ass poultry, my brother. Turn here."

The glorious aroma of fried chicken enveloped them as they entered the brightly lit eatery. The door had basically been slammed in their faces by the group who had gone in before them. Seemed too much of a chore to hold the door for the people behind them. A handful of uniformed employees scurried behind the counter, and there were at least a dozen customers eating at the tables. The television above the counter was off. For the time being, the world appeared almost normal to Rob. All seemed serene, folks were dining, some even laughing. There were the rude, non-door-holding bastards, and the only evidence of death was being loaded into brightly-colored buckets to be served with curly fries.

Some barely-audible instrumental versions of recent soothing hits filtered down from the ceiling speakers as the guys perused the take-out menus.

Music to calm the potential savage beasts, thought Rob.

"The main thing here is the sauce," said Paul. "If you get chicken strips, you can dip those fuckers all night long. The sauce, cousin, the sauce."

"Sounds good," said Rob, as he squinted to read the lighted menu sign behind the counter.

"Welcome guests! How may I help you?" smiled the girl at the register.

Rob admired her dedication to her job, as she almost surely either knew someone who'd been affected by the cannibalistic outbreak, or at the very least, she must've been worried that either the customer at her counter, or the fry cook to her rear, would suddenly want nothing more than to devour her. Yet, there she was, beaming—probably for minimum wage, too.

"Hi," said Rob, with a polite smile. "Would you happen to have orange soda?"

DANIEL O'CONNOR

Virginia

Dr. R. Anderson opened another Diet Mountain Dew. He sat beside his sister at a long conference table. His head was bandaged all the way around, a blood stain on the back of the gauze. Dr. V was now in a hospital gown with heavy packing over her bitten shoulder. A handful of other medical professionals were also scattered around the table, all watching a large monitor mounted on the long wall. A helmeted guard stood in each of the four corners of the room. The woman on the big screen was seated in the White House Office of Science and Technology. She preferred to be addressed by her full, hyphenated surname.

"Dr. Papperello-Venito, we've suffered a tragedy here today," said Dr. R. "We lost one brave security officer, and have had several employees injured . . . "

"So terrible, Dr. Anderson," she replied. "I can see that you and the other Dr. Anderson have both been through a great deal."

"Not just us. We have several folks still in medical, worse off than we are. We are going to need more security here, as there are currently not enough . . . "

"We are very thin on security, Dr. Anderson," she replied. "We are doing what we can, but both manpower and equipment are dangerously low since the attack. I'm sure you understand."

Rubbing her injured shoulder, V spoke up. "Excuse me, Dr. Papperelnito . . . "

"It's Papperello-Venito," replied the White House official.

"Yes," answered V. "It's a bit of a mouthful, to be honest. May I call you 'Dr. P'?"

"I'd prefer you did not."

"Excellent. You mentioned equipment. That button thingamajig on their wrists . . . "

V was pointing at the guard nearest her seat.

"Yes, the possible malfunction. Are you entirely sure you pressed it during your struggle?"

"Pressed it? I still have the imprint in my forefinger."

"We'll need you to send the entire unit to us for examination."

"Have you had other issues with these units, Dr. Papperello-Venito?" asked R. Anderson as he sipped his diet soda. "Also, it seems it's a bit of a crapshoot as to if an affected person actually has the time to activate their device."

"It's the best we can do at this point. The demand will be incredible. They're needed in safe zones, schools, police departments, the armed forces. People will want them for home use. Hell, there are already illegal knockoffs on the internet. We're trying to speed up production and outsource it, but the red tape is huge. One of your security team has offered to demonstrate the effectiveness of the device. Even the presidential detail uses them," she stated, ignoring R's question. "Please step forward Officer Clayton-Cromartie."

V looked at her brother, "What, another hyphenation? It's why I stick with my maiden name," she whispered.

The guard walked up and stood just behind the Andersons. Another helmeted sentry then moved into place behind the first.

"Please proceed, Officer Clayton-Cromartie," said Dr, Papperello-Venito.

The guard placed his hands briefly on the sides of his helmet, as if to ensure its snug fit, then calmly lowered both arms and pressed the button on his wrist device.

A brief click could be heard, and, though unseen by those in the room, a needle popped from beneath his helmet, pierced his neck, and sent him falling, unconscious, into the arms of his partner behind him.

"Excellent," said Dr. Papperello-Venito from her White House perch. "They are quite functional."

"That one worked," said R. "But the one my sister pushed didn't . . . "

"Please refrain from familial references in the work place, Dr. Anderson. Let's adhere to a professional code."

V. Anderson stood from her chair, despite her obvious pain, "Dr. Pappelito, rather than focus on how my brother refers to me, I think we should look into the fact that your fucking sleepy button only works some of the time. Not to mention that, in your brilliance, you just incapacitated another member of our security team, when we were weakened already. Your problem is that your mechanism is wireless. Wireless! At home I have to reset my wireless router every time we use the microwave. There is a section of my backyard that never has cell service. My husband set up our home with wireless speakers, so our "fancy" total home music system sounds just a bit better than a Mexican broadcast signal on an AM radio in Anaheim. Maybe in five or ten years, it'll all be better, but for now, why don't you run a ten-cent wire from the wrist transmitter into the goddamned helmet?"

"Wireless really sucks," added R. Anderson, Diet Mountain Dew in hand.

Dr. Papperello-Venito just stared.

"Good day, doctors," she said, as she ended her transmission.

The Andersons looked at each other. They turned their attention to their unconscious protector as V spoke. "When do you think he wakes up?"

"Who knows?" answered her brother. "But I will say that Dr. Pepperoni-Venetian could be a double tight ass. You know, both her persona and her physical composition. I'd like to see how feisty she is after she leaves 1600 Pennsylvania for the evening."

DANIEL O'CONNOR

Las Vegas

Rob and Paul each carried armfuls of chicken as they climbed the stairs to their motel balcony. Under Rob's arm was a bottle of Orange Crush from a gas station mini-mart. Upon reaching the balcony, it was all still there; the bird shit, the blood, the glass, and the body. Some insects had found their way to the wide-eyed corpse.

Reaching the door, Rob knocked.

"Who loves orange soda?" he yelled, hoping Cash's response would be "Kel loves orange soda!" —a famous line from *Kenan & Kel*.

He was hoping the food and drink might brighten the mood.

No answer.

He knocked again, harder.

Just the sound of a near-empty city bus rumbling down the boulevard.

"Cash! Teresa!" He was thumping the door with all he had.

"Relax, bro," said Paul. "They're probably asleep. Remember the weed."

"Teresa didn't smoke."

"Maybe she did after we left. Don't panic. Let me call T's phone."

Paul rested his chicken bag between his body and the window as he dialed. He gave a reassuring nod to Rob as he waited for the call to go through.

They heard the muffled sound of Teresa's ringing phone from within the room. By the second ring, Rob was putting the chicken and soda on the dirty balcony concrete.

After the fourth ring the call went to voicemail, and Rob was hurling his body into the door, trying to break it down.

"Help me out!" he yelled to Paul.

Bhong dropped his bag and drove into the door with Rob. Nothing.

"Step back," yelled Rob. He then slammed his foot into the door, right by the lock. Nothing.

"What the fuck?" he screamed, as he ran down the balcony, grabbed a slatted steel trash can, ran back, and hurled it through the glass window. The noise cut through the Las Vegas night, echoing through the parking lot below.

Rob was first through the window. A shard of glass sliced his forearm, but he didn't notice. Paul was directly behind him. In a blur, they first saw that the chair had been propped against the door lock, as it had been when they were in the room earlier. Next, they noticed that the TV was still on, but the girls weren't on either bed.

On the floor, just beyond the disheveled sheets hanging from the far mattress, were Cash's bare feet. They were motionless.

"God, no."

Rob bounded around to the far side of the room. That's where they were, both Cash and Teresa. Blood was everywhere; on the carpet, the side of the bed, on both girls, even on the nightstand and the wall behind it. A table lamp was broken on the floor beside them, next to Paul's bike helmet, which was on its side in the blood puddle. Rob rushed to Cash's side as Paul went to Teresa. Both were face down.

That's when he noticed the smell.

Gun powder.

Rob felt for a pulse on Cash's neck. He didn't know if he'd found one, or if it was coming from his own shaky fingers.

He turned her face-up. Her eyes were closed. He put his ear over her nose and mouth. Yes, it was there.

Cash was breathing.

He looked for the source of the blood. She had wounds on her neck, shoulder, and left arm and some scratches on her face.

"She's alive," he said, just as he turned to face Paul. He was about to ask about Teresa when he saw her face. Paul had turned her over, but immediately saw no reason to check for signs of life.

Teresa's eyes were open and red. Foamy vomit covered her mouth and chin. Blood poured from her nose. She had a bullet hole in the left side of her skull with a larger exit wound on the right. It was the source of the blood spatter on the nightstand and wall. The gun had been under her body but could now be seen by Rob and Paul.

They sat in silence for a moment, not knowing what to do. A warm, dry breeze filled the room through the broken front window, curtains dancing like ghosts. The room was lit by only the glow of the television.

Nick Nick Nick Nick Nick Nick Nick Nick Nickelodeon.

"I don't want any ambulance," mumbled Cash as Rob and Paul assisted her to the bed closest the window and furthest from Teresa's body, which Paul had covered with a sheet. A light had been turned on and the television off. Cash sat on the bed, staring at the dark, blank TV screen. Tears rolled down her cheeks, but she produced no sound. Paul tried to close the dancing curtains a little tighter. The glass shards crackled on the carpet beneath his feet.

"We have to get your wounds cleaned up, baby," said Rob. "You need to be examined . . ."

"Bites," she said, still staring at the blank screen. "They're all bites."

"Okay," he said. "A hospital . . . "

She put her bloodstained finger to his lips. "No."

Paul's phone was in hand. He'd been ready to dial. He returned it to his pocket.

"Take your phone out," she said, never looking at him. "You do need to call the police. I just killed the best friend I ever had."

Cash took the corner of the bed sheet and used it to try and remove the drying blood on her arms.

"We can get you all cleaned up, with all the best sanitizers, at a hospital. How 'bout it, Cash?" offered Rob.

"My name is Caroline."

She rubbed the sheet harder against her skin.

There was a sound by the window. Rob looked at Paul, who cracked some more glass as he stepped to pull the curtain aside. He nudged his head out, being careful to avoid the jagged remains that had sliced Rob's arm.

A coyote. The American jackal. Fangs bared, ears pointed, it tore at the bags of chicken outside their door.

"All good," said Paul, as he turned to Rob. "Just an animal."

"Before we call the police," said Rob softly, as he ran his hand gently along his girlfriend's hair, "why don't you try and tell me anything you might remember about what happened. I know you did nothing wrong, but we may have to be careful about how we explain this to the authorities."

Paul walked toward the bathroom, as to give a bit of privacy.

She looked down at her arm, still scouring.

"I shot her. More than once, I think. I murdered Teresa."

"No baby, it wasn't murder. I saw her face, and your bites. She became . . . she changed. That's clear."

"We were laughing, Rob. Just talking like any other night; watching TV. Then . . . " she stopped talking, stopped rubbing her arm. Rob just waited and tousled her hair. The bathroom faucet began running, heard through the open door.

"Just tell me the same way you'd tell the police," he said.

"She charged across from this bed to mine. Took us both to the floor. I managed to get up and run toward the door." She looked around the room, "Where is Paul?"

"What? Paul?"

"Where is he?" asked Cash. "He needs to call the cops."

The faucet turned off.

"He's just in the bathroom, Caroline. What happened after you ran toward the door?"

She looked up from her arm, gazed into Rob's eyes. "That's weird," she said. "You never call me Caroline."

"Cash," he said. "Can I call you Cash?"

"Whatever."

The water was running again in the bathroom. Cash resumed rubbing.

"She caught me before I reached the door. She was making loud, horrible noises. She was so strong. I turned to push her away . . . "

The tears came. They seemed to wash Cash out of her detached state. The tautness abandoned her body. The rubbing ceased.

"I grabbed whatever I could," she said. "I hit her with Paul's helmet. Over and over. She was tearing at me, Rob . . . "

From the bathroom, it sounded like Paul dropped a plastic cup. Rob glanced in that direction but quickly returned to his girlfriend.

"I know, Cash," he whispered.

"The helmet didn't faze her. I bashed the hell out of her, but *nothing*. We tumbled to the floor and the lamp fell on us. I tried to hit her with that too. I punched and kicked. She . . . she was ripping pieces off me."

Her head dropped into her stained hands. Rob exhaled. Helplessness engulfed him. The curtains flitted ethereally in the arid desert breeze. There was the ruffling of the chicken bags just beyond the shattered window. It meshed with the sonance of sobs and the babble of the running faucet. Rob took a peek at the oozing slice on his forearm, as he caressed Cash's quivering shoulder.

"Then I saw the gun under the bed," she wept.

He leaned closer and kissed the top of her head. She raised her eyes.

"I just had to stop it," she said, almost pleadingly. "Rob, she was hurting me so much. Biting and clawing. Choking. She was killing me."

"I know, sweetheart."

"I yelled, 'It's me, Teresa! T, it's Carrie. Stop!' But . . . she . . . just came for more."

He wrapped both arms around her, the blood from his wound knitting with hers.

"You did what you had to. Different times, different rules."

The small pink bathroom cup rolled out onto the floor of the main room.

"Paul?" said Rob.

No response.

"You okay in there?"

Just the dribble of the faucet. Cash turned to look toward the bathroom. Rob stood and headed cautiously for the running water. He paused by Teresa's covered body. The bike helmet and gun were beside her. He reached to pick up the helmet. Then he glanced over and saw Cash looking so helpless on the bed. He picked up the gun instead.

"Hey, Paul," he tried, one final time.

The absence of response had him stepping quietly toward the bathroom, 9 mm behind his back. He was almost at the pink plastic cup, as it rested on the soiled carpet. As Paul had left the door open, Rob wasn't sure if he should slowly peek into the lavatory or just quickly charge in. Various movie and TV cops flashed through his brain.

What would they do?

It just confused him.

He reached the doorway and decided to go with the slow, one-eyed peek.

There was Paul, standing and facing the mirror. He had one leg up on the toilet, head tilted back, and to one side, elbow firmly braced against the edge of the small sink.

Paul stared into the cloudy mirror. He was desperately attempting to pop a problematic pimple under his chin.

Rob immediately spotted the Hello Kitty buds in his oblivious cohort's ears. The tinny fast-paced music sounded as if one had thrown a rave within an aluminum kettle.

As Rob fully entered the doorway, he bent to pick up the fallen cup behind him.

"You guys good?" yelled Paul, music still assaulting his ears, "Carrie okay?"

He raised his left hand, giving Rob a hopeful thumbs-up sign, while keeping the fingers of his right hand around his pimple. Then he pointed to his headphones. "Wanted to give y'all some privacy."

Rob looked back at Cash. "All good, baby," he smiled.

She felt a tad better, considering she was still stuck in the worst day of her life, so she decided to call the police herself. Whatever fate awaited her, it was time to face it. She felt heart-shattering guilt over Teresa, but maybe Rob was right; she had no real choice. As Rob entered the bathroom to talk with Paul, Cash looked over at Teresa's iPhone, still there on the bed. She picked it up and tapped it. The device was still on Twitter. The prior trending topics had changed just a bit. *Walkers*, *#zombies*, and *cannibals* were still near the top, but a new phrase was currently the most popular topic on the country's Twitter feed. Some type of abbreviation. A cannibalized abridgement of an actual word. Chic slang for the suffering.

#Canni

"This idiotic helmet makes me nuts," said the cop. His face could not be seen through the visor. It was the same type of helmet worn by government security. No markings of any kind. No mention of Las Vegas Metro P.D. Had the same wireless trigger mechanism on his wrist.

He finally sat on the edge of the bed after interviewing Cash, jotting down notes. Another officer had questioned Rob just outside the open motel room door, beside what remained of the chicken bags, and a third cop spoke with Paul by the bathroom. Only one of the officers had the fancy new helmet.

Teresa's body remained under the bloodstained sheet on the floor by the bed.

The cop removed his headgear. He was sweating beneath it.

"I gotta take this off now and then; annoying as hell." He wiped his forehead and thick mustache as he smiled at Cash. "So you're sure the dead guy out on the balcony had absolutely nothing to do with the incident in this room?"

"I'm sure. I've told you that already."

"Yeah," said the cop, "but two rooms, two smashed front windows, two bodies . . . "

"Johnson!" came the husky bellow from the balcony, "Why is that helmet off your head again?"

"It's makin' me crazier than a funeral clown, that's why, Sarge."

"Well, you've had riot gear on before, haven't you?"

"Yeah, but . . . "

"No different. Do me a favor; put it on and keep it on. And a funeral clown is not a thing."

The sergeant's order, as usual, was framed as a request. He was medium height but quite broad-shouldered and he always spoke in command voice. As his subordinate grudgingly put the helmet back on, the supervisor pointed him toward the balcony door.

"Wait out there with the boyfriend. Keep your eyes on the rest of us."

As the officer left, the sergeant sat down on the bed.

"Caroline, I'm Sergeant Obarowski. I'm very sorry you lost your friend here today. It's obvious that you've been through hell."

"Thank you. That other cop was a little harsh. I'm not proud of what I've done, but I'm not hiding from it either."

"I understand."

"That cop kept asking me about what happened in the other motel room. I told him what I could, but I wasn't in that room. What happened here was not related to that . . . other than the same thing happened to the girl in the other room . . . "

"Don't you worry about all that," smiled the policeman. "The glass patterns corroborate your story; broken glass inside this room and outside that other room. Other things too, but I won't bore you with all that. However, despite my ego, I am not the final arbiter of these things, so we will need you and your friends to come down to the station while we get Crime Scene in here for some pictures and stuff like that. We might need to have you make a stop at the hospital and get those bites examined."

She stared off into space.

"What . . . um . . . what about Teresa?" she asked, quietly.

"The medical examiner's office will be removing her body, and then we'll go from there. It's a process, miss."

There was a good forty seconds of silence before Cash spoke again.

"How come only one of you cops has a helmet?"

Thick Sergeant Obarowski gave her a smile. "Not enough of them yet. We take turns wearing the ones we do get. Better than nothing, I guess."

"Oh."

"We have to keep them under lock and key. Seems they get stolen and taken home."

"I wish we had them."

Rob came in from the balcony, with the helmeted cop behind him.

"Do we really have to go to the police station, Sergeant? She has been through so much already."

"Look, young man, it's just a paperwork thing. A while back, this would've been a major case—two dead bodies in a motel. The local news would be all over this. But now this has become routine. You said the male victim on the balcony had been there for hours and nobody gave a rat's ass. Not surprised."

"But Cash—I mean Caroline—she could really use some food and rest, sir."

"We'll grab something for the three of you to eat and we'll get her medical attention, but we do have to eventually go to the station. All of your accounts of what happened seem very credible, but—and I'm not implying this is the case here—some folks have used this epidemic we're having as a chance to do away with people and claim self-defense. We've had cases where a true premeditated murder has occurred, and the perpetrator tried to claim that the victim had transformed into one of these, you know . . . "

"Cannis," said Cash.

"What?" asked Rob.

"She's right," said the cop. "That's a new street term. Short for 'cannibals'. Ah, whatever floats your boat."

"But you saw Teresa's body," pleaded Rob. "The way she looked with the . . . "

He waved his hand over his face.

"Yes. The eyes, the caked vomit," replied the police sergeant. "That's all in your favor. However, there is the issue of the weapon. I know we're in some kind of an ass-ways wild, wild west these days, but a stolen police weapon is still kind of a big deal."

"Sergeant," said a monotone Cash, "I told you that a police officer actually told us to take that gun. We witnessed that horrific scene on the highway with the three cops. The one who survived is the one who told us. You can ask him yourself."

"If we hadn't listened to that policeman," added Rob, "Caroline would be dead now."

"Officer Pruyn, get us on the list for the van," bellowed the sergeant to the third officer, who came out of the bathroom with Paul.

"Yes sir."

"The van?" asked Rob.

"Just for transport, young man," answered Obaraowski, "The three of us can barely fit in our former two-officer patrol unit, so we can't take you all to the station in our car. It's for your own safety as well. We're gonna have to secure you all in the van so that if one of you does exhibit a change of behavior, you'll all remain safe."

Cash dropped her head as she spoke.

"Am I going to jail?"

"I wouldn't worry much about that, miss," he said. "Do you know that we can't even keep two-person prison cells anymore? You have no idea the number of felons who are being released, just because the prison system literally has no room to lodge them safely anymore. Cruel and unusual punishment, they say. If they're coming out, you ain't going in, Caroline."

Rob gave her a reassuring smile, as Officer Pruyn stepped back to radio for the transport van.

Sergeant Obarowski's penetrating eyes gave Paul Bhong the once-over. "Nice Hello Kitty earphones," he said, without expression.

Paul quickly looked down to see them dangling from his pocket in all their pinkness. Before he could formulate a response, a loud wail came from the front door.

"What the fuck is all this?"

The man was blocked from entering by Officer Johnson. It was Mackey, the motel manager—or maybe it was Jackie. His hands sat on his hips, and the unopened bottle of orange soda rolled around by his feet.

It seemed to be a new sun, but in reality, it had been right there for over four billion years. It carried the new day through the police station windows. Taken at face value, maybe if isolated in a photo, it might be interpreted as reassuring, even cheery.

But this was not a Polaroid.

The musty stench of the crowded lobby taunted Cash's nostrils, staining the memory of the antiseptic air she'd underappreciated during her early morning stay at the hospital. She sat on a peeling hardwood bench with Paul to her right. To her left was a large, bald fellow with a fresh, rough, self-inflicted tattoo of a cross on his sweaty forehead. He smelled like olive loaf.

She tried to converse with Paul as the big guy feverishly fingered through the pages of a worn, black and white composition notebook. "They'll soon grow horns," he muttered to no one in particular.

The lobby was standing room only as the overworked cops tried to deal with a panic-stricken public. The police were, as usual, located behind a tall, intimidating desk with all doors to the work area behind the towering counter securely bolted. Now however, two helmeted officers stood on something no more elaborate than soapboxes, on each end of the lobby. In addition to their usual gun belt accessories, both men carried stun guns the length of a nightstick.

"They did your whole interview at the hospital?" asked Paul.

"Yeah, a detective even fingerprinted me and took my picture," she smiled. "I hope I never have to see that photo. What a mess."

"I'm sure you still look just beautiful," responded Paul.

Cash didn't answer. Though a compliment, it felt odd.

Olive Loaf Man had more to say, and somehow Cash welcomed the auditory break in the awkward silence. "Time, times, and a half," he growled, as he tore through his pages of faded ink.

"Well, they bandaged you up good," said Paul, trying to distance himself from his maladroit adulation.

"Yep. I hope they don't take too long in there with Rob. I'm the one who . . . " Her voice trailed off as a vision of Teresa's comforting face graced her memory.

"Mrs. Larkin," called out a desk officer. He was reading from a waiting list. A frail older woman stood and approached him.

The guy with the notebook wasn't done yet. "Only the roaches shall remain. Happened before—Triceratops, Stegosaurus. Extinction event, you fucking Mouseketeers. Deal with it."

Cash had no patience for all of this. She trained her big, tired, and empty brown eyes on him.

"How exactly is this an extinction event if it's only happening in our country? Quit terrorizing these people. Things are bad enough, jackoff."

He quickly closed his book and turned away from her. He mumbled under his breath as his teeth ground against each other.

"Switch seats with me, Carrie," said Paul.

"No, it's fine. Did they feed you and Rob? At the hospital, they gave me a piece of quarry rubble that they referred to as a bagel. All things considered, bad as it was, I loved it."

"I've never been much of a bagel guy."

"You ever been to New York?"

"No."

"Then, you've never really had a bagel."

"We got an egg on white bread and a cold coffee. Prisoner food they get from a diner."

"Lucky you."

"Never been back East. I do have friends up and down the East Coast. Well, internet friends, anyway. Mostly people who ride, or computer nerds."

She nodded.

"So," he continued, "what's next for you? Did they tell you anything?"

"They gave me a court appearance ticket. The date is like six months away."

"They charged you with something, then."

"I think it has to do with the gun. They basically told me not to worry. I told them I won't even be in Vegas in six months. Didn't faze them. The detective said in normal times I'd be held, or at least released on some pricey bail. They just let me go. No bail money or anything."

"Yeah, those appearance tickets are usually dated for about one month away. The backlog must be insane these days."

Cash gave him a look.

"I . . . I know people who get arrested," he stammered. "Not speaking from personal experience."

"Mr. Harris," called out the desk cop. A lanky fellow with a young boy beside him walked up to the officer.

" . . . unt," whispered the sweaty lunchmeat beside Cash, face buried in his notebook.

She was hoping that she didn't miss a *C* at the start of his grumble and convinced herself that he was not referring to her. She ignored it.

"They gave me a prescription for pain meds at the hospital," she said to Paul. "For the bites."

"Score!" he smiled, trying to lighten the mood. No response.

The big guy beside her was scribbling in his book and breathing heavily.

"I asked the ER doctor," she said softly. "I asked her if, since I was bitten, I was probably infected, or whatever . . . "

The scribbler tore out his page, crumpled it, and stashed it in his pocket.

"She told me that I was infected long before the bites, and that she herself and the cops and everyone else were also infected."

"Yeah," said Paul, as he touched her hand reassuringly. "We're all in this together."

She found the hand touching a bit strange, but it bothered her less than his previous oversteps.

A plainclothes cop emerged through the door, accompanying the frail woman who had been brought behind the desk moments earlier. He had his arm on her back, nearly holding her up.

"But I just want to sit here," she pleaded.

"We can't have that. We're overcrowded as it is, ma'am."

"It's the only place I feel safe, young man. I can sleep right in that chair."

"I can get you a van ride to a safe house. They're popping up all over the city. You can feel secure there, Mrs. Larkin."

"But my downstairs tenant, Harold, he says those places are not safe at all."

"These days, they're as good as it gets. At home, I can't even sleep with my own wife."

He led her out the front door into the Las Vegas heat.

"Dr. Hargrove," called out the uniformed desk officer.

The nonsensical note taker beside Cash stood. He looked right at her, giving her a clear view of the cross dug into his damp head, tucked his book under his arm, and walked toward the police desk.

"Doctor?" she said to Paul, her sleepy eyes widening.

"Probably just the name he wrote down on that waiting list. I can call myself Commodore, if I want, or fucking Rear Admiral."

From the face of the desk, the man turned back at Cash.

"Only happening in our country *today*," he said, mimicking her voice, "But what about tomorrow?"

The cab smelled like the Marlboro Man had fucked the St. Pauli Girl in the back seat, while permitting the driver to watch under the condition that he swear off deodorant forever.

Rob sat in the middle with Cash and Paul on either side, behind the partition.

"You'd think they'd have a closer police station than that," sighed Cash.

"They do," answered Paul. "But not with those friendly homicide detectives that we got to meet."

"And, worst of all, we don't have a gun anymore," added Rob.

The mention of a firearm, along with the word *homicide,* was not lost on the cab driver, who glanced in his rearview mirror.

"They are having NYPD tell Teresa's family," he added.

"What?"

"Babe, I didn't want you to have to do that over the phone, and I'm not close enough to her family."

"But strangers?"

"They lost Joy-Joy, and now Teresa," whispered Cash. "And I *killed* T. How can I ever face those people again?"

Rob intertwined his fingers with hers. "They'll understand," he said. "Nothing is as it was."

As Paul and Cash gazed out of their respective windows, Rob, sitting in the middle of the back bench, took note of the clear partition between them and the driver. Though the rest of the taxi interior was well-worn and had the scars of thousands of late-night Vegas transports, the partition appeared to be brand new; shiny, clear, not a scratch on it. There was a sliding window through which cash could be exchanged, and several small holes to facilitate conversation. Rob leaned forward and ran his finger along the holes as his mind flipped through various scenarios regarding Cash, marriage, and survival.

"You need seatbelt, please," smiled the driver, through the mirror. "People get hurt if I stop short. Break nose on divider. Please all wear seatbelt."

"Oh, sure," replied Rob.

He and Paul dug behind themselves for the belts, feeling all sorts of crumbs and candy wrappers as they searched. Cash's belt had been on the whole time, and her hands had already been sanitized.

"The partition looks pretty new," said Rob. "Hopefully you haven't been robbed or anything."

"Divider not for robbers."

The unlit neon clown was high in the sky and holding a pinwheel as he pointed at Circus Circus Hotel and Casino. Cash was trying to decide if the vintage display was happy or creepy as the driver continued, "Nobody is canni in my cab, yet. Thank God. Bad things happen to other drivers, though. You don't worry either, my friends. I never flip to monster while driving. No crashes. Thank

Jesus. One time I become monster at home, but I was alone. I wake up on floor and many things broken and smashed. Bad taste in mouth, stuff on face—but nobody hurt. Thank God and Jesus. Also, Uber and Lyft not safe for passenger."

"None of us have turned either," replied Rob. "You can feel safe too, I guess."

Cash's eyes were drawn to a car, up on the sidewalk, front end partially through a fence; the driver's head resting against the closed side window. No pedestrians around the car, no cops or hotel security in sight.

"That man might be hurt," she said loudly.

"That's one-man canni crash," he replied. "Nothing for us to do."

"But he . . . "

"People turn into monster, all alone in car. Then, the car crash. Monster stuck in car, growling, biting. Usually strapped in by seatbelt, too stupid to unlock belt or open door. Sometimes people watch from outside car—like looking into big cage or fish tank. Then after twenty minute, maybe longer, monster become person again and fall asleep. That man just sleeping it off. When he wake up, he call tow truck."

Cash looked at Rob, as the driver continued, "You all have seatbelt on, right?"

Fifteen minutes later the cab pulled into the parking lot of In-room Hobo. Rob dug some cash from his wallet and stuffed it in the money drawer of the partition.

"Thanks for the ride," he said to the driver. "Keep the change."

"Jesus be with you."

Cash emerged first, instinctively reaching out for Rob's hand behind her. "Oh, no," was all she heard from him as he flew past her, running across the lot.

An empty parking stall.

In the spot that was previously occupied by his '83 Malibu, there was nothing but a collection of glass shards.

It was gone. His car. His *father's* car. And all of the 8-tracks it contained. Everything his dad had left him. All gone.

Cash and Paul approached.

"Maybe it was towed, baby," she said, without believing her own words.

"No. They broke the window."

"Okay, we'll call the cops. There aren't too many cars like yours around. They'll find it," she said.

"The police aren't going to look for it. They aren't going to come here and take a stolen vehicle report. All of that shit is from a different time. Stuff like this is meaningless."

"He's right," added Paul. "We could probably go to the station, wait around for three or four hours and file a report that way."

"They still won't have the time or manpower to look for my car," said Rob.

Cash took his hand. "Tell them what it means to you. Your father . . . "

"People are fucking eating each other, Caroline," he said. "I've only lost a car."

"I know some dudes who I can ask to look around for it," said Paul.

"Uh . . . yeah. Thanks, Paul. That would be awesome," answered Rob without much enthusiasm.

Cash smiled at Paul and touched his arm. "That's very cool of you. You are one interesting fellow, Paul Smith-Bhong."

He just laughed. "It's not like they're Special Ops or anything, but they do find things. Is there anything I can do for you guys before I take off? I'm beat."

"All good," said Rob. "We just need that sleep we can never seem to get. I'll worry about everything else when we wake up."

"Cool. Give me a shout later, or tomorrow, if you want. I'll try and hit up those guys to look for your car before I crash."

"Thank you," said Rob.

As he turned to head for the staircase, Cash leaned in and gave Paul a quick hug. "Thanks for helping."

"Oh . . . sure," he replied with a smile, not expecting the brief embrace. "Maybe you guys would want to check in the office. They might've heard something, or there could be a security camera . . . "

"In this place?" said Rob without turning around.

"Yeah," answered Paul. "More likely a hidden camera in each room to watch people hump."

"Ewwww," said Cash. Paul gave her a grin and headed for his bike.

The front desk area smelled like fried onions and secondhand cleats.

"Didn't see or hear nothin', okaaaay?" yakked Mackey, as a watery condiment blend dripped from his chapped lips.

"Security camera?" asked Rob.

The manager shook his head as he ran his hand across his mouth, in lieu of a napkin.

"Didn't think so," said Rob.

"Well, we've seen kids just hanging out in your lot," interrupted Cash. "Maybe you should get a camera or hire a guard."

"We usually don't have no trouble, bright eyes. None at all, really," he replied, the words riding out on a caramelized belch.

"Did you notice . . . ?" began Cash, before Mackey interrupted her.

"No trouble till you all got here," he said.

"Listen, dude . . . " said Rob.

"You trashed the room," said Mackey. "Got cops running all around the place. You nearly got my brother killed by some big, naked, colored guy who was only gettin' his fuck on, not doin' nothin' wrong, okaaaay . . . "

"That big guy is now dead, you know," added Rob.

"Yeah, you all happened to be there when that happened too," coughed Mackey. "Then your other girlfriend winds up as a corpse, now you have stolen car problems . . . "

"Let's have a little compassion about our friend," said Rob, noticing Cash's face when Mackey referred to Teresa.

"What I need," said Mackey, "is for you two to be gone from the premises."

"Gone?"

"Yeah, gone."

"We prepaid for this shithole," said Cash, raising her voice, "and we haven't done anything wrong."

Cash was Brooklyn tough, but she was tired, angry, and losing hope. Rob could hear the slight change in her voice. Tears were on the way.

"Your pre-pay won't even cover the cost for the smashed windows and all the room damages." Attempting a show of force, Mackey reached down and gently placed his signed baseball bat on the counter. "You all are from New York, right? Did you know this bat is signed by Yankees legends Derek Jeter and Mariano Rivera?"

He grabbed a soiled rag and ran it down the bat, as if he were shining it up. "I really need you to check out, now."

Rob smiled, "One, we are going to our room and going to sleep. When we wake up, we'll leave. If that is not agreeable to you, feel free to call the cops. If and when they respond to your call, in maybe three days, we'll be long gone. Two, I'm no expert, but those signatures seem to have been signed by the same person."

Rob took Cash by her hand and they left the office, with Mackey examining the signatures.

They must've slept for fourteen hours. The room was now 3 AM dark, the night's breeze invaded through the shattered front window, only to be intercepted by the curtains, and there were blood stains on the carpet. Cash couldn't sleep anymore and her mind was filled with memories of her lifelong best friend. The school talent shows. The junior and senior proms. High school graduation. Trips to the beach. Those final, sweet words T had said about Rob.

Cash looked over at her sleeping boyfriend. He seemed to be in the same position all night, but she had fallen asleep first, so maybe not. He slept on his side, with his back to her—not the usual way he'd curl up close, with his protective arm around her. His pillow almost covered his head.

She didn't want to wake him since rest was in short supply, and she really didn't want to start this day in which they would have to search for a new place to stay and have no car in which to do it. She thought about a rental but didn't know how much cash would be available on their credit cards with new hotel fees and whatever damage charges Mackey decided to add to their bill now piled on.

She grabbed the TV remote and flicked it on, immediately muting the sound. Doing the time change math, she figured her favorite early morning reruns might be on now in the West. She ran through the channels until she found it.

Success!

The pretty woman in the black and white broadcast was hopping around like a trained seal.

Cash managed the slightest smile as she lost herself in *I Love Lucy*.

It was funny, even with the sound off. Cash probably would know most of the dialogue from memory anyway. The show had a calming, soothing effect on her. It provided her first real memory of television—well, maybe after Barney the Dinosaur.

She grabbed the bottle of sanitizer from the nightstand, along with a tissue and cleaned off the remote and her hands.

Cash often fantasized about living in a fictional world like Lucy's. It seemed like such a happier and simpler time and she'd thought that long before the current world almost literally went to hell. Lucy had a great best friend in Ethel. Cash's own Ethel was gone.

Lucy would've never killed Ethel. No matter what, she thought.

The guilt was coming back. Cash knew it would be there, just beneath the surface much of the time, but present nonetheless—forever.

Of course, she thought, *in Teresa's mind, she would've been Lucy, and I would be Ethel.*

A smile came, and then vanished just as quickly.

Ethel would've never killed Lucy either.

Beneath the blankets and pillows, Rob moved a bit.

Cash thought about the fictional relationship between Lucy and Ricky. They seemed so perfect for each other, so deeply in love. Cash did feel love for Rob but wasn't sure it reached the Lucy/Ricky level. Did any real-life romance? She knew—and Teresa had told her—how much Rob loved her. She never doubted that. But she would occasionally wonder if he truly loved her, or if he loved having her as his. He was too protective, sometimes overbearingly so.

The covers tugged a bit in the glow of the TV screen as he made some sort of muffled sound.

Probably dreaming.

When her mind drifted to his possessive behavior, and his issues with jealousy, she would often blame herself for being too picky. She knew women who were saddled with men who cheated, men who ignored them, even men who beat them.

Still, she wanted Lucy and Ricky.

She wanted Hollywood romance from *Pretty Woman* or *An Officer and a Gentleman*.

He needn't be a ringer for a young Richard Gere, but she was hoping for something more relaxed.

Love me, care for me, but don't own me.

She thought if Rob had just a touch of the free spirit within Paul, he would be perfect.

Thinking of Paul made her uneasy. He was too touchy, and a bit forward, but he seemed so effortless and liberated. She'd never met anyone quite like him. He was mysterious.

Rob moved again, but this time she heard a different sound; a metallic rattle. She thought of a tin cup against jail bars. He grunted too, but it sounded muffled.

She leaned over, but his head was still beneath the pillow.

Cash got out of bed, being careful not to wake him. Wearing a Homer Simpson t-shirt and a pair of sweats, she found her way around by the light of the television, as no outdoor illumination, streetlight or otherwise, could penetrate the heavy curtains. She crossed by the foot of the bed, her own body temporarily blocking the glow from *I Love Lucy*.

Another rattle.

As she got around to his side of the bed, she was standing on a bathroom towel; it had been placed over the dried stain of Teresa's blood. The darkness and her thick socks prevented her from realizing that fact, but the dim television glare did manage to illuminate Rob's figure on the bed.

She reached to remove the pillow that covered his head. The blankets were pulled up to his neck.

Ricky Ricardo pounded furiously on the congas, but the muted TV kept them silent.

She was careful not to wake him, even as she saw his head.

It was covered, like a Klansman, with an off-white pillowcase. There were crude holes cut out for his eyes and nose. None for the mouth. She could see his eyes were still shut. She pulled the blanket away just a bit. Around his neck was a protective wrap, fashioned out of tied-together t-shirts. Looked like a multi-colored neck brace.

She pulled the blankets a bit further down and discovered the source of the rattling noise.

Handcuffs. Obviously lifted, borrowed, or unofficially exchanged for the gun at police headquarters, Rob had gotten himself a set of cuffs and had shackled himself to the bed frame.

As she stood on the section of carpet where her best friend died, she recalled some of Teresa's last words. They were about Rob.

He is a bit overbearing at times, but he thinks he's protecting you, and he would never, ever hurt you, Carrie.

There he was, bound to the bed, completely helpless should Cash turn as Teresa had, his only form of protection being some shirts around his throat. But he had gone to great lengths to ensure that he would not hurt her should he transform while she slept.

Cash felt guilty about her Richard Gere thoughts and her Lucy and Ricky fantasy. She wondered if she had ever witnessed a scene of such selfless love.

Then she considered the possibility that Rob may not have stolen a handcuff key.

They carried their luggage down the steps from the bird shit balcony in the midday sun. Rob glanced over at the parking space where he'd last seen his car— as if it might've reappeared.

"I really can't believe you can unlock handcuffs with a bobby pin," said Cash, still in her Homer Simpson shirt and well-worn sweats.

"Do you mean you can't believe that cuffs can be opened with a bobby pin, or you can't believe that *I* can do it?"

"Oh, shut up," she smiled. "I'm impressed, okay?"

"It's much trickier if you're cuffed behind the back."

"Still, it's not something I thought you knew."

"Hey, I'm from Brooklyn."

Maybe he does have a little Paul Bhong in him, she thought.

"No more of that stuff, though," she said. "I could've really hurt you if I had flipped during the night."

"Nah," he smiled. "I love when you bite me."

"I'm serious. Either we're both cuffed, or no one is."

They approached the door to the motel office.

"Let me wait out here with the luggage," said Cash. "I hate the way he looks at me."

"I don't want to leave you alone."

"I'll be right here. You can see me through the freaking window, *Dad*."

There he goes again.

"I'd really rather you next to me," he said.

"Nope."

He stacked the suitcases up and looked through the window to be sure he'd be able to see her from inside. As he entered the office, he heard the TV in the back room. Sounded like porn. He was hoping for Jackie, who was a crude slob, but an improvement over Mackey.

"Hello?" he yelled.

"Harder," cried the girl in the video.

Rob looked back toward the window to check on Cash. She was scrolling in her phone and biting a fingernail. She wondered if Rob had ever contacted his pal, John G, to either cancel, or update their plans to meet. Rob had told her that John was not a guy who was always tied to his phone. Seems he was a free spirit.

There was a bell on the front desk and Rob tapped it.

Turned out to be the dinner bell.

Here came Mackey—or maybe it was Jackie—from the back room. His eyes were fiery, and he spewed blood, vomit, and flesh. He flew over the counter like an Olympian. His sweaty forehead slammed into Rob's face as they both fell backward into a display of Las Vegas sightseeing brochures and then to the ground. The last thing Rob saw before the canni was fully on top of him was Cash, still outside the window, twiddling on her phone.

If he kills me, he'll kill her next, was all Rob could think, *If I can just hold my own for a few minutes, maybe he'll change back.*

The attacker's teeth clattered above Rob's face, and his breath reeked—well, truthfully, it had always been pretty bad. Rob managed to get his forearm between their faces.

Let him chew on that for a few minutes.

His dripping canines were a bit longer than the assortment of other teeth he had. There weren't too many.

Which one of those dickheads had all the missing choppers?

Didn't matter. The teeth were digging into Rob's arm when he heard it.

Clunk.

The attacker went limp and collapsed onto Rob. He pushed him off and saw Cash standing there, holding Mackey's prized and possibly Jeter and Rivera autographed, baseball bat.

"I'm a Mets fan," she said, as she hurled the weapon back over the counter. Rob exhaled. Cash put her hand out to help him to his feet.

"We should call an ambulance for him," he said, as he stood.

"By the time they get here, he'll be awake. All he'll have is a headache. Your arm okay?"

"I'm fine. Let's call a taxi and find somewhere normal to stay."

Rob put his hand on the door handle. Sounded like the girl in the porn video screamed, "Smack my ass, Supreme Overlord." Then they heard another sound.

He came stumbling out of the back, eyes wide, a curtain of blood pouring from his ruptured throat. The *other* brother. Jackie. Or maybe Mackey.

He took two steps, then fell, face first, to the office floor. Rob hopped the counter to check on him. Cash kept her eyes on the unconscious canni.

"He's gone," said Rob, as the boisterous girl in the video pretended to climax.

They left the office and grabbed their luggage. The door closed behind them. The two brothers were sprawled on the tiles, the front desk dividing them.

The door opened once more. Rob reentered and dropped his room key on the counter. Then he left again.

DANIEL O'CONNOR

Virginia

"Yes, Santa Claus, there is a Virginia."

Dr. R Anderson was mumbling to himself as he pondered some graphics on a map of the United States on his desktop computer. He was focused on his home state.

He sat at a cubicle just off the bright and cheery kitchen in his ranch home. Fifteen feet away, his sister was plopped at the granite counter, her laptop, tablet, and several notebooks spread before her. Twelve feet from them was a small bathroom, which R had reinforced with several locks and a security bar. The plan was if either of them flipped the other would run and secure themselves in the bathroom. They could also then climb out the window if need be.

"What are you grumbling about?" she asked. "I can't hear anything with this racket."

She was referring to AC/DC's *Highway to Hell* album blasting from the living room.

"Racket? That's music, my dear. Helps me concentrate. Besides, we are supposed to have two days off because of our injuries. I deserve to have some enjoyment."

"Sure, let's just go out to the lake for some fishing while the country collapses."

"Not fair. I'm working with a head wound and everything," he said between Diet Mountain Dew gulps. "I might be concussed."

"Poor baby with that bump on your head," she answered. "By the way, by my calculations, right about now, a security guard at work is shitting out my right shoulder."

"Well, your brother is taking good care of you," he said, as he switched back and forth between his research and an internet motorcycle forum.

"I won't argue with that. No way I could get any work done at home with Joe and the kids."

"I know they miss their Mommy. They doing okay?"

"As good as can be while usually locked in separate rooms, all wearing goalie masks."

R left the chat room and returned to his work.

"I still think our focus, at least initially, should be to find some type of indicator as to when a transformation might happen. A warning sign. Would solve a lot of issues until we find a cure."

"We need a cure."

"I know. I just mean that it might be easier to find a marker . . . "

"A cure."

"If we look at these episodes as seizures," he said, "there may be warning signs that we haven't isolated yet. Odors, mood swings, even just an aura of sorts . . . "

"This isn't epilepsy."

"If we focus only on a cure, we may lose everybody. However, if we can predict when an individual is likely to have a cannibalistic episode, much of the battle is won. No more family members killing each other. No more soldiers attacking their own. No more vehicle accidents due to being infected. Then we focus on a cure, which could take years to perfect—the clinical trials, FDA approvals . . . "

"That's all out the window. If we find anything close to a cure, it will be implemented almost immediately. It has to be."

On his desktop screen, R watched grainy footage of seven or eight churchgoing men, all in suits, desperately trying to control, and pin to the floor, an elderly priest who had become canni while on the altar.

Alarming as it was, Dr. R had seen his share of horror in the United States Army, just like his father and grandfather before him, so his daily function was rarely altered by external forces or images.

"Hey V, ya feel like a calzone?"

DANIEL O'CONNOR

Las Vegas

The shelter had only been active for a few days and it already smelled like corned beef hash and piss. This one was in the gymnasium of a high school that had become the victim of Clark County budget cuts. The beds were in perfectly formed rows. There was a large section that consisted only of blankets on the hardwood. It was stuffy and warm; the air conditioning was on, but sorely in need of a tune-up. The shelter was quieter than Rob and Cash had expected, just the occasional cough and the echoes of crying babies. At strategic points throughout the cavernous room stood members of the National Guard, some with the masked helmets, some without. The woman by the check-in desk had introduced herself as Steph, but her accent transformed it into *Staph* for the two New Yorkers' ears.

"We walked here from Las Vegas Boulevard," said Rob as he wiped the sweat from his eyes. "We were tossed out of our hotel. Our car was stolen. Her best friend just died. We're thousands of miles from home. I just want to keep her safe."

Cash stood behind him next to their luggage.

"I am sympathetic," said Steph, as if trying to convince herself. She had the body shape and neck of a Narragansett Turkey. "I truly wish we could accommodate you folks. You've been through so much, but we all have. We must give priority to those with small children. We also try and care for our seniors. Between all of that, there just isn't room for young and strong people such as you all."

"I can work for you," said Rob. "You must need able-bodied help. I'll clean toilets."

"Sir, we really . . . "

"Let my girl sleep here, please. I can stay outside in the street . . . "

Cash interrupted. "That is not happening."

"She's pregnant," he said.

Staph gave Cash the once-over.

"How far along are you?" she asked.

"We just found out," said Rob, before Cash could respond.

The woman produced a clipboard with some papers on it. "You'll both need to fill this out and produce valid identification."

Rob was thrilled. He studied her neck jiggle as he reached into his pants to get his driver's license. He was reading the admittance paperwork when Steph's arm swung over it. Her triceps fat was doing the Tango Argentino with her neck. She dropped a home pregnancy test onto the paperwork.

"It's ten dollars for the test, and I have to go in the bathroom with your wife while she takes it."

Rob arched an eyebrow and sighed, but at the same time, he couldn't help but savor the thought that Cash had been referred to as his wife.

CANNI

Virginia

The roads had a touch of rainwater on them, but nothing too severe. Only a novice biker would have any trouble at all in this type of weather. It was more mist than rain.

But the skid marks were there, plain as day.

Along the dark path of the tire tracks they found the sissy bar and the luggage rack, twisted and scarred from scraping the road. Ten yards beyond them was the Guardian Bell. Also known as a Gremlin Bell, its purpose was to symbolically protect motorcycle riders from evil. Crafted from fine pewter, this particular bell featured the inscription *2ⁿᵈ Amendment Defender* wrapped around a depiction of the stars and stripes.

The black Harley was at rest on its side beside the damp and rusty guardrail, oil and gasoline seeping out like plasma. One helmeted rider lay prone on the slick pavement, beside the fallen Screamin' Eagle; another was on the far side of the guard rail, down a wet, grassy embankment—arms and legs bent the wrong way, like snapped twigs.

"This one's breathing!" yelled the EMT beside the Harley.

A lanky cop knelt beside the rider with the twisted limbs. The officer looked up from the turfy slope, his face dewy with drizzle. He had no idea about the potential gravity of his next words.

"Not this one," he said.

"He rode a bike his whole life. Could do it with his eyes closed. He was in the Gulf War, was in the Pentagon on 9/11. He saved my fucking life yesterday," she said, quietly, "and he's dead because of me. I killed my brother."

V. Anderson reclined on a hospital bed. Her right shoulder was still bandaged, and now her left arm was in a sling. Both arms were also wrapped as they had been torn up by the pavement. Her neck was stuffed in a hard collar. She gulped frantically from a water bottle.

"Well, you are lucky to be alive," said the attending physician. He was standing with two police officers and a representative of the government.

"I need to speak with Dr. Anderson in private, please," said the government man. He was a tall, thickly built, Mexican-American with a shaved head and bleached white teeth. V eyed his three-piece suit, speculating that the sales tax on it would likely have paid for the clothes her brother was wearing when he died.

"We've been told that Dr. Anderson should have top level protection," said the physician, "I believe the police officers need to remain."

"No," came the reply from the government man. "They will stand outside the door until I speak with her."

Without debate, the hospital doctor and the two cops walked out.

"I don't believe we've ever met in person," he said. "I'm Arturo Ochoa-Calderone. Please call me Art."

V's thoughts were all about her brother, but she couldn't help inwardly sighing.

Another fucking hyphenated name.

"My condolences, Doctor Anderson. Your brother was an asset to his country."

Was? she thought. She knew he was gone, but still, the past tense had her upside down.

"I don't mean to be callous," he continued, "but do you remember anything at all about the motorcycle accident?"

It was all a blank. She was quite sure what had caused the wreck, and there was nothing in her mind to indicate otherwise, yet she thought hard as Arturo looked on.

"He wanted a calzone."

"A calzone?"

"Yes. That's the last thing I remember. My brother wanted to get some calzones for our lunch. He must've somehow cajoled me into getting on the back of his bike."

"You didn't like the bike?"

"Not especially. Definitely not in times like these. He was a persuasive sort, though."

That *was* word again. She looked over at the wall at nothing in particular and gulped from the water bottle.

"So you can recall nothing after the calzone comment?"

"I don't even remember walking out the door. I just woke up here."

"I assume, from your prior comments, that you believe that you . . . "

"Yeah. I flipped. Went canni."

"How do you *know* that to be the case?"

"You kidding?"

"Not at all. I understand you have memory loss but being tossed off a bike could cause anyone to black out."

"Where is my brother's body?"

"Not to worry. That is all being taken care of, and with utmost respect. No need to be concerned. I promise."

"Has anyone called my husband?"

"We have not. Once we knew you were relatively okay, I made the decision to let you proceed with that phone call, whenever you like."

"Okay. Good choice there. I appreciate that."

"Certainly," he replied. "As far as you flipping, how can you be sure that you actually did?"

CANNI

"Mr. Ochoa, I . . . "

"Ochoa-Calderone. But call me Art."

"Okay Art, when I awoke, my mouth tasted like the asshole of an African Bush Elephant. Also, I am starving. My beloved brother has just died, yet I want nothing more right now than a trip to the fucking Olive Garden. But, the number one reason I know that I had a cannibalistic seizure is because a man who could handle any bike on any terrain and in any weather wiped out on a lazy afternoon ride to a pizzeria. I obviously went berserk on the back of his Harley, probably trying to chew his face off, which would have been quite impossible, as we both had full-face bike helmets on. Tell me, Art, when they found me, did I have vomit all over my mouth? Were my eyes completely and inhumanly red?"

"Yes. All of that."

"Can you smell the stench of my breath, right now, from where you stand?"

"Kind of."

"Then, Mr. Ochoa-Calderone, why the fuck are you asking me this shit? And do you have a Tic Tac?"

"Dr. Anderson, am I asking you anything that you have not asked of the volunteers that you and your brother have studied at Dr. Robert's *barn*?"

DANIEL O'CONNOR

Las Vegas

ALL FLIGHTS GROUNDED

That was the news headline on Paul's phone.

"Two separate passenger jet disasters within three hours must've been the last straw," he said.

"We couldn't fly home now, even if she wanted to," replied Rob. He and Paul were watching Cash as she dumped their empty soda cups into a curbside trash container. They had just eaten at the MGM Grand food court on Paul's dime. The three of them stood at the intersection of Las Vegas Boulevard and Tropicana Avenue, a crossroad that features more hotel rooms than any other in the world. Yet they had no place to stay.

Rob smiled at Cash as she turned from the trash can to walk back toward him. His back was leaning on the MGM. Behind Cash and across the street stood the Tropicana, and just across the boulevard loomed the Excalibur and New York-New York. For decades, this is where the excitement was, countless thrills and endless excitement for the hordes of tourists. Now, as Rob looked around, the quartet of buildings somehow brought him thoughts of the Four Horsemen of the Apocalypse.

As Cash approached him, hand sanitizer rubbing between her palms, he couldn't help but love her. Here was a world when, in normal times, many self-centered slobs would have just placed those empty cups by the wall of the MGM, or even simply dropped them into the street, or tossed them into the well-manicured shrubbery. Yet there was his girl, with the world going to hell, car wrecks all over the roads, people screaming in the distance, helmeted security forces running about, and jets falling from the skies—his girl was placing trash into a receptacle and washing her hands.

Yet doing anything normal, no matter how trivial, had an aura of reward.

"Sorry about those shelters, guys," said Paul.

"We took a collar. 0 for 4," answered Rob.

"Huh?"

"A baseball term. Never mind."

"Oh, like you struck out?"

"In a way."

"I would so let you crash with me, but I live in two rooms, dude."

"Don't even think about it," said Cash. "We'd be like sardines."

"That's not even it. We'd kill each other."

"Ha," laughed Cash, as if they were in prior times.

"I mean literally kill each other," replied Paul.

"Have you . . . ?"

"Gone canni? Not yet."

"Same with us," said Cash. "Maybe, we're all immune or something."

"Rumor has it that some people might actually be immune," said Paul. "Not sure what the odds are that all three of us would be, though."

Rob came off his wall-lean to tend to his suitcase that had toppled over on the sidewalk. "I wouldn't want one of us to realize that we are not immune by discovering the bodies of the other two."

"I may have a place for you guys," said Paul. "I've been debating it in my head for hours, but you should be the ones to decide."

"What?" said Cash.

"We'll take it," added Rob.

"Hold up. Not so fast," sighed Paul. "A shelter would have been much better, or a hotel . . . "

"Not a hotel," interrupted Rob. "She won't be safe in a hotel room alone with me."

"I bet she's been saying that for years."

"Very funny."

Paul looked at Cash. She was grinning. He continued, "There's this place. I went there to try and get some answers about your stolen car. I know some people. They trust me. Word is—and this is so unofficial that I shouldn't even be saying it—it seems that maybe no one there has flipped at all. At least not the area I'm talking about."

"That's beyond sweet!" yelped Cash.

"Is it some kind of shelter? Is there protection?" was all Rob wanted to know.

Paul avoided eye contact as he spoke. "You see, that's the thing."

Cash stepped off the bottom rung and moved away from the enormous concrete wall. Rob and Paul were at the bottom, waiting for her. The two suitcases were there too. Paul had left his bike in the MGM garage, but not without retrieving a pair of important items from it.

"I don't even know why we are bothering," she said.

"We can leave now, if you want," said Paul. "I just think this might be your best option, under the circumstances."

He put on his miner's helmet and turned on its light. Then he handed a flashlight to Cash.

"If Rob is the bellhop, you should hold the light."

Rob picked up the luggage. "Well, at least we have an hour or two of sunlight left."

Paul gave his cell phone a quick check as he answered Rob.

"Won't matter."

Cash turned on the hefty black Maglite as she studied the structure before her. There in the warm, bright Vegas sun stood the entrance. Ten feet high and equally as wide. The sunlight managed to creep about seven feet within, after which there was nothing but darkness.

"It has come to this. I'm going to live in the fucking sewer," grunted Cash.

"It's not the sewer system," replied Paul. "I promise. It's a drainage system for floods. Yeah, it rarely rains here, but when it does, it can come hard. This was built to funnel that water out."

"How long is the tunnel?" asked Rob.

"Tunnels. Plural. It's an entire system, varying in height and width. Tunnels, chambers, dividers, equalizers, drains, basins, manhole tubes. All leading to the Las Vegas Wash, and then, finally, Lake Mead. More than two hundred miles of underground . . . er, caves."

"Rob, there must be some other way," moaned Cash.

He dropped the luggage and put his arms around her, but he spoke to Paul. "And people actually live in there?"

"Hundreds of people live in there. I know a few of them. Yeah, there are some real fucking dickheads—I'm not gonna lie. Lots of drug addicts, degenerate gamblers, some criminals hiding from the law . . . "

"I'll take my chances in a shitty motel room, Rob," said Cash, as she headed for the wall rungs.

Her boyfriend held her back.

"Think for a minute, baby," he said. "Would I do anything that isn't the best for you? Let's just check this place out. I know it seems crazy, but let's recap our options here. You and I in a motel—one of us flips and stone cold kills the other one. You and I sleeping in the street, or in some abandoned building, or on a train back to New York—one of us flips and kills the other one. I know from my point of view that I'd rather you did not kill me, and I certainly don't want to kill you, because once I found out that I did, I'd off myself anyway."

Cash stared at her feet. "But we could chain ourselves up before bed . . . "

"What about during the day? We could flip at any second. We are tempting fate whenever we are alone together."

Tears.

"It's okay, baby," he said. "I won't let anything happen to you. To us. Paul said that, for whatever reason, the people in the tunnels haven't been flipping . . . "

"I said that *some* people, in a *certain* section of the tunnels *may not* be flipping. These tunnels are like a city within a city. There are different . . . let's call them neighborhoods, with different leaders and different structures. There are also lone wolf residents who do their own thing. But, if I can get you into a non-flip area, if there truly is such a thing, that's great. More importantly, I want to get you into a community, where they stand watch and look out for each other. It's like a shelter. You won't be alone."

Rob rubbed Cash's cheek and nodded.

Paul continued, "But, get the fuck out of there fast if it starts to rain."

They stepped into the darkness, the light on Paul's helmet and the one in Cash's hand leading the way. Cash noted that the ground was quite dry for a flood tunnel. The walls were covered in graffiti, at least for the first several yards. Then the wall artwork vanished.

"If this is the best place to be, why won't you be staying with us?" asked Cash. She could feel the perspiration on her neck, which seemed odd, since the tunnels could be twenty to thirty degrees cooler than the busy streets above them.

"I live alone in a tiny apartment," answered Paul. "If I had a girl, we'd be staying here too."

They'd been walking for less than ten minutes when they came upon the first split. Their vision was limited to just the areas illuminated by their lights, so they could have missed the dingy divide in the darkness. But Paul was familiar with it from prior visits.

"You want to avoid that tunnel," he said. "We need to stay to the right here. It's the first of several splits."

Rob and Cash gazed into the total blackness of the second tunnel. They could hear some distant dripping. Sounded like a leaky faucet, if the faucet were the size of a Civil War cannon.

"Should we avoid it because of water?" asked Rob.

"No, that's not it."

"Stop," demanded Cash.

The men halted.

"There is too much of this," she said. "Get out fast if it rains, don't go in that tunnel, lone wolf whatever-the-fucks wandering around. Plus, it's starting to smell gross in here, and I'm sweating like an old pipe. My heart is racing . . . "

"And you have an enormous spider on your shoulder," interrupted Paul. He swatted it off. "Don't worry, it wasn't a black widow."

"I can't do this," she said.

Rob lowered the luggage.

"Maybe we won't. Most likely, we won't," he said. "Do you think we can just go and meet the people Paul knows? If they have some system of watching out for each other, you can be safe. It might even be true that no one flips there. Maybe they are so deep underground or something that they haven't had the exposure the rest of us have had."

"Baby, that sounds crazy," she said.

"I know, but the whole country is crazy. We don't have any options."

"Maybe we could round up some people who would all want to stay in a hotel. We could work up a security schedule and all. We wouldn't have to live in the sewer," she said.

"Storm drains. Not sewers," added Paul.

Rob ignored him. "What people, Cash? We don't know anyone out here."

"What about fucking buses?" she asked. "Trailways, Greyhound. Whatever the hell. Maybe they have security on the buses now. We could take a bus back home."

CANNI

Bakersfield, California

One hundred and thirteen miles outside of Los Angeles, the engine of the charter bus roared. It had a pattern that was almost musical. There would be a brief, trebly whine when the driver hit the gas, but it would quickly inspire a crescendo of bass and drums. The term *Basso Continuo* kept creeping into his mind, but he wasn't sure if the description truly fit. His days of serious musical study were in the past, as he now devoted much of his time to the creation of culinary delights.

A cooking magazine rested on his lap as the engine fumes irritated his nostrils. This was a newer, *greener,* diesel bus, but a greasy stench stormed his nose nonetheless. The other passengers were probably oblivious, but he wasn't. An older woman had been sitting beside him on the first leg of the journey, but never retook her seat after the rest stop. Her perfume, however, remained.

Peach, plum, lemon, a hint of jasmine. Vanilla and patchouli were also present. And leather. Probably too much leather. The aroma of the leather seats was even overpowered by the lingering cowhide of the lathered leather. Not so much like the safety of grandpa's old recliner or the excitement of a new car. This scent was more reminiscent of having one's face shoved into the pocket of a sixth-grade bully's weathered baseball mitt.

The bus driver had been pretty good. No sudden stops or herky-jerky reactions. Almost never ran over those reflective warning bump lane dividers. That was one way that he judged the abilities of most drivers.

"My Lord, I have such terrible gas," whispered the woman to her companion, two rows behind him. Not only did he hear her hushed confession, he already knew about her digestive issues. He was willing to bet she had some microwaved White Castle burgers for lunch.

Thud!

He froze for an instant. But there was no follow-up scream, no panic, no stampede for the bus doors.

No canni.

Just a piece of dropped luggage four or five rows ahead, most likely.

He hadn't seen it fall. In fact, he hadn't seen anything.

Ever.

Blind since birth, he was often asked what he *saw. Shapes? Light and shadow? Black?*

"Nothing," would always be his polite response. "I see nothing. What do you sighted types currently *see* behind you? That is what I *see* in front of me."

People always had a hard time with that. Couldn't get their minds around it. Sometimes insisted he saw black.

"Nope. Not black. I see nothing."

He ran his fingers across his braille magazine, taking in Emeril Lagasse's tips on the use of citrus and sea salt. Nothing he hadn't read before. He liked a bit of repetition. It ingrained things in his memory. In days past, he'd surely have had some heavy cups on his ears, most likely enjoying the talents of Weather Report, the Mahavishnu Orchestra, or Return to Forever. If he'd smoked a bowl, he might listen to the ones he called *The Charlies*, Parker and Mingus.

But now, in the new America, he had to listen to the world beyond the headphones.

Always listen.

The sun was almost down. He could tell by the angle it hit his neck through the side bus window. He was waiting for darkness. In many ways it could be the great equalizer, should he need it.

The seat beside him—the one vacated by Ms. Leather—creaked. He heard the air escape from it as his own chair shook. Between all of that, and fact that he perceived a hardy exhale from an angle above his own ear, he'd deduced that a rather large person had landed next to him.

A brief, deep throat-clear and a scant rub from rock-sturdy triceps told him there was a physically formidable man in the next seat. The new neighbor might require a scant reapplication of deodorant, but his breath had been recently freshened.

"Mind if I set myself here, my man?"

"Oh, not at all," he answered. From the voice, the inflections, and trace of accent, he figured the fellow to be African-American, probably not directly from the South, but likely a generation removed from legit Southerners.

"I think my prior seat was about to surrender, man. This one seems stronger, ya know? There I was," said the big guy, "thinking I'm all gangsta for riding a non-security bus all by myself, and I see you sittin' here, calm as all shit, with a blind man's cane by your side."

"Well, I could be Matt Murdock," he grinned.

"Huh?"

"You read comics? That's Daredevil! My dad used to read them to me."

"Oh, yeah. Never read the comics, but I saw the movie and the TV show. Brother was a blind bad ass."

"That's me. Either that, or I desperately wanted a ticket on a pricey security bus, but they were all sold out and I sheepishly settled for this."

"Ride at your own risk, right?" laughed the large fellow.

"Had to sign a waiver."

"Same here."

"I messed with the guy and told him that, for the document to be legal, he had to read the entire three pages aloud to me, since I can't read it myself."

"He did it?"

"Started to, but I let him off the hook."

"Well, Daredevil, my mama raised me to look out for others. Big believer in karma, my mama. So, if someone on this bus flips, I'll make sure you get out alive. I was an O-lineman at UCLA. I can handle myself. The name's Willie."

The blind rider was about to introduce himself when he heard the commotion.

"Outta the fucking way!" yelled a cigarette-ravaged voice toward the front of the bus. There were some scurrying sounds barely more than two feet away. He grabbed for his cane and awaited word from his new friend.

The feet pounded up the aisle, toward the back of the bus.

"It's nothing," said Willie. "Looks like a couple of bros had too much to drink."

The foot traffic hurried past them and to the rear.

Willie continued, "One of 'em is taking the other to the head to hurl. Seem to be gettin' their Vegas on before actually gettin' to Vegas."

Exhale.

"You can snooze if you want, or listen to some jams," said Willie. "I promise I got you covered."

"That is very reassuring," he answered. "My only issue is, Willie, what if *you* flip?"

DANIEL O'CONNOR

Las Vegas

Cash, Rob, and Paul were twenty minutes into their black tunnel when they heard the scuffling. Every argument Cash had made for avoiding the tunnels had been shot down by the men. Their answers sounded idiotic, yet completely plausible. She marveled at the thought that when the best chance for a safe, relatively normal life rested in the damp bowels beneath Sin City, the world had finally turned into the shit pile we'd long been warned of.

"Okay, what the fuck is that?" whispered Cash, as she spun the head of the Maglite toward the sound.

The noise in daylight might not have been particularly noteworthy. Here in the moist darkness of the unknown it was terrifying.

They called them *equalizers*. Basically large holes in the side walls of some of the tunnels, used to facilitate overflow.

The scuffling came from the other side of the wall, beyond the first equalizer. Paul walked toward the hole. He could easily climb through it, should he desire.

"Wha . . . What are you doing?" asked Cash, keeping her voice hushed.

"Going to see what the noise is."

"No! We should keep moving. Quietly moving *away* from the noise."

"We have to see if it's an actual threat, then deal with it."

"What are we, Navy SEALs? If it's a canni, we should avoid it until it flips back to human."

Paul ignored her and stuck his illuminated head through the hole, miner's helmet-first.

"Rob," she pleaded, looking over at where she knew her boyfriend stood. She couldn't see him in the blackness because her light was trained on Paul, and the hole.

No answer.

"Rob?"

She swung her light to find him. She saw the luggage. No Rob.

Her body grew cold.

"Paul, I don't see Rob," she said.

He didn't respond either. She swung her light back to the equalizer. Paul was gone, likely through to the tunnel beyond the hole.

Now there was more noise in the adjacent drain, where Paul might be. She had no choice but to gravitate toward it. Her body felt like ice. She wanted to be near Paul since Rob had vanished. She dreaded each step she took toward the hole, but anything was better than standing in the middle of the black tunnel alone.

Her foot stepped on and audibly cracked a hypodermic needle near the wall.

She ignored it and approached the equalizer. She sensed a slight breeze coming through from the next tunnel. She wasn't about to climb through without peeking. The flashlight went through first.

Scanning the darkness with her shaky spotlight, she could see a figure up ahead. The figure also held a light, though not nearly as bright as hers. It was illuminating something on the ground. It looked like a long puddle, or small stream, of sorts . . . but it appeared to be *moving*. The distant light source initially blinded her from identifying the person holding it.

She squinted as she stepped through the equalizer.

It was her missing boyfriend. The light was coming from the flashlight app on his phone.

"What is it, Rob?" she asked, no longer bothering to whisper.

"Come here, Cash," he answered. "Look at this."

She hurried toward him, her body warming a bit. Puddles splashed beneath her. This tunnel was oddly wetter than the one from which they'd come.

"Where is Paul?" she asked, on her approach.

"Down there," he said, pointing vaguely into the black behind him.

Cash saw no sign of Paul's miner's light.

"Down where?"

"Further down somewhere. Look at this, baby."

Cash followed the light app's glow to the wet ground and trained her more powerful Mag on the area.

Crayfish.

Lots of 'em. Scurrying through the shallow puddles and thin streams. Tiny lobsters living not in the Louisiana bayou or the swamps of Madagascar but in manmade caves below the Vegas Strip.

"Okay, that's weird," said Cash. "But those creepy crawlers weren't the ones making all that noise. Why are we wasting time here, Rob?"

"It's fascinating," he replied. "Paul's looking around for the source of the noise. If he needs me, I'm right here."

Footsteps. Splashing.

Both lights left the crayfish and swung down the tunnel. Here came the bouncing light from the miner's helmet. Cash exhaled, relieved to see Paul.

Wait. That is Paul, isn't it?

It was surely a light from a helmet. The helmet was certainly on a head, but the glare was too much.

I'm just being paranoid. Of course it's Paul. I think.

He was coming faster.

"Paul?"

He was almost on them.

"Paul?"

"What's up?" he answered, just as he reached them.

Cash placed a hand on the damp wall to steady herself. Her heart felt like a kick drum.

"You freaked me just a bit, Paul," she said.

"Sorry. Fucking crawfish!" he replied. "There's a joint nearby called 'Hot n' Juicy' . . ."

"The noise," interrupted Cash. "Did you find whatever was making that noise?"

"Nah. Probably just a dweller. Most of them are as harmless as those craws."

Cash slid her head into Paul's view, appearing washed out in the bright beam from his helmet. She squinted.

"*Nobody* is harmless anymore."

"You're right," he replied. "But there is also something I call *storm drain paranoia*. I had it when I broke my tunnel cherry. And that was *before* anyone could kill you at any time."

It was then that Cash peered into the shadows behind Paul. There stood a figure; pale and unshaven, with a thick old jersey scarf around his thick old Jersey neck. Cash could hear faint rumblings of the traffic above their heads and the occasional clunk of a manhole cover, when pummeled by the tires of an especially weighty vehicle.

"Yous like da mudbugs?"

"Fuck!" screamed Cash, as she and Paul spun around.

"Interesting little bastards," said the man, as he was hit by all three light sources. "Sometimes I watch 'em like they was in a fish tank. They'll lay on their sides, crawl out of their entire skin, and then eat da fuckin' thing. Oh , I'm sorry, miss. Forgive my language. Then again, you just said basically da same word. The root word, anyway."

"Dude, sneaking up like that is not cool," said Rob.

"Sorry. Wasn't sneakin' up. I just move around quiet, I guess. I'm Joe."

Paul moved toward him, "Hey, Polish Joe! It's me, Paul Bhong."

"Oh, yeah!" he answered. "Ain't seen you in a while. How's things?"

"Well, you know. These are my friends, Rob and Caroline."

"Pleased to meet yous. Yous exploring da tunnels or movin' in?"

"Not sure," said Rob.

"It ain't so bad here, all things considered. Polish Joe," he said, thrusting out his arm for a handshake.

Rob found himself studying the man's hand for filth, but there was none. Just callous—both on Joe's big palm and maybe in Rob's trepidation.

"Hello," said Rob, as he shook hands. "Nice to meet you. This is Caroline."

"Hi," said Cash, not willing to cross the handshake barrier just yet.

"So, you're Polish?" asked Rob, trying to make conversation.

"Nah."

Paul laughed as he spoke, "Polish Joe is from back east. New Jersey, right?"

"Well, Jersey, by way of Long Island," he answered.

"My friends here come from Brooklyn. They're your neighbors, Joe."

"Brooklyn?"

"That's true," smiled Rob.

"Well," asked Joe, as he took something from his pocket and approached the crayfish puddles, "are yous da expensive coffee, vegan, Arcade Fire, MSNBC, Brooklyn people, or da old school, egg cream, Roll n' Roaster, stickball-playin' Brooklyn people?"

"We're the kind who don't need to validate ourselves to random tunnel-dwellers," answered Cash.

"Okay. Old school Brooklyn. That's good. Though a simple 'Go fuck yourself, hobo' would've been more authentic. Yous might be a mixture of old and new Brooklyn."

Polish Joe sprinkled some granules over the water.

"Shrimp pellets," he said. "Da mudbugs go nuts for 'em. Of course, they'll eat anything at all. Seen 'em consume each other when times are tough. That's why I try and feed 'em when I can. Of all da creatures, from man to mouse, they're da only ones I truly care about down here. They don't bite ya like da rats, steal from ya like da people, or crawl all over ya and also bite ya like da roaches and da black widows."

Cash tapped Rob on the shoulder.

"I'm ready to sleep in a dumpster, gas station bathroom, or the freaking *House of 1000 Corpses*, as long as we are above ground."

"Big picture, Cash. Bugs and mice are the least of our problems. I'll figure something out."

Rob turned to Polish Joe, hoping to bring something positive to the moment. "We hear that people aren't flipping down here, underground."

Joe kept his eyes on the crayfish as they bumped and clawed their way to the pellets.

"Well, that's some horseshit straight outta Yonkers. I seen an old timer go *batso* by da double barrel drain under Excalibur. Tore da place to hell. I took off in da other direction and slammed my head into a pipe. See here."

He pointed to a scabbed-over gash on his forehead, before concluding, "They found him dead in da Flamingo Wash."

Paul responded. "The people in the bunker say no one has gone canni in their community."

"Canni?"

"Yeah, that's what they're calling it now."

"Hmmm. Ain't heard that. Anyway, you mean them brainwashed souls in *Archie Bunker*?"

"Well, they call it *Artsy Bunker*, but yes. Word is that everyone there has remained fine, and that they are very secure with self-policing, or whatever."

"That could be true. I don't go down that way. I take the long way around, just to avoid them. Could be a big fuckin' lie too. More brainwash shit. I got no love for that Don Russo nutcase. Craziest bastard I ever seen and I seen everything the five boroughs and Palisades Park had to offer. Also, steer clear of da old witch in da big pipe."

With that, Joe took a handful of the dried pet store shrimp pellets, and ate them. Through falling crumbs, he added, "And fuck Lindenhurst."

Rob, Cash, and Paul watched Polish Joe head back into the shadows. They couldn't see a thing without their lights, yet he wandered away as if he had the sonar of a Smoky Mountain cave bat. They climbed back through the equalizers into their original tunnel.

The luggage was gone.

"Of course," said Rob. "Why would the suitcases still be here? Everything else has been stolen."

"Sin City," replied Cash.

Rob scanned his phone flashlight around the tunnel.

"Save your battery," said Paul. "That light is the only reason to have a phone down here. Don't expect any service."

He shone his miner's light to assist Rob. Cash folded her arms. "Do you two actually think someone picked the luggage up and moved it eight feet across the tunnel? It's long gone."

"Maybe they rummaged through it and discarded whatever they didn't want further up the drain," answered Rob.

"It's gone," she repeated.

Paul trained his light far down the tunnel. It seemed endless.

"Maybe not," he said.

They had been trudging through the dank cavern for twelve minutes since the luggage went missing. It felt like an hour.

"You mean there is no faster way in or out of this place?" asked Rob. "We have to do this whenever we come and go?"

"There are faster ways," said Paul. "I'm not too familiar with them, though. Also, the way we came is the way I've always come, and it seems safer."

"One whacked-out crank who consumes pet store pellets and some luggage thieves. That's the 'safe' route?" groaned Cash.

"Yes, it is."

Cash felt cold again.

"This 'bunker' we're going to . . . " began Rob.

"Artsy Bunker," said Paul. "If you are accepted there—and I am owed a huge favor—you should be safe from the common dangers of the tunnels. Nobody fucks with Don Russo, or anyone who has his blessing."

"This Russo dude, if he is so powerful and feared, why does he live down in this shit? You wouldn't find Vito Corleone living like this," said Rob.

Paul chuckled. "The *only* rules and laws down here belong to Don Russo. There are no police, no surveillance cameras, and no one who doesn't either follow or fear him."

"The cops are never in here?" asked Cash.

"Almost never. They clear the place out every New Year's Eve. Security precautions for the millions celebrating above. Wouldn't want a WMD going off under Caesar's Palace. They come down if they're hunting for a big time criminal or a high priority missing person. That's pretty much it. They generally leave the tunnel dwellers alone. Better to tuck them underground than pestering the tourists above. That's where the major coin comes from, sucka."

"Everyone fears this guy, but he owes *you* a favor?" asked Rob.

"He owes my dad a favor, but I'm gonna collect it for you guys. My dad is an attorney and he's the main reason that Russo is running this place instead of some prison exercise yard."

Cash shone her light on Paul. "Is this any better than prison?"

"For him it is. He's the big cheese. He loves it. He couldn't live by prison rules. He does what he wants, society be damned."

"I've heard that song before," said Rob. "John Gotti, Al Capone. They always wind up taking a fall."

"He's not really like them," said Paul. "They flashed what they had. Expensive suits, fancy cars. They craved attention. Don Russo doesn't want any of that. He just wants life on his terms. He doesn't conform to anything. Don't think of Gotti or Capone. They did certain things that are expected of all people in civilized countries; had families, appeared in public, wore clothing."

"Wore clothing?" asked Cash.

Paul adjusted his helmet light and kept staring down the tunnel as he replied. "Don Russo doesn't wear clothes. Too conformist."

"What does he wear?" she asked.

"Nothing."

"So this *Don* title is because he's like a Mafia boss or something?" asked Rob.

"No. His name is just Don Russo. It's not a title. Is *Rob* a fucking title?"

They spotted an apartment of sorts up ahead. Two beds, a bookshelf, clothes rack, television with a wire running up the concrete wall behind it. All items were elevated, being set upon crates, to minimize water damage. Of course, if a true flood came barreling through, it could all be gone in minutes.

Cash was particularly intrigued with the tidily arranged living quarters. She assumed it did not belong to Don Russo. There was, after all, a clothes rack.

"Hello?" yelled Paul, hearing nothing but a faint reverberation in return. "We are just passing through," he continued. "Not looking for any trouble."

No response.

They moved closer, nearer to the beds, which were neatly made. Sheets and blankets tucked under.

"I don't like to sneak up on anyone," said Paul, speaking softly now. "People can overreact. It feels almost like we're trespassing."

"So, this isn't the bunker we're headed to?" inquired Rob.

"Oh, no. This is just home to a couple of independents. Most of the tunnels are like this. The bunker is the only area that I know of that has any structure."

"So these people can leave their TV and all of their possessions unattended, but we put suitcases down for five minutes and they're in the wind?"

"Tunnel etiquette. This is their home."

Ten minutes later they had arrived. The tunnel split into another double-barrel. It was the tallest and widest that they had come across. They were greeted in the glow of their lights by two men, one rather stout, and a scent that was either potent marijuana or skunk.

"There's a way to go around," said the first guy, pointing. He didn't sound outright unfriendly, and maybe even more professional than expected, considering he looked like a hot shower might be in order. "This is a private camp."

A tattered silver and black Oakland Raiders curtain hung behind them, keeping their group's home hidden. Beyond the drape, however, there was light.

"We're here to see Don Russo," said Paul.

The men sized him up.

"You been here before? Your face is memorable," said the second man, his hot breath revealing the mystery smell to be cannabis, unless he had just consumed a Palawan stink badger. He had a large growth protruding from just behind his right knee, under his cutoff shorts. It was redder than the rest of him, rough and chafed, about the size of a basketball.

"My name is Bhong. Paul Bhong," he looked back at Rob and Cash, giving them a 007 grin. "Pay no attention to the man behind the Raiders' curtain," he added. Despite everything, it brought a smile to Cash's lips, her strawberry balm glistening in Paul's light.

"Why you wanna see Don?"

"Would you please do me a solid and just tell him I'm here. I think he'll see us."

The men looked at each other. "I'll go," said Skunk Breath.

As he disappeared behind the Raiders curtain and into the light, the remaining man called to the parallel tunnel. "Spats," he yelled.

Out of the blackness of an equalizer hole appeared Spats' head. "What?" he asked, as he spotted the three visitors. He stared for a good long time. Probably not at Rob or Paul.

"Just be aware that I got *overheads* here, Spats. You and Yurman just be on your toes there."

Spats kept ogling Cash. Rob heard the grate of his own teeth as he watched, jaw clenched, through the light from Paul's hat. Then Cash whispered in his ear. Her breath was candy-sweet. It calmed him.

"In case this hasn't crossed your mind," she hushed, "we are waiting here, surrounded by some type of doped-up security detail, just hoping for the chance to have an audience with some deranged chieftain of the sewer, who is, most likely, swinging-dick naked."

Rob pondered that as he stared back at the man who gawked at his girlfriend.

"Well," offered Rob, "it's really not the sewer."

They walked among the beds. All were up on crates. It wasn't a five-star hotel, but it was nearly the equal of some hostels they'd seen. Lights of varying types were on the walls and atop some old and occasionally water-damaged tables and dressers. On some of the beds were people. All types. Most of them thin and pale. Some played cards or read; others slept. Few made any eye contact. Their clothing was generally tattered, yet most items were folded neatly in piles or hanging from lines.

Strawberry incense filled the air. It concealed the marijuana smell, for the most part. The pleasant scent had Paul craving a frozen daiquiri. Rob's thoughts were of Cash's lip balm.

Skunk Breath—he had not yet introduced himself—led the way. He moved briskly for a man with a substantial leg growth, though his left leg brushed against it with each step. Cash's mag and Paul's helmet light were turned off. The wide tunnel had ample space in which they could walk, even with the beds all against one wall. A handful of men and a couple of women stood along the other wall, near a collection of worn, rusty bicycles. Rob assumed this was more of the *security* that Paul had talked about. He looked for weapons of any sort but saw none. He wasn't too concerned about the basic quality of life in the tunnels and didn't give a thought to the lack of privacy or apparent drug use. He was focused on only one thing: keeping Cash safe from potential cannis.

Including, and perhaps especially, himself.

"Have you ever filmed in here, Paul?" asked Cash. "This could go viral."

"Yes. Don Russo then danced on my phone."

A bit further along they heard the music. Some type of old disco maybe, with lots of keyboards. None of them recognized it.

There were more black Oakland Raiders curtains. One read, *Las Vegas Raiders*. They surrounded a large section of a tunnel that had to be fifty feet wide. They created three false walls to go with one true concrete one at the back, making a room-within-a-room; well, within-a storm-drain. The music came from behind the curtains. Silhouettes of dancing bodies could be seen. Colorful light escaped through breaks in the curtains, as did pot smoke and laughter.

"Wait here," ordered Skunk Breath, who disappeared behind the Raiders cloth.

Cash stood there, inhaling the weed, and the strawberry incense. She was up to her elbows in hand-sanitizer. She scoured the wall behind her looking for spiders and roaches or any moving shadow. None were seen, but she could still feel them on her, sliding on her sweat. This veritable tomb on the nether side of Earth, awash in clashing scents, crawling with vermin and lunatics, somehow housed a group of people who, in the current state of life, found themselves dancing and laughing. They weren't grabbing baseball bats, ready to fight off the next canni. They weren't searching out refuge and help, only to be turned away. They also probably hadn't killed the best friend they'd ever had.

CANNI

Las Vegas

The bus reached the station without incident. There was almost a collective sigh among the passengers. The sober ones, at least. A couple of the drunks had to be roused by the driver, a stone-faced fellow with a sweaty brow and four strands of carefully-combed brown straw. His midsection had grown wide over the years; wider than what seemed symmetrical for the rest of his body. Looked as though his waist had expanded around him through decades in that driver's seat. It was almost like he'd buttoned his uniform over one of those long-haul coach tires. Henry was his name. His damp forehead surely came with the task of transporting a cargo of ticking time bombs from L.A. to Vegas, all while wondering if he might have an episode himself and possibly steer his bus off the side of a mountain. A driver with his seniority should have automatically qualified for the routes that came with security, but there were always those elements of ass-kissing, nepotism, palm-greasing, and fair-haired superstars, to muck up the way that life should actually roll. Henry had grown tired of the fight. He was just a quiet and dependable worker. Never caused a fuss, never sought attention. Just got his passengers from A to B as easily as possible.

The passengers were filing down the center aisle of the bus, one behind another. Henry stood outside, at the bottom of the front door steps. His smile appeared to be more of a clenched jaw, as if he were examining his teeth in a mirror. He uttered something to each exiting passenger.

"Goodbye, now."

"Enjoy Las Vegas."

"Thanks for riding with us today."

Inside the vehicle, Willie stood with his new sightless friend. He helped him slip his backpack on.

"Let 'em all get off," Willie said. "I'll lead you out at the end."

"Thank you kindly, but I can . . . "

"I won't hear of it," said Willie, "I'm six-foot-six and three hundred and eleven pounds, and I'm terrified ridin' this death trap. I can't imagine if I wasn't able to see. We're gettin' off together. Now, you got my phone number. You call me if you need anything while I'm here."

"I will, my enormous friend. Thanks for everything."

"I still don't believe you don't carry a phone."

"It's not my thing. Most of those bells and whistles don't chime for me."

As Willie led his friend down the bus steps, toward the Las Vegas night, the blind man could smell that the leather-perfumed woman had just disembarked, as had the inebriated men. Henry stood beside the open front door at the bottom of the vehicle's stairs. He reached out to assist Willie in helping his friend navigate the final steps.

"Thanks for riding with us. Enjoy Las Vegas," said clenched-jawed Henry.

"Sure will," grinned the young man with the dark glasses and thin white cane.

Willie thanked the driver for his assistance and stopped to say his goodbyes to his new pal.

The football player's hands felt like weights on his slim shoulders. He could feel Willie fixing his backpack straps for him, as he spoke. He smelled the Alien Fresh Jerky that Willie had loaded up on at a famous tourist stop during the ride. This one was hot and BBQ as it colored his buddy's breath.

"I hope you find your sister, Willie," he said.

"I will. She's run off in the past. Fancies herself as a star. Not sure if dancin' on a pole makes someone famous, but, in her mind . . . Well, I'll find her. I done it before."

"If I can help in any way . . . "

"Yeah brother, you don't know what she looks like, can't see for shit, and you don't even own a phone . . . You're hired!"

They laughed. A wave of beef jerky hit the smaller man in his face.

That's when the blind man was stunned by what he first thought to be a punch to his jaw. He tumbled to the pavement as the first screams rang out. He believed he heard Willie's voice within the commotion.

"Willie?" he yelled. He felt the pain of his backpack pushing into his spine as he hit the ground. His dark glasses had come off and his cane was lost. He reached for it, to no avail. He felt that strange "punch" again, but now could tell it was not a fist. It was much larger. It was breathing.

It was trying to wedge its way between his shoulders and jawline.

It wanted his neck.

He hunched his head into his shoulders, trying to prevent it. He smelled an Italian hero sandwich. Some might call it a hoagie or a sub. Regardless, he inhaled ham, capocollo, provolone, salami, cigar smoke remnants, and fresh vomit.

Then he heard Willie for sure.

"Oh, hell no, muthafucka."

What the sightless victim could not see was that Henry the bus driver was on him, mouth foaming, trying to tear into his neck. The thick-waisted bus operator had tossed three-hundred- pound Willie aside like a Girl Scout as he went for his target.

Now, Willie was back and lifting the canni as he did so many barbells in his days at UCLA. Unfortunately for Willie, to a canni one neck was as good as another, and Henry turned his painful, insatiable hunger to the big guy.

Now they were both atop the blind man; canni on top, Willie in the middle.

He felt all the weight on him—well over five hundred pounds. This pressed him harder onto his backpack. He endured the struggle and heard the groans and growls. For the first time in years, he felt helpless. Willie could be heard cussing, and Henry just sounded like some type of bear or wolf. He knew he might be able to wiggle out from under this, but even then, how could he save Willie?

As the struggle continued above him, he heard his big friend scream. Then he felt it, all warm on his face.

Blood.

Not his own, but dripping, perhaps pouring, from above.

"Help us!" he yelled, wondering to where an entire coach full of passengers might have vanished. They were close enough to be watching and yelling. Of that, he was sure.

He wiggled out from under the attack, reaching out, feeling around on the ground for his cane. He heard what sounded like a light metal rattle, probably after being kicked, and he went for it. There it was. Though at that moment, he'd happily trade his thin, aluminum cane for a thick, blackthorn walking stick, or maybe even a guide dog along the lines of Cujo. Nevertheless, he picked it up and started flailing at the top of the pile, at the canni.

"For God's sake, somebody help us!"

The infected Henry paid no mind to the cane strikes as he bit away at Willie, a piece of arm here, a chunk of clothing there. The former lineman did a good job of protecting his neck, yet this bus driver, whom Willie could normally incapacitate in seconds, was in this state, many times stronger than his victim.

He must have struck the canni a dozen times with his cane before he was shoved aside. He smelled booze.

"We got this," was all he heard.

He stepped back, knowing he could offer little help to the sighted in a case like this.

The drunkards who had spent the ride in alternating states of sleep, drink, and regurgitation, had come to help. They grabbed the canni from behind and began to lift.

"Push, big man," one of them yelled to the supine victim. Bloodied and tiring, Willie enacted his best bench press. Between the three of them, Henry was wrestled to his feet. Luckily for all, he seemed more intent on feeding off Willie than tossing them all around like so many flies. His teeth clattered away inside his foamy mouth, the blood on his double chin pale in vibrancy against the redness of his gaping eyes.

Behind them all was the idling charter coach. The front door was still open.

"Push him towards the bus," bellowed one of the drinkers.

They gave it their all, with Willie bull-rushing the canni as if the college lineman was clearing a lane for his tailback. The attacker was beginning to move backwards as he bit at the top of Willie's clammy head.

Willie managed to speak as he and the drunks pushed with everything they had. "Hey, Daredevil," he said, panting and groaning as he surged, "find me, get behind me, and shove like hell, brother."

The blind man was at the back of the pile instantly, adding all of his strength to the thrusting effort. Another fellow, in a mechanic's uniform, grease and all, with a name patch on his shirt that read *Eddie V*, dashed from the bus depot to help. Two women, clothed like they'd just left church on Easter Sunday, leaped from a wooden bench to join the charge. The canni was forced into the bus. He tripped backwards over the steps, and they were able to slam the door shut.

There were seven people pressed up against that door, yet it still began to open.

Until it shut again.

It was a tremendous struggle. Canni Henry punched his arm right through the thick, tinted glass on the top half of the door. He felt around frantically, clawing and grabbing at air. The folks pressing against the door were all hunched low, staying below his swinging reach, as glass shards showered upon them.

"Stay low, Daredevil," shouted Willie, concerned for his sightless friend behind him and ignoring his own dizziness and weakened knees.

The canni began to wriggle and clamber through the window frame. More glass fell. The jagged remnants slashed his skin as he tried to squeeze through the smashed outlet, grunting and growling with hunger. His bloodied hands swung just above the faces of the door-blockers. Shoulders and above, he was now out above his crouching adversaries, chunky fluid pouring from his mouth and onto their heads and faces.

As they prepared for the next battle, and the inevitability of a fat, wild cannibal landing on top of them, he got stuck.

The enormous spare tire of flab around his mid-section could not fit through the window. No matter how hard he pushed and writhed, he was unable get his bloated core past the shattered opening.

It took a while for the door-blockers to realize that Henry was stuck. They still had to apply pressure to the door lest it swung open, but there they were, all bent over and pushing, with a roaring, leaking, bleeding canni wedged into the window frame above them.

A horn honked frantically as an old pickup truck drove up onto the sidewalk, bright head beams glaring. It maneuvered into place and began to back slowly toward the front bus door. As it inched closer to the bus, the folks by the door moved aside, with the dazed and injured Willie having the presence-of-mind to grab his blind friend's hand. The pickup was right up against the door, denting it a bit. The canni wiggled and screamed as it hovered above the truck's bed, halfway out the window.

The group all either sat on or collapsed to the concrete ground, exhausted. They didn't take their eyes off the canni, though, in case it did flop out of that bus.

The pickup driver got out of his truck. He was a frail senior, much older than even his ride. He removed his wire-rimmed glasses, spit on the lenses, and wiped them with a hanky. Returning them to his wrinkled face, he stared at the scene before him.

"The devil's work," he said.

All was quiet—save for the trapped cannibal, lots of breath-catching, and at least one hushed prayer. The hope was that Henry would return to normal in a few minutes and they'd deal with excavating him from his jagged glass cage. Someone would need to call for paramedics, but these days, the wait was eternal.

One of the church ladies, her lovely pastel outfit now wrinkled and covered in fluids, took out her phone. She wasn't older than forty, but she had a Jitterbug cell with giant buttons. After she pressed the first one, her companion, in an equally pastel and filthy dress, stood straight up, eyes wide, and roared. She vomited all over herself, turned to the group, and in a haze of disorientation, decided whom to eat.

Before she could choose her victim, her church-going best friend dropped the Jitterbug, stood, and gave her a blast of pepper spray right in the eyes.

The newly-infected woman ran in circles, screaming and clawing at her eyeballs. She bounced off the rear of the charter bus as her fellow canni continued his violent struggle at the front door.

"Blinded bitch," burped one of the exhausted drunks from his spot on the ground.

"What?" asked the sightless man, as he had his arm around the injured Willie.

"Not you, bro," whispered the lineman.

The female canni bolted across the waiting area, swinging her arms and biting at the air. She slammed into the side of the depot building, fell down, and then struggled back to her feet.

His shirt patch read *JD*. He was the second mechanic to emerge from the building. He brought with him a tire. No rim. Just a tire with a donut hole in the middle. He sauntered up to the crazed and blinded female. Raising the big rubber wheel high, he slammed it down on her. Perfect fit. It wrapped around her like an enormous Hula Hoop, settling tightly just below her shoulders. Her arms trapped against her sides, she toppled over to the ground, temporarily sightless and temporarily starving. She chomped at the air, with her tire permitting her to roll in a circle, she as the axle with only one wheel.

There they all were, on the ground, at night. Bus and pickup headlights on. One canni trapped in a Greyhound, one wrapped in a Goodyear.

"Can we please get an ambulance for Willie?" said the blind man, hugging his injured friend.

The church lady picked up her Jitterbug and, hands shaking, dialed again.

The attackers were both still frothing and groaning, each neutralized—one literally and one figuratively—by spare tires.

DANIEL O'CONNOR

Las Vegas Drainage Tunnels

"Don Russo will see you now."

The music was lowered, but not entirely turned off. People filed out from behind the Raiders curtains. Most of them eyeballed Rob, Cash, and Paul as the partiers broke off into various directions within the tunnels. There was the occasional smile, but many seemed to be sizing up the visitors as possible intruders. A couple of them did point at Paul, or pat his shoulder, as they passed. He was happy that some remembered him.

They followed Skunk Breath behind the curtains.

The lights, in a rainbow of colors, still danced. A couple of small, battery-powered color globes continued to spin. There were no beds, dressers, or makeshift closets to be seen; only some homemade cabinets holding the stereo setup and rotating disco balls.

Other than the one who had led them into the area, there were three more men waiting there. None paid them any mind. Two of them chatted with each other while the third scanned an iPod that had a long RCA cable running from it to the stereo receiver. That fellow, they deduced, was Don Russo, as his tattooed and naked ass stared them in the face from the far wall. Everyone else was clothed. As Russo turned, Rob first thought he was a black man. Then he was pretty sure he was a white guy, maybe Italian. Then, he changed his mind again, deciding that Don Russo was probably black. Cash didn't try to guess. She was too busy trying to keep her eyes above his waist.

He held the iPod in his hand as its long cord tethered the music player to the stereo. He looked like some kid hanging on to a stringed kite handle, if the kid was two hundred seventy pounds and looked like he just strode out of San Quentin without his clothes. He stared at his three visitors but said nothing. His glare seemed to last all night, but was, in reality, just over a minute in duration.

"Feets don't fail me now," he said, to no one in particular, yet he was eyeballing the three.

Rob and Cash didn't know whether to ignore the odd comment, laugh, or look to Paul for guidance. They chose the latter. Paul smiled, so they did their best to follow suit.

"Hello there Paul Bhong, Smith, or whatever the fuck," said Russo, "How's dad?"

"Ah, you know."

"Come over here," said the naked man, waving his hand, the iPod, and the black cord.

"Wait here," said Paul to his two friends, as he stepped toward Russo.

Once Paul reached him, the tattooed leader raised the volume on the dance music again, preventing Rob and Cash from hearing their conversation.

They had an animated discussion, with Paul turning back to look at his friends more than once. Skunk Breath had joined the two other men in a separate dialogue several feet from their boss.

"*We got a funky situation*," sang the vocoder-ized voice over some pounding drums that blasted from the stereo.

Finally, Paul returned to his friends.

"Okay, so I explained your situation," he said, music still pumping.

"Cool," said Rob, giving Cash a smile.

"The thing is," said Paul, "they aren't too stoked to add members that they consider to be *overheads*; you know, not legit tunnel dwellers. He sees you guys as a product of the current situation—the infected. He said you would have never set foot in here prior to the incident."

Russo tapped his feet at the other side of the enclosure, mouthing along to the lyrics. "*We got a funky situation . . .* "

"But you made it sound like he owed you a favor," answered Rob.

"Well yeah, but, um, he's protective of his people down here. Trust is a big deal."

"Trust?" snapped Cash. "One of these skells stole our luggage!"

"*Skells?*"

"It's her Brooklyn coming out," said Rob. Cash kicked his shin.

"Well, I doubt it was these guys who took your bags," replied Paul. "These tunnels are loaded with people. Russo's crew are just a small number of them."

"So, he doesn't want us?" asked Rob.

"I didn't say that. Also, I bet he can get your suitcases back by tonight. Don Russo is extraordinarily persuasive."

"Okay, so what does he want?" asked Cash, hurriedly wiping off something that she felt, but could not see, on her wrist.

"I'm just the messenger," said Paul, "but Mr. Russo has requested a sexual favor as a show of good faith and trust."

Rob pulled Cash to his side. He sized up the three male Russo-followers in the "room". They were all rather thin, not fully nourished. He might be able to take them all, especially if Paul helped. Russo was another matter. He wasn't exactly an Adonis—layers of fat had grown over his muscle—but he had an aura of strength and looked like he could more than handle himself.

"You have to be as fucking crazy as that asshole," said Rob to Paul. "Do you think for one second that I would let that dirty freak anywhere near my girl? I'd rather die right here."

Paul looked back at Russo.

"*We got a funky situation*," sang the naked tunnel dweller, seemingly oblivious to all else.

"Rob," said Paul, staring straight into his eyes, "he wants the sexual favor from *you*."

Rob found himself on his knees beside Don Russo's bed. Cash and Paul stood behind him. He was going through the luggage which had been returned to them as soon as Russo sent word out into the tunnels that he'd consider it a personal favor should these possessions reappear.

"Looks like everything is here, Cash."

She patted his head as she stood beside Paul.

"Thank you, Mr. Russo," said Rob.

"Feets don't fail me now," he replied.

"Huh?"

"That was the album playing when you all crashed our jam. I say *album* loosely 'cause it was on some bullshit computer file instead of a thick slab of vinyl, but it was Herbie Hancock's *Feets Don't Fail Me Now*. 1979. A lot of folks hate that record because they thought it was beneath the jazz master to drop a simple disco joint, but we like it 'round here."

Rob looked up at the naked disco lover, who sat cross-legged on his mattress. Skunk Breath stood near the bed.

"Thank you for recovering our luggage, Mr. Russo."

"All good. That's what we do down here: take care of each other. Also, sorry about the blow job request. No hard feelings that you refused. Probably my fault, but I have no patience for fence-sitters."

Rob turned to Cash. "Fence-sitter?" he mouthed.

"It's the art of the deal, right?" continued Russo. "Ask for the moon, settle for some cheese." He picked at the graying-brown curls atop his ample head. Neither Rob nor Cash could determine his age. He could have been anywhere from thirty-five to fifty-five.

"So, since you're mechanically inclined, we got a few generators that shit the bed. Get them up and running and you've earned your entry into our safe little community. As for Cash here . . . "

"Caroline," she corrected.

"Noted. We'll find something for *Caroline* to do, too."

That sentence, mostly in the way he uttered it, had her feeling dirtier than all the insects and rodents in the tunnels combined. Rob zipped the luggage and stood beside his girlfriend—maybe more in front of her—keeping her away from Russo.

"Skunk here will show you to your mattresses," said Russo, "We had a couple of friends go out for some silver mining a week ago Tuesday and they never came back. Their loss is your gain."

They actually call this fucker "Skunk"? was the first thought in Rob's head, quickly followed by *Silver mining?*

Then, nobody said anything. For quite a while.

Nobody.

CANNI

"You're overwhelmed," said Russo. He repositioned his exposed penis without a thought to the fact that four other people were in front of him. "It's an adjustment, living down here, but you'll get used to it. We seem trapped, but in truth, we're free. You'll see."

Midnight traffic bounced on the manhole cover above them. The penis adjustment had Rob standing even more prominently in front of Cash, shielding her as the Secret Service did Ronald Reagan after those shots rang out. This did not go unnoticed by their host.

"Yeah, keep your girl safe," he said, long fingernails picking at his scalp, "I'm the loco one, right?"

Rob's every muscle wanted to get Cash out of there, but his brain told him otherwise.

"I'm a lunatic because I refuse to wrap myself in the clothing of your people?" asked Russo. "You were born naked, brother. So was Miss Brooklyn behind you. Would it bring you comfort if I wore a nice shirt and pants? I used to. But, that bare, exposed, newborn me was doing just fine. Then your society wrapped me in your shirts—the ones woven from racism, sexism, and homophobia. The trousers, the dungarees, britches, pantaloons, if you like, they were stitched with poverty and greed, with patches on the knees for lifelong groveling. Yes, be afraid, modern day lovebirds, I am the crazy one."

Rob and Cash were assigned separate beds; side-by-side, but with a small dresser between them. The furniture was chipped and peeling, with a bit of duct tape securing one of the drawers. Everything was elevated on bricks and blocks. Paul was still with them as they examined their living area. Also standing there was a short, stout fellow with piercing blue eyes and almost no teeth. He was known as Hoffman and had a bit of an accent, probably German. Skunk had passed the newbies off to Hoffman so he could return to his post at the south entry of Russo's bunker.

"I will try to allow you privacy, but I must be nearby. It is how we all stay safe," said Hoffman.

"What do you all do if someone turns?" asked Paul.

"Well, we have strength in numbers," answered their protector. "We have sacks for over the heads, some mace, other things, too. We have had nobody become cannibal in our home, so luckily we have not had to use anything yet, on our own people."

"So no one has flipped in the tunnels?" asked Rob.

"In the tunnels, I think yes. In our area, no. We will not permit anyone, especially monster, to enter our area. You and the young lady are safe here."

He gave them a wide, generally toothless grin and stepped away.

Cash pulled the cover back on her mattress, seemingly inspecting for bugs. Rob moved closer to Paul and whispered, "Thank you for this. This place is crazy

106

as all fuck, but I feel I might be able to keep her safe here. Especially since it seems that Russo prefers my ass to hers."

"Don't be so sure about that," answered Paul. "He enjoys girls, too. You'll probably see him in bed with three at a time."

"Well, it's not gonna be with this one," said Rob.

Four hours later, with Paul long gone, Cash half-slept in her bed, tossing about. Her sneakers were still on. Rob knew she was having more nightmares about Teresa. He studied her from his mattress, sitting straight up, eyes heavy but focused. The watchers had just switched shifts and they had patrolled this section several times already. Still, Rob felt he should protect Cash as she slept. He wasn't ready to trust anyone.

The tunnels at night were noisier than he'd expected, mostly from the Las Vegas traffic overhead. When there came a sound that originated from within the tunnel system, it seemed to reverberate throughout.

The echo drifting through as he watched Cash twist on her bed was that of a distant barking dog.

CANNI

Washington, D.C.

It is not often that a canine can be found in the Cabinet Room of the White House, but there sat a rigid, black and tan Belgian Malinois in a leather harness. Beside the large dog was his handler, wearing a dark-visored helmet. Four other similarly-attired agents stood throughout the expansive room. At its center was an oval mahogany conference table with twenty leather chairs, all filled. Suits, pant-suits, and military uniforms with lots of *scrambled eggs* and *fruit salads* adorning them. Bronze Stars were not in short supply. Pens and paper sat in front of each attendee. No computers. A handful of lower-level staff ringed the table, carrying plastic bags.

The early afternoon sun shone through the Rose Garden windows as the President of the United States cleared his throat and spoke.

"Who ordered the Cheesy Gordita Crunch?"

"I did, Mr. President," responded the Vice Chairman of the Joint Chiefs of Staff.

The Commander-in-Chief closed the wrapping and handed the taco to an aide who carried it to the general.

The Secret Service dog licked its chops.

"Not sure how I wound up with the Gordita Crunch," said the president. "Does everyone else have what they ordered?"

"Yes, sir," came the responses.

"Good, then. Where were we?"

"All non-essential personnel please vacate the Cabinet Room," said the Chief of Staff in his best command voice.

The staff members who had brought the Taco Bell bags into the room quickly exited to the hallway.

"Warren," said the president, "are we closer to finding the people behind this?"

"I can say that we are, sir." replied Warren Hamburger, Director of the Central Intelligence Agency. "Now, I don't mean in general; I mean the exact scientists who concocted this menace, and the people who paid, coerced, or ordered them to do it. They had literally *hundreds* of pilots who spent years preparing for this. But we are closer. Not there yet, but getting better intel every day. Every hour, in fact."

"Good. It can't be that hard to find someone with both the genius and malevolence to carry this out. I want them."

George Edward Bernard Collins was not a president who would talk around an issue. He got where he did by saying what he meant. He won the election by minimizing the talking points and engaging voters by being as close to a "regular guy" as a presidential nominee could be. Being African-American, he steered clear of race talk, saying that it should not be a central issue of his campaign. He wanted to focus on being an American, as all of the voters, regardless of skin tone, were. He would joke that he had blown the chance to be the first black president anyway but was proud to be the first unmarried POTUS elected since Grover Cleveland, and now he would just like to be an effective American President.

In private, he would tease staffers that he was, however, the first *full-blooded* African-American U.S. President. "No white in these veins," he'd say laughingly. If made public, such a statement might be fodder for the Sunday talk show circuit, and even produce whispers of racism and impeachment, but it was, to his mind, simply a goddamned joke—something with which the American people may have lost touch.

President Collins had the country on the right track. Unemployment was down, along with gas prices. Wall Street had been doing well, likewise the housing market. There had been relative peace as far as military involvement went. World leaders had taken a liking to him. He could sense that the great majority of Americans, regardless of political party, saw him as a wonderful young president, not just a wonderful young *black* president.

He had also planned to be married in office, and in the White House; the first such wedding since President Cleveland's in 1886. It was going to be a doozy.

Then, all of this shit happened.

He knew that there would always be those who hated the United States of America. No matter the president, the party in power, or the state of the world in general, there forever would be those who despised freedom, and were sworn to topple it.

This, *The Flyover*, had been their most devastating attempt yet.

"I want to tell you all something," he said. "A few of you are already aware of this, but I want everyone in this room to know: yesterday afternoon, for almost forty-five minutes, Vice President Montgomery was the Acting President of the United States. I spent part of that time trying to kill and eat my security detail. The rest of that time was spent recovering and being cleaned up. I remember none of it, but I am still here, as are the Secret Service members who subdued me. I want to thank them and the vice president for a job well done. The point of all this is that these bastards who did this, they did it to *all* of us. Their attack has infiltrated the White House. We need to find them, and we need an antidote for what they created. There are no other options."

He looked over at his vice president, who returned his nod. Owen Walfred Montgomery had known the president since he was his history professor at Princeton. The veep was twenty-eight years older than his boss but found that the teaching dynamic was a fluid one, and he had received at least as much knowledge from his former student as he had instilled.

They had many a private joke that could never be made public, such as when President Collins referred to him as "O.W.M.", which was public knowledge, he wasn't just referencing his initials. He was lovingly calling him "Old White Man", which is precisely—though not in those terms—what the pundits proposed as a running mate for the young black hopeful. Always good to have someone who looks a lot like prior presidents standing beside anyone who might not fit the male, white, seasoned mold.

Vice President Montgomery, on election night, told his boss that his dream was to see the day that we had our first gay president. The newly-elected commander-in-chief responded, "Have you seen those powdered wigs on our forefathers? Come on, dude."

That was the closeness of their relationship. It made for a smooth one-two punch atop the Executive Branch. There was no filtering. No time to fret about feelings.

Make it happen.

That was their mantra, and they each had a little sign on their desks that would remind them of those words every day.

"Where do we stand medically?" asked President Collins to no one in particular. He took a long sip from the purple straw in his icy Baja Blast.

"We've had an incident with two of our top researchers, Mr. President."

The words came from Dr. Papperello-Venito. There was no Taco Bell meal in front of her.

"How so?" he asked.

"The Andersons, from Dr. Robert's *barn*. One is deceased, the other injured, but she will be back to work. She apparently had an episode and her brother is dead as a result."

"We can't have this," he responded. "We don't want *any* deaths, but we certainly do not want our top people—those who might lead the way out of this—being lost. We have to protect these people, maybe keep them apart from each other in some way . . . "

"Sir, it was an off-duty situation."

"There can't be an *off-duty* anymore. Everything we have built since 1776 is on the line. All of those who have given their lives for our country deserve for us to prevail."

"I would like to say, sir, that though the Andersons are—or were—a bit different, and maybe not my favorite people, they were working from home, on their own time, still going above and beyond for our country when he lost his life."

Another doctor dryly interrupted, "He was getting a calzone."

"They were taking a fucking lunch break," snapped Papperello-Venito. "Is your 7 Layer Burrito any different, Gordon?"

"Okay, settle down," demanded the president. "Please see that Dr. Anderson is recognized for his sacrifice. Now I know we have a whole lot more than just a brother and sister team working on this. What else can you tell me?"

"Some of the incidents are lasting longer," she replied. "Some of our case studies have been experiencing episodes of longer duration."

"How long?"

"Some have been nearly an hour," she said.

"God," groaned the president.

The guard dog barked, startling most of the room.

"Everything okay?" asked President Collins of the canine-handler.

"I believe so, sir," came the reply from under the visor.

"And, more importantly," continued Dr. Pepperello-Venito, "one subject has remained in the cannibal state for twenty-one hours thus far, has not slept, and has not returned to normalcy as we speak."

The president exhaled. This may have been his deepest fear: the possibility of irreversible flipping. For a moment, the only sound came from the panting Malinois.

"Listen people," he said, "We've got citizens medicating themselves with sedatives and booze. And I mean folks who have not done this before. You can't buy pepper spray anymore. All sold out. Half the time it doesn't even work on these things. Doors are being locked from inside and out. The locksmith business is booming. Never mind just killing each other, the average Americans are having episodes and running blindly into traffic, or off cliffs, overpasses, or bridges. You want to talk about the economy? One of this morning's financial papers went with the headline, YOUR STOCK BROKER ATE MY STOCK BROKER. I don't know, is that funny?"

"Terrible," mumbled Vice President Montgomery.

"You know those *secret* drug tunnels between the U.S. and Mexico?" continued President Collins, "People are now using them to sneak *out* of our country. Even with the borders closed both ways, don't you just get the feeling that somehow, someway, this is going to eventually become a worldwide issue? I hope to God not, but we have to anticipate the worst."

"Still no signs that the infection is transmitted by contact, or any means other than the initial exposure from the flyover, sir," reminded Dr. Papperello-Venito.

"Good news is always welcomed, Doctor," he answered, though sounding skeptical. He sipped his Baja Blast. "A new wrinkle," he continued, "is that there has been quite an uptick on murders. People are trying to use this situation to kill whomever they'd apparently always wanted to off. They try and pass it off as self-defense against a cannibal attack. Of course forensics can determine if the murder victim had been in an altered state at the time of death, but we just don't have the time or manpower to keep up. Hell, are you all aware of how many convicted criminals we have been putting back on the streets since this happened? We can't keep two to a cell anymore. You think cellmates were killing each other *before* all of this? So, we have no room to keep them safe, and they are back on the streets. The tentacles of this attack are extending farther and deeper than we had imagined. Every aspect of our daily lives has been altered. If we do not resolve this matter quickly and definitively, our country, our freedom, and our lives, are doomed."

The big guard dog let out a deep growl and took a few steps toward the far end of the mahogany table. His helmeted handler held him back. All attention was now on the Belgian Malinois. The president looked down toward those in the area of the dog's interest.

"Everyone feeling okay?" he asked.

All nodded or smiled. He turned to the dog handler.

"Does the animal sense that someone might be about to flip?"

"Unknown, Mr. President. It is a possibility. Also it might just be the Taco Bell."

DANIEL O'CONNOR

Las Vegas

The morning sun always found its way into the tunnels. It wasn't a monumental display of light by any means, but through various grates and manhole covers, tiny beams would dart down from the heavens and dance like the slimmest of spotlights, occasionally being blacked out by passing traffic, be it vehicular or foot.

As Cash opened her eyes, one of these dancing beams landed on a pretty young woman who stood beside her bed, smiling.

"Good morning," she whispered, "I'm Phaedra."

Cash was slightly startled, and the first thing she did was look over at Rob. He was there, sitting up on his mattress, pillow propped against the wall behind him, but he was sound asleep.

"He watched you for a good five hours before he nodded off," said Phaedra in a hushed tone, "We should let him rest. I can show you to, for lack of a better term, our *bathroom*. You can also wash up and brush your teeth, Caroline."

Cash rubbed her eyes, "You know my name?"

"Sure. You're one of us now."

"I don't think we really need to hold hands," said Cash as Phaedra led her through an adjacent tunnel.

"Of course," responded the soft-spoken girl with the flowing red hair. She abandoned her grip on Cash's cold hand, but her smile remained. Cash sized her up to be about her equal in age, but she was either unburdened by the fact that life had led her to the tunnels or she was one hell of an actress. Also evident to Cash was that this girl's hair was shiny and clean, not matted with filth like many others below ground. She looked as though she could be a mermaid. Maybe one who had been on dry land for too long.

"Most folks don't even think to bring a toothbrush, but I'm happy you did, Caroline. We have unopened extras if you needed one, though."

"I have floss too."

"Super! So, I am going to show you our lavatory facilities. In other words—buckets."

Cash had figured that she and Rob would just find a way to use some casino restroom whenever required, but she hadn't realized how long of a trek it could actually be to exit the tunnels and walk to civilization. She then fixated so much on the word *buckets* that she ignored whatever Phaedra said next. Additionally, the word *buckets* began to change shape in her mind so much that it began to appear almost as if it were not a word at all. Surely it wasn't spelled the way she always had thought. It didn't look right. "Blah blah blah BUCKETS blah blah blah BUCKETS blah blah," seemed to be what Phaedra was saying.

Cash needed to refocus.

"Drugs, honey?" were the first words that brought her back.

"What?"

"Not to pry, but you seem spaced. Are you stoned, Caroline?"

"No. No way. I don't use drugs. Maybe a little weed, but that's all."

"Oh, okay. Most folks are down here because of drugs. Some gambling, but mostly drugs. We don't judge. Don Russo won't stand for people who can't contribute, though. The drugs can't interfere with chores. That would crumble our society."

"Sorry, but what did you say your name was?"

"Phaedra."

"So Phaedra, I am not even, like, awake yet. This is a lot to process, you know?"

"I'm sorry. You're right. Let's just concentrate on the *buckets*."

Somewhere down the tunnels, a sound.

It was there, then gone. Silent. Could have been some kind of engine, or even a deep voice, or growl. With the echoes and muffled noises of the city above, it was difficult to identify.

"The thing about these tunnel sounds," said Phaedra as they stopped, "is that it's so hard to tell how close they are. I've been here for two years and I still can't tell. Once upon a time, there was what sounded like a *toilet flush* and it seemed so far away, but then it was right on us."

"*Toilet flush?*"

"Oh, sorry. Especially with me showing you about the *buckets*, and all the lavatory talk, I understand your confusion. Totally my fault. A 'toilet flush' is when a huge flood comes though and washes everything out: people, belongings, everything. Luckily we are usually prepared, and they don't occur all that often. We are in the desert, after all. But when they happen, they totally, totally happen. I've seen people drown."

Cash's fears of possible Cannis in the distance were replaced by the threat of a flash flood.

"Shouldn't we get out? I have to get Rob!"

"Oh, no. That's not a flush at all. Look at the light streams coming in. The sun is out and strong. No clouds mean no rain. No rain means no floods."

Cash's thoughts returned to default mode: fear of Cannis.

"We all do our share of cleaning the *buckets*, Caroline. Even Don Russo. We take turns bringing them out of the tunnels and washing them out. It's tedious, distasteful, and the worst job, but it needs to be done. Others—meaning folks who are not part of our Artsy Bunker—just do their business in certain sections of the tunnels, creating a disgusting mess that draws all the worst vermin. It never gets cleaned out until there's a flush."

"So, when there's a flush, we have to deal with waves of floating waste?"

"Oh, that's the least of our worries if we are caught in a flush."

Cash was getting itchy. She could feel a skin-crawl coming on.

"There is a way to get way less *bucket* duty," said Phaedra, stroking her crimson locks. "I don't do it much anymore."

"How's that?" asked Cash, rubbing each arm with its opposite hand.

"Well, Don Russo gives out the assignments, of course. He really enjoys handsome people, be they male or female. He always calls me the "fairest of the fair". Says I'm the loveliest girl in our world. I'm sure that will change with you here, but that's fine," she smiled.

"He bases assignments on physical appearance?"

"Not entirely that."

"And, by the way, you are very pretty, Phaedra. I'm sure you'll still be the fairest to him, if that matters to you."

"It shouldn't, but it does. People would say I have daddy issues. Oh, follow me through this chamber; it leads to our shower—well, actually a long garden hose that we have attached to a spigot behind an abandoned warehouse up above. I hope they never get their water turned off!"

They stepped through the in-wall opening, into the next tunnel, a smaller, narrow space.

"So Russo is a father figure to you?" asked Cash.

"Ha! Not at all. People blame daddy issues for a variety of things. I never knew my real father. According to my mother, he was a famous singer. I promised her I'd never tell anyone who he is. Or was. He's dead now. Died out here near Vegas, but I never met him. I can't say for sure if he's my father, but *supposubly* he is."

"FiveFourThreeTwoOne," yelled Cash, quickly, while counting on her fingers.

"What the heck was that?" laughed Phaedra.

"Nothing," answered Cash, inhaling deeply. She rubbed her arms frenetically.

"Are you okay?"

"Yeah. It's a tic. When someone says that word, or non-word, actually. I count back in time to before they said it."

"What word?"

"I can't say it."

"*Supposubly?*"

"FiveFourThreeTwoOne. Motherfucker! Sorry, that just came out. But please don't say it. It's not even a word."

"Of course it's a word, silly. I don't even know what you mean, Caroline. You nutty girl."

"The word is *supposedly*. Listen: sup-pos-ED-ly. That's the word, not the other one."

"Sup-*pose-UB-ly*."

"FiveFourThreeTwoOne. Please don't try again. Let's just move on." Cash counted on her fingers, rubbed her arms, and took three deep breaths.

"Anyway," continued the redhead, "I don't think of Don Russo as a father. He's my lover. He enjoys making love to attractive people. I know he'll want you immensely. If you become one of his lovers, your chores and assignments will be much easier. You'll be one of his favored followers."

Cash stopped walking, but continued scratching and rubbing.

"Phaedra," she said, "show me how to clean the shit buckets."

Thump, thud, smack. Thump, thud, smack. Thump, thud, smack . . .

In Rob's nightmare, those were the sounds he endured as Cash was having sex with an unknown hooded man as he was forced to watch while tied to a chair behind a huge glass wall. As the coitus concluded, the man rolled up the bottom of his hood and took a large, bloody bite out of the back of Cash's shoulder.

Thump, thud, smack.

Rob opened one eye as he awoke. Nothing moved but his eyeball.

Thump, thud, smack.

He was grateful that the sounds were not emanating from his nightmare scenario, yet he was not thrilled to discover their actual source.

There was Don Russo, naked, leaning against a tunnel wall. He was throwing a small ball, on an angle, at the floor. It would then hit the far concrete wall and fly back into his meaty hand.

Thump, thud, smack.

Despite the unusual and potentially unnerving sight, Rob had other concerns. "Where is Cash?"

"No worries," said Russo. "She's being shown around by a lovely young lady."

He continued to bounce the ball as Rob stood.

"Can that 'lovely young lady' stop a canni attack?" asked Rob, dryly.

Skunk and Hoffman stood off to the side as Rob began to head off into the tunnel system. Russo stopped bouncing the ball.

"Hold on, partner," said the naked leader. "I promise she is safe. We ain't lost nobody yet."

Rob stopped walking and said, "Can you at least tell me which direction to go?"

"You made me stop bouncing my ball," said Russo. "I once did it over a thousand times straight without a fuck up. Sounds simple, but there are so many variables; you get tired, lose concentration, it takes a goofy bounce. Sometimes even the simplest things go wrong if you do them enough times. Law of averages."

"*Cash!*" yelled Rob as loudly as he could. It echoed through the tunnels and startled many of the inhabitants.

"Holy fuck!" said Russo. "Chill, brother. We don't operate like that down here, all high octane shit. Your girl is fine." He turned to his men. "Go get her and Phaedra."

Skunk and Hoffman took off. Rob began to follow them. Russo grabbed his arm. His grip felt like a bear claw. Rob tried to pull away.

"You can go if you want," said Russo, "but you'll feel better and learn something if you let her return without you. You won't be able to watch her twenty-four-seven down here. Not possible. You need to see that she is safe even if you aren't beside her, Rob."

Russo loosened his grip. Rob looked in the direction taken by Skunk and Hoffman. His body actually leaned that way, but his feet remained firm.

He stayed.

"Cool," smiled Russo. "Now take a deep breath. She'll be back in a minute. She was being shown around and taken to wash up. No men around her, just our girl Phaedra."

Rob still stared down the length of the tunnel, though he couldn't see much.

"I'll wait maybe five minutes, then I'm getting her," he said.

"Sounds fair," answered Russo as he held the little ball up to Rob's face. "I know you're from Brooklyn, but you're kinda young. So, do you have any memories of the Pimple Ball?"

"The what?"

"Pimple Ball."

Russo held it up to Rob's eyes. A rubber handball. Quite dirty, but it was once white. There were small bumps all over it—'pimples'—and it had stars at what would be its North and South Poles.

"Yeah, so?" mumbled Rob.

"These were the greatest. I grew up in Philly. They were the shit, Rob. These little bitches could be bounced crazy. Before computers and all that crap, we could play all day with these things. All kinds of different games. Then, when the air finally went outta the ball, we'd cut it in two and play Halfball. All we needed was a broomstick."

"I'm not sure . . . "

"Look, buddy," Russo held the ball up close to Rob's eyes. "I used to have a few of these. They all went flat. This here one is the only Pimple Ball left in Artsy Bunker. It's almost like a miracle to me because it's still full of air."

"Cool, I guess."

Don Russo placed his chapped lips on the dirty ball and kissed it. He then took two steps and fired it with all his strength down the long, dark tunnel. It went so far that they didn't even hear it land.

Then, Russo and Rob stared at each other.

For too long.

"Cash!" Rob yelled, louder than before.

"Aw, geez," sighed the nude Russo, "I did all that for nothing. You said you'd give her five minutes and you didn't."

"I said five minutes before actually getting her. All I did was call her name."

"Okay, I'll give you that. I wanted you to see that the Pimple Ball was important to me. It was with me every day. But I just let it go. If I'm meant to have it again, I'll come across it. If not, life goes on. Maybe I'll find another ball down the road."

"She's going to marry me. She's not a rubber ball."

"Fair enough. I'm just saying to let things happen. If they are not meant to happen naturally, then I promise, you don't want them to happen. It'll all go ass-ways. The whole 'square pegs' bullshit."

"Why were you playing ball beside our beds in the first place, Mr. Russo?"

"Let me get to that in a minute. Did you ever see a Pimple Ball by the side of the road when you were growing up?"

"Uh, I don't know."

"Tennis ball?"

"What does this even mean?"

"Please don't say 'golf ball'."

"I can't remember. None of them, okay?"

"That might be the best answer! I say you can judge how spoiled a person is by the balls found on the streets where they lived. Golf balls would mean a silver spoon in the ass, ya know? Living by a golf course. If you didn't see no balls at all, you're probably a good dude. Shit, even I saw Spaldeens, Pinky Balls, and Pimples, and I grew up in squalor."

"And you were playing ball beside my bed for what reason?"

"Yeah, that. Well, I came to wake your ass up, and if I got a ball, I'ma bounce it."

Rob was looking down the tunnel as he spoke. "Why wake me at all?"

"These tunnels are filled with slackers: drug addicted gamblers who have been sucked up in slot machine tornados and deposited right here, just like Dorothy and Toto. Except this ain't Oz. They wander around down here like zombies. No structure, no hope. We don't want those types in our bunker. Sure, we got addicts and gamblers, but the ones here have a purpose. We have chores and duties that keep our society running. The lazy ones can fend for themselves in the other tunnels. We want the workers."

"So, the ball-bouncing was my work bell."

Russo laughed heartily. "Yeah. But you can clean up and grab breakfast first. This ain't a sweatshop. We have lots of fun down here. Have some drinks, smoke some stuff, dance parties, free love for those who want it. We just get our work done first. I'm hoping you can fix those generators. My boys will show you the ropes as to the washing up and bathroom stuff. That's where your Miss Brooklyn went with Phaedra."

"I'm just worried when I'm not there to protect her. I know you can imagine how crazy this is for her. Just coming down to these tunnels is weird enough, but with the threats we all now face with this disease, or whatever it is . . . "

Russo placed his hand on Rob's shoulder.

"Listen," he said. "Truth be told, it's Phaedra—down that tunnel—and me right here that's in danger. We've been living below in our little piece of America where no one has flipped. You and your girl are the dangerous ones because you've just come from above, where the monsters are."

Rob, perhaps as a reflex, turned his attention to the traffic noises above their heads. He hadn't considered the prospect that he and Cash might be a danger to those who've welcomed them beneath the chaos. He certainly didn't trust Don Russo, or anyone in the tunnels. Hell, he wasn't even too comfortable with Paul Bhong. Yet so far, they had all conspired to do exactly one thing: keep Rob and his girl as safe as possible.

Well, that and the request that Rob give Russo a blow job.

"You guys have been great," said Rob, "but it must be about five minutes by now. I'm not saying that your people are a threat, but I need to have Cash with me."

"I had an enormous bong once," said Russo. "It was beautiful, all Rastafari colors. I cherished it because it came from a Marine buddy of mine. He had the most wonderful and powerful Rasta name too. I was so damned jealous."

"What was his name?"

"Bob."

"Bob?"

"Yeah. Like Marley. Those fuckers had the most common names, but made them so badass; Bob Marley, Peter Tosh, Jimmy Cliff . . . "

"Yellowman?"

"Shit, Rob, you know Yellowman?"

"Well, I've heard of him . . . "

"Real name: Winston. Nice try, though."

"Cash?" bellowed Rob down the tunnel.

"On the way back, Rob," came the distant reply. Hearing Cash's voice usually increased his heart rate, but in this one instance it slowed it down.

"Thank Christ," mumbled Russo. "Listen, bud: I loved that bong. More smoke flowed through that thing than the fucking chimney at Chernobyl. One night, long before I lived down here, while listening to Canned Heat and watching *The Mary Tyler Moore Show* on mute, some chick knocked it to the floor. It was in pieces. I blamed no one. It was an accident. The next day I glued every damned piece back together. I still have that bong. I'll show you later. It's not as pretty as before and it has scars all over where I reconstructed it. But you know what? The smoke still flows through and I get just as stoked as before. It's not perfect, it was damaged, but it still functions once I made sure to put it all back together."

"Is this the final metaphor of the day, Mr. Russo?"

"Okay. I see."

"I just . . . I must admit that I don't understand how your story pertains to me."

"I'll be more direct. You've been here exactly one night and the whole place sees that you are, well, I was going to say you were wrapped around that little girl's finger, but it's more than that. You are wrapped around her like a boa constrictor, squeezing till she can't breathe, wanting only to consume her. You are the one actually at risk, Rob. What I mean is that if the day comes that she smashes the blood-pumping *bong* that resides deep inside your chest, you can still patch it back up and get high on the rest of your life. The scars will remain forever, but you must find a way to keep smokin', motherfucker."

Rob had no answer. He was shocked that Russo had sensed his greatest flaw and deepest fear in such a short time. He was puzzled as to why the society's leader would even care enough to offer advice. He was also coming to terms with the fact that Don Russo had apparently served his country as a Marine. If Rob hadn't shied his eyes from Russo's perpetual nakedness, he might have noticed the tattoo over his heart: a Battlefield Cross that consisted of a helmet sitting atop a rifle, with two boots below. The inscription above read: FOR THE FALLEN.

Russo was covered in ink, from an Oakland Raiders logo, to the quartet of symbols that adorn Led Zeppelin's fourth album, to an elaborate portrait of most of the cast from the old prisoner of war comedy television program, *Hogan's Heroes*. But it was the Marines artwork that covered his heart.

Cash had returned. Her hair was wet from washing. Rob loved it that way. Like when she'd stride out of the ocean at Rockaway Beach.

"This is Phaedra," said Cash, as she gave her boyfriend a hug.

Rob smiled at the young woman, extending his hand. "Rob," he said.

The redhead gave a broad smile as she clenched his palm between both of hers.

"Come Phaedra," said Russo, "Let our new friends have some moments together before their workday begins. Someone will come to show you where to wash up, Rob."

As the pair left, Cash said, "Workday? I thought we came to Vegas for a vacation."

"Why didn't you wake me?" asked Rob. "You ran off without me."

"Because you stayed up all night, staring at me. You need to sleep too."

"I wasn't staring. I'm just trying to keep you safe."

"Rob, we came down here because supposedly it is safe. They watch over each other. That is basically the only positive in being here. If you can't embrace that, we should just go back above ground and take our chances protecting each other. We won't be together all the time down here because we're going to have different chores, or whatever."

"I'm going to request that we have the same jobs."

"Oh, I'm going to fix generators?"

"No. But when I get that done, I'm going to ask if we can do the silver mining."

"That again? You found out what it is?"

"Yeah. They have people go into the casinos and check all the slot machines for unused credits. Sometimes they get just a few cents, but there have been times where they've gotten hundreds of dollars, just left in the machines by drunken gamblers. They do this every single night."

"Hmm, so we can either dump buckets of human waste or stroll through air-conditioned casinos, printing out tickets? No way the new guys can get that cushy job, Rob. You're smarter than that."

"Two things: don't you think some of these unwashed types get tossed out of the casinos . . . ?" Rob hushed when two dwellers of that variety cruised by on safety patrol.

"If we stay clean," he continued quietly, "no one's gonna notice us on the casino floor. We could be there all night. Number two: remember that the casinos are *up there*. They are not in the supposed 'safety' of the tunnels. We'd have to walk the streets to get there and count on their security to protect us once inside. Even cops have been flipping, so there is no guarantee there. I don't think the silver mining gig is the prize it once was. Hell, Russo himself said two of them never returned from their last trip."

"I'm confused," said Cash. "You say everything is about keeping us safe . . . "

"Keeping *you* safe."

"Whatever. But if we go up to the streets every night, doesn't that defeat the purpose of being here?"

"I don't even know anymore. If I can watch you while you sleep and be beside you when you're awake . . . "

"Rob. Baby. Listen to yourself. If all of what you said were to take place, you might be the one who kills me."

"But . . . "

"Or, I'll kill you. I've already done away with my best friend . . . " She sat down on the mattress, her head in her hands. Rob came to sit beside her and stroked the ringlets in her damp, sandy brown hair. She'd been doing reasonably well considering the events of recent days, but every now and then the horror fought its way to the surface and consumed her.

"To think we thought it sucked back home," she said.

"I didn't think it sucked."

"I'd give anything to just be back the way we were," she explained. "Being a paralegal, going to school at night. It was hectic, but it wasn't really so bad. You could keep working toward opening your own auto repair shop. Teresa would be there. We were always there for each other."

"I know, baby."

"This was supposed to be a fucking vacation."

"Well, it would be just as bad back home. The whole country is screwed. At least we can still get our Las Vegas wedding done, if you want. I know John G is gonna call me when he's here. I guarantee that crazy fucker is still coming, all ready to be my best man."

It was too late to suck the words back in. Rob had done it again. Yes, the best man might still be en route, but Cash had shot and killed her maid of honor.

DANIEL O'CONNOR

Washington, D.C.

President Collins was erect in his chair within the Situation Room of the White House. The vice president sat beside him, and they were surrounded, horseshoe-style, by their national security team. There was no Taco Bell in sight. It was not yet afternoon rush hour in Washington D.C., but half the world away in the Middle East it was well past midnight. An unexpected sandstorm had kicked up, but it was not enough to deter the U.S. Navy SEAL teams. The White House leaders watched two separate screens as their armed forces converged simultaneously on two modest homes, some thirty miles apart. The president had expected maybe some flash grenades and a whole lot of yelling, but that was not to be. It was more like some deadly surprise party. A quick and quiet entry, night vision goggles giving his men the edge they needed. Finally, some screams, a religious proclamation—neither from the SEALs—and a barrage of *pops* that sounded like fireworks, but certainly were not.

Then, silence.

The president, safe as could be expected within the fortified White House, felt his heart thumping as fast and loud as he'd ever experienced. Even after he gave the go-ahead, he did not want any of his troops wounded or killed, but he thought he had the spine to deal with such a result if it happened. If not, he wouldn't have applied for the job.

"Two under, two expired," came the first transmission.

"Five under," was the report from the second location.

"Let's hope the dead ones aren't the primary targets," mumbled someone in the Situation Room.

"Liberty team intact," came another transmission.

Then: "Vesey team intact."

"No American casualties," translated a military officer standing near the president.

A sigh of relief, followed by more silence as the SEAL teams prepared to extricate themselves along with their prisoners and the two bodies.

One could actually hear the faint sound of a ticking clock on the wall to the right of the commander-in-chief. As the White House staff watched the specialized Navy units proceed to a quartet of Sikorsky Black Hawk helicopters, two per location, another sound began to battle the clock as the chief silence-breaker.

The panting dog.

Tick, pant. Tick, pant.

President Collins looked over at his helmeted guard and the dog attached to him. He smiled.

"You might want to give *Lassie* a cold drink, Harold. That is Harold in there, correct?"

The guard raised his visor, "Yes, Mr. President, it's me," he smiled, revealing his face briefly before lowering his faceguard again.

"Get that puppy some water," laughed the president.

"Sir, unless that is a direct order, I request waiting until this meeting is concluded."

"Not an order, Harold; just a suggestion from a guy who loves animals. I'm sure you know best."

"Liberty on helos."

"Vesey on helos."

Applause from the Situation room, and one dog bark. The SEAL teams were safely aboard their helicopters and on the way to a U.S. airbase with prisoners in tow.

President Collins put his hand on the shoulder of Vice President Montgomery. "Owen, those guys are amazing. They pull these things off so matter-of-factly. In and out within minutes; coming back safely."

"Yes they do, Mr. President. We would be nowhere without our armed forces. The entire free world depends upon them, whether they know it or not."

The VP's words hung in the air with the boisterous cheers, many decibels above the ticking clock and the panting dog.

President Collins leaned in closer, "I don't feel worthy to be called their commander-in-chief. If I were on that raid, I'd be like a lost kitten compared to those men."

"George," responded the vice president, pulling his younger friend closer, "your strength lies within having the fortitude to make the calls. You have to face the American people when things go wrong. I've watched you telephone and personally visit the newly-widowed. You *are* the commander-in-chief, and the men and women of our military honor and respect that fact. Vince Lombardi wasn't much of a football player. He certainly wasn't going to run the sweep for the Packers. But the Super Bowl trophy bears his name. The team takes their strength from their leader. You exude that strength. You must never doubt that. If you waver, so will the team."

"I won't," he answered. "They are just so monumentally impressive that I have my 'fanboy' moments. I can always count on you for a good slap in the face. Even with my history papers at Princeton."

"Well, I just remember your blank stare when I asked you to name the U.S. Presidents who were members of the Whig Party."

The president grinned. He patted his second-in-command on the back. The cheering began to subside with a collection of hugs.

Then came a transmission from one of the Black Hawks.

"Security issue on Vesey Two helo."

The room went still.

The deep grunts and muffled thuds of a struggle blasted through the transmitter.

"Do we have video on the chopper?" asked the president.

"Working on it, sir."

"We have a canni situation on Vesey Two," stated the helicopter pilot, calmly and clearly.

The conflict grew louder.

"Almost have video."

"Possibly more than one infected threat," offered the pilot.

The noises coming from the chopper seemed more concerning than the placid tones of the pilot's voice would indicate.

"Video now."

The shaky and grainy image showed two helmeted SEALs bounding wildly about the chopper's cramped interior. At least five other members of their team tried to subdue them. The only passenger strapped into a seat was the one prisoner they carried aboard Vesey Two. He wore no helmet and his eyes were wide. He screamed something in his native tongue. The only other words came from the pilot.

"Vesey Two requesting permission to land. Situation red."

"If you need to, do it." came the response, "Be fast, because they will be on your ass."

"*They* are not the prime concern at the moment, sir."

The president turned to one of his military advisors. "Shouldn't they have all been belted into their seats? How can we have a couple of infected SEALs tearing up that chopper?"

"Sir, I can only assume that they flipped before they strapped in. Once they are onboard in a situation like this, they secure any prisoners, then themselves, but they will lift off before they are all seated. Time is an issue in a mission like this."

"But *two* of them becoming that way simultaneously?"

"I have no answer for that, Mr. President."

"Sir," added another official, "it might just be a function of probability. If these events are increasing in number and/or frequency, the lone attacker at any given location might soon be the exception, rather than the general rule."

Those words fluttered in the air of the Situation Room as the helo did the same above the desert. The transmitted image from Vesey Two was dark and pixelated.

"Non-lethal force!" was the garbled message.

President Collins spoke again to the staff in the room. "Maybe the stress level of a mission like this can trigger the infection. I assume we are looking into that."

"Of course, sir. But to SEALs, this is like our grocery shopping. At home, they are people; on missions, they are machines."

"Non-lethal!"

"Get him outta the fucking cockpit!"

The image went black. Transmissions ceased.

Nothing for nearly forty seconds, then:

"This is Vesey One. Vesey Two is down. Crashed. Rescue/recovery to commence."

The three other Black Hawks headed toward the crash site. Video from one of them appeared on the White House monitors. The sandy terrain was a mass of fire and black smoke, helo pieces strewn everywhere.

The only sounds now were the ticking clock and the panting dog.

Two hours later, long after a particularly thirsty canine was awarded a cold bowl of water and a hefty can of food, the president and vice president entered the Oval Office. Already within were two helmeted guards along with a man and woman in blue janitorial gear. The man, a middle-aged fellow with rough, dark skin—apart from a large, pink burn scar on his right cheek—emptied a trash can into a wheeled bin. He blinked a lot. The female was a blonde, no older than twenty-three. She ran a vacuum across the thick oval rug. It sucked up any lint that tainted the plush presidential seal. She shut her Hoover off when Collins and Montgomery entered. The older fellow went right on with his cleaning duties, but she froze, staring at the world's most powerful man and barely noticing his second-in-command.

"Let's go," said one of the guards, as he pointed the cleaners toward the door. "My apologies, sirs. We did not expect you at this time."

The young woman unplugged the vac, not bothering to roll up the cord as she moved as fast as she could. She knocked over the upright, whispering under her breath as she retrieved it. She then nearly jogged out of the room, dragging the machine behind her. She did manage to smile at President Collins; maybe even batted an eyelash.

The older janitor never even glanced at the two dignitaries. He casually returned the small trash can to its place beside the most important desk in the free world, got behind his rolling dumpster, and pushed it slowly toward the exit, blinking and grimacing along the way. He quietly whistled something. The president, his mind racing with other things, still picked up on the melody as something from his childhood but couldn't pinpoint it. Under different circumstances he'd have asked the custodian right then, but it wasn't the right time.

The female porter stood outside the office, waiting for her slow-footed partner. She was still smiling.

When both were finally beyond the room, they encountered a third member of the cleaning crew, also wheeling a trash bin. An officer began to close the heavy white door.

"You guys too," said the president to his protector.

"But, sir . . . "

"If you hear a racket, come in and do what's necessary. But for now, outside, please."

"Yes, sir."

They left. Collins and Montgomery were the only people in the room. They sat down, not at the desk, but on two cream-colored couches that faced each other across a small coffee table. The table sat beneath a large bowl of fresh fruit. The president grabbed an apple and tossed it to his friend. He then took one for himself.

"When Cannis take down our SEALs, we are in big fucking trouble, Owen," said the president.

"George, the SEALs could've handled it, but they chose not to kill their infected brothers. They tried to subdue instead of eliminate. Fatal error."

"They're human."

"Ten of our best, gone just like that."

"Not to mention the loss of a captive who could've been an enormous asset in getting to the bottom of this shit. Whoever concocted this pathogen, or whatever it is, might know how to reverse its effects or even just minimize them."

"Well, as you heard, the thinking is that our mission did not get any major players, but maybe we grabbed someone who can send us in the right direction."

"Time is of the essence and our SEALs just took a major hit," replied the president.

"Our guys will do their best to get the right info."

"I know."

"George, I am fully aware that you are opposed to enhanced interrogation . . . "

"You can say *torture*, Owen."

"Whichever, you might want to think about adjusting your displeasure barometer in a case like this."

President Collins rolled the apple around in his palm, peeling off a dangling piece of red skin.

"You've been my educator and my friend for decades, Mr. Vice President," he said, "But even you have no answers as to why we are despised by so many."

"Well, I don't claim to have all the answers," he replied, "but, I always have the obvious ones. Here in our land, we strive to treat women as equals, we have progressed in the understanding that skin color is the most insignificant difference imaginable, and we have recognized that marriage between two consenting adults is a right to all. Most of those who hate us, also hate all of the above. I don't mind being despised in the company of all of that."

"Looks like we'll be hated for a long time, no matter how we explain ourselves."

"For certain. You know, if these people who wish to vanquish us ever become infected themselves, they will quickly discover that your flesh, though slightly overcooked, and mine, horribly under-done, the meat of my Ellen, and your Madison, and that of my straight son and my gay son, all taste exactly the same."

"Truer words never spoken."

"And the world will witness your White House nuptials. You tell Madison not to worry. That wedding will happen. It's just been delayed. And my grandson will be the ring bearer. He's been practicing already."

"I believe you, Owen. How is that little tornado of a boy?"

"My Gregory. He's just amazing. Killing it in first grade. I will be taking him to his first baseball game come summer, God willing. He's a Nationals fan. I tried to get him over to the Phillies, but his dad won't have any of that. I think the team wants me to throw the first pitch, but I'm gonna require that Gregory be right beside me."

"Well, I know you'll toss a better fastball than I did."

"George, I think Gregory can throw a better ball than you."

DANIEL O'CONNOR

Las Vegas

When Cash awoke the following morning not much had changed. There was Rob, half-seated in his bed, sound asleep. She had noticed him sitting there and watching her as she tossed before dawn, but she was too exhausted to argue over the same issue again. Now the tiny spotlights of sun squeezed their way through any crack, vent, or crevice and shimmered through the darkness of the Las Vegas tunnels. On her way to wash up she ran into Paul, who had been coming to check on her and Rob. She explained that Rob was still sleeping and that their schedules were screwed because of how he guarded her at night. She learned that Russo had requested a favor from Paul; that he go on a "junkyard run". The purpose was to obtain various parts, vehicle batteries and the like, that could be of use to the community.

Paul asked Cash to go with him.

If she thought about it for too long, she would have likely refused, but she wanted some time out of the tunnels. Rob was out cold, and the trip represented a bit of freedom to her. Mainly, Cash wanted to see daylight. She told Phaedra and some others to tell Rob where she went.

Paul's helmet didn't fit her perfectly, but she still felt safer with it on, and she was grateful that he was kind enough to go without head gear so that she might wear it. Blasting through the sunny Las Vegas streets had her temporarily forgetting all the bad in the world. They were headed not to the junkyard but to Paul Bhong's apartment. He'd told Cash that he couldn't carry all of the parts Russo wanted within the limited storage of his Harley. He'd have to borrow his buddy's car which was at his apartment complex. Somewhere not far from the M Resort and Casino, they passed another bike that was flat on its side in the middle of the parkway. No rider. It was a reminder that Cash didn't need. She knew that should she or Paul flip while riding, disaster would follow. Still, she was having a large case of the "fuck its", and the warm, dry breeze felt wonderful. She also noticed that, with her arms around his waist, Paul's midsection was hard and taut; more so than she'd imagined.

And she had imagined.

Cash had never been on a motorcycle before. She'd been too afraid, much like her thoughts about flying. But she enjoyed sitting atop the roaring Harley. It made her feel free.

They stood outside Paul's apartment.

"Give me just one second," he said as he entered, leaving the door open a crack and Cash standing behind it.

She heard Paul's footsteps scurry across the floor behind the door. There were some squeaking noises, perhaps metal-on-metal. Something sounded like a coiled spring, then some muffled thuds. More footsteps and Paul was back, opening the door.

He hadn't lied when he told Rob and Cash that he lived in a tiny dwelling. It was basically a studio, with a small bathroom off to the side. Kitchen appliances were against one wall, with a sofa, one chair, and a desk with a decent-sized computer monitor atop it on the other side of the room. No traditional television or stereo system. Everything was based around the desktop.

"Well, now you see why I couldn't offer my home to you guys," he smiled. "We'd have killed each other. Even before the canni epidemic."

Cash laughed. The air-conditioning felt nice, too.

"Please have a seat," he said, pointing to the couch.

"Is this where you sleep?"

"Yeah. It's a fold-out. I closed it up while you waited outside. Tried to be gentlemanly and all."

Point scored.

Cash looked at the bathroom.

"I would kill to take a shower."

"Oh, uh, um . . . sure. Let me check for shampoo and body wash. There are clean towels. I have a hair dryer . . . "

"All good, Paul," she smiled. "Anything will be better than a garden hose in a sewer. I brought my toothbrush too."

"Oh, okay. Let me show you how to work—what am I saying, you know how to work a shower."

She could sense that the normally confident and cool Mr. Bhong was not quite as slick when alone with one female.

"I will go and borrow the car while you shower. I'll be back in like five minutes."

"I'll be showering for longer than that."

"Yeah, right."

"I mean, I live in a subterranean tunnel, dude."

"Sure, Carrie. Shower for as long as you like. I have some online stuff to do too."

She heard the apartment door close just as she turned on the water. It took a few minutes to warm up, so she used that time to brush her teeth. It was probably the most dimly lit bathroom she'd ever occupied. There were three vanity bulbs above the sink, but two were burned out.

Typical single dude.

Stepping into the shower, the hot flow from overhead felt wonderful. The lock on the bathroom door didn't work, but she got it to stay closed, and she didn't expect Paul to burst through and jump into the shower with her.

It may have briefly crossed her mind, but she didn't expect it.

As she lathered up, Cash thought about how she'd one day love to have one of those fancy showers with four or five nozzles blasting her with water from all directions. She loved being clean, and that would be the epitome of a good wash.

It was kind of sexy, too.

She never felt better or more alive than when in a steamy, soapy shower. Her brain told her that had to change. She had to appreciate life and take everything she could from it. There were too many fears, too many hang-ups. But they were difficult to overcome. Worse so since what happened with Teresa. Maybe this new world with the specter of sudden and immediate death being a constant would show her how to live, no matter how many days remained in her coffer.

As she rinsed some scented soap out of her eyes, she noticed that the dim bathroom seemed to have brightened. She pulled aside a section of the blue plastic curtain.

The new illumination was coming through from the main room.

The door was opening.

"Paul?" she asked, as anxiety clashed with arousal.

No reply.

The door inched open a bit more. She could see the invading light; it shone upon her clothes and underwear, which were neatly stacked upon the closed toilet lid, but there was no shadow within.

"Paul?"

Silence.

"Okay, very funny. Slasher film garbage. You got me, okay?" she added.

The door stopped moving. No sounds came from the other room. She turned off the shower water.

Then the only sound came from the droplets that plopped behind her.

"Warning: if that's you, I am gonna be pissed."

Then an entirely different thought came through.

What if it isn't Paul?

She studied the small room for a weapon. Could she pull the towel rod off the wall? Would it be worth it? The heavy lid over the toilet tank—that's the one.

Cash grabbed the big bath towel and secured it around her wet body.

After a bit of hesitation, she quietly emerged from the bathroom. She saw no one at first. It's not like there were many hiding places in the tiny apartment, and there was one comforting thought:

Cannis don't hide.

There was one spot where the wall ducked in, over by the kitchen area. It was the only place anyone could be where she couldn't see them. She moved toward it, water running down her legs, beneath the towel, and onto the tiled floor. She held the off-white slab of thick, toilet porcelain with both hands. It was cold and damp. Her hands were shaking.

The entry door flew open.

There stood Paul, car keys in hand.

"Whoa! What the fuck, Carrie?"

He took a half-step back behind the door.

"Thank God," she said, lowering the toilet lid.

"You okay?" he asked.

"Yeah. The bathroom door opened and I . . . "

"Damn. It always does that. I live alone, so I really . . . "

He walked over to take the lid from her hands. He stood right in front of her. Her in that towel, wearing no makeup, and her wet hair. It may have had almost the same effect on Paul that it had on Rob. Almost. As he took the lid, his pinky grazed hers. Her eyes glanced up at his. Beads of water slid down like teardrops from her bare shoulders to the towel that covered her from chest to thighs.

Paul inhaled deeply and walked away with the porcelain cover.

"You know how ironic and racist it would be if you killed a Korean with china? You could start World War III like that, Caroline. My people are like tigers, yo. Keepin' it straight since '48. I was born during the Seoul Olympics. That makes me South Korean royalty, girl."

She had to laugh at his nervous rambling.

"You were born in South Korea?" she asked, skeptically.

"South . . . er, California. But I can still represent."

"By using the name *Smith*?"

"I hear you. I just get tired of the shitty jokes. You know, 'Hits from the Bhong" and stuff."

"Right. Screw those morons. You did mention a hair dryer."

"Yeah, I have one. You know it's better to let it dry on its own. There's no humidity here. It won't get all, you know, whatever that is that girls try to avoid."

"Still, the dryer would be great," she grinned.

"Cool," he said as he fumbled through a desk drawer, locating the dryer, "Take your time, I need to catch up on some stuff," he added, powering up his desktop.

"You wouldn't have a flat iron?"

"Come on, dude. Do I look like I'm in a boy band?" he replied.

She giggled and returned to the bathroom, pushing the door almost-closed. He thought he heard her towel hit the floor, knowing he may have walked away from a chance at witnessing it.

Then he put on some headphones and she ignited the noisy dryer.

The bathroom mirror was foggy, and the faint light of the one working vanity bulb wasn't much help. Still, Cash wiped the mirror clear and went to work on her damp, tussled locks. The

door remained open just a crack, and she heard nothing but the whir of the

12-volt dryer motor. "On Melancholy Hill" by Gorillaz was the song that filled Paul's head. He signed into an internet forum of which he was a regular. It was titled NO CAGE.

He typed under the name *Paul Rider.*

"*Super hot girl naked in my bathroom right now. I am typing in biker chat. Story of my life.*"

"*u b fucked dude,*" came a reply.

"*She's cool too. Didn't shade me about my shitty apartment.*"

"*tell her u put all ur cash into ur bike. that'll make her hot n sweaty.*"

"*Dunno if you are fucking with me or serious, but that is what I do with my cash lol.*"

Paul scrolled through some other posts:

"*Best bet I've found is an AGM, along with a BatteryTender plugged into it every night. HD sells a good one (and probably most expensive), as does AutoZone . . .*"

"*prob a dead battery. Just buy a stock OEM Yuasa battery and be done with it.*"

"*yo, Paul Rider, you heard from RA? He aint been on. Wanna ask about Sturgis this year—if this fuckin world still functions.*"

Paul responded, "*Nope. Haven't seen him on. He's prob busy.*"

"*better hope he don't find out u r 2 chickenshit to nail dat hottie in ur toilet. RA will road rash your ass.*"

"*It's not that,*" wrote Paul. "*even if she'd bite, she's got a fiancée. Or at least a boyfriend—IDK. Wouldn't be cool.*"

"*Whaaaaaaaaaaaaaat? Hit it. The world is ending, bro. U risked ur life just bringin another person into ur home. She owes u.*"

Paul looked over at the door, it was still just a bit ajar. A portion of the damp towel could be seen on the floor behind it. All he could hear was the music coming through his Koss headphones.

He turned his attention back to the monitor. He scrolled around for other biker posts.

"*Anyone ever tried 'Dyna Beads'? I've never tried em. I'm just getting comfortable with electric start.*"

He signed into his YouTube channel, *Bhong Rider,* to check for updates.

21 subscribers.

CANNI

Las Vegas Tunnels

"This is bullshit, man," growled Rob as he barreled quickly through the tunnels, holding his phone high, trolling for a signal.

Phaedra hurried behind him, the occasional ray of daylight causing her red locks to glow.

"But Paul is your friend." she offered, "You seem overly concerned."

"Paul is a fairly likeable guy who we've only known for a few days. The word 'friend' is a bit strong at this point."

"But he brought you to us. He's keeping you and Caroline safe."

"Forgetting the whole 'friend' debate, if Cash is going around Vegas with just him, neither of them are safe. Is that so hard to understand?"

He stopped abruptly as his phone indicated a possible signal. Phaedra gave his back a caress.

"You are so wound," she said. From behind, her hand went to his right shoulder, while her other palm landed on his left. She squeezed them tightly.

"Your shoulders are too rigid," she whispered, "Strong, but bound with tension."

His brief signal vanished.

Cash, her hair still a bit damp, sat in the passenger seat of a black Santa Fe. She tapped the electronic door lock on her armrest. Paul steered them into the junkyard.

"We're driving through the main entrance?" she asked. "I was under the impression we were stealing things."

"We are."

He pulled his borrowed SUV up to the guard booth. A large female filled the entire space. She was reading porn and smoking a cigar. Her clip-on tie had come loose and dangled from her shirt button. Paul lowered his window.

"Russo," was all he said.

"Uh-huh," replied the woman, without looking up.

They drove in.

Cars everywhere. Trucks and buses, too. Some in neat rows, others stacked on top of each other. Some just burned-out shells. Miles of refrigerators, washers, and dryers.

"So, just the name Russo gets you in?" she asked.

"In some places."

"That's crazy. We're talking about a homeless, perpetually naked, sex addict."

"He gets things done for people. They return the favor."

Cash pressed the door lock button one last time, just as her phone rang. An Electric Light Orchestra "Telephone Line" ringtone.

"Rob is probably freaking out," said Paul.

"It's not Rob," she replied, looking at her screen. "It's my aunt. A video chat."

Cash took a deep breath, fearing the worst. She touched the answer button.

"Hi Aunt Margie. Is everything okay?"

Cash knew immediately that her aunt was in a hospital. The wall behind her was bare and harshly illuminated.

"As okay as can be," smiled Margie. "We are all just concerned for you, and your uncle and I wanted to see you and know you're safe."

"We're doing fine, Aunt Margie. No need to worry."

"And Rob is good?"

"Yep."

"And Teresa?"

Cash went cold. Teresa's family had been notified of her death, but this was the first realization that her own relatives were still unaware. She wasn't ready.

"Um, how is Uncle Reg? We've been thinking a lot of him."

"He's a trooper, Carrie. You know that. I'll put him on, but first the girls want to say hello."

The camera panned to Cash's cousins, Laura and Jennifer. They were a couple of years her junior, and maybe the closest relatives she had. They were actually her friends, and she missed them. Seeing their faces made her forget where she was, and that Paul was sitting beside her.

"Hey ugly!" said Laura.

"Why didn't you take us to Vegas, bitch?" joked Jennifer.

"They have enough pole dancers here," she answered.

"You should know."

Cash smiled broadly. The girls made no mention of the evil that had consumed the country. For a few seconds, all seemed normal. Then Aunt Margie had the phone again.

"Carrie, here's your uncle."

The screen was now full of Uncle Reg. He sat on his hospital bed, frail and colorless. Cash remembered he'd always had a deep tan. He'd been a man of strength and vibrancy. A proud cop.

"Reg, it's Caroline. Talk to her!" ordered Margie.

Incoming Call—Rob, read the screen message below her uncle's face. She had no real choice but to press the red button.

Decline.

Cash heard Paul's fingers tapping the steering wheel, and she didn't know if it was his habit or a sign of impatience. She also didn't care.

"Hi, Uncle Reg!" she said loudly, adding her brightest smile.

His eyes turned up toward the phone camera lens. He stared.

"It's Caroline," she said. "I miss you!"

He continued to stare without expression. She noticed that Paul's finger-tapping had ceased.

"Caroline?" responded Uncle Reg, as if trying to place the name.

"Hi!" she said again, not knowing what else to add. She repositioned her phone, hoping he might get a better view of her face, to help him recall. A portion of Paul came into view behind her, but she didn't take notice. It was just a glimpse of his hands on the top of the steering wheel, motionless, not tapping.

Uncle Reg's eyes widened. He stared into the camera lens. He was looking past his niece. He raised a shaky finger.

"Look . . . behind . . . you," was all he said.

Cash was surprised by her uncle's words, but she obliged him and turned her head. There beside her sat Paul Bhong doing nothing special.

"Rob," said Uncle Reg. "Hello, Rob. Caroline and Rob."

Not knowing what to do, Paul flashed a huge smile and waved.

"Is Rob there?" said Aunt Margie. Cash could hear her cousins' clamoring as well. They all squeezed into frame, shouting out greetings to Rob.

Then they saw Paul and his grin. He flashed a two-fingered peace sign.

"Rob is back at . . . the . . . hotel," said Cash, moving the camera away from Paul.

"Who's that?"

"Is Teresa with you?"

"That was our friend, Paul," answered Cash.

"Where are Rob and Teresa?"

"Uncle Reg, I am so happy to see you. I can't wait to come and visit in person again. I'm gonna sneak in some of those brownies. And freezing cold milk. Whole milk. Not that low fat junk they give you over there."

"Brownies," he said. "Caroline and Rob."

"When will you be home, sweetie?" asked Aunt Margie.

"Not sure yet. Taking it day by day, with all that's . . . you know."

"I know, dear. Be careful, all of you. The girls are telling me to ask if there might be a ring on your finger, but I told them . . . "

"No ring."

Awkward silence. Paul began tapping his fingers on the wheel again. Cash was searching for a way to end the video chat.

"Brownies," said Uncle Reg.

"Yeah, brownies for sure," smiled Cash. "Okay, guys, I have to go now. I love you all and will see you soon!"

"We love you, Carrie! Nice to meet Paul. Give our love to Rob and Teresa!"

She ended the call and sat there, pressing the door lock button. The sound played off the beat of Paul's finger-tapping.

Paul loaded a car battery into the trunk of the Santa Fe. He placed it beside five others.

"Russo loves his batteries," he laughed. "Recharges them with some small solar panels and a charge controller."

"He's got it all figured out, huh?" replied Cash as she leaned on a junked, simulated wood-paneled 1978 Dodge Aspen. Behind her were the rows upon rows of discarded vehicles. In front of her and behind Paul and the borrowed SUV were rows of everything else. Plenty of refrigerators, washers, and dryers. Almost everything was worn and rusty, yet the bright Vegas sun bounced off of all of them, almost proudly.

"I think I see a portable generator," said Paul. "Russo would love to have that baby. I don't know if he cleared it with the owner, though. Batteries are fine, but I don't want to take anything that hasn't been agreed upon."

"We are in a junkyard, Paul, not the fucking Louvre."

"No. Deals are deals. Russo lives by his word. You don't know the etiquette of the underground homeless, Carrie. You're lucky."

"I'll help you lift it."

"No. Seriously, I have to ask first. I can't call Russo. He has no phone. No reason to with no service in the tunnels. I'm gonna walk back to the guard booth. I'll ask her if it's okay."

"No. You keep doing the grunt work. I can go talk to the porn queen. Better than loading batteries. What do I ask?"

"Just ask if we can take the generator. If she doesn't know, maybe she can call the owner of the yard."

"Cool. Don't go anywhere," she said. "This place is huge. Be right there when I get back."

"I'll be here. Don't get lost. Hit my phone if you do."

Cash headed off in the direction of the main entrance, recalling that they entered through the gate and made one right, then a left. She strode through the sun-drenched graveyard of all things deemed worthless, gazing at the tall, chain-link fence that ringed the entire property. She accepted that she was in a salvage yard, yet if she merely stepped through the gate, she was not. She wondered how long it would be before those gates marked no differentiation.

Paul Bhong was staring at her ass.

He stood there with a crusty battery in his hands, but he was watching Cash stroll away in her cutoff shorts. Some decent part of his soul told him it was the wrong thing to do, so he turned his attention back to a different trunk, the one he was loading. He'd had a history with trunks. Always found the best stuff locked in the back of junkyard vehicles. Sometimes even cash.

Cash made her second turn and she spotted the front entrance and the guard booth. There was something on the pavement beside the booth door. A bit of movement.

As she came closer, she realized it was the pornographic magazine. There is was, flat and open on the ground. The breeze was turning the pages. It landed on a shot of three people standing; two men and a woman. The female was in a handstand.

The guard booth was empty. The front gate was still open. There was no *back in five minutes* note.

Paul was opening trunks. He recalled some of his greatest finds, besides money. There was a great set of vintage Klipsch stereo speakers, a box of more than a hundred Hot Wheels toy cars, even an object that he later learned was an articulated robotic arm used by NASA. It was his greatest scrap score, and he sold it to a collector for a thousand bucks. He didn't give *everything* he recovered in the junkyards to Don Russo.

About forty yards behind Paul, in the direction Cash had gone, something scampered past the row of vehicles. It bounded rapidly. He thought he'd heard something, but when he turned, it was gone. He stood for a minute, wondered if there might be a loose junkyard dog. Then, the thought of a possible canni crossed his mind.

He was hoping for the junkyard dog.

Paul took out his phone, about to call Cash. Then he thought better of possibly setting off her ELO ringtone if canni or canine lurked nearby. He also didn't want to start the noisy engine of the SUV, so he walked, trying to have his feet barely touch the ground, toward the front gate.

Cash walked too. She almost called out for the guard. She almost grabbed her phone. Like Paul, she caught herself in time. They were adjusting to a new world. She felt a chill despite the nearly ninety-degree heat. She told herself that she was overreacting. Surely, the guard would come walking up any minute and they'd both have a laugh. Then she recalled how the portly female security officer didn't look like someone who might ever actually have a laugh.

Cash made the first turn. All appeared fine. She'd just have to walk this row, make a left, and Paul would be there in sight, loading that trunk. They could just hop in the Santa Fe and leave.

All she could hear was the sound of her own feet. She was treading as lightly as she could, but to her, she sounded like Godzilla on the streets of Tokyo.

If a cat jumps out at me now, I will scream like I'm on a fucking birthing table and apologize to every shitty horror movie director who has ever walked the earth.

Cash heard every twist and turn of the Las Vegas breeze as it whipped in, around, and through each piece of junk in that yard. Anything that could sway swayed. Anything that could flap flapped. Whistling wind is a real thing, and the haunting sound took Cash back to a literature class where she had learned of the Fable of the Seven Whistlers; a septet of birds who would warble the high tones of impending death.

She studied the hills of salvage, searching for anything with wings.

With nary a bird in sight, she'd made it to the final turn. As she took a left onto the final long row, she saw Paul walking toward her, thirty yards away.

But it was what was behind her friend that caught her attention. She slowed her walk.

It was the junkyard guard.

She was standing way back by the Santa Fe, her back to both Paul and Cash. Paul had no idea she was there. He was smiling at Cash and about to speak. Cash put a finger to her lips and pointed. Paul remained silent and turned to look behind him. Cash stopped walking altogether.

They both hoped that the guard might have been just out looking for them and was waiting by their SUV.

But then they saw the large officer leap, in one bound, like a cat, to the roof of the vehicle. It shook under her weight. Her back was still to them, but she began to turn, surveying the yard from her higher vantage point.

Vomit landed on the rear window of the SUV, like the droppings of a pterodactyl. Even from their distance, Paul and Cash could see the red eyes.

And those eyes locked on the both of them.

The Santa Fe trembled again as the infected guard leaped off. She fell as she landed, but looked up again, teeth bared and dripping. Her clip-on tie flapped in that whistling wind.

"Cash, run!" yelled Paul. "Don't wait for me!"

He was a good twenty yards behind her as they both took off. They knew the super-charged canni could easily run them down, so finding a hiding place was essential. They also each knew that technically they need not be faster than the canni, only faster than one another.

Both simultaneously dismissed that thought.

Cash ran as fast as she ever had. She heard pounding footsteps to her rear. She hoped they belonged to Paul, but if he had taken shelter already they might not. Cutting sharply to her right, she darted into a sea of taller junked vehicles; vans, trucks, and the like. She dove and rolled.

PARE SI HAY NIÑOS

That was the brightly-colored sticker that was peeling from just above the bumper, that in turn was just above her feet. Cash had slithered beneath an old GMC ice cream truck. It may have leaked oil during its final moments, but you'd have thought it bled vanilla swirl due to the number of red harvester ants that shared the ground with Cash. They were quickly on her arms and legs.

With little choice, she let them have their way. Her thoughts flashed back to a film she saw at Bishop Kearney High School. The documentary depicted birds in the process of *anting*. The feathered creatures would intentionally sprawl on a mound of ants, inviting them to crawl all over their bodies. There were several theories as to the purpose of this ritual, but none of the experts could declare, with any certainty, the exact reason why birds would choose to do this. It helped Cash to envision herself as a blue jay.

Then the footsteps came.

The oddity was they were on either side of the truck. To Cash's right, the row she had just run down before cutting across the line of trucks, she saw a pair of high-gloss work shoes. They obviously contained the feet of the infected guard. They paced, as if unsure of which direction to go.

Cash, prone and trying to ignore the biting and stinging of the ants, turned her head to the left. There were Paul's blue Adidas sneakers. He was still; likely listening for the steps of the canni on the other side of the ice cream truck. Figuring that it would take the insects much longer to devour her than the canni, Cash felt relatively safe beneath the truck. She wasn't even sure the hefty guard could fit under there if she tried. Though she didn't discount the thought that her hunter might be able to toss the entire vehicle on its side.

She heard the work shoes scurry away. The Adidas remained.

Knowing that it would probably scare the hell out of Paul but figuring it might help save his life—*as long as he didn't scream*—she reached out from under the truck, envisioning her arm as a wing as blue as Teresa's eyes, and grabbed hold of his ankle.

"FuckingMotherFucker," he said, but in a whisper.

Good job, buddy, thought Cash before she stuck her head out. Paul looked down to see her face, stained with dirt and harvester ants.

"Come under here," she whispered.

"Uh, no thanks," he answered. "I have a better idea. Come on out. Fast!"

She thought about it for a second, but those scumbag ants were the clincher. She crawled out, wiping the bugs from her *wings* as she stood. Paul brushed a couple from her cheeks. She shook her hair violently, sending more insects into the wind.

Paul put a finger to his lips. He slowly slid open the door to the ice cream truck. He sent Cash up the steps first. Without thinking, he soon realized that his hand was on her right buttock as he pushed her into the truck. Despite everything, she knew it too. He followed her inside and gently closed the door.

The truck smelled like the hot fudge of a sewage treatment plant and was, more or less, an oven. Most of the old ice cream equipment was still within.

"You okay, Carrie?" he whispered.

"Yeah, except I might be itchy for the rest of my days. You?"

"All good. We should be safe here until she passes out, or whatever."

He had just finished the sentence when the canni returned. They watched while hunched down near the truck's side window, the one where countless ice cream cones had exchanged hands.

The canni seemed intently aware that people were nearby. It leaned north and south without going anywhere. A pained roar came from its foaming throat.

It lifted a refrigerator, perhaps in frustration, and launched it at a junked school bus that sat beside the ice cream truck. Windows shattered as a second roar exploded.

Even stronger than I thought, mused Cash. *Or are they getting stronger?*

The diseased security officer's head pivoted quickly. Her breaths were heavy, as her crimson eyes scanned for food.

Cash wondered if the canni had recall from before the seizure. Did she remember that two people were in the junkyard and sought them as prey as soon as she turned? Or was it coincidence that they first saw the canni by the SUV?

Paul picked another ant from Cash's hair.

The canni moved closer to the truck. They ducked down further. Paul considered videoing the goings on.

Cash's ELO ringtone went off again.

She and Paul both fumbled for the phone as it tumbled to the floor, near the dying ant.

Incoming call Rob

There was no choice but to press the Decline button again. Paul understood why she did it, but he also noticed that she hadn't tried to call her boyfriend in the time between when she refused his previous call and the start of their current predicament.

The more important immediate issue hinged on whether the canni had heard the Electric Light Orchestra jangling, in the dreadful, tinny cell phone sound from the debilitated custard wagon.

It ran its hand along the side of the truck, gurgling as it listened. Neither Cash nor Paul knew if it had noticed the ringtone. They were frozen in a crouched position, heads on either side of the service window, as their predator lumbered by the glass pane. They both knew that even if they avoided the hungry canni outside the truck they might not be safe from the ones gestating within each of them. If one of them flipped in that confined space, the other would be dead in minutes.

They could hear the thud of the hand taps along the white body panel. They appeared to be moving toward the back of the truck, then they grew louder again. Neither Cash nor Paul dared peek out that window. Paul crawled over to Cash's side, remaining under any possible view from the outside.

As they knelt, he whispered, "I was thinking what Rob might do here. If that thing starts to come through the door, I will occupy it as best I can. You will break this window and climb out. Here are the car keys. You run like hell . . . "

Striking like a canni, Cash grabbed Paul's face. She firmly planted her lips on his. She held tight as his mouth opened to match hers. It quickly moved from a kiss to a *real kiss*. Paul's hand slid to the back of her head, pulling her closer. They barely noticed that the canni had moved on. The tapping ceased, but the kiss continued. Despite the lingering danger, Paul felt that embrace down to his toes, some areas more than others. Maybe the danger enhanced it.

When they released, Cash was gazing into his eyes. His brain was scrambled. He thought of how much he enjoyed that moment. He was almost unsure if it actually happened. He thought of Rob, and if he would ever learn of it. *Would there be any more of this?* He then remembered that there was something nearby who would like nothing more than to kill and eat him.

Cash stood. She moved quickly away from the window and unbuttoned her shorts. She lowered them to her knees.

Paul jumped to his feet and opened his belt.

This is going to happen, he thought. *And in an ice cream truck.*

"Whoa there, buddy," smiled Cash. "Slow your roll. There is an ant crawling up my butt. That is the one and only reason my shorts are down."

"This is fucking ridiculous," growled Rob. Sweat covered his reddened face and soaked through his sleeveless white shirt. He stood beside Phaedra, both baking in the sun. They and a handful of others were dumping buckets of waste into the sewer drains.

"It's just one of the chores," replied Phaedra. "It gets easier."

"It's not the buckets. It's that I am trying to do this while I have no clue where Cash is or if she is even alive."

He took his phone out and walked away from the others. Phaedra followed behind. He yanked his soiled shirt off as if it were aflame and dropped it on a loose fence post. Phaedra got a look at the deltoids that felt so firm. When he turned, pressing his phone screen, she saw the pectorals. Not Mr. Olympia, but well-proportioned and quite defined. Perspiration had him nicely oiled. She kept a respectful distance, but soon saw that his call wasn't answered. Again.

He sat against the hard, sun-drenched wall, his shadow sitting beside him. Phaedra approached.

"It's not really break time," she smiled. A wavy strand of her red hair danced across her face.

"Tell them they can fire me."

"Come on, silly. They all know we need to clear our minds sometime. Everyone down here has some major problems. You know that. Hang on a sec."

She jaunted over to the nearest tunnel, disappearing into its inviting shade. Rob noticed a long-tailed lizard that stood motionless on the far wall. Its small body was gray with dark crossbars. Nature had designed the creature to blend in with desert creosote brush, but there it was, in the sun on a white concrete wall, deceiving nary an ant or spider.

In a moment Phaedra emerged, carrying a bottle of lime Gatorade. Ice chips fell from the frosty container. It looked beautiful to a thirsty Rob. He also happened to notice that Phaedra's emerald-colored shirt almost duplicated her eye color. When framed by her crimson locks in the stunning brightness, she looked to be an angel.

"Here ya go, Rob. I wish I had a little something to spike it up," she laughed.

"Thanks, Phaedra."

He eyed his phone, though it didn't ring. He chugged the icy refreshment, downing half the bottle in one gulp.

"That was sweet. Here, you can have the rest. You can drink from the other side of the rim if my germs freak you."

He handed her the bottle. She drank from his side.

"Caroline will be back and healthy," she said. "I bet her phone died."

"Maybe."

"This is still cold," she said, as she put the bottle to his forehead. "Feels good, right?"

"Yeah."

She moved it from his head to his bare chest, her emeralds glancing up at him as she pressed it to his heart.

"Deep breaths. Settle down, and all will be well. I promise."

"Why are you being so nice to me?" he asked.

"That is how humans should be, right?"

"It is, but I don't encounter it a lot."

Phaedra held up the bottle for Rob to sip. He did so without regard to any possible germs. She placed her other hand on his biceps as she spoke. "My mother used to say something, it was a famous quote," she said. "It was, 'The true measure of a man is how he treats someone who can do him absolutely no good'. Now, I wish they had said *person* instead of *man*, but it's still a great quote."

Rob managed a smile. He said, "My father used to say that to me. I was actually going to finish the quote with you, but that would've been beyond tacky. Do you know who said that?"

She nodded. As she opened her mouth to respond, he decided that this time he would say it along with her. They spoke concurrently.

"Samuel Johnson," said Rob.

She said, "Ann Landers."

They laughed together. Rob looked over at the lizard on the wall. It hadn't moved.

"There is good within us, Rob. I mean, within people."

"Some."

"Most."

"I can't go that far," he replied.

"It's just that this disease has ignited the bad," said Phaedra. "We need something to empower the good."

"You think that we all have some evil inside, and this virus has just amplified it?" he asked.

"I don't know that 'evil' is the correct word. Maybe it's 'greed' or 'narcissism'. When people become monsters, they only want to serve themselves. They want to consume. They want to devour you and make you a part of them, forever. Nourish themselves at all costs to others. The tall guy who pushes in front of a small woman at a concert; the fit person who parks in a handicapped stall to save a few steps; a canni is just these people on some super-steroid."

"But good people turn," said Rob. "My friend Teresa was a caring person. I've seen her give her last dollar to the hungry. She volunteered at soup kitchens. You know that TV ad where you can sponsor a child in Africa with a monthly contribution? She had, like, three of those kids. Now, she's gone."

"Sounds like she was a beautiful person."

"Yet, she became one of those zombies."

Phaedra squeezed his sweaty biceps as she responded, "They are definitely not zombies, Mr. Muscles. Zombies are thoughtless shells, returned from the dead. The canni are we."

"I meant that they eat . . . "

"It's not *they*, Rob. It's *we*."

He looked at his phone again.

"When I was little, my mom used to make us root beer floats," said Phaedra. "We'd snuggle up and watch scary movies. Now you know that I love quotes, so it should be no surprise that I remember movie lines."

"*They're coming to get you, Barbara,*" he offered.

"Good one, but way off base. You can't shake that zombie thing, can you?"

"Maybe not."

"Do you remember this quote, Rob? I hope I get it right . . . '*Even a man who is pure in heart, and says his prayers by night, may become a wolf when the wolfbane blooms and the autumn moon is bright*'."

He stared for a moment, letting a fresh breeze soothe his face.

"Yeah, kind of. The whole wolf part gives it away. Guessing it's not from *Dracula*."

"Now yet again, I wish they had said *person* instead of *man*, but it still applies."

"How?" he asked.

"Can't you see?" she asked. "That is canni. You and I, Caroline, and everyone else; we are all Lawrence Talbot. The wolfsbane has bloomed. The difference is that our full moon glows every day, all day, and all through the night."

Rob sat silently. Phaedra followed his stare to the far wall. She spotted the lizard. It remained motionless, as if it could wait for all eternity for an unsuspecting insect to approach.

"The dudes at concerts who put their girlfriends on their shoulders, blocking the views of people behind them," said Rob.

"The concert dudes and their shoulder girls," smiled Phaedra. "All of them are canni."

"But my main flaw, my weakness," he said, "it is not based in evil. It comes from love."

"You are consuming her, Rob."

She rested her hand on his glistening chest as she continued. "Even a man who is pure in heart."

Her words lingered until Rob's phone blasted them from the air. Same ELO ringtone as Cash. He snatched his cell as that lizard would an ant. He didn't recognize the number.

"Hello?"

Phaedra stood and walked away, to give him some privacy. She could still hear Rob's voice, but not that of the caller.

"Johnny? Hey, what's up? Are you in Vegas, dude? Cool. How have you been dealing with all of this? I can't even imagine . . . "

Phaedra watched the lizard as Rob spoke to his friend.

"We're actually not in a hotel, bud. Long story. I'll explain when we hook up."

Rob listened for a bit, then replied. "There's some stuff I'd rather tell you in person. Let's meet up on Thursday. I don't have my car—that's another long story."

As the conversation continued, Spats, one of Russo's men, approached Phaedra.

"There are folks sweating their asses off on bucket duty while you and the new guy are playing footsie. Maybe you two could get back to work. We rely on each other here, you know?"

"We will, of course. He's new to all this. Let him have his phone call and we'll be back working. He's going through a lot right now."

"I can't relate," deadpanned Spats, "because my life is all big tits and unicorns."

Phaedra spoke as he walked away. "Thank you, Spats."

"*You* ain't on a phone call."

As Spats rejoined the others he shook his head. Most of them glanced at Phaedra then went about their chores. Rob stood, still looking at his phone. His call was over, and there was still nothing from Cash.

"Feel like getting back to work?" asked Phaedra with a smile and head tilt.

"Why not? Nothing else for me to do."

"Not to pry, but the call was unrelated to Caroline?"

"Unrelated to her blowing me off. It was my friend John G. He's our best man."

Rob stood and dusted himself off. He and Phaedra headed toward the other workers. On the far wall remained the lizard, placid as the pyramids.

Paul loaded the final items into the back of the Santa Fe. Several yards behind him, Cash held a water bottle to the mouth of the security guard who minutes earlier had wanted to kill her. The woman sat on the pavement, her back against a rear tire of the ice cream truck. Her shirt and dangling clip-on tie, were soaked with vomit and sweat.

Gulping the water, the guard took a breath and yelled over to Paul, "Yeah, you can take the fucking generator."

The drive back to the tunnels seemed eternal. Cash and Paul had barely exchanged a sentence since the kiss. Each of them was within their own racing mind. Neither knew if anything more could or should come of this. Then there was Rob. They both knew his world could be shattered if the moment ever repeated or propagated. Maybe even if it didn't. Still, Paul had to stay true to his own identity. He cleared his throat as he drove.

"Cash, just sayin', but I was so down to play anteater."

She shook her head with a slight grin, gazing out her window, noting that he addressed her as Rob would.

He wondered if someone with the true first name of Winthrop had ever strolled through a drainage tunnel lugging two buckets of shit. It was as Rob pondered that in the darkness that he heard her voice forty yards away, just outside the entrance.

Cash.

He couldn't decipher her words, but he knew it was her. Never before had relief, frustration, and anger assaulted him in unison. He put the buckets down and started quickly toward the sunlight. Cash's laugh echoed through the tunnel.

This stopped Rob, and he turned around and retrieved his pails of human waste. He carried them toward daylight at a snail's pace. With each step, the voices of Cash and the others became louder and clearer. She giggled some more. Then, he heard her ask about his whereabouts.

"His slacker ass is on bucket duty, *supposubly*," replied one of the men.

"FiveFourThreeTwoOne," stuttered Cash. Rob knew she was now into her finger-counting, arm-rubbing, deep-breathing, ritual.

"Da fuck?" came the man's reply.

As Rob moved toward the light, some more conversations were heard.

"Where'd you get them wheels, Paul?"

"Oh, it's my bro's car. Took the bike to my place and switched over to the Santa Fe."

"Your place? With Miss Brooklyn? Sweet, my playa!"

Rob stopped.

He lowered both buckets to the dusty ground. Then he turned and trudged deeper into the darkness.

Rob sat on his bed, feet up. He stared at the thin streams of light that darted in from the city above. Dust particles danced within the rays, like leukocytes. He heard the footsteps, and knew the pace of her walk.

"Hey," said Cash.

"Hey," answered Rob, eyes remaining on the light.

"I tried to call a few times," offered Cash, "but your service . . . "

"You went to Paul's apartment?"

"He had to get a car, and I took a shower . . . " she immediately realized her answer just made it worse.

Rob turned his eyes to her.

"You took a shower? Okay. Then why do you look filthy? You've obviously been rolling around in the dirt or something. Your hair is a mess too."

"Things like that happen when you're hiding from someone who wants to kill you."

"Fuck. I knew it."

"Knew what?"

"I knew that if you left here without me you'd be in grave danger. What happened?"

"We were getting things at a junkyard . . . "

"You and Paul?"

"Yes. The gatekeeper of the yard turned canni. I had to hide under a truck. I got dirty, okay?"

"What did Paul do?"

"I couldn't answer your calls because I was in hiding."

"Did Paul do anything to protect you, or did he just look out for himself?"

"He was going to fight while I climbed from the truck and ran to safety, if it came to that."

"You said you were *under* a truck. You were *in* a truck?" he asked.

"Both, for fuck's sake! I'm lucky to be alive and all you can do is cross-examine me? You're not even happy to see me? What, are you afraid that I had a little time to breathe? A little time to know what the world is like without you draped all over me?"

"That's just great. Sorry that my love is labeled as suffocation. You're part of the choir. I've heard that song from Phaedra too—even from that insane Russo. I guess I'm the asshole."

"Well, sometimes you are."

"Maybe Paul is the guy for you. You guys can have an open relationship. Maybe you need a guy who doesn't give a damn about you but just likes your ass or something."

"Typical Rob. There you go. He can't possibly like my personality or my smile or eyes. Anyone who isn't you just wants to get laid, I guess."

Rob sat up. He looked at Cash, standing there all soiled.

"So he does like you?"

"I didn't say that. I . . . I don't know."

"Fucking liar," he growled.

"What?"

"You heard me. You're a fucking liar. I can't stand liars."

"Okay, I'll be honest," she said, fixing her tussled hair. "I kissed him."

Rob felt it all at once. Fire in his face, ice in his body. His mouth turned to sand and his throat narrowed as if underfoot. He thought he might be flipping, as he had never felt this way before. He considered yelling "*Run*".

But he couldn't speak.

All he could see were imagined images of *The Kiss*. That, and worse. He realized that, if he was becoming a canni, it would have already happened. This pain, this metabolic change, was something different. It was a steaming brew of sadness, anger, fear, and the fiery death of trust. He stood, and walked to the far side of the tunnel, further from Cash. The streams of light were now between them, like prison bars.

"He's alone with you for an hour, and the first chance he gets, he kisses you."

"That's not correct," said Cash.

"Really?"

"I told you, *I* kissed *him*."

Cash sat on her bed, legs tightly together and arms folded.

Traffic pounded the streets above them, rattling the manhole covers.

Expecting a barrage of questions, Cash tried to prepare her answers before they were needed. It surprised her that Rob had but one singular question.

"Where, exactly, did this happen?"

Rob couldn't recall the last time he'd ridden a bicycle. He had grabbed the sturdiest-looking of the bunch of tunnel bikes. It smelled of strawberry incense but felt like rust. He hadn't said a word to Cash since he asked her for directions to the junkyard. She had no answer, but Phaedra knew exactly how to get there.

He rode alone through the brisk night, wearing the black New York Mets jacket that Cash had given him long ago. He had never been much of a baseball fan, but if Cash loved that team, so did he. He knew that she was safe in her tunnel bed. Unless she took off with Paul again. It had been the most awkward of evenings. He had remained near her, but neither spoke. For his part, he didn't know which questions to ask. But mostly he feared the answers.

He had little money left, and he was feeling guilty over the fact that he'd just spent a chunk of it at Walmart. Plus, he gave ten bucks to a stranger to guard a bicycle worth half that while he shopped. Everything he'd purchased was stuffed inside the clearance-sale Ariana Grande knapsack strapped to his back. Hey, funds were low.

The ride had been long and lonely, but at least he hadn't seen any Cannis. At one point he'd heard the pounding of charging footsteps behind him. They were fast and he had to pedal like hell to distance himself, but he never looked back. So technically, he hadn't *seen* anyone who wanted to kill him this night.

Not yet, anyway.

I can probably return the wire cutters for a cash refund.

That was his first thought upon his arrival at the closed junkyard. A section of fence had already been pushed in. Might have happened in the dim and distant past, or earlier this night.

He knew one thing was of the utmost importance before entering this or any enclosed area in which he was not welcome.

First, you shake the gate.

He rattled it a bit initially, then, hearing nothing, he gave it a great waggle.

Again, dead air.

Not a guard dog to be seen.

I can probably return the chuck steak for a cash refund.

With the bright colors of the Las Vegas Strip sparkling in the distance, in stark contrast to the near blackness of this industrial area, he slipped through the fence. He wondered if the junkyard dog had exited the same way and who, or what, had come through the chain link in the first place.

He didn't see any cut marks on the fencing. It looked to have been forced, as though a tank had crashed it, albeit the hole was too small for that.

It was more the size of a human.

His newly-purchased Maglite had found the guard dog. At least some of it. It was probably a great Doberman specimen as it lived. Its ears had been cropped and tail docked. Cruel procedures to Rob's way of thinking, but nothing when compared to what some canni had done to it. *I can probably return the big flashlight for a cash refund.*

PARA SI HAY NIÑOS

Rob thought briefly of the disemboweled dog as he stared at the bumper sticker of the ice cream truck. He sat atop an old, decommissioned police car; a Plymouth Fury from the 70s—just another dead thing, like every other piece of matter in the yard. From the roof of the vehicle where the cherry top once spun, Rob watched the truck—the wheeled den where Cash betrayed him—go up in flames like a Salem witch.

Cash may have cheated on him and he could never undo that, but that didn't mean that the location of the transgression had to stand forever. It could burn like the couch that took his father. The brown sofa, the location of so many childhood beatings, went up in flames along with the man responsible for them. Sometimes Rob wished that his mother—the one who walked out on his family, which led to his father's drinking, which led to Dad falling asleep with a burning cigarette—could have been the parent on that microfiber monstrosity when it ignited.

Now he imagined Mom in that ice cream truck. She was wrapped in every misery he could recall: the day she left and the one-sentence note she'd left behind, the way Dad transformed into a monster, the memory of walking in on his own prior girlfriend having phone sex with some stranger from Indiana, and now the image of Cash, the person he thought would be the antidote to all of the other miseries, sliding her tongue into the mouth of Paul Bhong.

The same lighter that ignited the truck was now tickling the tip of a big, fat joint that Phaedra had given him. He sucked it in, legs folded, atop the erstwhile police vehicle, his cheap Ariana Grande knapsack beside him. The burgeoning fire brought some life to the cadaverous junkyard. Rob's senses were aroused. The flames were brilliant and the crackling resonant. The spice of the burn raced up his nostrils as its torridity enveloped him like a womb.

Moths came.

They flittered about the outline of the blaze, twinkling like the stars above. Maybe they were just insects, but Rob was happy that they'd arrived.

Because they were life.

By the third hit of his spliff, Rob was feeling it.

Phaedra has some quality shit.

The start of his high arrived at the same time as the canni.

It was a woman. Some nondescript lady who might be any soccer mom or middle school teacher. Normally Rob would not give this unremarkable organism a second glance, but she was the only other human around, and she was covered from chin to feet in blood. Probably the dog's. A Michael Kors tote still dangled from her shoulder. Mocha.

She, like the moths, was drawn to the flames.

Rob thought about running, but he knew she'd catch him before he could get to his bicycle. Maybe it was the cannabis, but he wasn't too scared. The monster hadn't noticed him and was staring intently at the burning truck. He felt almost invisible in the darkness, though the glow of the flames would sometimes hit him like a strobe. He remained motionless and contemplated the cremation of his broken heart.

Motionless, save for the elbow-bend that carried the herb to his lips.

The truck had a death rattle of its own. Things within were popping and falling. Rob's body was warm, inside and out. He enjoyed the absence of concern.

Burn, motherfucker, burn.

He considered the moths. He knew some of them undoubtedly flew directly into the flames and were turned to dust. Hell, they do it at any porch light. Yet, others appeared to continue circling the fire, avoiding direct contact. Were these the more intelligent ones? Were they just the lucky moths? Was it all a matter of chance? Would even the encircling moths eventually wind up in the fire?

Rob evaluated all of this, inhaling smoke from both his arsonist creation and Phaedra's fatty, when a vision of Cash, her eyes the warm color of that Kors bag, grinning in Paul's tightening arms, bum-rushed his mellow.

Just before his returning anger peaked, the canni caught fire.

DANIEL O'CONNOR

The arm of her light sweater went up. She spun in a circle, like one of the moths, screaming, teeth clattering. Rob watched for a couple of seconds before his hazy mind understood that this canni was a human being about to be burned to death, and that Rob the arsonist was about to become a murderer. He slipped down from the car roof just as the canni went to the ground, sweater flames spreading.

The smoldering infectee spotted him and struggled to stand. It was then that Rob struck her across the head with his Maglite. He didn't know quite how hard to hit a human head in order to cease consciousness but avoid death. Adding a human in this physical state to the equation just complicated matters.

He hit her pretty fucking hard. As she went down, he could feel the flames. She began to get back up. He blasted her again. This time it was lights out.

Except for the fire.

The unconscious canni was ablaze and the truck beside her an inferno. He looked for anything to douse the flaming woman.

It had to be his Mets jacket.

He removed the garment that Cash had given him on one happy Christmas morning. Onto the canni it went, smothering the fire. The infected woman would have some serious burns, but she'd probably survive. He'd call an ambulance as soon as he could find a phone. He grabbed his knapsack and headed for the bike.

As he walked away, the Mets jacket remained atop the canni, withering beside the pyre of the ice cream truck.

CANNI

Virginia

In the first minutes of her first day back at work deep beneath Dr. Robert's Virginia barn, Dr. Anderson stood in the research center's kitchen, pouring coffee with her good arm. To the side of the room by the snack and soda machines stood a helmeted guard.

The doctor tried to inhale the scent of her brew, but she got perfume instead. The lovely Dr. Martinez had come up behind her.

"How you feeling, V?"

"Oh, pretty beat up, inside and out, but aren't we all?" she smiled.

The smile was genuine, but mostly because she was thinking of what her brother might have said about their attractive co-worker, and her aroma.

"Well, I am glad to see you back," said Martinez. "We need you."

Pouring some sweetener, V responded, "Any significant changes?"

"Oh, yeah. Number twelve has died of an apparent stroke . . . "

"Twelve? Wasn't he only in his twenties? Relatively healthy?"

"That's him. A bit of a *papi* too. Buff."

"Wow."

"That's not the worst of it."

Dr. Anderson's coffee stopped just short of her lips.

"Nine and sixteen," said Martinez, "have gone canni, and have not switched back."

"For how long?"

"At least thirty-six hours by now."

"Crap," said V as she put down the Styrofoam cup. "And we now call them *Canni* in here?"

"Not officially. Not on paper."

Anderson ignored her coffee and headed toward the doors that led to the work area. She stopped to study the guard standing by the vending machines. Glancing down at his wrist she said, "Still rocking the wireless, eh?"

He gave a shrug and a slight tilt of the head.

Just as she stepped away, she noticed the soda machine. The Pepsi, Diet Pepsi, Mountain Dew, Gatorade, and Aquafina pushbuttons all shone green.

The button beside the Diet Mountain Dew selector flashed red. EMPTY.

DANIEL O'CONNOR

Washington, D.C.

Vice President Montgomery carried four straight-backed chairs one-by-one from the side of the room and placed them in front of the Oval Office desk, facing President Collins.

"You know we have people who do that, Owen," smiled Collins.

"Yeah, well, I got it."

"Is this a surprise party or something? Who's coming?"

The VP threw up a forefinger as if to say '*give me a minute*'. He turned to the two helmeted guards by the closed doors. "I'm sorry, but I'll need to ask you fellows to wait just outside, please."

The officers began to move, then stopped, looked at each other, and turned to the president.

"That's fine," said the commander-in-chief. "We have our emergency buttons, and while I'm not speaking for the vice president, I can scream like an infant. Just remain by the doors but in the hallway."

As the guards headed out, Vice President Montgomery added, "Please let the gentlemen behind the door in as you exit."

The president raised an eyebrow as the men entered: CIA director Warren Hamburger, his boss—the Director of National Intelligence, Retired Admiral David R. Lamb—and the pink-scarred, dark-skinned, usually-blinking White House janitor.

"Please be seated, gentlemen," said the VP.

President Collins adjusted his seating position. He studied the two department heads and one custodial employee who sat before him. The pair of directors greeted him with nods and a verbal "*Mr. President*". The janitor grimaced and blinked.

"Well," offered the president, "this is certainly different."

"Yes, it is, sir," answered the vice president.

"Are you sure the Secret Service needs to remain outside?" asked Collins.

"More so than ever, actually," responded Montgomery.

Collins pulled his executive chair right up to his desk. The vice president alone remained standing.

"Mr. President, you are aware that Retired Admiral Lamb has led our naval forces, including the SEALs, for many years," he began.

"Of course."

"Admiral," continued the VP, "what is your opinion of our SEALs?"

"They are mammoth. They are selfless. They have no fear. I would walk through Hell with one SEAL beside me."

"My thoughts as well," answered Montgomery. "All that being said, Admiral, would you have any suggestions with regard to any other unit that might be more successful in our quest to locate, and capture alive the men and/or women who created, implemented, and unleashed this demon upon our country so that we might gain information into a possible antidote or potential cure?"

"I do. Mr. President, do you remember the coordinated bombs attacks on the Florida theme parks or the sarin gas release in the Vegas casinos?"

"What? There have been no such incidents."

The janitor grimaced as the admiral replied.

"Exactly. Because we have a unit that stopped them both."

"What unit?"

"Sir, they do not have a name."

"Okay," responded the commander-in-chief, "I'm sitting here, being told by a retired naval admiral that there is an unnamed tactical unit that has stopped attacks that I, as president, have never heard of, and, no disrespect to anyone, a member of our cleaning staff, who has never uttered a word to me, is sitting in on the meeting. You know the old elephant in the room saying? Well, it's here, and it seems to be shitting all over me. What in hell are you all talking about?"

"I didn't even know any of this until yesterday, sir," said the VP.

"Alright," answered the president. Then he turned to the janitor. "Did you know about all of this?"

He blinked feverishly and nodded as the admiral answered for him. "Sir, there is something about our friend here that you . . . "

"I asked *him*, Admiral. Now, sir," he said, turning to the janitor, "it is not commonplace for a member of the cleaning crew to be present at a classified meeting. The Secretaries of Defense and Homeland Security are not even here, so I assume you have something of great value to add to all of this. I am asking you, and you alone, to tell me what it is."

The custodian squirmed in his seat, beads of sweat bubbling on his forehead.

"Come on," said President Collins, "don't be shy. I hear you whistling all the time. It's quite tuneful, too. Why exactly are you here, sir?"

The sweating man leaned forward a bit, eyes watering. He spoke. It all came so quickly.

"FuckYouPresident. EatMyAsshole."

The man was already waving his arms as Collins stood.

"I'm sorry, Mr. President. I . . . I . . . can't control . . . "

The VP interrupted, addressing his boss by the name he'd called him for decades, "George, this man has a medical condition. It's why he limits his verbal communication. The whistling helps him control it."

"You knew *that* too?"

"Again, found out yesterday."

"Okay, so what does he have to do with the nameless unit?"

"I run it," said the janitor.

"Ah, that's more like it," answered the president. "I don't blurt out swear words all the time. Sometimes they come and I can't control them. It's like a cough or a sneeze. If I'm quiet or whistling I do better. I apologize in advance for anything I might say. The words are not a reflection of my inner thoughts or feelings. They are merely words."

"So, you aren't really a janitor?"

"Well, Mr. President, yes and no, sir."

"Explain."

"I work here part-time on the custodial staff as my cover. There are other unit members employed in various capacities as well. SuckMyBlackCock."

"Dear Lord," mumbled President Collins. He looked at his vice president, then at the two agency directors. "Is this all legit?"

They all affirmed.

Turning back to the custodian, Collins asked, "What is your name?"

"Joe Isley, sir."

"Is that your real name?"

"No, sir."

"What is your real name?"

"I am not at liberty to say."

"Okay, Joe Isley. So you lead some super-secret team of Avengers that do not even report to the president . . . "

"Several presidents have not known about this team." interrupted VP Montgomery. "Vice presidents as well. It's a need-to-know basis."

"Did Obama know?"

Montgomery had no answer, so he glanced at the admiral. The retired naval officer nodded. Then added, "Not during his first term."

"Mr. Isley," said the president, "I think you know that I don't sugarcoat anything, so I will ask you: how, with your verbal condition, can you possibly lead a team like this?"

"Sir, I think that should show you how good I am. I have this burden, yet I am still the one chosen to command them."

Collins sat back and tapped his fingers on his desk. He still couldn't quite process the scene before him. He looked into Isley's eyes.

"Quickly, Mr. Isley. Let's say that in this instant, you learned that you must get me out of the White House to save the world. Everyone in the building is against you, including myself. Go!"

"I would impale your hand to that desk with your letter opener. As you dealt with that, I would kill the three men beside me with your fancy pen. You may or may not have pushed your button by then, but I would expect those two guards outside to come rushing in. I'd be waiting for them, maybe with this chair as a weapon. I would kill them with their own guns, take those weapons, maybe their body armor, too. I would then retrieve you, sir, and take you out of the office and to the tunnels, hoping I could do so with minimal engagement, but feeling relatively safe with you as my hostage."

The president stopped tapping his fingers.

"Damn." he said, "Not gonna lie. That was impressive."

"FuckDatAss."

"Okay, then. You know the White House tunnels?"

"Somebody has to mop them, fuckface."

"Oh, boy."

"Sorry, Mr. President. I don't usually do it this much. I'm a bit nervous."

"You get nervous?"

"Not in the field, sir."

"Then why now?"

"Because I am in the Oval Office in a meeting with four men whom I greatly admire attempting to save the country that I love so."

President Collins pondered that answer while casually moving the silver letter opener further away from Isley. He then turned to CIA Director Hamburger.

"Warren, you've been noticeably silent."

"Yes, sir."

"Let's hear it."

"Well, if you are asking, while I do appreciate their effectiveness, I do not support certain methods and I am not a proponent of zero accountability. They basically answer to no one. To them, waterboarding may as well be a footbath, and I am quite sure that they would kill anything from an old woman to a newborn to achieve their goals."

"Ouch. What say you, Mr. Isley?"

"I respect Director Hamburger's opinion. He is a patriot and a man of honor."

"But what about all of the baby-killing and such? You have the head of the CIA saying that you all are too brutal. That's some crazy shit right there, no?"

"Anything we may do is thoughtfully considered beforehand. The potential reward must exceed the deed. I will not mislead you, Mr. President, our country is facing virtual extinction. My team, if implemented, will do anything to prevent that."

"Right. What I don't understand is how you function. Who pays you? What about your families? What do they think you all do?"

Isley grabbed a hanky from his pocket to mop his brow. "None of us have families. They either think we are dead, missing, or they never gave a damn in the first place. We have no real friends besides one another. But we are well-paid and live like kings, truth be told."

"Where does the money come from? I've been slicing budgets since I first sat in this chair."

"Well, I'm not a financial or budgetary expert, but, you know when you hear folks complain that the Pentagon pays two thousand dollars for one little box of nails?"

"Yeah."

"We are the nails."

President Collins could see Admiral Lamb's grin.

"Another secret." said Lamb, nearly whispering. "We sometimes call them The Nails."

"I see." said the president. "So then why was it that our SEALs were the ones who killed Bin Laden?"

"The public needed to see that," answered Lamb.

"If I may add," responded Isley, "the SEALs then wrote books and movies about the whole thing." He put his hanky away. "We don't kiss and tell."

"Mr. Isley, you know that attractive young female custodian who is always smiling at me? Is she a part of your team too?"

"She is a cleaning lady, sir."

"Gotcha. Just wondering. So, is my blessing required for you all to track down those behind this?"

"Yes. Just a verbal affirmative."

"If I don't agree, then you don't act?"

"That's correct, sir. We are ghosts, but we are your ghosts."

President Collins looked at the men before him. Director Hamburger was the only one who failed to make eye contact.

"What's next?" asked the president. "You all gonna tell me that we actually have aliens at Area 51?"

No response.

"Great. Well, considering the unique nature of this threat," said Collins, "I realize that extreme measures must be taken. If there is an asset that our country has, I'd be neglectful if I offhandedly dismissed it. On the other hand, I'm not a fan of just torturing and killing folks who may not be directly involved in terrorism. We are a civilized people. Gentlemen, I know time is short, but I'll need even a small segment of it to think clearly about this. Gut reactions are sometimes overreactions. So, Mr. Isley, when I've made my decision, I will tell Admiral Lamb, and if we need to speak again, it will be arranged. How does that sound?"

"SuckMyBlackDick."

CANNI

Las Vegas

"Suck my white dick."

These words were whispered into Rob's ear from behind as he sat at the restaurant table.

He didn't flinch. He turned, knowing exactly who would be standing behind him.

"What if it wasn't me sitting in that table, asshole?" smiled Rob.

"I'd either have a broken nose or a date. Maybe both. Hey, you said first table by the casino entrance. I trust you."

The American Coney Island hot dog joint sat snugly inside the D Las Vegas Resort and Casino, right in the middle of the bustling Fremont Street Experience. The gambling hall had an old Vegas vibe but with all of the modern amenities. The music was loud, the dancing girls pretty, and the drinks strong. But all of that was just beyond the restaurant entrance. This was still a family-friendly dog and fries restaurant.

"Glad you could make it, Johnny," said Rob.

"Hey, a deal's a deal."

"Come sit, brother."

John G felt the table edge and sat, across from Rob. He put his white-tipped cane down beside him.

"So, where is Cash? You know I'm dying to meet her."

"Yeah, more on that later," said Rob. "How have you been, bud?"

"Well, I'm in a nice room here. A corner king! Great deal, too."

"You're staying *here*?"

"Yeah."

"So why didn't you just give me your room number instead of meeting down here?"

"I think you need a room key to come up. Security, you know."

"Oh, okay. How's things otherwise?"

"Decent. I made a new friend. Oh, and the bus driver who brought me here also tried to devour me. My new buddy saved my ass. Big guy. Linebacker or something."

"What? Are you alright?"

"Fine. My friend—Willie is his name—he went to the hospital, but he's out already."

"Why didn't you tell me on the phone?"

"No biggie. That's the new world, right?"

Rob took a sip of soda from his icy white cup.

"This must be beyond horrifying for you, John."

"No more than you, brother. Maybe I'm better off. I can't actually see these fuckers when they flip ugly."

"Lunch is on me, by the way." said Rob as he stood. "What can I get you?"

"Well," replied John, "you do know that I study the culinary arts. My palate has matured quite a bit lately so, without being rude . . . "

"Stop jerking me off."

"Two dogs with everything, and a gyro. But wait a minute: I want to know about Cash. Where is she?"

Rob took another hit of cola.

"Well," he said, probing the edge of the plastic cup lid, "you know my car that I was always talking about?"

"1983 Chevy Malibu. You think I'd forget?"

"The car is gone. Stolen. My dad's tape collection too. And now it seems so is my girl."

"What? But, the wedding . . . "

"Yeah, the wedding. Seems that might have been nothing more than my own personal fantasy, Johnny."

"Cash is really gone?"

"Well, not entirely, but we barely speak. She hooked up with a guy who is supposed to be our friend. He set us up where we're staying right now."

"Where is that?"

"In the drainage tunnels under the city."

"Drainage tunnels? Sounds like an awesome friend."

"It's an odd thing," said Rob, lowering his voice. "Nobody in that little tunnel area has flipped."

"Really?"

"Nobody, John."

"Underground tunnels. Is Teresa living there with you, too?"

Rob sat back down.

"Teresa . . . "

"Is she gone as well? Dude, you were gonna hook me up with her!"

"John, Teresa . . . she . . . she's passed away."

"Oh, my God. I am . . . so sorry. I don't even know what to say. This trip has been hell for you, Rob. Your friend has died. That's worse than everything else combined."

"Cash killed her."

CANNI

Washington, D.C.

President Collins raced down the hall. His necktie was over his shoulder and pointing back at three members of his helmeted security detail, who fought hard to keep pace. Two further guards manned a set of metal doors toward which Collins was headed. They pressed a code as they spotted their commander-in-chief, and the entryway opened with a blast of air.

Once inside the White House Medical Unit, he was intercepted by two members of its staff.

"Where is he?" asked President Collins, breathing heavily.

"Sir, he's in the trauma center, we . . . "

Collins brushed past the clerical staff, knowing that if he hadn't been greeted by a doctor or at least a physician's assistant or registered nurse then they were all possibly in a code blue or similar situation. He noticed a pattern of blood droplets that led to the trauma room.

He was there in seconds, and his worse fears were realized. The entire medical staff seemed to be behind the glass, all working feverishly on Vice President Montgomery. Collins could barely grab a glimpse of his friend as he lay there, motionless, surrounded by medical personnel, tubes, wires, and covered in blood.

Collins stood there alone with his security detail and the WHMU clerks keeping a respectful distance. He knew that some of Owen Montgomery's family had come to visit him at his White House office today, but why were none of them here with him now?

He looked over at the unit clerks.

"Who did this?"

They both turned their heads toward another room in the unit. Collins walked toward it; there was no longer a need for running. As he approached the glass, he could see Montgomery's son and daughter-in-law in an embrace. Then, he saw little Gregory, his Washington Nationals shirt soaked with blood. The boy sat in a chair, being tended to by a nurse. She was cleaning caked vomit from his lips and chin.

George Collins' thoughts quickly turned the way his mentor would have wanted: they veered from personal to presidential. He pondered how terrorists previously would have had virtually no chance at attacking a prime target while he or she was safely ensconced in the White House, but now with their latest assault, they have had the vice president's six-year-old grandson do it for them. He looked again at the trail of blood on the hallway tiles.

Young Gregory spotted the president through the glass and, probably not fully aware of what he had just done, lifted his small, trembling hand to wave.

By the time Collins mustered a smile for the boy, he knew that Joe Isley would be required to do some mopping.

DANIEL O'CONNOR

Las Vegas

Rob had anticipated difficulty in leading his sightless friend through the dark tunnels, but it was almost as if John G were showing *him* the way. The only advantage Rob had was at the tunnel splits, and that was only because he'd been through them before.

"Darkness: the great equalizer," smiled the blind man.

They had happened upon Polish Joe. Rob was about to introduce him, but his only words were, "Fuck Lindenhurst, fuck the geese, fuck Pat Benatar." They kept moving.

Some of Russo's men weren't thrilled with an unannounced visitor, but Rob didn't care.

"Mildew, marijuana, urine, and strawberry," said John, almost to himself.

They reached Rob's living quarters, and on her bed, reading a Barbara Taylor Bradford novel by flashlight, was Cash.

"Hey," said Rob.

Casually looking up from her book, she saw the fellow with the cane and dark glasses. He was smiling broadly. She put the paperback down and stood.

"Hello," she offered. She shot Rob a look that said *Who is this?*

Before John could reply, Rob said, "Cash, this is my buddy, John G."

"Oh? Oh! So nice to finally meet you, John. Rob calls me Cash, but my name is actually Caroline—or Carrie." She wanted to say *Rob, why the fuck did you never mention that he was blind?*

"I only know you as Cash so I really do want to call you that," replied John, "Also, damn you Rob, she is gorgeous!"

Rob smiled at the puzzled look on Cash's face.

"Oh, I *know*," continued John, "I know that Scarlett Johansson is absolutely killer; not because others tell me, but because of her voice and the way that she breathes. Your sound is different than hers, but I can tell, Cash."

"Um, well, thank you, John," she answered. As she absorbed John G's flattery, she realized that the fact that Rob never mentioned his friend's lack of sight is because he would never mention her OCD issues when describing her to others, nor would he bring up in conversation if a friend happened to be diabetic or HIV positive. It wasn't how Rob saw them. None of that was at the essence of the person. Rob had told her that John was funny. He was a good cook. Maybe a tad eccentric, with his disdain for cell phones and the like. Rob told Cash that John was a great friend who would go the extra mile for others. Winthrop Robert was blind to the fact that John was blind.

This was one of the qualities that drew her to Rob in the first place.

"So, how is life in this subterranean hotel?" asked John.

"Not too bad," she replied. "They leave a Molly on our pillows each day."

"Really?"

"Nah. But they should."

"Imagine taking a Molly just before a flip," pondered John.

"We haven't flipped John, remember?" answered Rob.

"Oh. Even before you settled down here?"

"Nope."

"Shit, I flipped twice. Once in my room at the D Hotel. I thought I broke my nose, but apparently not. I did completely destroy their lamp. I could've blamed it on the whole 'blind' thing, but I came clean. They were cool about it. New way of doing business, I guess. Luckily, I was alone and didn't hurt anyone but myself and the lamp."

"Shhh," said Rob, "If they hear that you're a flipper they'll drag your ass outta here, bud."

"Did you bring him here on that freaking bicycle, Rob?" asked Cash.

"Yep. On the handlebars."

"Screw you, liar," said Cash. She was grinning just a bit.

"John paid for a taxi. We tossed the bike in the trunk."

The music started. Seems Don Russo had the makings of another party down in his area.

Funkadelic.

"Hell yeah," said John G. "This place might be as cool as Fremont Street."

"We have fewer hobos," answered Cash.

"Can we get involved in that party?" asked John, "I haven't smoked a bowl in months."

"You haven't done any hard labor down here, John," said Rob, "but I think if you made a monetary donation to the greater good, Russo would happily let you join us."

"I can do that."

"Sweet. Let's go. You in, Cash?"

"Nah. I think I'll just chill here," she said.

"What? Just a little grass?"

Grass as far as the eye could see. Who'd have thought there was a place like this in the desert? When you're trespassing on a swanky private golf course just before sunrise, it seems the entire world is blanketed with lush, healthy turf. Rob may not have been able to convince Cash to attend Don Russo's latest dance party, but when the party was over, she couldn't wait to get out of the tunnels and had hitched a cab ride with Rob and John to drop John back at his hotel. When they passed by the course though, Cash suddenly had the urge to be alone with Rob. John hadn't minded, and Rob seemed eager to bail as well. The driver let the couple and their bicycle out by the golf course before heading back to Fremont Street with John.

Unprotected sex had gained an additional meaning; being out of the tunnels and its true protection in numbers or its debatable protection from flipping meant that Rob and Cash were now at the mercy of fate as to whether either might kill the other.

Cash's thoughts ran the gamut from her family back home to her indiscretion with Paul along with visions of her own mortality and that of everyone she knew. She inhaled the sweet scent of the lawn below her and had her head tilted back, eyes on the glittering stars above.

Rob's mind was almost blank, still buzzing from Russo's weed. He did love how Cash looked in that worn, gray tee that read PROPERTY OF THE NEW YORK METS, even more so when, like right then, it was the only thing on her and she was on him. He didn't notice that there was a sky full of twinkling stars above and he smelled no grass. At the moment, he had no idea who Paul Bhong was, and had no interest in pondering mortality. His girl, if she still was his girl, was right where she belonged, and he hadn't been sure this would ever happen again. This was how he liked it, just the two of them, with no one else able to intrude or endanger.

Two of his favorite people ever were his Aunt Janet and Uncle Bob. One of them, he had forgotten which, told him that life was like a jet on a runway: it would crawl at first as it waited for takeoff, but then it would accelerate, pinning us back in our seats, as it blasted off the surface and into the sky. He knew that he and Cash were at the age that came just before liftoff, and he wanted it to stay nice and slow, especially at times like this. There was nothing bad at that moment. There were no viruses, no deaths, and no Cannis. There was only Cash.

Their amorous rapture, the brilliant sunrise, and the powerful sprinkler system, all erupted as one.

As he came to his senses, he had a question.

"Wanna start a band?"

She smiled, "What would we call it?"

"The Indifferent Dead."

"I don't get it."

"You know, there's the *Walking Dead*, the *Evil Dead*, the *Grateful Dead*; always a catchy adjective . . . "

"So?"

"Never mind. How about The Mark Cuban Missile Crisis?"

Rob knew that though convivial and cordial most of the time, Don Russo had a reputation that instilled fear in the street people of Las Vegas. He had his own rules and would not bend. Hell, the fucker never even wore clothes.

As he and Cash returned to the tunnels, muddled whispers filled the unusually dank air that Russo had just handed out some severe justice to a dweller who had betrayed him. The man was banished from the tunnels—*all* of the tunnels—and sent to fend for himself on the streets after, and if, an ambulance retrieved his unconscious and bloody self from the Las Vegas Wash.

He got off easy.

Word was that those floaters who would turn up outside the tunnels after a flood would more often than not be the same folks who wound up on the wrong side of Russo's ongoing dance party.

Don Russo was extraordinarily persuasive.

They had a saying down below: *go with the flow.* You either did it, or you did it.

As they moved through the tunnels toward their living quarters, Rob and Cash were faced with a barrage of images. Residents were moving a bit faster than the norm. They passed Russo, glimpsing only his bare ass as he hosed blood from his hands. They came upon Paul Bhong. Rob was formulating exactly what to say to the man who'd at a minimum kissed his girl when Spats came out of the dark, carrying a portable radio. The broadcast was fading in and out.

"Holy shit, man." said Spats. "Big Mex is saying that the vice president is dead."

"What?" gasped Cash.

"Who is Big Mex?" added Rob.

"Man, Mex is the best radio dude in Vegas. You New York types wouldn't know."

"Is he reliable?" asked Rob.

"Yes," interjected Paul. "If you live in Vegas, you know Big Mex."

"I may not be the smartest fucker," said Spats, "but everyone is questioning the popularity of Big Fucking Mex, and I just told you all that VP Montgomery is fucking dead."

Rob abandoned all thoughts of confronting Paul. Temporarily.

"What happened to the VP?" he asked.

"This reception is for shit, but it sounds like he got Cannied by someone on his staff or something, and died from his wounds."

"We can't even keep our vice president safe. Holy shit," said Paul. "Where did it happen?"

"Right in the White House."

"Fuck."

"Can you get any other stations on that radio? Like a news channel? Just to confirm," said Rob.

Spats answered, "The president is going to speak soon, *supposubly.*"

"FiveFourThreeTwoOne," yelled Cash, as she counted on her fingers and sucked air.

"Damn it," sighed Rob.

Cash was rubbing and shaking as they reached their sleeping quarters. Paul followed to the rear of the couple.

"You okay, Cash?" he asked.

Rob answered for her, as he set her down on her bed. He never turned to face Paul. "Her name is Caroline. She is Cash only to me. Don't ever forget that."

It was then that Paul realized that Cash had already told Rob about their moment.

"I came to tell you about it, Rob. I wasn't going to be dishonest."

"Save it."

"I just want to say . . . "

"Now's not the time," barked Rob, finally turning to look Paul in the face.

What ate at Rob most was the fact that he still had no idea how far that liaison actually went, and he battled internally over whether he truly wanted to know.

Paul reached out, hoping for a handshake, even if no words were to be exchanged. Rob stared at Bhong's outstretched arm but didn't move.

Then came Phaedra, eyes wide with excitement. "The Witch of the Wash is talking! She's talking!"

Cash seemed to regain clarity with the appearance of Phaedra.

"What?" asked Rob.

"The Witch of the Wash," answered Paul, knowingly. Rob ignored him.

"Who is the Witch of the Wash?" asked Rob, eyes on Phaedra.

"Come," she answered, "Let us all go and see!"

As the crimson beauty headed down the tunnel, Cash stood. She leaned into Rob and

said, "You mean there's a witch in these tunnels not named Phaedra?"

He smiled and asked his girl, "Do you wanna go see?"

"Hell, yes."

"Wanna start a band?"

"What would we call it?"

"The Linda Blair Witch Project."

She smiled. "Okay, that one wasn't bad."

They hurried after Phaedra, with Paul once again behind them. As they stomped through the darkness, Paul spoke. "The witch lives in a pipe in a tunnel wall. She's been here since before any of these people, even Russo. They thought she was mute."

"She lives in a pipe?" mumbled Cash.

Paul answered, "Yeah, Cash—er, Caroline. It's a long pipe, plenty wide for her to crawl around in. Polish Joe mentioned her the first day I brought you guys here."

They approached something that initially appeared to be a waterfall of sorts, but turned out to be a bustling wall of gnats. As they hurried through the barrier of insects, they saw ahead that Phaedra had stopped in one of the double-barrel tunnels. A handful of other dwellers had gathered, staring into a pipe that was maybe four feet wide and the same distance off the ground. As they reached the group, Cash gazed into the deep tube.

The inside had been painted white. Despite the bright color, one could only see a few feet into the pipe before the shadows took over.

"Her pipeline deepens to forty feet," said Phaedra. "She is within."

Cash began rubbing her arms.

"You want to go back, babe?" asked Rob.

"Why is the pipe white?" she asked.

"You wanna see the witch?" bellowed one gawker. "I can shine my light in."

"No!" yelled Phaedra.

Cash took a step closer to the pipe, before reiterating her question, "Why . . . is the pipe white?"

"Caroline," said Phaedra, "it makes it easier for her to see the insects."

Rob chuckled, "She's supposed to be a witch and she's afraid of bugs?"

"The important thing is that she spoke today!" said Phaedra. "Who heard her?"

"I did," came the reply from several.

"What did she say?"

"Something about seeds."

"Seeds?"

It was then that a fair-sized spider known as a Carolina Wolf wandered into the whiteness of the pipe's edge. Its legs were thick; some looked almost like thumbs. All gray and furry. It crawled up the side of the circular metal duct until it stood upside down at the top.

The hand came from the shadows deeper within the pipe. It was old and wrinkled. Long, cracked nails. Slow and deliberately, the fingers corralled the spider and extracted it from the white surface, back into the blackness.

"Seeds," was the only word uttered before the chewing began.

The same hand that had grabbed the insect emerged once again, this time placing flat on the damp pipe's bottom, seemingly for balance. Her face, mostly hidden behind stringy hair, the color of roadkill, came just partially into the light. Her eyes were not seen, but her pointed jaw, still grinding the Carolina Wolf, was quite visible as she spoke.

"Seeds. Fossils."

"Okay," whispered Cash to Rob, "we are getting the fuck out of these tunnels."

"Seeds. Fossils. Time capsules."

Phaedra cleared her throat, "Ma'am, we were not aware that you could speak. Are you in need of anything? We are a community down here."

The crimped hand floated up and brushed aside the greasy strands that had blocked her eyes. She studied Phaedra, then Cash, then back to Phaedra, as she chewed.

"Seeds. Fossils. Time capsules."

She cast her gaze upon Cash once again. Never looking away, she backed into the lightlessness of her dank domicile and swallowed.

DANIEL O'CONNOR

Brooklyn, New York

Weeks earlier

Rob and Cash stood together on the concrete steps that led to the front door of a basement apartment, just across the street from Marine Park. Remnants of a two-day-old snowstorm melted around them in the afternoon sun. The water droplets sounded like a ticking clock as they fell from the leaky gutter above.

Parked at the curb and surrounded by vehicles that had been sullied by the storm was Rob's 1983 Chevy Malibu, freshly washed and waxed. The sunlight bounced off of it like a disco ball.

Rob and Cash looked as bright and shiny as the car. They smiled broadly in their green plastic derbies, covered in shamrocks, as the door opened.

"I am a bad-ass superhero!" she said, her face hidden behind a child's drawing. The artwork depicted a slim blonde girl in a bright green costume, with a yellow cape. T-BIRD, read the inscription, in red, white and blue crayon.

"Happy St. Paddy's Day!" yelled Rob and Cash.

The drawing was lowered, and there behind it, clear blue eyes engineering the most beautiful of smiles, was Teresa.

"Happy St. Patrick's Day!" she replied. "You feelin' my superpowers? I can fly!"

"My son knows she is going to be a flight attendant," came a voice from inside the apartment.

"Come on in," said Teresa. "My cousin Joy-Joy is here!"

The couple entered, passing through some green and white helium balloons, to see the back of Joy-Joy's head as she watched TV. It was a news broadcast with the screen segmented into four; in one corner was the anchor, and the other three were labeled MANHATTAN, BROOKLYN, and ALBANY. Within each of the latter three were teams of investigators in hazardous material suits, complete with headgear and breathing apparatus.

"They should not have canceled the parade. That's just giving in to terrorism," said Joy-Joy. She stood and turned to face the visitors.

"I know I've met Caroline, but I don't believe I've met her gentleman friend," she smiled as she walked around from the couch. "Joyce McDougald. Call me Joy, or Joy-Joy if you like." Cash gave her a hug, and she shook hands with Rob as he introduced himself.

"I've heard a lot about you," he said. "Islip, right?"

"East Islip," she answered. "They canceled our local parade too. Schools are closed. I was going batty at home. I told my husband it was his turn to watch the kids. He always takes this week off so we can do the parades and stuff. I wanted to come see T before you guys head out west. Hubby can work on our slow-draining sink and hang with the kiddies today."

167

That was a lot of info for one breath, thought Rob, yet he was charmed by Joy-Joy's radiant smile and rosy cheeks. He couldn't find a speck on her wardrobe that wasn't green, either.

"We won't even need a parade," he said. "We'll have our own party right here!"

"That's the spirit!" beamed Joy-Joy.

Rob turned to Teresa, "I brought the CD."

"CD?"

"With the potential wedding songs . . . "

"Oh, God," sighed Cash.

"I could've found them on my phone," replied Teresa.

"Screw that," said Rob.

"You're lucky they're not on 8-track," added Cash.

"Teresa, please tell me that you do still have a CD player," said Rob.

"Yes, Robert. I do. I might also have a VCR around here somewhere . . . "

Joy eyed the CD as soon as he presented it.

"Fleetwood Mac?" she asked. "Cool. That one doesn't look familiar, though."

"Well, it's . . . "

Joy started singing. "*She is like a cat in the dark, and then she is the darkness . . .* "

"This one is more recent," said Rob. "It came, like, almost thirty years after that one."

"For real? Wow. Well, play it, I'm ready to dance! I brought my Irish Drinking Songs CD, too!"

By the time Rob was finally able to play the songs the green beer had begun to take effect and Cash's cousins, Laura and Jennifer, had arrived. They'd all listened closely to "Bleed to Love Her", but minds were wandering and alcohol was flowing for "Steal Your Heart Away".

"Which one do you prefer, Carrie?" asked Laura.

"I don't know. Remember these are *Rob's* choices . . . "

"What are you doing about a dress?" was Laura's next question.

"We're just *considering* getting married in Vegas," replied Cash. "If we do, it will be spur of the moment."

"I'll marry you, Rob," smiled Jennifer. "If my cousin drags her feet, I'm swooping right in."

Rob smiled, as he thought Jen was adorable, but he grew frustrated that no one was actually listening to the song.

The TV was muted but the images of the hazardous material investigators continued.

"Oh my God, this blackhead is going to become a basketball," sighed Teresa, as she stared into her hand mirror. "Rob is trying to set me up with his friend John when we get to Vegas, but he's gonna see this monstrosity on my face and run the other way."

"He won't notice," said Rob, still annoyed at the general lack of attention being paid to "Steal Your Heart Away".

"Are you flying JetBlue?" asked Joy-Joy with some green beer still on her lips. "I hear they have seats that lie flat."

"We're gonna be driving," replied Teresa. "A great way to see the country!"

"Good for you! Plus, who knows what these animals will do next? This could be anthrax or Ebola. Who in hell knows?" wondered Joy-Joy as she watched the muted television broadcast.

"With or without terrorists, Carrie ain't flying. That's for sure," added Laura.

Cash grabbed a leprechaun balloon and bopped her cousin on the head.

"I'm just jealous," laughed Laura. "I wish Jen and I were coming along."

"We can all fit," said Rob, as the song ended and he ejected his disc. "It'll be tight, but you're all pretty skinny."

"If only," said Laura. "We need to be here for Dad."

"For sure," answered Rob.

"How's he doing?" asked Teresa as she walked over to rub the shoulders of both sisters.

"Good days and bad."

"Please give him my love. Uncle Reg was always the coolest guy in the room," smiled Teresa. "I'm gonna come see him as soon as we get back."

"He'd love that," said Laura.

"But, in the meantime, you go kill it in Sin City," added Jennifer.

"Remember," smiled Laura, "what happens in Vegas . . . "

CANNI

Las Vegas

Present

"... stays in Vegas," whispered Cash. Her lips were chapped and dry. She sat in the darkness of her tunnel bed, feeling all alone in the world. The memories of a prior month seemed decades away. The sun was about to rise. Exactly twenty-four hours since she and Rob made love on the grass, less since she had seen the Witch of the Wash. Yet, those images along with her remembrance of St. Patrick's Day in Brooklyn, had conspired to deprive her of sleep. She'd thought she was hallucinating moments before, as she saw Phaedra whisk by in a beautiful white wedding gown. It was explained to her that the bridal attire was used to garner sympathy in casinos while silver mining. Surely a new bride couldn't be a homeless person scrounging for change. Cash was also feeling a rare touch of excitement, as Rob told her that John G was footing the bill for a taxi to take them around Vegas. John had said, "I'm fucking blind and I can't stand the darkness of these tunnels. You guys must be ready to explode." She looked forward to the respite.

She heard voices in the distance.

"The most brilliant business decision ever? Easy. The person who came up with the instructions: *lather, rinse, repeat.* They doubled their profits just by telling fuckers to use their shampoo twice as much."

It was Rob's voice. Then she heard John's reply. "I've saved some coin by not being able to read that canni shit."

"I don't know—is that really canni?" asked Rob.

"Seems so to me. Gouging consumers."

The voices grew closer. She could hear the tapping of the cane.

"Well, they're not forcing anyone. It's more like a suggestion. You know what is real canni? Dickheads who leave their shopping carts around the parking lot, instead of putting them in a stall with the other carts. Letting the wind blow them into people's cars. That's some selfish canni shit right there."

"Agreed," said John.

They reached Cash, who was sitting on her bed. Just behind them were Hoffman and Skunk, but they continued on through the tunnel.

"Hey, babe," smiled Rob. He guided John to sit on his bed. The sun was just beginning to stream down through the grates. Broken light kindled his face as he spoke.

"Good morning, Carrie. Ready for some fun today?"

"Am I ever. Thank you, John. We need to get out of this cage."

"A cage is not a cage until the door is locked."

"Wow," said Rob. "That is some heavy shit."

John answered, "A noose is but a rope until it's used."

"You're a smart dude, John," said Cash. "I see why Rob likes you so much."

"Well, Rob always gets the girl," smiled John, the light flickering on his dark glasses.

"We are going to pay you back for this, bud," added Rob. "I promise."

"Don't be a dick," said John. "We have to look out for each other since we are now seemingly in the middle of the food chain, I guess. You're watching out for me every minute we're together. I think the least I could . . . "

He stopped talking and grabbed the edge of the mattress with both hands. His cane fell to the floor as he squeezed hard.

"Oh, shit," said Rob, as he went right for Cash. He grabbed her and pulled her off the bed, wondering which direction would be the best escape route.

A loud grunt from John just as Rob decided to take Cash in the opposite direction of the Witch of the Wash. His blind friend fell back onto the bed.

"At least he won't be able to see us." said Rob. "We'll come back and get him squared away when he flips back."

"Canni!" they both yelled. It echoed through the subterranean channels.

"He can't see anything," hollered Cash. "Don't hurt him. Just stay clear!"

They heard Skunk and Hoffman running back their way. Then they heard John.

"Stop . . . you two dickheads," he was breathing heavily. "I'm not flipping, you cocks."

He was still grunting as his friends stopped running. Rob had Cash remain with the arriving Skunk and Hoffman, as he cautiously walked back toward John. He was still flat on the bed, covered in sweat, fighting to suck in the musty air. The light strokes from above were no longer on his face, but across his chest.

"What's going on with you, bro?" asked Rob. "Let me help you. You need a hospital?"

John's dark glasses were crooked, but they still covered his eyes. He reached out, searching for his friend. He inhaled deeply. Rob took his hand. It was damp and cold.

"Rob," said John between breaths, "I . . . I think I can see."

CANNI

Washington, D.C.

President Collins sat alone in the Situation Room. He had never been in there without accompaniment. It seemed vast and cold. His trusted aid and mentor was gone. Though he was the most powerful man in the world, he'd always had his friend Owen to lean on. Maybe even hold his hand, in a manner of speaking.

Collins had just left an Oval Office meeting with Admiral Lamb and Director Hamburger. They'd told him he should head to the Situation Room regarding a *maintenance issue*. That code was used because uniformed and helmeted Secret Service guards were present during that discussion. The president chose to exclude his advisors from his present location so that no security need be in the room. He was all alone. His protectors stood outside the door.

He realized that he'd never been the one to activate the monitors before. It took a minute, but it wasn't much harder than figuring out how to work a strange television set.

Four monitors lit up. A handful of others remained dark. It was obvious that someone, probably Hamburger or Lamb, had set it up that way before Collins had come in.

There was a face in each monitor. Live.

One featured Joe Isley, not in any custodial uniform or even camouflage, but in a plain, white t-shirt. It appeared damp and soiled. The other monitors separately showed two men and a woman. Collins had expected to see people of middle-eastern decent, but only one of the men fit that profile. The second man and the woman were quite pale. He correctly pegged the fellow as a North Korean. Wasn't that difficult. His guess on the woman was Russian, but he'd soon learn that she was born in the United States of America and of Irish/Italian descent. They were all at least forty years of age.

"Hello, Mr. President. We got 'em."

"Can they see me, Joe?"

"No, sir."

"Are you telling me that these are the actual scientists?"

"Yes, sir. We also retrieved two laptops, three thumb drives, and a cellphone."

"You got them already? How is that possible?"

"We work hard. We go in a straight line."

"Any casualties on your team?"

"Nothing major," he answered, through a grimace and several blinks.

Collins studied the three images. They looked tired. Disheveled. Maybe a little frightened. There were no signs of physical injury on any of them.

"They don't look like you roughed them up much."

"They were our prizes, Mr. President. We treat them as gently as possible.

When it's their turn to speak, things might be different, motherfucker. My apologies, sir—my affliction."

"Right. I honestly can't grasp this; the fact that you've caught them all."

"Regretfully not all, sir. We lost one. He died trying to use children as a shield."

"I see. And those children?"

"We go in a straight line."

President Collins paused. This was something that went against all he had ever stood for. He had to balance whatever Isley's team may have done against the probable impending death of the country he loved so. His finger tapped the console.

"Joe, have any of them mentioned a possible cure for this?"

"We have yet to reach the questioning stage. I thought you and your staff might want to be involved in that."

"Almost no one on my staff knows you exist."

"They don't have to know *who* brought them in. But also— GoFuckYourselfCunt—they might not have the stomach for what may need to be done to get them talking. Again, my apologies."

"So, these scientists haven't said anything to you, yet?"

"Apart from cussing us out, not really. That mid-East extremist scumbag says the same thing over and over, for now anyway."

"What is that?"

"Check it out, sir."

With four blinks and a grunt, Joe Isley left the frame for a minute. He then appeared in one of the holding rooms to the side of the darker-skinned captive, who was chained to a table. He motioned to someone off-camera to raise the mic level.

"You got something to say, murderer?" asked Isley of his prisoner.

The man looked at him, then turned his attention forward, as if knowing that someone important was watching. He smiled. His eyes were black as a shark's as he spoke directly to the president whom he could not see.

"You die as canni, no?"

CANNI

Las Vegas

They were giving John G some water. A crowd had gathered around him. Even Russo was there. The sun wasn't fully up yet, but even so, Skunk, Spats, and Hoffman were taping cardboard over any overhead slots that let the light shine through. Russo's orders.

John would lift his dark glasses for a few seconds then drop them down again. He grimaced each time.

"Give him some room, guys. Please," asked Rob.

"This shit is crazy, bro," said Don Russo.

"Should we get you to a hospital, Johnny?" asked Rob.

Cash's hands covered her mouth.

"No. All good," answered John. He lifted his glasses again. Eyelids opened. Tears poured. He closed and reopened his eyes a few times, but the glasses remained off. Phaedra joined the group, along with two more young women.

"I'm seeing shapes. No. I'm seeing even more than that."

John was breathing heavily. He poured sweat.

"Have some more water," said Rob, crouched before him. As Rob held the cup, John grabbed his arm.

"Brother," said John, "I'm not gonna do any corny shit like run my hand over your face, and I'm sure as shit not going to sculpt you, but Rob, I can fucking *see* you right now."

Smiling broadly, Rob lifted the cup.

"Say something," said John. "I want to see you use that familiar voice."

"Um, hello . . . there . . . John. Have . . . some . . . water."

"What the fuck with the slow talking? I'm gaining sight, not learning how to speak."

Everyone laughed.

"Sorry," chuckled Rob. "Do you really see me?"

"Yes. I mean, I'm guessing this is what you'd call blurry, but I do see your features." He closed his eyes again and wiped away the moisture.

"You okay?" asked Rob.

"Yeah. This is just a whole lot to take in. I don't know what the hell is happening to me."

He opened his eyes again. He scanned the darkened enclave. A horseshoe-shaped crowd stood before him. His gaze fell upon one female.

"You're Cash."

"That's right," she smiled.

"Wow," he sighed. "You *are* beautiful."

She blushed a bit and it felt wonderful to hear as she wasn't feeling her prettiest, considering the circumstances. Her confidence didn't soar for long though as John spotted Phaedra.

"Wow," he sighed. "You are beautiful."

Then the leader came through the crowd. "John, I am Don Russo."

For the sake of history, the fourth human image captured by John G's eyes was that of Don Russo's dangling genitalia.

CANNI

Virginia

Deep beneath Dr. Robert's barn, Dr. Martinez sat across from V. Anderson. V couldn't help but notice those dark eyes that had mesmerized her late brother so. Damned if Martinez didn't smell fantastic, too.

"Remember the huge discussion about admitting patient number eleven to our study because he had prostate cancer?"

"Sure do. He had a fairly low Gleason score."

"Yes, but he had a high PSA and was enlarged."

"Okay."

"V, he doesn't have cancer anymore."

"What?"

"His PSA is under two, and his prostate is small and sturdy."

"Well, a biopsy . . . "

"Done. No sign of cancer."

"Well," asked V, "could the rumors be true?"

"Did you see the woman on the news who said she just got up from her wheelchair and danced?" wondered Dr. Martinez.

"No, but I saw the kid who said he'd been deaf since birth but was now listening to Kanye on headphones."

"Did he say which was worse?"

V chuckled as she stood. "And what the hell is going on in the North Wing?"

"Not a clue."

"It went dark, and my card won't let me in anymore."

"Same."

"I understand the whole need-to-know scenario," offered Dr. Martinez, "but we are all working towards the same goal. How can we be excluded from whatever they are doing over there?"

"Can you cover for me?"

Anything called The North Wing just sounds too serious. In reality, it was one section of the underground compound, separated, like all the wings, by a single locked security door. Twenty feet from that door stood a vending machine, one of the several frequented in better times by R. Anderson. He was irreplaceable, but his Diet Mountain Dew was not. It was back in stock. V sipped one for the entire half hour that she had eyed the wing's door from her position of cover. The vending machine stood directly between her and the security door. On prior days, the sight of her lingering there might have caught the attention of anyone watching the security monitors, but now, as long as you weren't eating anyone, there wasn't the time nor the manpower to even give a fuck.

Thirty-two minutes in, the door opened.

V tossed her soda can into the trash as she bolted for that entrance. The exiting man had his back to her as she squeezed her foot in to block the door from closing. He was wearing janitor clothes.

Joe Isley felt her trying to rush past him and he shot his arm out to block her way.

"Pardon me, ma'am. Restricted area," he smiled, with just the hint of a twitch. Her foot remained.

"I know two things," she said. "One is that I am involved in top level government research at this facility, and two, no custodial employee would give a damn if I entered the North Wing."

"Not sure about all that, ma'am. Just doing as I'm told."

They remained wedged in the doorway as she replied. "You see the ID badge pinned to me? Why don't you have one?"

"I do," he smiled. "Must have left it in my car, motherfuckingscumbag."

Stunned by his response, V responded as her brother might have, with a shot to Isley's jaw. He saw it coming, but used it, and her included concentration, as an opportunity to kick her foot out of the entryway and close the door. Taking a jab to the face for a chance to secure the wing was an acceptable swap for Joe Isley.

"I deserved that, ma'am. Sorry for the insulting words. My tongue is the cross I bear."

He turned and walked away, leaving Dr. Anderson at the locked door, mouth agape.

CANNI

Las Vegas

The image that had been saved to the phone was that of a stunning blonde beauty. Rob had run far enough to get service, captured the picture from the internet, saved it to his photo collection, dimmed the screen significantly, and ran back.

Now John G was sitting on the tunnel bed, gazing at the illuminated face of Scarlett Johansson. "Wow," he sighed. "She *is* beautiful."

The crowd around him laughed. Don Russo's genitals bounced with his guffaws. John took his eyes from Scarlett's image and looked around at the group of tunnel-dwellers. They were the first people he'd ever laid eyes on. He assumed they weren't the cleanest or most well-groomed folks that he'd likely encounter, but here they were, living like this in this new world, and they were all happy and excited that he had gained vision. He spotted the large, roundish lymphedema that grew from Skunk's leg. Even absorbing his first visual evidence of human anatomy, he knew that mass of fluid and blood vessels to be abnormal.

The group sported a variety of skin tones, from pale to dark. He was pondering how something so trivial could be the trigger for so much wrong in the world when he saw the man at the far back just behind everyone else and thus a bit more blurry. He had a fair but tanned skin shade. John didn't know it, but it was Polish Joe.

He also didn't know that Joe was canni.

Then came the growl and the vomit. Polish Joe tore into the pack of tunnel dwellers. Screams and chaos. Rob immediately went to Cash. Polish Joe went to Phaedra. His teeth were clattering, scraping against her forehead and nose, when some of the men leaped upon him. He tossed them aside like a handful of kittens and was back at Phaedra. Before he got to her soft, white neck, Skunk hit him with a blast of pepper spray. Joe let go of Phaedra and spun wildly. The men tackled him again. He went down, reaching and grasping for anything he could eat.

He found Skunk's right leg. From the tunnel floor, he reached up blindly and found the textured, rough skin of the man's lymphedema. Its texture was not unlike that of the Pimple Ball that Russo had chucked down the tunnel. A can of shrimp pellets fell from Joe's pocket and spilled out.

With men upon him, Polish Joe was still able to thrust upward and sink his vomit-coated teeth deep into the bulbous flesh of Skunk's elephantiasis.

The eruption of the scream came along with the explosion of blood, fluid, liquid proteins, cellular debris, and bacteria. The concoction spilled all over Joe's face as he tore off a chunk of the substantial mass. He'd severed nearly one hundred blood vessels with his one bite. Skunk went to the ground reaching for his leg. He was almost convulsive. Red fluid went everywhere. Spats, Hoffman, and others tried to subdue Joe with little success. John G, during his first minutes of sight, joined the other men atop Joe. Rob was torn between joining the fray or remaining in front of Cash. He stayed.

Polish Joe got a hold of Hoffman's wrist. With his teeth. They sunk in, along with much of the fluids from Skunk's punctured growth.

"Out of the way!" yelled Don Russo.

The men scurried from atop Joe. Hoffman slid to the side, his arm still in the jaws of his attacker.

They heard the pump action, then the blast.

Russo blew a hole in Polish Joe's chest with a 12-gauge Remington. In the tunnels, the blast sounded like something from an atomic test site. The echo went on for too long. Joe's blood mixed with Skunk's and formed a fresh lake of death.

The dwellers were stunned, but Russo got them refocused. "We got to tie off Skunk's leg above the knee and get him to a medic. He'll bleed out. Now! Take Hoffman, too."

As he stood there naked but for the shotgun, he inhaled the scent of gunpowder and realized what many were thinking.

"I had no choice." he said. "We couldn't dance around with him while Skunk bled. We couldn't lose our best security men trying to corral him. Who knows what might've happened? He almost got Phaedra, for Christ's sake."

Skunk was loaded into a wheeled office chair and rushed toward the closest exit. Hoffman ran along side, wrapping up his own wrist. Spats and some others moved toward Polish Joe. He was flat on his back, motionless, with an enormous hole in the middle of his chest.

"Drag his body to the wash feeder," ordered Russo.

The spilled shrimp pellets crunched under the feet of those who grabbed onto the fallen dweller.

Cash was frozen in the same spot since it all broke out. She finally looked to Rob and spoke. "So much for nobody flipping in the tunnels, then."

Russo heard and responded as if insulted. "Polish Joe was not part of our bunker. He was a loner. None of our people have turned into that. None." All Rob could think of was the phrase, *Fuck Lindenhurst.*

A trail of blood and pellets remained in the wake of Joe as he disappeared down the tunnel. John G still couldn't see well enough to accompany Skunk and Hoffman or even to drag Joe to the wash. He sat back down on the bed.

Cash put her hand on his shoulder as Russo presented more orders.

"Rob and John, with so many gone, I'm gonna need you men to work security right now."

Before they could reply, a call came from down the tunnels. "Hoffman went down, we need more help getting the injured topside!"

"Shit," sighed Russo. "Rob, I need you to go help them. Those men need treatment."

Rob froze. He didn't want to leave Cash. He thought about taking her, but that would mean leaving John behind and, in Rob's mind, alone. His newly-sighted buddy would still be too slow to tag along on a hospital run.

As if reading his mind, Russo, still brandishing the shotgun, interrupted. "Don't make this more confusing. If you take Caroline or *Eyeballs* with you, you guys are done here. We don't tolerate selfishness. We need people here to keep the place secure."

"Go," said Cash.

Rob's brain ran through all possibilities.

"I'll watch out for her," said John, "and she'll do the same for me."

"They'll be fine," said Russo.

Rob took a deep breath and looked Russo in the eyes. "Give her the gun," he said.

"Whoa there," replied Russo.

"You want her to act as security," said Rob. "Hand the gun to Cash."

"I don't even know if she can handle . . . "

"I can," she said.

Russo scratched his scrotum.

"We need help!" came the voice from the tunnels.

"They need me," said Rob. "I'll go as soon as Cash gets that gun."

"Fuck the world," sighed Russo almost passively. He handed the Remington to Cash. She stood and became rigid and alert, as if receiving some sort of commendation.

"Keep 'em safe, babe," smiled Rob. Then, he was gone.

John looked over at Cash. The shotgun appeared much larger than it had when Don Russo held it. He stared down at the blood, fluids, skin chunks, and shrimp pellets that covered the ground.

John G put his dark glasses back on.

Rob had expected bright sun, but he welcomed the overcast as he, and six others, including Phaedra, pushed Skunk and Hoffman in separate office chairs toward Flamingo Road, and Desert Springs Hospital. The journey wouldn't be short, but there had been no response from the overloaded 911 system, and no one was stopping as they tried to flag down passing vehicles.

That was when they spotted the idling and occupant-free swimming pool service pickup outside a supply shop.

People are still using their swimming pools? was Rob's initial thought. He then debated in his mind if that was a positive or negative comment on society. He hadn't reached a conclusion by the time they had loaded everyone in and stolen the vehicle, with Rob at the wheel.

John G had gained the power of vision, yet with his glasses on he still relied on his other senses, the ones that had comforted him for his entire life. Based on the scent of the air, the feeling on his skin, and the methodical sound that the others had yet to hear, he was the first in the tunnels to know.

It was raining.

Cash, standing guard like G.I. Jane, looked up at the cardboard that Russo's men had taped over the small openings. Coming slowly but increasing rapidly through them were the drops of water.

What neither Cash nor John knew was that the rain had begun twenty minutes earlier in the surrounding hills, and it came hard. Now all of the accumulated rainfall was headed down to the valley. Coming toward the drainage tunnels like Niagara Falls. The thunder blasted almost as loud as the shotgun had minutes before. John and Russo flinched. Cash didn't blink.

In the Desert Springs emergency room, Rob couldn't actually hear the TV news broadcast over the chaos. The staff had taken Skunk and his deflated lymphedema into the back but had not yet turned their attention to the pale and unconscious Hoffman and his wrist. Rob did, however, spot the words FLASH FLOOD ALERT on the screen.

The original plan was to return the stolen pickup to the supply shop where they'd hijacked it, but now Rob raced past that location with Phaedra beside him. The rains were heavy and the visibility poor. They had left the others to stay at the hospital with their wounded comrades. As the pickup approached the tunnel entrance nearest their bunker, it created waves on either side, as if in a flume. Phaedra rubbed Rob's shoulder as the tunnel opening came into view. She gasped.

There were people everywhere, standing or squatting in knee-high water.

And that was *outside* the drainage tunnels.

The water could be seen blasting out of the underground maze like something in a white-water rafting ad. Rob was out of the truck and running—never turning off the ignition.

"Cash?"

He splashed down to where most of the crowd stood, still gasping for air and completely soaked.

"Cash, where are you?"

She was nowhere to be seen.

He found John G.

"Buddy, are you okay?"

John nodded.

"Where is Cash? Was she with you?"

"She was at first," answered John between gulps of air, "but then . . . she was gone. I don't even know what happened. The water took us all. I called out to her . . . "

Don Russo was doubled over, sucking wind. He had the shotgun, though.

"Where is she?" asked Rob. "Did she get out?"

"I don't know. I can barely breathe. Not sure if we lost any."

"You managed to save that fucking gun."

Those were Rob's last words before he waded toward the tunnels. He was trying to decide if he'd be better off trying to swim when John yelled out, "Rob, there are canni everywhere in there! It's fucking nuts! Be careful!"

As Rob entered the tunnel system, he had but one tool: the flashlight app on his phone.

The tunnels already smelled different. It was as if the water had dredged up everything that was foul and made soup. He waded against it. He knew it must have been much stronger before, when it washed everyone out.

Almost everyone.

He was in near-complete darkness and activating his light app when the first body floated by face down. It was a man. He thought about checking on him on the small chance he was breathing, but feared that Cash might be drowning at that very moment. He trudged onward.

"Cash!"

Her name echoed down the tunnels. All he heard in return was his own voice. Then from a distance came a growl.

Fuck me.

The deeper he went, the more insects he spotted on the walls. His light focused on roaches and spiders, who seemingly had been more aware of the impending flood than their human counterparts. They'd sought high ground before the waters reached the drains. He carried on against the black tide. Just as he was about to call out to Cash again, it came out of the water.

Canni.

Rob tightened for battle.

It was an older man, unfamiliar to Rob. Water poured off of him as he gasped for air. Then, just as Rob was deciding what to do with his phone, the man submerged again.

Okay, this is worse.

Preparing for an attack on his legs, Rob heard a splash behind him. The canni had resurfaced. This time, however, he held an obviously dead and partially eaten Spats in his arms. He went back to feeding, ignoring Rob, before the water took him away again.

"Cash!" he yelled once more.

The water rippled. Rob shone his light.

Rats. Maybe a dozen of them. Pretty good swimmers. They drifted past Rob, swimming with the flow. They had made the rational decision to head for the exit. Rob continued on in the opposite direction.

He could tell that the sun was breaking through the clouds because shards of light had begun to filter through to the tunnels, just a few rays here and there. He pushed forward, putting his phone away; the incoming light, though not much, was enough to guide him, and he wanted both hands free. He could feel himself stepping on *things*. His mind ran the gamut from hypodermic needles to dead rodents to severed body parts.

"Caroline! It's Rob! Are you here, baby?"

Nothing but echo and the thrash of rushing water. Rob felt it in his knees. He was winded. Every step was a mountain climb. He had to keep his eyes trained on the water before him lest something else surface and attack. He wouldn't allow himself the thought that Cash might have perished, either from the flood or at the hands of a canni. If he dwelled on that, his remaining strength could abandon him.

The slivers of light helped him along. They also illuminated the breathing thing behind him which lowered itself upside down, like a drenched bat. Rob never saw the canni with its feet wedged into an overhead grate. Never knew it was there—until it dropped to the water.

Rob heard the splash, got soaked by the wake, spun around, and saw nothing but the ripples.

Then he felt it at his legs.

He tried to kick free. No luck. He tossed his phone into the mouth of a dry overhead pipe, sucked in as much air as he could swallow, and went under.

The canni was trying to gnaw at Rob's legs, right through his pants. Rob had his eyes open, but tunnel water had much less visibility than the average lake or swimming pool. Still, he'd rather have his attacker biting at a pant leg than his throat, so Rob pushed hard on the thin man's balding head, in an effort to keep it down.

The strength of the canni was apparent and Rob was growing weaker. He knew he couldn't fight for long. Its head was moving higher.

As the hungry assailant rose, mouth agape, Rob knew that he had filled his lungs with air before submerging, but the canni's lungs were likely filling with water with each attempted bite. Rob wrapped himself around the infected man's head, bringing it into his chest, and he went down on his back, betting that his strong young lungs would outlast his attacker's. He could feel the movements of the canni's mouth against his shirt but hadn't felt the sting of a bite. It seemed more intent on devouring Rob than in surfacing for air.

As the struggle continued, the thought crossed Rob's mind that the canni might outlast him. Maybe it could remain submerged longer than he, no matter the amount of water it took in. All at once, panic struck. Now Rob fought to emerge and suck for air but he couldn't break free.

If he knew that Cash had died in those tunnels, Rob might have just released his air and taken his chances at joining her in eternity, but there was some hope that she was alive and he couldn't abandon her this way.

As his air escaped, his thumbs searched for his attacker's eyes.

He found them and pushed. He didn't expect to go that deep, and it felt like jelly. Instinctively, he pulled them both out. One thumb had an easier time than the other.

Regardless, the canni let go and Rob blasted through the surface. He was dizzy and choking when the monster came out of the water. One eye socket was just a bubbling fountain of blood, but the other was worse: an eyeball swung from it like a hypnotist's pocket watch.

Face covered in blood, it opened its jaws wide. That's when Rob saw why he hadn't been bitten.

The fucker didn't have a tooth in his mouth.

It clattered about and stumbled away aimlessly. Rob sucked in some more air, took his phone from the pipe, and marched on to find his girl.

Outside, Don Russo, his people, and other tunnel-dwellers continued the battle to regain their strength and faculties. The sun was high and strong, but the water remained and they were all still in it, to varying degrees. At least the temporary lakes at street level were nearly still. It was through these waters that Paul Bhong arrived on his Harley.

Rob was nearly shot. He'd gained some momentum from his battle with the canni, but that temporary rush had vanished and his legs were like rubber. He carried on through the black tide, saving his phone battery and using the trickle of available light from above.

Just past a divider in the distance, something forced him to activate the flashlight app. It moved slowly but was steadily approaching.

"Cash?"

It was a faint hope but proved to be wishful thinking. This figure was larger, broader. Rob trained his light on it. Something seemed off. The bright beam seemed to pass right through it. Rob considered stopping, but every second mattered and this approaching being possibly stood between him and Cash.

After another moment of convergence, the light hit it just right. A chill wrapped around Rob as he saw the face, pale as fresh snow. It stepped closer. The spotlight hadn't shone through any solid matter. There was a hole.

Here came the bloodied frame of Polish Joe, without haste. Much of his chest was absent. Don Russo had blasted through it with his shotgun. Rob tensed, ready for more combat. He hastily shoved his phone into another pipe, knocking some cockroaches to the drink below. His cell quickly came riding back out on a rush of water and more roaches, splashing into the depths. Joe was ten feet from Rob.

Shitfuck.

Joe was upon him.

Then, he was behind him.

Polish Joe, bloodied, white, and missing his middle, walked on, never so much as glancing Rob's way.

There was no time to digest what he'd just seen, so Rob pressed on sans flashlight app.

"Cash?"

The echo had become familiar.

Up above, Russo and his tunnel neighbors had their situation officially confirmed as serious by something that had become almost as rare as Halley's Comet.

The police had arrived. Lots of them.

"There are people still in the tunnels." yelled Paul. "They're in there with Cannis."

The cops unloaded rafts from the back of a truck.

Rob's body ached. He wondered how much longer he could hold his own against the waist-deep current. He doubted he could survive another canni encounter. The tunnel seemed darker than ever. To his left was a large pipe opening that was different from all the others. He'd seen it before. The white paint gave it away.

It was home to the Witch of the Wash.

Rob assumed that, since the giant pipe was high in the wall, the witch may have decided to ride out the flood within. He considered that Cash may have also crawled in to escape the waters.

He peered in.

He already missed his flashlight.

"Cash?" he yelled, then, "Hello, ma'am? Are you in there? Have you seen anyone else?"

A ruffling sound was heard. The rushing water was loud, so he leaned his ear in closer to the pipe. The sound grew closer. There was some light filtering in from high, but it didn't reach within the pipe.

"Can you hear me?" he yelled.

She began to come into view. He first spotted a wrinkled hand, then the matted strings of gray hair.

"Ma'am . . . " he began.

Before he could continue, he saw the blood. Her face was down, dragging against the pipe's bottom. The blood was pouring from her neck. It covered her shoulders. Her limbs were limp, yet here she came, gliding toward him as if being pulled.

Or pushed.

Amid the ruffling in the pipe and the rushing of the water came the gurgled strain of heavy breaths. The witch slid closer. Soon her arms dangled from the edge of her circular steel lair. Rob could tell that her head was almost fully detached. Much of the flesh from her neck was gone.

She dropped out of the pipe, brushing against Rob's torso to the rambling tide below. He watched her wash away, but only for an instant. That's when another arm came out of the darkness of the pipe, blood up to the elbow.

"Cash?"

This time, he uttered her name as a whisper.

His love's face emerged from the blackness. She was alive.

Morosely, she was also a full-on canni.

The rafts full of cops had entered the tunnels.

Cash glared at Rob. She was still chewing and swallowing bits of the witch. Blood dripped from her chin, red as her eyes. He took three steps back.

"Hey . . . hey, baby. It's Rob. Let's be chill, okay?"

Her eyes remained fixed on him, but she seemed most intent on loading a last clump of skin and fat into the salivating froth of her gaping jaws. Rob hoped they could just wait out her episode without her attacking and then walk out together. The look in Cash's eyes hinted at other outcomes.

He heard shouts in the distance. "Metro Police! Is anyone here?"

Rob considered calling out to them, but he feared that should Cash pounce on him the cops might shoot her. Would they use a Taser? Some type of tranquilizer dart? He didn't know, and despite being in Vegas, it wasn't the type of gamble he wanted to take.

She finished her swallow and inched closer to the edge of the pipe. Her eyes focused solely on Rob, like a mountain lion ready to pounce.

He steadied himself. "Carrie," he said, "let's chill. Your boy would like to live a bit longer, if that's cool with you."

Her neck arched back. Head went high. She exposed her teeth.

"If we can hang on for just a bit," he said, "this will pass, and the cops will take us out. Then we can find a way back home."

She lifted her butt. Got on all fours. Her head came back down and one hand lifted, almost reaching out toward him.

"We can go back to Brooklyn," he said.

For an instant, he thought he might be getting through to her. His hope faded when her mouth snapped open like a leatherback sea turtle.

"Cash!" he barked more firmly. "We were going to . . . "

She rocked back with a deep growl. Rob knew that her next motion would be a forward spring and a powerful leap from the pipe.

"We were going to get married, baby . . . *supposubly*."

Her motion paused. The pinky on her left hand began to tap feverishly on the bottom of the pipe.

All the cops in the rafts wore full-face helmets. It wasn't for convenience. They paddled through the tunnels, slicing past the rats and the roaches with a large tactical lantern guiding their way. They had come upon a couple of *floaters*—police lingo for victims of watery deaths—but there had been no one for them to save.

Their light beam bounced up and down with the movements of their vessel. They had it trained ahead, but it would also hit the tunnel ceiling and the surface of the dirty water. Just past a divider, they spotted a figure. It seemed oddly configured, different than a human body.

"Get the light on that!" bellowed a sergeant.

At first, it looked like some kind of walking cross. Coming into closer view and being better lit, the image became clear.

It was Rob. He carried Cash in his arms, the way he'd always envisioned their honeymoon threshold. She was unconscious, arms dangling. He'd summoned some kind of strength that he'd only heard about in stories. He had become the mother who hoisted the car off of her pinned child.

"Make sure he's normal," offered one cop as they rowed closer.

"He's squared away," replied another. "You ever see a canni carrying someone to safety?"

Rob said nothing as the officers took Cash from his arms and placed her into a raft. He tried to climb in behind her but found a hand on his chest.

"Hang on, buddy," said the voice from beneath the facemask. "We need to get you into the other boat. Those officers will help you in."

He wanted to protest. Wanted to say that he needed to ride with his girl. Wanted to remove the cop's paw from his chest. There was no more energy within. Before he knew it he was in the second raft. Went face first. The feeling of being off his feet, of having his legs out of that fucking water, was euphoric. If he could only muster the strength to smile.

For most of the ride toward the exit his eyes were closed. He could hear the voices of the police and the rush of the water. The rocking of the small vessel was surprisingly soothing. As the smallest bit of strength returned to his body, he raised his head, looking for the other raft. Looking for Cash.

He found her boat just a few yards behind, being rowed their way. Relieved, he lowered himself again. It was as his head returned toward the bottom of the raft that he discovered something bobbing about in the water and bumping up against his ride.

Once outside, the police and EMT crews placed Cash onto a stretcher. She remained unconscious. They had a cart ready for Rob as well, but he decided to walk. Pale, scratched, and bruised, he spotted Don Russo, Paul, and John G among the crowd. Russo's shotgun was gone; ditched into the water when the police arrived. There were a lot of people milling about, all of them exhausted. Rob then realized exactly how many folks called those tunnels home.

CANNI

"Gums?" was the first thing he heard as he approached the group. It came from the mouth of an older woman. He ignored it and went to John.

"You okay, Johnny?" he asked, his knees wobbling.

"Yes. I'm fine. Is Caroline . . . ?"

"She'll be okay. As long as she wakes up as herself."

"Gums?"

Russo spoke. "You seen Spats in there?"

Rob nodded, then added, "I'm sorry."

"Shit," replied Russo.

"Gums?" asked the woman, again. Rob looked over at her. Her mouth was agape, and devoid of teeth.

Russo interjected, "They called her man 'Gums'. You can guess why. You see him in there?"

Rob felt dizzy. His heart was pounding. He knew he'd seen her man and had taken his eyes out. He wasn't sure how to reply.

"Maybe," he said. "There were some people roaming around. It was dark."

He saw her face change. It relaxed. She sensed hope.

Paul stood there, ignored by Rob. He watched as his shaken friend turned again to Don Russo.

"I found this, Russo," declared Rob. "It came back to you."

He reached out and revealed something small and wet in his upturned palm. It was Don Russo's Pimple Ball.

The naked man accepted it with a smirk. Then, with a splash, Rob collapsed to the muddy ground.

He sort of knew he was dreaming, but it was terrible all the same.

"Hey baby," said Cash to Paul. She cooed it again, more slowly. Her underwear was pink.

"Come on," was all that Paul replied. His underwear was gone.

"Baby . . . " she hushed one more time.

Rob opened an eye. The room was brightly lit and he was flat on his back.

"Baby," said Cash, "I'm here."

"Come on," said Paul from someplace beyond Rob's vision. "Come on, buddy. Wake up."

There was Cash at his bedside, a little sliced and diced, but she was herself, and not some crazed monster.

"Cash," was all he said. His throat felt like sand, and he was unsure if this might actually be the dream.

"It is me, Rob. I'm here. You saved my life."

He tried to process it all, but his brain was hazy. Cash continued. "You were dehydrated and exhausted, baby. You'll be fine, though."

His eyes moved to check if she was wearing nothing but pink underwear. Not the case, so that was good. She leaned in closer. "I have some great news. I haven't told anyone else yet."

He studied the scratches on her cheeks; lines dug by the nails of the witch. It gave him fuzzy thoughts of Tic Tac Toe. Her lips were against his ear, touching, as she whispered.

"I think I've found the cure."

He lost consciousness again.

CANNI

Virginia

The list had been hand-scrawled. The top right corner of the page sported a half-circle imprint of the damp bottom of a Diet Mountain Dew can.

We are trying everything but are under-staffed.
Some subjects have remained in altered state for much longer. Some may be permanent.
Some seem to have prior health conditions reversed. For lack of a better term: Cured.

Activity around the facility had been so busy and behavior so odd that V. Anderson had come to her own conclusion: the president was coming. She assumed she might have to meet with him face to face for a progress report. The opportunity didn't thrill her.

The rumble came quickly. V went to investigate. Doors opened. A herd of helmeted security entered. She thought she spotted a glimpse of President Collins within the wave of armed beef, but he was immediately ushered past that goddamned door to which she had no access. The slim frame, and stern face, of Dr. Papperello-Venito came at her quickly.

Here, thought V, *another brilliant medical mind—as is Dr. Martinez—that my brother fancied in a wholly non-medical manner.*

She still wore her smile of remembrance as the White House doctor extended a hand.

V spoke, "Nice to see you, Dr. Pepper . . . er Papper—"

"Papperello-Venito. It's not that difficult."

Fucking hyphens, thought V as she shook hands with her superior.

President Collins alone walked into the holding cell. The woman, all smooth skin and raven hair, was chained to a desk. Despite recent wear and tear, she appeared at least ten years younger than her forty-two years. There was the hint of an eyebrow raise and a slight dropping of her lower lip at the sight of the world's most powerful man.

"Eileen O'Dowd," said the president.

"*Doctor* Eileen O'Dowd," she replied, brow returning to place.

"Forgive the oversight," he answered. "I decided that if I came . . . "

"Where's the other black fuck? Your designated baby-killer?"

"Black fuck? I had you pegged for many things, but white supremacist wasn't one of them."

"Well, he is black, and he is a fuck of all fucks, so I'm actually just stating fact."

"He's a patriot."

"Patriotic baby-killer."

"Not to get off on the wrong foot, but 'baby-killer' is all over your resume, Dr. O'Dowd."

"Yours too."

"I came to see you personally. No threats of violence against you or your family. I just came to see if I can understand the motives of you and your colleagues and to see what we can do to put an end to all of this. I don't have the luxury of time, so there'll be no song and dance. We need a cure or an antidote. We need it yesterday. You've made your point, I would guess. The world has taken notice. Now, let's move forward from here. No one that you love or that I love has to die. No one needs to be interrogated. No need for me to call on that 'other black fuck'. Just you and this 'black fuck'. I came to you first because you were once an American, but I will offer the same to the two men we have in custody. There is no need for any of you to die, either after a trial or in the course of events."

"Mr. President, you're full of more shit than a Diaper Genie. You opened by saying there would be no threats of violence, and five sentences later you mentioned my death occurring 'in the course of events'. Try your luck with the others. I would be honored to die for our cause."

President Collins tried door number two. The North Korean scientist said nothing. No statements, no proclamations, no anti-American jabs, no "black fucks". Nothing.

In the third room, despite twelve minutes of questioning, the dark-skinned doctor had only one thing to say to the U.S. commander-in-chief.

"You die as canni, no?"

"I'd say 'yes' to jazz, but not fucking smooth jazz."

"We have to agree, and we have to agree right now."

The four helmeted Secret Service Agents were new to this type of arrangement.

"Anything except hair metal and boy bands."

"I don't care at all."

"Nothing after 1989."

They stood in a circle. President Collins was about to have a confidential meeting with a guy they only knew as a White House custodian. They'd ordinarily be ordered to wait outside the door. With the new risks involved, a system had been implemented whereby they could remain in a room, but they had to have loud music piped into their helmets so they would be unable to hear the conversation but could still act should anyone become a monster.

"I'm pulling rank. It's gonna be old school funk. After this, we'll set up a rotating schedule."

Collins stood there with his arms folded. "Gentlemen," he said, "I'd like to get started."

"Yes, sir," answered the team leader, fumbling with the headset controls. "We're ready."

CANNI

The agent lowered his face shield. Collins recognized the strains of the Gap Band's "Jam tha Motha", but it wasn't so loud as to be distracting. The president then took a seat next to Joe Isley. They stared at the three monitors, each framing one of the captured scientists.

"You are a good man, Mr. President," said Joe.

"You think? I mean, do you *really* believe that?"

"Yes, sir, I do. You didn't have to come down here. Didn't have to personally meet with these murderers. Your kind heart brought you here. Tried to spare them the horrors to come."

Collins had already noticed the piece of luggage on the floor beside Isley's leg.

"Well Joe, I know that we are different, but you are a good man as well. I don't believe that you enjoy what you do for your country, yet you do it without hesitation."

Isley exhaled. "Sir, it sometimes gives me pleasure."

"I'm betting it's not actual pleasure. Could be a form of satisfaction."

"Maybe, cockmouth. Sorry, sir."

"All good, Joe. What actually brings you pleasure?"

"Hmmm. Don't know. Used to be a good game of chess."

The security detail tapped their feet to the funk.

"Chess?" smiled the president. "I enjoy that. Not that I'm any good. Maybe one day we could have a match."

"I haven't played in years. Many years," answered Joe. His left foot touched the zippered bag beside him.

"So, let's do it. Once we get past all of this."

Joe Isley was honored at the invitation, but he didn't reply. He desperately wanted to open his bag and deploy its contents on the three who sat in the holding rooms. His armpits grew moist. The hushed and trebled beats of the security helmet funk sounded like a ticking clock.

"Why did you abandon chess, Joe?"

"Oh, I don't know, sir."

"Yes you do. You don't have to tell me, but if you let it out, you might just have the desire to play again."

Isley wondered which option might get him and his bag into those rooms sooner.

"Sir, promise me that you won't use any of what I tell you to find out who I really am."

"Joe, if I really wanted that, I probably could have done it already."

"In grade school, I was a chess champion. Best in the county. Got an enormous trophy."

"Okay," smiled Collins. "Perhaps we shouldn't play."

Isley was focused. Ignored the quip.

DANIEL O'CONNOR

"I practiced against my sister's boyfriend, Troy. He was older, a high school senior. Good player, but I was better."

The muffled music ticked along.

Isley continued. "Troy liked me. Was very impressed with my game. I worked lots of 'em; King's Indian, either attack or defense, Alekhine, you name it."

"I've no idea what any of that is."

Joe didn't pause. "One night, we played to a draw. One of Troy's better games. I said goodnight to him, my sister, and our parents, and went to bed. Had school early the next day."

Isley's leg was around his bag and drawing it closer.

He went on, "At 12:17 AM, Troy woke me up. He told me he was sorry. As I shook the cobwebs from my brain, he took me around the house, holding my hand. He led me to my parents' room and then to my sister's. Troy had murdered them all. Slit their throats. He and everything else was covered in blood. At first, I couldn't even stand. Went to my knees. I assumed that he'd kill me next, but he told me that I was meant to do great things in this world. Said something about me being the first black International Chess Master. He told me my future was bright, and he wished me luck. Like I said, at first I couldn't even stand, but pretty soon I could. After Troy gave me a hug, with that blood getting all on my clothes, he turned to walk out the front door. Well, Mr. President, I killed him then and there with that big, heavy chess trophy. Broke his head. Broke the trophy. Broke my hand, too. Don't know how many times I hit him. He sure couldn't be recognized. Looked like jelly and bread."

Collins sat silently. He gazed at the monitors, at the people who had attacked his country. The security officers tapped their feet ever so slightly to the music. Joe Isley wasn't completely done, though.

"Twat."

A nap had long been customary for V. Anderson after a long day's work; much more so in recent weeks. She awoke in the guest room of the home that belonged to her late brother. A phobia had developed soon after she blamed herself for his death, so she avoided her husband and children. She was intent on not killing any of them. Draped in the Pittsburgh Steelers jersey that her spouse had given her long ago, she sprang from the bed.

CANNI

Las Vegas

In the hospital lobby, Cash was on the phone with the Centers for Disease Control and Prevention.

"Well, I have waited on hold for more than an hour," she said. "Maybe that shows how serious I am."

"Miss," replied the CDC rep, "with all due respect, that just shows that you are determined. It has no bearing on the credibility of your information. However, please tell me all about your cure, and we will add it to the hundreds, maybe thousands, of others, and we will eventually get to it. That's the best I can do."

Cash bit her lip. "Okay, the cure is as follows; fill your mouth with water, place your thumbs in your ears, forefingers pressing your nostrils together, hold your breath, jump up and down and swallow the water."

"Great," sighed the rep. "That's your solution for the virus, then?"

"Virus? I was calling about hiccups."

She hung up with a customary "Asshole".

DANIEL O'CONNOR

Virginia

They were just pliers. The kind found at any Home Depot. Joe Isley held them up to the light for no reason other than to watch it reflect off the tool. Well, maybe to heighten the tension for the Middle Eastern terrorist, who sat naked and chained before him. Isley then sat on the floor, sans mat and placed his left hand on the man's cold foot, sans glove.

"Theoretically, I know I should probably have you strapped to a table with me hovering over you in the dominant position," said Isley. "But, I prefer this view. I can get right up close to the toe."

The room wasn't particularly large, but it was barren, so there was a touch of echo to Isley's words.

"You have nice, long toenails," he continued, "so I can probably get them off without hammering a skewer between nail and toe. That's a bit of good news for you, I suppose."

The chained man ground his teeth then spat at his captor.

Joe Isley placed his pliers down and got to his feet. He went over to his small piece of luggage and retrieved a rag. As he moved behind his prisoner and gagged him, he offered more words. "The thing about gags is they muffle screams. I was hoping for some nice, clear howling, so now we'll both have to work a little harder for that, okay? Don't disappoint me."

The scientist wiggled and grunted as Isley went on. "I will do you the courtesy of asking you one final time, and please take note: I will not do any moronic shit like asking you the same thing after each toe; I'm going to go through all ten pretty quickly. So," Isley cleared his throat, "are you prepared to tell us everything you know about the virus, its creation, and any possible cures?"

He retrieved the pliers, put his hands on his hips, and waited.

No response, so Isley grabbed his bag.

As he sat back down on the floor and clutched his captive's foot again, he had some final words, "Full disclosure: it's not going to be toenail, toenail, toenail—it's going to be toenail, toe, toenail, toe."

Joe Isley removed a large pair of clippers from his luggage.

75.

That was the number worn by "Mean" Joe Greene during a Pittsburgh Steelers' four-time Super Bowl championship dynasty in the late 1970s. A soft-spoken gentleman off the field, Greene would wreak havoc on the gridiron, tearing through anything in his path to attack whoever possessed the football.

V. Anderson's self-reinforced sleeping quarter featured mattresses up against the walls, three bolt locks on the door, and boarded-up windows. A telephone sat, hidden within a bolted closet.

She had flipped to canni three times, including the incident that caused the death of her brother, and she feared that she'd become a "perm", as some referred to infected victims who remained in their murderous state. Her family had strict orders that if they hadn't heard from her for forty-eight hours, they should send authorities to investigate this particular room. Her kin should not, under any circumstances, come to check on her themselves, and they should warn the responders that she was likely in the mind of killing anything in her path.

She bolted from her sleep in a manner so fierce that she would have swatted Joe Greene away like a pollinating honeybee.

DANIEL O'CONNOR

Las Vegas

Cash's phone was in Rob's hand. He sat in the hospital lobby, speaking with a White House operator.

"Yes, I probably sound insane, and I know you get a lot of these calls, but if you can put me through to someone with some authority—I am not asking to speak with President Collins—I can tell them what we know."

"Sir, just leave your name and number with me, along with your comment or suggestion and I will forward it to the proper agency. We do appreciate your taking the time to contact the White House."

"Comment or suggestion? Oh, never mind."

CANNI

Virginia

"That is one fine-looking toenail," smiled Joe Isley.

His captive's yells were muffled by the rag in his mouth, but his eyes screamed for him. Sweat synthesized with tears. Isley held the nail, clasped by his pliers, up to the light. Blood poured from the parent toe.

He peered into the eyes of the terrorist, said nothing, placed his pliers down, lifted his heavy pair of clippers, and lopped off the entire nail-less toe.

V. Anderson hurled herself against the bolted door. She clawed at the wood as she growled. If this canni version of herself had access to even ten percent of her normal brain capacity, she would be out of that room in seconds, free to hunt, kill, and eat whomever she desired. But she had learned that these creatures seemed to be almost totally about physical strength and the innate desire to hunt and survive. In her usual state, Dr. Anderson feared that these mutated beings might eventually gain more ability to reason and analyze, but at this moment, she was nothing but a raging bonehead.

She slammed her skull against the door.

DANIEL O'CONNOR

Las Vegas

Hospital lobby. Paul Bhong had reached the KTNV news desk.

"I will tell you," he said, "but we want it to go national."

"I can't promise you that," replied the young news intern. "I can tell my boss, and she can run with it if she chooses. We might mention it on the air—the local news—if it passes muster."

"This is crazy important. You do know that, right? We might have a freaking antidote for this whole mess, brother."

"I know you don't want to tell me, but I have to ask: is this the elderberry syrup and vodka thing?"

"What?"

"Lily of the Valley? Mistletoe?"

Click.

CANNI

Virginia

Isley had added a tourniquet by the ankle, but with three toes gone it was getting messy all the same. The fourth toenail refused to come off in one piece.

"Shit," sighed Joe. "Now I have to use the skewer and hammer on this one."

The scientist grunted. He shook his head violently. His face was soaked and pale. He hurriedly mumbled something through his gag. Seemed different than his prior verbalizations. With skewer in hand, Isley had a question. "You wanna tell me something?"

The man nodded frantically.

"Okay, then," huffed Isley as he got to his feet. He went around just behind the doctor and loosened his gag.

"Let's have it, then," demanded Joe.

"I . . . I . . . will tell your leader. I will tell the president, only."

Joe Isley returned the rag to his captive's mouth, sat down, and shoved the skewer beneath the man's half-toenail.

"Wasting my time. That ship sailed for you, homeboy. You tell me now. No one else will be here for you."

DANIEL O'CONNOR

Las Vegas

John G held Paul's phone in his hand.

"Yes," he said, "I would like you to connect me with Ms. Oprah Winfrey."

Click.

CANNI

Virginia

Isley's prisoner was howling again, eyes wider than ever.

"You ready now?"

He nodded feverishly. Isley pulled the gag out.

"Speak."

The sweat-soaked scientist gasped for air, then closed his eyes before he spoke. "I will tell you exactly what I wanted to tell your president."

"Let's hear it."

The man opened his dark eyes and stared directly into Isley's.

"You die as canni, no?"

After one final skull slam against the bolted door, V. Anderson collapsed to the floor.

DANIEL O'CONNOR

Las Vegas

Paul Bhong was on the phone with his mother.

"Trust me, mom, it's legit—at least it really seems to be. No one gives a fuck—sorry—no one wants to listen to any of us. No one. You're a respected doctor. Maybe they will pay attention to you . . . Yes, I understand that you're putting your reputation on the line, but if we are right, you'll have done something wonderful for humanity. Just think about it for a bit. Think medically. Maybe it will make sense to you. Please."

CANNI

Virginia

Joe Isley was sweating almost as much as his prisoner.

"Well, that's ten toes. Not sure if what you got now can still be called feet. Maybe hooves? Shit, what do I know? Anyhow, you're a tough prick. In some ways, I admire that. Not enough to give a *fingerfehler* fuck about you or to ease up in any way but still, nice job. So, my crew is gonna come in now, take you to medical so you don't die, let you mend for a bit, then we'll get back at it."

The scientist was barely conscious, but he mumbled something through his rag.

"I know," answered Isley. "You're probably thinking that I'm going to take your fingers next, but you've proven that you've got a decent tolerance for this sort of thing. I have other plans. Hang on. Sneak preview!"

Isley disappeared behind a door. The toeless man opened one eye. What he saw next was a bit blurry, but there was no mistaking it. Isley returned with a blindfolded teenage boy. The kid had headphones on, hands in his pockets. His captor guided him to the middle of the floor; actually had him standing in the blood, and upon the severed toes.

The bleeding man howled as he recognized his son. Isley marched right up to his delirious detainee and whispered into his ear.

"He's next."

V. Anderson had been unconscious for hours. The first things she noticed when she awoke on the bedroom floor were her nail gun of a headache and how her mouth tasted like a yeti's taint. She thanked the universe for permitting her to emerge from the cannibalistic state yet again and wondered how many times might be the charm before she would be doomed to remain trapped in that hell permanently.

Three sliding bolts later, she was at the bathroom mirror staring at the bruises on her forehead. After a colossal dose of Colgate and Listerine, she was in her late brother's sunny kitchen and de facto workspace. She schlepped past the array of laptops and notebooks, both hers and her sibling's, and advanced to the coffee maker.

With her caffeine brewing, she stared back at the laptops. Ambling across the tile, she tapped her brother's device and it lit right up. There had been something on her mind for days. R. Anderson had been an immensely popular figure on the internet, though never under his real name, and his online friends deserved to know that he was gone. If she didn't tell them, who would?

She knew he always forgot his passwords so he had them saved, and she could quickly access his favorite sites and chatrooms. As she began to inhale that calming scent of coffee, she came across some of his inbox messages:

Hit me up bro
New Harley documentary on Netflix
thx 4 the Sabbath cd!
I'm a horny coed hungry for cock
Okay, that one was spam.
Where u been, R?
RA—Sturgis maybe?
U work for govt right? I have cure 4 canni. No bullshit

V shook her head and went to grab a cup for her java. Midway to the cabinet, she stopped. There was her bruised face staring at her from the microwave glass. She, her brother, their entire team, and many others had toiled night and day for a mere seed that might lead to a cure for this monstrosity. Surely, some internet gearhead wasn't going to suddenly become Jonas Salk.

But, yet . . .

This guy—well he typed like a guy—knew that her brother worked for the government. R told that to almost nobody. Yeah, he probably told him he was a mechanic for the department of something-or-other, but still, there was some small level of trust involved.

V ran through what might have been her brother's responses to her indecisiveness.

Don't waste your time, sis. Think logically.
You think my friends are idiots? Contact him! What do we have to lose?
Click on that one from the horny coed.

CANNI

Las Vegas

Upon leaving the hospital they journeyed directly to the Fremont Street casinos. Those people back at the tunnels would need assistance and silver mining was one way to help. Rob and Cash took the east side of the Four Queens gambling hall and Paul and John G handled the west. Truth be told, John still couldn't see clearly enough to spot any credits left behind in a slot machine, not in these dimly lit casinos, but he tagged along with Paul just to supply company, and perhaps guard his six against any possible canni attacks.

Eight cents. Twenty cents. Eighty-three cents.

The tickets printed out rapidly—some were accompanied by tinny music or animated explosions of coins—no matter the meager total of the cash-out. Rob and Cash were shocked by the number of slot machines that contained money deemed worthless by gamblers. They strode through the aisles holding hands; one checking the slots to their left, the other to their right. They giggled almost uncontrollably.

As Cash tapped an illuminated square button for a two-cent ticket, she noticed that security had already spotted them. Her smile faded. Then the guard looked away. Maybe he had larger concerns in the current climate, or maybe he was sympathetic. As she pondered, a heavy Midwesterner emerged from a nebula of cigar smoke.

"Hey y'all," he smiled. "I been on a roll for twelve hours. Get yourselves some chow now."

He presented Cash with a pair of twenty-dollar bills and was gone before she could respond.

"Sweet!" said Rob, still chuckling.

Cash was staring at her reflection in one of the nickel machines. She held forty dollars in charity, and two dollars and nineteen cents in assorted cash-out vouchers. There was a time not long ago that she and Rob stood out among the tunnel people. They were cleaner, brighter, and perhaps more alive. Her casino reflection had her looking worn. The dirty screen added to a perception of grayness in her current appearance. She had always been in color. Now she was black and white.

Paul arrived at his apartment after dropping his friends back at the tunnels. He stank of smoke; cigarettes from the casinos, marijuana from the ride in his borrowed car. He'd wanted to help his underground friends reestablish life in the drainage caverns, but he had a more important task at the moment.

But first, a shower.

He scrubbed himself down, his mind drifting to the fact that Cash had showered in this very stall on that day when everything changed in their relationship. He wished to have all of those thoughts evaporate within the steam. He had work to do.

His hair wet like fresh black ink with a white towel around his waist, Paul sat at his laptop. One message immediately stuck out:

Important news RE: RA.

He opened the missive.

I am RA's sister. Call me VA. I regret to inform you that my brother has passed away. Paul read that line three times before he could proceed.

Please forward this information along to his other internet associates. I am sorry for the impersonal manner, but that is the essence of online groups anyway. I read your message about the virus and your claim of a cure. If this is some sick biker joke or something, please stop. If you truly believe on the soul of my brother, and your friend, that you have some pertinent information, then reply to this message with more details and some evidence. Do not make light of my brother's memory by jerking me off. Thank you.

He inhaled deeply, trying to gather his thoughts for a heartfelt reply, albeit one that didn't contain too much information. Rob and Cash had made it clear that since no one had given them the time of day with regard to their supposed antidote they now wanted to involve only serious people, and they wanted something in return. The sudden news that his cyberspace buddy, RA, was likely deceased kept pecking at his brain like a hungry raven. The fact that that brain was also floating in a marijuana haze didn't help at all. His typing commenced at the same time that his doorbell rang.

His friends wouldn't normally appear at his door without a warning text, especially at this late hour, and it certainly wasn't the mail carrier. He opened the door and his mouth fell open.

"Mom?"

He'd seen her not too long ago before the world flipped upside down, but here she looked smaller, frail. She immediately disappeared into his embrace.

"You called for a doctor?" she whispered.

She had barely left her home since the day when, in her cannibal state, she brutally killed her beau and his teenage daughter at a barbeque. Dr. Anita Chuang knew her son needed her help, and she would do what she could by driving to Vegas from her Lake Elsinore home. It would be done in memory of Edgar and Verde, her victims.

The next morning the tunnels were returning to norm. People scurried about with boxes and salvaged furniture. Their subterranean world was doubly damp and offered a thicker stench than before the flood.

"Dank and stank," was how Skunk described it upon his return from the hospital, obviously cured by the virus; with nary an after-effect from the chunk gnawed out of his lymphedema.

Rob awoke on a pile of blankets where his bed once stood to the sound of Cash rushing in with her phone in hand. John came behind her. Hoffman, another instant-recovery patient, was just behind them. Cash and John had been outside where the reception is better. Hoffman followed them as they reentered the tunnels.

"Someone is gonna see us, Rob!" she screamed.

"Huh? What?"

"A U.S. government official from Washington. We're going to meet with her in person!"

"Are we going to Washington D.C.?" asked John. "I want to see the White House."

"The Pentagon!" added Hoffman.

"Fuck that," said Rob, rubbing the sleep from his eyes. "*The Exorcist* steps."

"What?" asked John.

"I know you haven't been able to watch movies, bud. We're gonna change that. But there's a huge flight of steps in *The Exorcist* that are located like ten minutes from D.C., and I am fucking going."

"*Those* steps!" nodded John. "They're in the book, too. Both braille and audio."

"Guys, chill," interrupted Cash. "We're not going to Washington. She is coming out here.

We have to meet her at some location near Vegas. Paul has all the details."

"An actual bigtime official is traveling across the country because she talked to Paul Bhong?" asked Rob. "You sure he isn't just stoned?"

A naked Don Russo strolled in as Cash replied. "The government lady spoke with Paul's mom, who is a well-respected doctor, and she vouched for us without revealing our discovery. Two hours later, they called back—probably after researching her—and said okay."

"*Our* discovery sounds all sweet, Caroline." said Russo. "See what I did there—'*Sweet Caroline*'? But other than you three and the Asian kid, and now his mom, it seems, none of us—your friends who keep you all safe—know what the fuck you all are talking about when it comes to this so-called cure."

"We *can't* tell anyone else yet. If word gets out, we'll lose our leverage with the government. We do have a list of requests, and we will present them to the officials before we reveal our secret."

"Lookin' for that payday, girlfriend. I feel you," he answered.

"It's not about a payday. I want a flight home; a safe, private jet back to New York for Rob and me. We want John to get home, too. We also want help for everyone in your community down here."

"Government help? For us? We gettin' free cheese and shit?" he deadpanned before quoting James Brown, "*I don't want nobody to give me nothin', open up the door, I'll get it myself.*"

"It's not like that," she responded.

"How you all gettin' to that meet-up?" inquired Russo as he picked at his navel.

"Um, I'm guessing that Paul will probably drive us."

"Drive who? You three and Paul's mother?"

"That sounds about right."

"Okay," he said, glancing at whatever he'd removed from his bellybutton, "but you know there's broods out there. Fucking flocks of 'em. Perms. They're forming up in bunches. Killing in packs now. My thoughts are that you might need an escort. Some kind of backup in case you're attacked." He looked at Rob. "Am I making sense, bro?"

"But why would you want to do that?" asked Rob.

"Look, be straight with me, you two." said Russo. "You think you have some cure, but only you guys know about it, which means that maybe you all are protected but the rest of us are still sitting ducks . . . "

"Not the case at all," added Cash.

"Says you. The thing is, if the rest of us down here had anything at all to do with this cure—if it is a cure—we should be involved in this all the way through. We get you to that meeting safe, maybe they let us in, maybe not . . . "

"Not."

"Maybe. But right after you tell those Washington people. If they actually believe you, then tell us next. You tell all of my people who have kept you safe and fed you since you got down here. Spats died fighting for us; fighting for you. We want to know before Anderson Cooper and the fuckers at Fox News."

"I'll think about it, okay?" replied Cash.

Russo was back in his navel. "And we'll expect more than government cheese."

More than thirty hours later, night again fell on Las Vegas, and it was time to go. Just outside the tunnels, the motorcade prepared to roll.

This was no parade of government vehicles, but a collection of motorcycles and cars to take Rob, Cash, and the underground dwellers to the big meet. Paul stood beside his red Harley as Don Russo and Phaedra approached the black one that they would share.

"I want you to know, Paul," began Russo, "that because your mother is coming with us, I did seriously consider wearing some briefs or shorts or something out of respect. But then it dawned on me that she is a seasoned medical professional, so she won't be fazed by one naked man."

"Hmm," grunted Paul, eyeing the new black high tops on Russo's size 4E feet.

"Also, and I'm not cracking wise, but do you think that maybe, when we're all done saving the world, that if I supplied the glove she might give me a prostate exam?"

Paul put his helmet on and got on his bike.

Hoffman had a Harley as well. Rob sat behind the wheel of a six-year-old Ford Explorer with Cash by his side. John G occupied the back seat next to Dr. Anita Chuang. Behind them was a Chevy pickup driven by Quinn, a Gulf War veteran who'd been down on his luck and taken in by Russo the previous winter. Beside him sat Skunk; his healing lymphedema prohibiting him from riding a bike. Two old vans completed the caravan, packed with Russo's followers, supplies, and anything deemed too valuable to leave unguarded in the tunnels; prized possessions, items of daily functionality, and an enormous load of weed.

In the Explorer, noticing its popped ignition, Cash had a question.

"So, all of these vehicles are stolen?"

"Um, Paul owns his bike," answered Rob.

"What if we all get arrested?"

"How exciting!" blurted Dr. Chuang from the rear.

"Russo said all the cars and bikes will be returned when we get back," said Rob. "He explained that the true owners would want to do their part to help us, if only they knew the situation."

"Now I see how Russo brainwashes everyone around here," she answered.

"Cash, my car was stolen, my dad's tape collection was stolen, *we* stole a police handgun, *I* stole a fucking swimming pool service truck . . . "

She slid over and rested her head on his shoulder as she spoke. "And I stole Winthrop Robert's heart."

Her words had him unable to find his own. Dr. Chuang looked at John G and they both beamed. "Awww," sighed the doctor.

The trio of Harleys thundered as they led the procession like the tip of an arrow toward Interstate 15.

Heading north behind the lights of the Las Vegas Strip, they found the freeway to be nearly empty. There were some abandoned and totaled vehicles strewn about along with a few slow-moving taxis. There was almost no chance of any traffic enforcement as the police were overrun with more pressing matters. The further they motored from the strip, the darker it got.

"You've been very quiet," said Dr. Chuang, tapping John's wrist.

"Just a little nervous, I guess."

"Nervous about the ride? Or meeting Washington officials?"

"Well, some of that, I guess, but," he exhaled, "mainly I'm wondering that if our cure turns out to be legit, will *everything* change?"

He turned toward her and she looked directly into his eyes. It was clear that she knew immediately, but he said it anyway.

"Will I go back to being blind?"

Just after their second freeway and before the final road portion of their journey, the group pulled off for gas. Hoffman went around with some credit cards. Nobody asked where he'd acquired them, but they could usually be found in a wallet, right beside the driver's license that would provide the holder's home zip code and access to any gas pump.

There was just a single employee at the station and he was bolted within to prevent any canni entries or exits. There were no other patrons around to see the group drinking water and eating jerky; would have been hard to decipher through the clouds of marijuana smoke anyway. Puffing at gas pumps had fallen a notch on the day to day risk meter.

The group had not encountered any wild canni on their trip and certainly none of the fabled herds of perms. There did soon come some rustling in the brush just beyond the old gas station, though. But between the black of night and the haze of smoke it wasn't going to be easy to see.

"Who got the flashlights?" asked Russo.

Quinn and Skunk came by with a hefty Mag and handed it over. Russo clicked it on and pointed it at the brush, which swayed slightly in the light desert breeze. That's when they heard the steps; several of them. Grunts, too. Snorts.

The head of the first one came through first, chewing. Cattle. Half a dozen of them; sauntering sluggishly athwart the bramble. The first group in the bovine parade seemed not to notice or care that the trailing cow trembled as it marched, trying to shake the parasite that rode upon its back, gnawing at its bloody withers.

Cash had witnessed more than a lifetime of horrors in recent days, but the sight of the helpless cow falling over under the crunching chaw of something that resembled a raging scarecrow had her in tears.

"Does anyone have a gun?" she cried.

"We can't kill him, baby, he can flip back. He could be someone's father," said Rob.

"The poor cow," she sniffled, "I want to shoot the poor cow."

"We have no guns," said Russo, his ass gleaming in the Silverado's high beams. "Lost my boomstick in the flood."

The skinny, denim overall-clad farmer tore at the animal's flesh.

"Can we do anything?" she asked.

"Best we can do is get back on the road and maybe change the course of this plague. This here is just nature. Usually it's a wolf that would take down a cow like that . . . "

"We're all wolves now," interrupted Phaedra, drafting her smoke toward the moon.

"Let's get rolling before that hungry hayseed gets tired of Bessie and sets his sights on us," said Russo.

The final road, a thin stretch with one lane in each direction, was much darker than the major highways had been. It looked like it would wind for miles before vanishing into the distant mountains. The headlights of the row of vehicles looked almost like the scattered rays of sun that would filter down through the tunnels. The three bikes led the way with Paul at the tip of the arrow. From the back seat of the Explorer, beside John G, Dr. Chuang watched her son ride.

"You see, it's my Paul leading, not that Russo character."

John squinted. "Yes," he said, "though maybe Russo is staying back because Phaedra is on his bike. Could be looking out for her safety."

"He could always put the young lady on Paul's bike and take the lead position himself," she answered.

"Hmmm."

"Paul's always been a leader," she said. "Such a good kid. He didn't have the greatest family life, with his father and me. There was always drama."

Cash turned her head to listen. Rob's concentration was on the murky road ahead.

Anita Chuang continued. "He would withdraw into himself. Study computers. Read biker magazines. I knew he was hiding. Hiding from reality. I should have done more . . . "

"Your son is a good man," smiled Cash. "You did an awesome job with him."

Rob changed the subject. "No sign of any groups of perms," he said. "We may have caught a break there."

Cash had a question for Dr. Chuang. "Was Paul a good student?"

Before she could reply, Rob had a request. "Cash, can you read those texts with the instructions?"

"The ones Paul got from that government lady?" she asked, getting her phone out.

"Yes. The only instructions that I could possibly be talking about."

She ignored his attitude and found a text. "*Go to the new mini-mart, not the older inn. The town is basically mobile homes, the inn, and the mini-mart. The mart is the only new structure . . . *"

A late model white pickup pulled up alongside them with no lights, on the wrong side of the road. It paced them. Cash didn't notice it but the others did as she continued reading the text.

"*Go in the mart. No matter the hour, it will be open for you . . . *"

The pickup took off, blasting past the bikes ahead and into the night as Cash read on.

" *. . . Ask the counterman if he sells Buitoni Instant Pizza. After he answers, tell him your toaster is broken anyway . . . *"

The first road sign on the two-lane trail was just ahead.

" *. . . Then, purchase a Snickers bar with almonds. At that point, the counterman will give you further instructions.*"

DANIEL O'CONNOR

The beaming rays of the Explorer landed on the green rectangular route sign. It was covered in a variety of stickers, many old, some partially scraped off. Still, the white letters were plainly visible.

EXTRATERRESTRIAL HIGHWAY

The caravan pulled into the small parking lot. There was barely enough space for the vehicles to fit. The sign on the building was not a monument to creativity.

MINI-MART

Don Russo stormed over to the Explorer as Rob and the others were getting out.

"Why are we stopping here? We're almost there!"

"Did you ask Paul?" replied Rob.

"He told me to ask you."

"This is where we were instructed to stop."

"Oh, come on," huffed Russo. "You know, I know, and my dead Uncle Billy knows that we are right down the road from Area 51. That white pickup parked up ahead in the dark ain't no coincidence. You telling me this meet-up is gonna be at some fucked up 7-Eleven?"

"I just don't know, Mr. Russo."

"I thought we were all gonna go inside Area 51," he sighed, sounding more like a child than the leader of the tunnel-dwellers.

"I don't know that any of us were going to be in Area 51, but I do know that the specific instructions state that Cash and I are to go in this store along with John, Paul, and Dr. Chuang. That's it. They said if anyone else walks in with us, there is no meeting. So, you and the crew need to wait out here, or you can drive back home if you want, but we have to follow orders."

Russo scratched his shoulder. "I haven't followed orders since I was discharged from the Marines."

"Well, guess what? Like it or not, you are now serving your country again."

Rob tugged on the door. For an instant it appeared to be locked, but then came a *click*, and he pulled it open. As they stepped in, a bell chimed, as it might at any convenience store. The place was well-lit and smelled as clean as it looked. The man behind the counter appeared to pay them no mind, staring at his phone, seemingly in gamer mode. He was certainly under thirty, bearded, wearing a beanie and a black Misfits rock tee.

"Hello," smiled Cash.

He gave a slight wave, eyes never leaving his phone, fingers tapping away.

The group walked separately about the three short aisles of the modest emporium, glancing around, examining random goods on the shelves, not knowing what to expect. The young counterman never raised his head.

Cash whispered to Rob. "What are we waiting for? Let's just do it and see what happens."

They waved at the others and all five approached the head of the store. Rob tapped the wrappers of some Little Debbie snack cakes just beside the counter. The bearded fellow looked up from his phone. His dark eyes were trained on Rob. He appeared to be of Middle Eastern descent. He flashed a wide, friendly smile.

"What can I do for you?"

Rob cleared his throat "Uh, do you have Buitoni Instant Pizza?"

"Nah."

Initially baffled by the concise response, Rob continued, "Oh, because my toaster is broken anyway."

Rob cautiously placed a Snickers bar on the counter—with almonds. The clerk eyed the candy bar and put his phone down. Cash then dropped four more snacks on the counter.

"Can we just add these to it?" she smiled.

The store employee rang up the purchase.

"We *do* have to pay," whispered Cash to Rob, as if they'd discussed it earlier.

He put a few bucks on the counter and waited while the bearded man placed the items into a paper bag, neatly folding the top of it and handing it to Rob. Then, nothing for maybe five seconds, which felt like five hours.

"Have a nice night," the employee said. "Leave that way, please."

He was pointing at a small brown curtain that hung over a doorway to the rear of the store.

"Sweet," grinned Paul Bhong.

"Thank you," added Rob, brandishing the sack of candy. The small group shuffled toward the hanging drape. Rob led the way and pulled the curtain aside. They entered.

It was a storage room; nothing special. Stacked boxes, musty smell, dimly lit. Wrinkled poster of Kate Upton on the far wall. The five of them stood in a semicircle, not knowing what to do. Would they be followed through that curtain by Dr. Anderson and some government reps? Paul peered back through the curtain, into the store. The counter dude was still there; still playing with his phone.

Then they heard the noise. Kate Upton was moving. So was the entire wall that she adorned. The newly-exposed room was the antithesis of the storage area. It was bright and sterile. Cramped, though.

As they walked in, exiting the stuffy grayness of the back room, the group collectively realized that they were in an elevator. John G closed his eyes, shutting out the intense radiance. Rob searched for floor buttons. There were none. The lights above them hummed. The door slid closed behind them and entire lift shook. They were going down. Next, the lights went off.

Outside the mini-mart, there was quiet. Maybe too much of it. Don Russo stood beside his bike and stared in the direction of the white pickup that sat facing them, lights off, thirty yards up the road. He couldn't see it, but he knew it was there. He also knew that with Rob's group gone, he still had about fifteen of his crew with him but without a single firearm. Beyond the short reach of the mart's parking lot light, there was complete darkness. Yet, he could sense movement in the brush. Be it the desert breeze, coyotes, Area 51 security—commonly known as Cammo Dudes because of their desert camouflage attire—or something much worse, it gave him an idea.

"Maybe we should all get inside these vehicles and lock the doors."

After a brief flash of red, the normal lighting returned in the elevator. The movement stopped ten seconds later. The door glided open. Awaiting their arrival were two people in lab coats and two large helmeted guards. Just behind their greeters stretched a long tunnel. A two-car tram sat idling with a helmeted female driver at the wheel.

"I'm Dr. Anderson," she said with hand outstretched. "Thank you all for coming." She introduced the man beside her, adorned with small eyeglasses and a large pink polka dot bow tie, as Professor Daniele. One of the guards lifted his face visor. It squeaked like a rusty cemetery gate.

"I am Lawrence. My partner here is Maurice. The tram operator is Curly."

Dr. Anderson's eyebrows rose, apparently finding the security introductions a bit unnecessary.

"We are going to need your phones," said Lawrence, holding out a plastic bag. The group complied, with Rob stating, "John and I don't have phones."

"We know," answered the guard. "You were scanned in the elevator. We are only interested in recording devices or weapons. You're all good."

"Figures," sighed Paul, another viral video opportunity gone.

The guard squeaked his visor back down over his face.

V. Anderson had a question for the group. "Did you get the Snickers with almonds?"

Rob opened the paper bag and Cash reached inside, searching for the correct bar. She handed it over to a smiling V.

"Thank you," she said, dropping the candy into a lab coat pocket. "Let's hop into that oversized golf cart, shall we?"

Russo had his flashlight sticking out the window of the Explorer. He shone it into the brush, looking for anything that moved. Phaedra sat beside him with Hoffman in the back seat. He trained the light up ahead, on the pickup. It just sat there, engine running. There seemed to be two silhouettes in the cab. *Probably Cammo Dudes*, he figured as he shut his light.

"I wanna go in that store," he said. "I'm hungry. You guys want anything?"

"Nah," said Hoffman.

"I want to come with you," answered Phaedra. "I'm tired of just sitting here. It's eerie."

"Okay," he said. "Hoff, lock the doors when we get out."

The two of them exited the SUV and walked across the small lot toward the store.

There came three loud yelps, followed by a long, pained howl.

"What the fuck?" grumbled Russo.

"Coyote," smiled Phaedra. "Alerting the rest of its group to its location."

"Hmmm," he replied, as he tugged on the front door of the mart. It stuck at first but opened on the second attempt, after the *click*. They strode in and headed toward the refrigerated section across from the counter.

"No shoes, no shirt, no service," said the counterman, eyes on his phone.

Russo did an about-face and stalked toward the counter, with Phaedra behind.

"I got shoes on, partner; it's where I keep my money."

"You are otherwise naked," replied the shopkeeper, eyes now on the pair. "The lady may make a purchase. You need to wait outside."

"Technically," said Russo, then standing right at the counter, "if I was to put on a shirt, I could make a purchase."

"Your genitals are exposed."

"The sign mentions shirts and shoes, bucko. You sell any of them goofy alien shirts? I could put one on."

"We don't sell shirts. Or pants. Or alien anything. Now, if you don't leave, I'll be forced to phone the Lincoln County Sheriff's Department, and they absolutely hate to be called out here in the middle of the night."

"Let me buy the food," said Phaedra to Russo. "Go outside now."

"Our peeps came in here," said Russo to the counterman, "but they never came back out. Where'd they go?"

The shopkeeper dialed his phone.

"Okay, chill out now," said Russo. "I'm leaving. She's buying. One thing, though; every single place we passed in this town has some kind of Martian or E.T. stuck to the building. How come you got nothing?"

The tram ride through the tunnels was longer than they'd thought. They finally disembarked and proceeded to another elevator. Everyone got in, with the exception of Curly, the female driver. There were nine in all. Dr. Anderson, Professor Daniele, and the two guards stood facing their visitors as the lift ascended.

Awkward silence.

"The new world," said the professor, adjusting his bow tie. "Everyone faces each other in elevators."

The door opened. They stepped out to find themselves at another door; a heavy steel contraption. The professor took a card from his coat pocket and swiped it through a reader on the wall, twice. The door rumbled open. Before them was a maze of hallways, branching out in all directions. It was all stunningly bright, albeit with no sign of people. Daniele tapped a button to close the door behind them.

"Too sweet," gasped Paul Bhong. "Area 51."

"No, Homey," replied the professor.

"Homey?" laughed Paul, putting his fist out to the professor for a bump.

"I wasn't referring to you as a *homey*, sir. That is the name of this place; Homey Airport."

"Doesn't look much like an airport," replied Paul, putting his fist away.

V. Anderson winked at him, nodded, and silently mouthed the words *Area 51*.

The steel door thundered as it closed behind them. Then came the squeak of Lawrence's face shield. "Don't tweet about this when you get home. We'll be watching," he said through a grimace that he passed off as a smile.

Squeak. Visor down.

The hallways were basically frozen. Frigid air blasted down from the vents overhead. Cash shivered. The cold brightness reminded her of when her Uncle Reg took her to an Islanders/Rangers hockey game when she was a little girl. The PBA tickets had them sitting just off the ice. She was chilled that night too, but her uncle bought her an official jersey, and she wrapped herself in it while munching popcorn. The jersey got her feeling warm, her uncle had her feeling safe. She tried to channel all of that as they approached yet another door, with red lettering.

POST INCUBATION SPECIES IDENTIFICATION

Professor Daniele grabbed the handle, and stared into Paul Bhong's expanding eyes. He pulled it open.

It was a cafeteria.

"Never gets old!" laughed Daniele. "Wish I had a picture of your faces."

Phaedra walked toward the SUV, munching an apple. Russo got out of the vehicle and opened her door for her. She tossed a banana back to Hoffman.

"I should march back in there and beat that dickhead's ass," huffed Russo. "Like my money's no good for him."

"Come on now. He's cool. He was born in Santa Monica and listens to punk."

"He told you where he was born?"

"Yep. I asked. Doesn't hurt to be friendly."

Russo tore open a bag of corn chips, popped some into his mouth, and turned the flashlight back on. The pickup remained in the same spot up the road. He turned the light toward the roadside, hoping to see coyotes. Up the closest hill among the cactus and yucca trees moved something larger. Looked like a woman with long, stringy hair. She wore a dirty and torn pink housedress. There appeared to be no purpose in her walk. She'd amble slowly one way then just change direction, only to return to her original path a moment later. Russo's light beam was right on her, but she paid it no mind, as she continued up the hill in the darkness.

The cafeteria was large but empty. Two workers in kitchen garb, a man and woman, toiled behind the counter. There were several long tables, all empty save for one. As Professor Daniele led the group toward the chosen meeting spot, the singular person awaiting them arose from her hardback luncheon chair.

"Welcome. I am Dr. Papperello-Venito, from the White House."

They all shook hands and exchanged pleasantries, and, once seated, the White House doctor spoke again.

"Not to be curt, but time is, of course, a factor, so before you reveal your information to us, I understand you have certain requests—dependent, obviously, on the premise that your information is of value."

"Are we so insignificant that we must meet in the lunchroom?" asked Rob.

"Hey now," said V. Anderson, "you're in Area 51, aren't you?"

Squeak.

"Homey Airport," interrupted Lawrence the guard, as he lowered his faceguard with another creak.

"Rob," added Cash, "if we were unimportant, the boss lady from Pennsylvania Avenue would not have come all this way."

"Maybe," replied the doctor, "I just wanted to visit Vegas before we all go tits-up. Please just tell us what you want."

"There is something I want to say that is more important, just in case you think we are a bunch of idiots or scam artists," said Cash. "We have lost people. I shot and killed the closest friend I've ever had because she was in the grips of this disease and was in the process of slaughtering me. Dr. Chuang?"

"I became infected and ended the lives of my fiancée and his daughter."

John G added, "I was attacked by a stranger and had my life saved by other strangers, all while I was blind. Then, I was granted eyesight only to see the worst things I could imagine."

Rob cleared his throat. "I used to work with a guy called M.B. A master mechanic. Single father, a little older than me. He taught me a whole lot about engines, and even more about life. He opened up his own shop, in Pennsylvania, offered me a position, but I couldn't leave New York; certainly wouldn't leave Cash. M.B.'s daughter is an adorable little thing. She has challenges, bound to a wheelchair. She killed her father in their backyard."

The government employees turned toward Paul Bhong. "My mother spoke for me as well," he said. "I've had canni experiences, but nothing to compare with my mom or my friends. Maybe you experts should talk."

V. Anderson reached across the table and put her hand on Cash's. She then looked into the eyes of Dr. Chuang. "I have been in this seizure state more times than I'd like to remember. My brother, an American hero, died as a result of one. He died because of me."

She turned to her boss, Dr. Papperello-Venito. The supervisor responded, after a moment. "Well, we lost our vice president. He was a friend, but it is a loss for our entire country. We've lost Navy SEALs. I mourn the loss of Dr. Anderson's brother, who worked tirelessly for the cause."

"My man, RA," sighed Paul.

"As for familial losses," continued Dr. Papperello-Venito, "just a distant cousin. Hadn't seen him in decades. He was a public works employee up in Minnesota. Operated a snowplow."

They turned to Professor Daniele.

"Also a distant cousin," he said, leveling his pink bow tie, "FBI agent. Done in by a serial killer. Unrelated to all of this but painful and tragic nonetheless."

Russo downed the final corn chip, and let the empty bag fall to the floor of the SUV. Phaedra had nodded off beside him, as had Hoffman in the back seat. The slow-walking woman in the hills had long moved on. He reached again for the flashlight and trained it on the desert.

Nothing.

Then, he moved it toward the white pickup. It was still there as the light hit it, only now it was moving. Not driving, just moving. Rocking in place. It was too far away for Russo to hear any sound. The rocking—hell, it was almost bouncing—had him thinking that maybe the two security officers within were fucking. It had crossed his mind to explore Phaedra in the Explorer, but he didn't want Hoffman to be there for it.

His mind raced about sex a bit more, until he came to the conclusion that one of the pickup's occupants had flipped and was currently murdering the other. Seconds later, all movement ceased.

"So, you want a private plane ride back to New York," said Dr. Papperello-Venito, "get John back safely to Cali, find a secure, decent place to live for your tunnel friends. That's it, right?"

"I guess," answered Cash, "though Rob did have his car stolen . . . "

"And I have a brave friend who is searching for his sister," added John.

"Done, done, and done," replied the White House doctor. "If, and only if, your information is of any true value. We have all been through misery, and I have no doubt about your intentions. I respect that you brought a medical doctor with you and we are ready to hear you out. I must add, though, that your credibility has been diminished in my eyes, including your own, Dr. Chuang, because each and every one of you have responded to our invitation and entered our government facility stinking to the Milky Way and back of cannabis."

V. Anderson and Professor Daniele nodded in agreement. The three officials scanned the five visitors across the table as the two guards looked on. One by one, Cash, Rob, and their friends did proud the grins generated by both Cheshire Cat and the Joker of Gotham City.

V dropped her Snickers bar on the table.

"No fucking way," she mouthed, almond nougat on her teeth.

Squeak.

Dr. Papperello-Venito turned to snap at the intrusive guard with the noisy face shield.

There stood Lawrence, face contorted, eyes afire, dripping teeth bared.

"Run!" screamed the second officer, Maurice, as he charged at his infected partner. Chairs toppled over as everyone bolted in all directions. Rob had Cash by the hand, heading for the kitchen. The two workers had already vanished. Paul took his mother in a different direction, north, with Doctors Anderson and Papperello-Venito not far behind. John G found himself heading toward the east doors with Professor Daniele. The canni lifted his partner and tossed him over the abandoned table, watching the others scatter like roaches in a light beam. The hungry attacker growled, searing eyes darting from runner to runner.

The only one not fleeing was the fallen guard, just getting to his knees. The canni chose him and leaped over the table. Professor Daniele spotted this just as he and John reached the door. He paused. John grabbed him. "Professor, let's go. I'm sure help is on the way."

"I . . . I . . . " mumbled Daniele, aware that there was but a skeleton crew of security for this wing, at this hour. His body tensing, he grabbed John's hand, "*I hid in the clouded wrath of the crowd; when they said 'sit down', I stood up.* That's Bruce Springsteen."

"Cool, but Bruce also said *Born to Run.*"

Daniele shoved John out the door, saying "Get out while you're young."

Just before he ran toward the canni, Professor Daniele had one final decree, "*Growin' up.*"

John found himself alone in a hallway. He wasn't sure where his friends were, after the scattering. Blasted with icy air and intense light from above, he slinked along knowing that some doors could be opened freely, but important ones, like exits, required a pass key.

Where to hide in the kitchen? The first under-counter doors that Rob pulled open contained the two cooks, each doubled over and brandishing an enormous knife. He closed them and moved on with Cash's arm in his grasp. His plan was to find a place for his girl and then go out and find John. They spotted another sub-counter pair of doors and opened them; nothing within except some pots. Working quietly, the pair transferred all of the cooking gear to the floor, hoping that a canni wouldn't use deductive reasoning should it stumble across the lot, and thrashing noisily through the metal minefield could alert the hidden as to its location. Cash hunched in. Rob kissed her as he prepared to close the doors and hunt for John.

"Don't go," was all she said.

Rob knew exactly how tough his girl was; he'd seen it for years, but it had become more apparent in their current situation. Yet as she looked up at him from within the cabinet there was a pleading in her eyes. He truly loved John, but how could he leave Cash there, alone? He struggled to stuff his tall, broad-shouldered frame in beside her. His body was a pretzel, but he was going to ride this out beside her. He convinced himself that John was probably safe somewhere with the others. He rationalized that there was probably some room containing a half-dozen people ready to defend each other, so it wouldn't be prudent to leave Cash there on her own. He reached to pull the cabinet doors closed behind them.

"Wait," she whispered.

She popped out quickly and grabbed a large jug of cooking oil, bringing it with her as she ducked back in and closed the doors.

The stuffy, cramped janitorial closet housed five buckets, four mops, three brooms, and two Washington, D.C. doctors.

"We should be okay," whispered V. Anderson. "If he doesn't stumble across us for fifteen minutes or so, he'll likely revert back and pass out."

"If we don't succumb to these bleach vapors first," replied Dr. Papperello-Venito.

"Shouldn't a security team be here momentarily?"

"The professor said it was a skeleton crew, but one would think . . . "

"I hope those kids are all okay," answered V. "We signed up for this; they didn't."

"They're not actually kids. We have servicemen and women younger than they are."

"Yes, but *signed up* is again the key phrase."

Dr. Papperello-Venito produced a packet of tissues, handed one to her associate, and stuffed two rolled pieces into her nostrils. Muffled sounds could be heard outside in the distant halls. It was impossible to decipher them clearly.

Adjusting her impromptu nasal filters with her left hand, Dr. Papperello-Venito placed her right on V. Anderson's shoulder. "I want to tell you," she whispered, "that your brother was a good man. You already know that, but I haven't had the opportunity to offer you my thoughts."

"Thank you, doctor. I appreciate that."

"Might I add," she said, clearing her throat, "that he was not at all unattractive, in that veteran biker manner of appeal."

V smiled. "He said you harbored a criminally hot body under all of that business attire."

"Well," she replied, repositioning her tissues, "I'm pleased that my calisthenics have paid dividends."

Not evident in the dim closet was the rosy transformation of her cheeks.

"The snowplow operator. The one in Minnesota," she added. "He wasn't a cousin. He was my first love. His name was Bill Smith."

Cognac cherry was the color of the monster. It weighed nearly 400 pounds, and it took everything they had for Paul and his mother to push it across the office floor and wedge it against the door. They sat beside each other atop that executive desk, ready to hop off and push back should anything attempt to enter their temporary haven. The room was packed with leather furniture; the walls covered with framed certificates, paintings, and prints, all too difficult to discern with the lights off. Still, Dr. Anita Chuang recalled her own less ostentatious medical office. She missed it.

Paul's mind raced, wondering about the status of the others; mostly Rob and Cash. Mostly Cash.

"I should have been less *doctor* and more *mom*."

It seemed the words came from nowhere, but Anita had long stored them in her heart.

"What?"

"I will speak for your father, too," she added. "We wanted to give you the best life by working hard and providing, but . . . we lost sight of the big picture; both of us."

"Nah," he said, "I'm lucky to have you. Don't wither on me now. You is a hard ass thot."

"What does that mean?"

Paul laughed, "Just some uneducated banter. I'm teasing. If I heard anyone else call you that, I'd straight fuck them up."

Anita knew that when her son felt emotion he'd default to comedy. She'd reached him. Her head went to his shoulder.

John G found a room with an unlocked door. He entered quietly and kept the lights off; still his greatest equalizer. He crawled behind a long couch and came to rest face-down. There was Abraham Lincoln on the floor, staring at him. How much loose change might be behind every piece of furniture in the United States if we were to total it up? For John, there was merely a single, dusty penny, but it was on heads.

So that's what President Lincoln looked like.

John wanted to tell Abe that he feared for his friends, feared for Professor Daniele, feared that any cure for the canni epidemic would return him to a world of darkness. He genuinely appreciated his saved mental image of Scarlett Johansson. Which of her movies to watch first? Was she even still alive? Had she turned canni? Was she possibly a perm? Was the infected guard who ran loose among his friends also a perm? Would they all have to hide until help came?

Would help ever come? Would it be too late? His heart was racing beneath the sofa.

Then, he got an idea.

The way out, the *actual way out*, required a pass key, like the one Professor Daniele had. He was going to find him if he was still within and alive. Instantly, John and the penny were gone.

With Lincoln in pocket, John was out in the bright hallway again, trying to stay near the walls but heading back toward the cafeteria. He saw security cameras above, stern in his belief that if he'd stolen a paper clip, the infantry would come from all directions, yet the place was church mouse central.

Cash's hands were cold. Rob did his best to warm them, ignoring the cramping of his right leg. He felt like they were in a magician's trunk, awaiting the saw.

Cash whispered, "Remember when we pounded Teresa with the snowballs?"

He managed a chuckle. "In the alley, with her cousin Susan."

"Yeah."

She was smiling.

"I miss the alley," he said.

"People think you're nuts when you say your best memories are from a back alley in Brooklyn," she added. "They picture things from movies, not kids playing sports, listening to music, having fun, eating pizza, building friendships, breaking hearts."

He took his hand from hers and crumpled a fist. "Here's to the alley gang."

Her hands had warmed. She too, made a fist, and touched it to his.

"Alley gang," she whispered, "forever."

John entered the cafeteria. He found the scent of floor wax and disinfectant to be holding strong despite all of the blood. Tables and chairs were overturned and strewn everywhere. He attempted the impossible task of calling out in whisper.

"Professor Daniele?"

Cash found herself in a rainbow. When she and Teresa were barely teenagers, they and their friends would often head from their back alley to the bowling alley. It was called Rainbow Lanes. That was the time Rob came into their lives as well. She could still smell the rented shoes, hear the music, and taste the French fries. Her mind was filled with the clattering sound of the toppling pins when she noticed through the darkness of the tight cabinet the ashen incarnation of dread across Rob's face.

It wasn't clacking bowling pins; this sound came from the pots and pans on the floor outside their sanctuary. Something was moving.

CANNI

The next sound they heard was the pounding of their hearts.

The cabinet doors were pulled open. Rob was about to launch into battle when he saw one of the kitchen workers who had also been in hiding. The man was still clutching an enormous knife, but he managed a smile though his broken English.

"You come now. All quiet. Monster no here."

Rob and Cash exhaled together.

"Thank you," said Rob.

The kitchen worker continued. "We go to exit. If monster come back, we . . . "

With a swoosh, a crash, and a growl, he was gone. Lifted and carried away as if hit by a train. Pots scattered and his knife dropped to the floor. His scream faded into the distance with the pounding feet of the canni.

"Professor Daniele?" repeated John, a bit louder. He tried to sidestep the blood on the cafeteria floor. Treading over some fallen chairs, he spotted a pair of shoe-clad feet protruding from behind a toppled table. Approaching with caution, he next saw the suit-clad legs, followed by the bottom of the lab coat, and the shirt within. It was when he observed the pink polka dot bow tie that he knew he'd found his man.

But, north of the knotted neck accessory, remained nothing.

No head. Only a burgeoning basin of blood and a mangled pair of eyeglasses.

While cursing the worst aspects of eyesight, John forced himself to frisk the professor's body for his pass key. It fell out along with an almost-empty pack of orange Tic Tacs. Only one mint remained in the clear plastic case. John pondered that the professor never knew that he was carrying what amounted to an hourglass of his final days in his coat pocket. He suddenly felt compelled to consume that crowning mint, and he did.

Then he saw Maurice, the fallen guard. He was prone—either dead or unconscious—arms in a grotesque composition of fracture, yet there was no visible blood in his vicinity. Tucking the pass key into his pocket beside Lincoln, John approached Maurice. He felt for a pulse—four times, in four locations—and was finally satisfied that the carotid artery had some thump to it. Ear to nose, he heard the cadence of shallow breaths. He realized that Professor Daniele likely died so that Maurice, a man deemed lesser on the dubious totem pole of life, could live.

"Hang on, bro," he whispered, knowing that his words went unheard. "I'm going for help."

Rob and Cash had a dilemma: should they remain in the cupboard and close the door or take off in a direction opposite of the galloping canni? Cash was startled, and perhaps inching toward shock, at the sight of the white-aproned cook being torn away from their view, like a bunny in the talons of a hawk.

"It's okay, babe," was all Rob could muster.

She stared blankly at the strewn pots and pans—the bowling pins of her altered state fantasy—when the ersatz bowling ball slowly rolled into view, heretofore dropped by the canni.

The wide-eyed and jaggedly torn off head of Professor Daniele.

Deciding that the infected guard might still be in the immediate area, John moved in the opposite direction of the way they'd all entered the section. He moved north along the main hallway, searching for doorways equipped with a pass key scanner.

Rob had thoughts similar to his childhood friend.

"We should go further in, away from this area," he whispered to Cash. He gripped the large knife that had done the cook no good; she lugged the jug of cooking oil. They stepped back into the cafeteria and saw the fallen Maurice— still unconscious, but still breathing when Rob checked. They peered at the shoe-to-bow tie section of the professor. They noticed the empty Tic Tac case and they continued through, out the other side, and entered the long hallway, northbound.

Doctors Anderson and Papperello-Venito, having heard nothing for what they surmised was over twenty minutes, could no longer endure their insufferable bleach closet. They cracked the door to see Rob and Cash headed their way.

"Do you know a way out?" asked V.

"No," replied Rob. "Have you seen John?"

"We haven't."

"Paul and his mom?" asked Cash.

"No one," said Papperello-Venito.

The doctors joined the couple on their hallway expedition. V had her key ring balled up in her fist, with the two sharpest constituents protruding from either side of her middle finger. Papperello-Venito brandished something she had not clutched in decades: a mop handle.

John was further up the same hallway as the others, but they could not see him because he had veered just slightly left. He had come to two portals that required a pass key; the one directly in front struck him as just the passage to yet another long hall, but the one that branched to his left might be an exit. It had large letters on the door, for a start. He had no idea what they were, as his only form of reading had been braille.

Recalling the method the professor had used on the initial entry door, John took the plastic pass key from his pocket and swiped it twice. It rumbled open. He entered a surprisingly small, insignificant room, which immediately presented him with a second door, another card scanner, and more lettering, even grander in font than the previous.

He gave it the first swipe.

Behind him, the door that he had not chosen, that may have led to more hallway, opened. Rob, Cash, and the two doctors could see it as they approached. Their bodies stiffened, then quickly relaxed, as they beheld the vision of a half dozen armed and helmeted security officers.

As the rescue team entered, they were greeted with the sight of John, to their right, swiping the card at his door for the second, and final, time.

"Noooooo!" came the screams of the security detail.

Their semi-automatic handguns raised in unison, aimed squarely at John—or the opening door behind him. The lead officer charged at the *Close Door* button as John scurried aside.

Too late.

They came as a pack, charging like enraged bulls from a bucking chute. They trampled the guard before he could close the door and just as he and the first three Cannis perished in the bullet barrage from the rescue team. They rode out on a smell not unlike that of a flatulent hippo.

John G, hunched in a darkened corner, covered his ears, involuntarily recalled his youthful, sightless fear of older Brooklyn kids blasting off mats of firecrackers. As he gagged on the stench and stared at those block letters, indecipherable to him, on the door he'd just opened.

DANGER—PERM CONTAINMENT

From their vantage, Rob, Cash, and the doctors witnessed a wave of hungry, permanently altered Cannis—at least twenty of them—engulf, and commence to devour, the entire security team. Final shots were fired blindly, serving more as funereal salute than forceful solution.

Rob's group did an immediate about-face. He dropped his kitchen knife as he spun, reached to grab it, and sliced the tip of his forefinger. It bled but he felt nothing. He knew they needed to exit the area before the feeding perm herd spotted them.

All it takes is one.

A single perm happened to glance to his right after cracking several teeth trying to chew through a riot helmet. He stood, still cloaked in portions of the Men's Wearhouse suit he'd donned for his banking job on the morning he flipped, trained his red eyes on the four runners, and growled. Several of his covetous consorts raised their heads.

"They see us!" yelled Cash. "Faster!"

All members of the herd who were not getting their share of security meat stood. They came running.

"Fuck!" screamed Cash.

"That sounded like Caroline," said Paul to his mother. He hopped off the cognac desk that barricaded the door to the hallway. "Help me pull this. We have to see."

With the fleet pack of perms gaining on them, Cash unleashed her cooking oil. With the opened jug held behind her as she ran, she swung it side-to-side, like a wagging tail. Her canola carpet bomb slicked their wake as they spotted Paul's disconcerted face jutting from a doorway fifty feet to the fore.

"You gotta let us in, bro," yelled Rob.

"No shit. Come on," responded Paul.

Behind them, the Cannis went as airborne as the disease they carried. Their speed and impetus worked against them on the oil-soaked floor. Up, they went, then down, some sideways against the walls, like trying to run hurdles on a hockey rink. Upon landing, the oil would also cover their hands and knees, inhibiting efforts to regain their footing.

Paul opened the door as far as it would swing before it hit the edge of the bulky desk. The light from the hallway streamed in with his friends. Rob held the door as Cash, and the pair of government physicians, climbed over the cognac counter, then, he followed. Anita Chuang's eyes were drawn to the newly-illuminated office walls. There, in the au courant proportions of light, in the thick of a cognac frame, hung *Camille on Her Death Bed*.

Paul, Rob, and the others, pushed the desk until it closed and reinforced the door behind them. Dr. Chuang stood alone, brushed spellbound, as the Monet returned to darkness.

In the hall, most of the permanent cannibals had regained their balance. Their soles remained slimy, so they advanced more tentatively in their march. The remainder of the perm herd lingered back over the remains of the security team, feeding.

"Are you guys all okay? Rob, it looked like you were bleeding," said Paul.

"Yeah, it's nothing. Sliced my finger. You and mom doing all right?"

"All good," he looked over at his mother, standing in the darkness and staring at the far wall, arms at her side.

"Mom?"

No response. Paul turned to Rob. His heart revved like a Harley. The forced air from the vent above felt frosty on his skin. It was too dark for the others to detect how white he'd become.

Still clutching the knife in his bloodied hand, Paul called out a different name—loud enough to be heard, but hopefully not by anything outside the door.

"Dr. Chuang!"

She turned toward him, sniffling. "Sorry," was all she said, in a whisper. Paul went over and embraced her.

"I'm fine," she said. "I got a little overwhelmed; paranoid from the cannabis, maybe. I'm not accustomed to it."

The perms trudged just beyond the office door. In no hurry, they treaded cautiously upon their lubricous footing. They could be heard by the group hunkered behind the barricaded entry. The sound of stomping, sliding feet was almost tolerable, but if there was to be the slightest hint of a tap, brush, or God-forbid, pound, on that door, hearts would stop.

One after another, with fecal waste sliding down their legs, they toddled by, hunting for the warm, pulsing blood and raw, fibrous flesh that they lost out on in the security ambush.

Within the darkened office, the six internees were all pushing up against the desk lest anything try to crash through.

In muted timbre, Paul had a question for Rob. "Where is John?"

"Don't know."

"And the professor?"

Rob closed his eyes and shook his head.

"Aw man. There should be a rescue team soon, right?" asked Paul.

Rob leaned in closer. "They just ate the rescue team."

"As long as these things don't know we are in here, we'll be okay," whispered Cash. "Sooner or later, even if it takes hours, someone will come for us. It's a government facility."

"But what about John?" asked Rob.

"I don't know," she replied. "If we open this door now, we all die. That wouldn't be much help for John. If we give them all time to pass, when we are reasonably certain they are gone—if that ever happens—then we can go find John."

"Do we even know that your friend is alive?" inquired Dr. Papperello-Venito.

"We don't," said Cash.

"I see."

The doctor's message was clear to all.

The perms continued to pass. It took several minutes, with them negotiating the oily footing, but the initial herd was moving further away from the office door. Problem was, the second group had just finished devouring the rescue team and had begun to move down the hallway. Some struggled as they came upon the spilled cooking oil, but they managed it well. They were covered in the lukewarm blood of their victims, yet their hunger remained. Soon, the second group reached the office door, but like the coterie ahead of them, they ambled past it, unaware of the potential feast within.

The slowest of them all was a heavyset fellow in a torn, soaked, and filthy

Vegas Golden Knights jersey. Never gifted with a flair for balance, he went down face-first, shattering an eye socket. It didn't faze him. Something else had garnered his attention.

A drop of blood on the floor. His thick tongue emerged, like a famished leech, to taste it. Then he saw another and another, leading like breadcrumbs to the office door. On that door was a partial handprint; more blood. Rob's blood. The thing crawled over and began to rise. It steadied itself by placing a hand against the office door. The touch barely rattled that fortified barrier, but inside it sounded like the end of the world.

"Oh, no," whispered Cash.

"They might move on," answered Rob.

"Maybe one just brushed against the door," added V. Anderson.

The rattling stopped. Dr. Chuang opened one of the desk drawers. She armed herself with a steel letter-opener. It was dull at the edges but came to a decent point. The only sounds in the room were her stealthy closing of the drawer, and the rushing respirations of the six office occupants. As they leaned against the desk, Paul put an arm around his mother. Rob's head rested on Cash's. He could feel her trembling. He tried to take solace in the quiet; hoping the immediate threat had subsided. As his own heart pounded, he sensed the increased pulsation in his bleeding finger.

My bleeding finger.

The thought engulfed him so rapidly that he was convinced he could hear his blood droplets crashing to the floor. He understood that if he was bleeding on *this* floor, he had also certainly bled on *that* floor.

"Oh . . . my . . . G . . . "

The door thundered!

Some of the captives shrieked. Then came the relentless pounding and the growls. In the hallway, the parading perm closest to the one at the door stopped and turned, as did the next and the next.

The entire brood took notice and headed toward the office door. The initial horde, the ones who'd missed out on the security feeding and who were now stationed much further down the hall, also reversed course. They too advanced toward the alluring hinged entry, constructed from oak, adorned with a fresh crimson handprint.

"Oh, no," was all that Rob could muster as reality dawned. He knew that the six of them, and one heavy desk, would not be able to hold off even two or three perms, much less a horde. His body shivered as the door shuddered. His mind raced at the thought of no future with Cash. Her death had always seemed so abstract, especially at this young age. And to die like this?

The door cracked. Screams from within the office.

This just fed into the frenzy of the perms. The door crack quickly became a hole as a bloody fist crashed through it. Rob slammed his knife into the invading hand, more than once. It did not withdraw. Blood from the canni poured down onto the desk as more punches battered the door. Cash realized that since they'd entered the facility, there was one thing that none of them had seen.

A fucking window.

She turned her head, trying to scan the office walls in the darkness. A second fist crashed through the door. She ran from the desk and hit the light switch. It was temporarily blinding, but the dark no longer provided any shelter, so what was the point? The walls and everything else were flooded with light. She patted it all, in some faint hope that a window might appear. Framed certificates tumbled to the floor as did *Camille on Her Death Bed*. The Monet print landed on its side, against the wall, rendering Camille horizontal. Cash found a flimsy door and opened it to see a tiny closet. She closed it. As the entry door began to buckle, Cash was forced to confront reality; there were no windows anywhere.

She rushed back, tears falling, to resume her position pushing against the desk.

Sweat coating his face in the fluorescent light, Rob looked into her eyes. "Sweetheart, I'm going to need you to go over and get into that closet."

"No."

"You have to. Take as many of the others who will fit. I'll fight these fuckers for as long as I can. Maybe they'll be satisfied with me and won't even notice that closet door."

"I'll stay with you," said Paul. "Mom, you and the other doctors go with Caroline. Go to the closet."

The growling head of the Golden Knights perm came forcefully through the large hole in the door. Dr. Chuang hopped on the desk and slammed her letter opener into its shattered eye socket. She shoved it through to the brain then yanked it back out. The perm fell out of view.

"I'm not abandoning my son," she said.

Another canni immediately replaced the fallen one, ripping a large piece of the door away. Several distorted faces, and more bloody hands, came through. Paul took the pointed tool from his mother and flailed away, as did Rob with his kitchen knife.

"We don't have much time!" yelled Rob. "Get yourselves in that fucking closet!"

None of them moved.

"Cash," he said, still swinging his knife, "don't do it for me, or for yourself; get in that closet for your Uncle Reg, for Laura and Jen, for your family, please."

"I . . . I . . . I don't . . . "

"There is a vent in the ceiling," he said. "Paul and I would never fit through it. All of you women just might. Get a chair, stand on it, use a coin or something to unscrew the plate, try to rip it off, anything. It might collapse if you all get in it, but maybe it won't, and you can crawl to another part of the building."

Dr. Papperello-Venito dropped her mop handle, grabbed a chair and hopped on it, fumbling through her lab coat pocket for a coin. The entry door was falling apart, the cognac desk being shoved further into the room. Cash ran, not to the closet or the chair, but toward the back wall, black Sharpie marker from the desk in hand. She touched the felt tip to the area from which the painting had fallen.

Rob, with a clattering canni hanging onto his left arm as he stabbed its head with his right, had a final declaration.

"Have a beautiful life, Cash. I love you."

Dr. Papperello-Venito was having no luck using a dime as a screwdriver.

"Shit," she cried as she tried to pull the plate cover off the ceiling vent. Her fingers bled as she tried to wedge them under the edges.

The first perm was fully within the office. Rob and Paul shanked it in tandem as the second climbed in. Dr. Chuang picked up the fallen mop handle and thrust it like a spear at the invaders. Figuring that light gave them no advantage, V. Anderson went to the wall switch and slammed them off. She still gripped her jagged keys between her fingers like a poor man's Wolverine, pondering whether to use them to fight or to sever her own jugular. She thought that if she was to never see her husband and children again, maybe, despite her scientific mind, she might soon be reunited somewhere, somehow, with the brother she'd just buried. Her boss now hung from the overhead vent plate, which remained securely attached. The last thing V saw before the room went dark was Cash's unfinished Sharpie graffiti.

cure 4 canni is

The third and fourth perms blasted in. Twenty more battled to be next. Just as darkness seized the office, save for a scintillating stream from the shattered, canni-filled door, Dr.Papperello-Venito was blasted from her vent-hang. She fell to the floor, driven down by a choking nebula of murky smog pouring from the overhead duct system from which she'd just disengaged.

A grand bonfire of skunks.

It filled the room in seconds. Smoke was prominent in the hallway as well. This was a monumental and dedicated onslaught of prime marijuana, far beyond anything ever witnessed by Cheech or Chong. The sudden absence of light combined with the eruption of burning cannabis inflicted a level of disorientation on the perms and humans alike. Some hit the floor, others walked into walls. But two . . . two kept stabbing.

Nostrils smoldered. It was like inhaling thorny chunks of pungent, baked earth. Visibility quickly approached zero within the office. The dominant sound was that of dry, barking coughs. The six humans knew to get as close to the floor as possible for the freshest air; the perms did not.

Cash had already dropped the Sharpie. She clearly heard the hacking of coughs and knives. A strange calm overtook her despite the deadly anarchic state of affairs. She felt anesthetized and prepared to succumb. Her hope was that if the perms got her now, she'd welcome death from a benumbed cloud of unconsciousness.

Heaven was cold, wet, and shrill with maddening cacophony.

That was the initial estimation as surmised when Cash opened her eyes. She shivered under the pelting rain. Lights flashed then died, only to resurrect. Some type of torturous dog whistle gnawed at her ears. She could focus neither her vision nor her tools of reason.

Next, she turned her head. The strobe effect teased her as it would light her locale for just seconds at a time. She fought to get to her knees, head whirling, thoughts scattered.

Bodies were everywhere, many covered in blood, now diluted, and covering the soaked floor in a pinkish glaze.

Fire sprinklers.

Now she was gaining some clarity. The overhead smoke detectors had kicked in. The flashing lights were part of the deal as was that fucking pig squeal of an alarm. She knew that Rob and her friends were within that grotesque paperchain of humanity, but was he, or any of them, alive?

The smoke remained in the air but had ceased its invasion. Still unable to stand, Cash took to crawling. Watery blood stuck to her hands and knees. With each lifeless figure she encountered, the initial goal was to discern them as friend or foe, then determine, in the former case, if they were alive, and in the latter, to hope to God not.

This was more difficult in practice because Cash was stoned out of her ass. *Don't wake a fucking Canni.*

It was her way of focusing. She sloshed through the water and smoke, gingerly trying to avoid any meaningful contact with a body until she could see it clearly. The first three were all perms; one obviously dead with the letter opener deep into its throat. Cash came upon Dr. Papperello-Venito, supine, sprinkler rain falling into her open mouth. Leaning in, she listened for breaths, but the shrieking alarm made it impossible. Cash steadied herself, tilted her head, and watched to see the doctor's chest rise with each inhalation. What she didn't notice was the canni rising to its feet behind her.

She crawled on, looking for Rob. She found his kitchen knife stuck deep into the ear of a big rancher type who sported a horseshoe print shirt and a colossal belt buckle. As she crept along, the scent of the cannabis began to lessen, replaced by the potent stench of human waste that came packaged with every perm.

There was Rob, face down, the emergency lights flashing on his left cheek. He looked pale and there was definitely blood seeping from his nose. She scurried over a couple of perms to get to him, abandoning all reason. The figure that stood unseen behind her took a first step. It was a female, probably late twenties;

her top half was adorned only by a bra, with a black pleated shirt below. Shit slithered down her legs.

Cash reached her fallen boyfriend.

"Rob!" she clamored into his ear, trying to rise above the alarm but not wake the deadened. Getting no response, she grabbed his head. There was a wound on his chin. Looked like a bite. She'd seen those before.

"Wake up!" she exclaimed, tapping his cheek.

The bra-clad woman behind her took another wobbly step.

Rob's eyelid lifted just a bit.

"Cash?"

"Yes, it's me. Be quiet. There are Cannis all around, passed out. You okay, babe?"

"Uh, what?"

"Are you okay? Are you hurt?"

"My face hurts. My hands, too. Also, I might be completely fucking fried."

She smiled, "Me too."

Rob's eyelid lifted the rest of the way. His iris slid over, changing focal power to absorb the image behind his girl. The wobbly woman encroached, eyes wide. He tried to get to his feet.

Beating him to it was Dr. Papperello-Venito, who had apparently become reacquainted with that mop handle. She rose as tottering as the others but with the mental clarity to bombard the shirtless female across the back and head with that wooden stick. Blow after blow walloped, pummeling her to the floor. The doctor's tattered blouse would rise each time she hoisted the weapon, revealing a Minnesota Vikings tattoo just above her right hip. The mop handle finally snapped in two, and the White House doctor continued pounding with the shortened piece that remained in her grip. The battered woman staggered to her feet and ambled out through the hallway passage where the office door once stood.

Papperello-Venito held the base of the mop handle high and, as water drenched her from above, unleashed a deafening wail that vanquished even the din of the fire alarm.

Rob was on his feet when he looked at his left hand. His pinky and ring finger were gone, blood pouring from the stumps. Unaware, Cash moved to comfort Dr. Papperello-Venito and take the jagged handle from her possession.

"It's okay, doctor," she said.

"Time is racing," was her reply, mascara dripping from her eyes.

"You're having a bad trip, doc. You did good. We're all pretty high. We're gonna try to get out of here, okay?"

"Time is fast . . . but the clock is slow."

Others were stirring now, friends and foes alike. Dr. Anderson sat up as did the stranger beside her. Rob, holding his hand up to have gravity slow the bleeding, noticed that Paul was almost on top of his mother. He'd probably passed out while fighting for her life. There was a sizable gash across her forehead. Paul grunted as he came to. He had several long scratches down his face.

"This blows," was all he could muster.

"We'll need to wrap that hand, Rob," said Cash, trying desperately to appear calm as she noticed it. "Let's see if those fingers are on the floor anywhere."

"Nah," replied Rob. "If they're floating around in this blood and canni shit, I don't want 'em."

Dr. Anderson sat staring at the strange young man beside her. He gazed back, directly into her eyes. Minutes before, he'd wanted nothing more than to devour her; now, he quietly rose to his feet and walked out through the shattered door.

Dr. Anita Chuang moved. Her eyelids lifted.

"Mom, you okay?" smiled Paul as he studied the injury to her forehead.

The doctor stood up, much sooner than anyone anticipated. She wobbled and reached for her head, feeling the pain.

"Mom!" said Paul.

She ignored him and moved purposefully toward the back wall, stepping over bodies along the way. Her son stood and trudged toward her. Before he could reach his mother, she had summoned the strength to lift *Camille on Her Death Bed* and place it back on the wall where it had hung for years, now cloaking Cash's epitaphic inscription of *cure 4 canni is*.

The six of them emerged in the hallway, some bloodied, some limping, all drugged. Heads were a bit clearer but visibility was not. Smoke hung in the air, denser toward the top half of the corridor. They brought with them the knife, letter opener, and broken mop handle. Rob's hand and Dr. Chuang's head had been crudely bandaged in some rags found in the office closet.

The goal was to find John G and then an exit. Their steps were measured, using each other for support, wondering how they might possibly survive another battle should there be one.

Cash was the first to detect the group coming toward them in the distance. With the spread of smoke, she could only see their legs and feet, but even those were unclear.

"Ahead," she whispered. The others began to notice. V pushed those Wolverine keys back through her grazed knuckles. Rob wiped his bloodied, bitten chin and extended the arm of his three-fingered hand to move Cash behind him.

Moving closer, it looked to be four of them approaching through the mist of marijuana. The first three wore black military grade full face gas masks. The fourth, lagging slightly behind, had no mask, in fact, he wore nothing but shoes.

Don Russo grinned like he actually enjoyed this shit. The first to remove his mask was John G.

"How 'bout we all get the fuck out of here," he said.

Some members of the group almost collapsed with relief.

"Johnny!" smiled Rob.

The two remaining guerillas in this ad hoc rescue team, both packing semi-automatic handguns were Curly, the female tram operator, and the young, bearded fellow who normally manned the convenience store cash register.

"Dude," smiled Paul, at the sight of the counterman.

Using his best hero voice, the store clerk responded. "They call me Huballa."

Grinning through his pain, Paul asked, "Who exactly are *they*, bro?"

"Oh, you know, people in general. Co-workers, gamers."

"You all did this—the smoking vents?" asked V.

"You a government lady?" inquired Russo.

"I am."

"Your president owes me a fuck load of country club Mary Jane."

The whole group was back up in the convenience store, ravenously tearing at candy bars and potato chips. Rob turned to Huballa, who still brandished the handgun.

"You have to remember," said Rob, Lays crumbs falling from his lips, "there are two of your guards still down there; one with broken arms. Also, there might be a kitchen worker . . . "

" . . . and some of those perms might be human again," added Cash, with Hershey's chocolate stuck to her teeth.

"We'll have a team arriving shortly," offered Curly, hand on her holstered firearm. "We'll get them."

Huballa added, "We are going to get you all medical attention, and we will then transport our Washington doctors to McCarran Airport, and all of you to wherever you choose."

"Don't you have more security in other parts of the complex that could've come in sooner to help us?" asked Rob.

"I can't comment," replied Curly.

Don Russo leaned in to Rob, pointing the remaining half of his Twinkie. "Makes you wonder, don't it? If they couldn't send more help for a perm outbreak in your part of the complex, how fucked up must be whatever they are guarding in the other areas?"

Silence.

"Hmm," sighed Russo. "Well, brother," he said to Huballa, "how's about unlocking that door so I get outside to my girl and our peeps?"

"Done," was the reply, as the counterman walked toward the remote locking device near the cash register.

Rob wiped some caked blood from Cash's cheek. She, like the rest of the group, was an unabridged mess.

"There's gotta be a bathroom in back. Let's get you cleaned up. You must be freaking, baby."

"It's okay. I can wait. I'll wash when they're taking care of your hand."

He embraced her snugly, the throbbing of his wrapped finger stumps echoing his heartbeat as Russo's naked ass trudged out into the black night.

Within four seconds, Don was banging on the door. Huballa clicked him back in.

"They're all gone," said Russo, through a blank stare. "I don't see nobody. Phaedra, Hoffman, none of 'em."

"Are the cars still there?" asked Rob.

"Yeah."

"Okay, let's go check it out."

Rob looked to Huballa and Curly, as they were armed.

"We have to stay here," said Curly. "Our job is to protect people on the property. You are all welcome to remain."

Rob looked over at Paul and John. They got the message: they were going outside with him and Russo.

"You stay here with the doctors," said Rob to Cash.

"Screw that," she replied. "All for one."

Anita Chuang stood from her spot on the tiles. "I'm going out with my son."

Dr. Anderson, also plopped on the floor, leaned into Dr. Papperello-Venito, "That large naked fellow did participate in saving our lives."

"By roasting some pot?"

"Yeah. That roasted pot is the reason we aren't two piles of bones, doc."

"All right," groaned the White House M.D. as she wobbled to her feet.

"Doctors," said Huballa, "we are responsible for your safety. I need to ask you to stay inside. Well, actually just the two of you," he added, pointing at the government employees, and excluding Dr. Anita Chuang.

Anita smiled at her son and his friends. "Looks like we are the *real* Expendables!"

"We are all going out," said V to Huballa. "You and your guns should really come too."

"Not our decision," said Curly. "Rules and procedures."

The poor man's Expendables filed out the front door.

"We'll be right here," yelled Huballa, as he and Curly stood by the entrance, just behind the glass. "Come running if you have to."

The first thing Rob noticed was that the driver's side window of the Explorer—where Phaedra and Hoffman had been—was a shattered mess. The group approached it together. The night was so still that they could hear each other's respirations. The SUV was empty, but Russo spotted the flashlight on the ground beside it. He retrieved it and shone it toward the Cammo Dudes' white pickup, the one that had been bouncing fiercely not long before.

Both passenger side doors were open.

"Well, toss my fuckin' salad," sighed Russo.

"What is it?" asked Paul.

"I think one of them Cammo Dudes turned Canni Dude in that truck, unless they were just fucking. He might've come out. Not 'come out' as in 'gay', but in actually exiting the truck."

Paul and Rob exchanged a glance.

"Let's check the other vehicles," suggested Rob.

Russo directed the light at Quinn's pickup. Empty. They moved on to the first, and smaller, of the two vans. Rob went around, intending to open the rear doors.

"Hold on," said Russo, as he walked over and shone his light through the nearly black back windows. "Looks empty, but I can't say for sure."

"How about this?" offered Rob. He put his mouth by the window and asked loudly, "Is anyone inside this van?"

After no response, he pulled the doors open. Empty. All that remained was the larger and taller cutaway van, the style often used for ambulances. It had carried most of their supplies and all of their weed. It featured no windows in back. The entire group approached. V had those jagged keys back between her fingers. Rob and Russo put their ears to the doors but couldn't pick up a sound. Cash looked back at the convenience store, hoping for a glimpse of armed backup. She couldn't see the inside of the shop with any clarity but reassured herself that Curly and Huballa were standing there, and that they would disregard rules and procedures should they have to save lives.

"Is anyone in this van?" asked Russo with a tap on the door.

"Yes," came the reply.

"Who is this?" responded Russo.

"Quinn."

Rob and Russo pulled the doors open. The whole crew was shoehorned within, looking terrified. Quinn, Hoffman, Skunk, and Yurman were closest to the doors, all brandishing knives. Phaedra, and the rest, crouched behind that first line of defense.

"Careful," said Hoffman to Russo, "there's one out there. It came running from that pickup; smashed our SUV window. We barely got out. Lucky us, its arm got caught in the glass. Gave us enough time to rush over here."

Russo panned the flashlight around, scanning the brush for any movement. Rob pulled Cash to his side.

Dr. Papperello-Venito had a suggestion. "Let's get everyone out of the truck and get them inside that store as quickly and quietly as we can."

It was then that a cold drop landed on Russo's bare shoulder. He glanced over at it, before turning his eyes upward. A substance was passively trickling from the edge of the van's roof.

Russo, while pointing, whispered to the group within the truck. "Up there?"

"We *did* hear something earlier," answered Skunk, tightening the grip on his knife.

Don Russo stepped up onto the rear bumper, depressing the van even closer to the ground, his dangling testicles now more prominent for all to see. He placed his hands on the edge of the roof, avoiding the dripping puddle. Going to his tiptoes, he lifted his eyes just above the rim of the roof.

Cammo Dude was sprawled face-first and unconscious. Vomit oozed from his mouth, forming a gelatinizing river that flowed to the chunky puddle which then dribbled over the edge of the truck. A Common Nighthawk pecked at the more fibrous components. Russo stepped down.

Glaring into the van, he had to laugh. "Look at you bitches, all huddled in there because one fucking canni came at y'all. Look here at Rob, Caroline, Paul, the other guy, and their doctor squad."

The group within the van studied the filthy, bloodied, and bandaged contingent; Phaedra gazing into Rob's eyes.

Russo placed his hand onto Winthrop Robert's shoulder as he continued. "You folks have no idea what these badass muthas had to deal with in there. Perms, not just Cannis, and I couldn't count how many I seen. Some knocked out, some stone-cold deceased. All thanks to this dirty half-dozen."

"There are seven of us," said Cash.

"Well, then . . . *Magnificent*," replied Russo.

"And my name is John."

"Right."

Hoffman and the others began to disembark in awe of the tale told by their leader. Russo used the event as a tool to toughen and tighten his crew of tunnel-dwellers.

"These, er, *seven* are real life heroes, my peeps, and we, by extension, have played a role as well. Be proud of yourselves regardless of that chicken shit, hiding in the van sequence of events. Y'all did good. Any questions?"

After a moment, Dr. Papperello-Venito, still feeling the effects of the marijuana, raised a hand. "Sir," she asked of Don Russo, "why, in the name of Hippocrates, are you uncontestably naked?"

In the distance appeared the lights: police vehicles, heavy trucks of some sort, and a large white bus.

Kevin Edward wore a suit too pricey for the neighborhood. He still smelled of body wash and hair gel, and his eyes had that *I was rushed out of bed this morning* tightness all around them. But he shook everyone's hands and had a knack for speaking through an expanded grin.

They were all on the white bus.

"We will get your motorcycles, phones, and supplies back to you by tomorrow," he smiled. "We will turn a blind eye to the other vehicles and return them to their rightful owners. It is imperative that we get you all out of here together, on this bus. The doctors from our nation's capital will be escorted to

McCarran Airport, then the rest of you will be taken to the locations of your choice. We have some medical personnel and equipment in the bus rear until we get your injured members to a hospital. No healthcare costs will be incurred by any of you. You will be contacted in the coming days with further instructions."

"You suits owe me hella weed," yelled Russo from the third row of seats.

"Understood," replied Edward. "I thank you all for signing the nondisclosure agreements."

"I hand wrote about that chronic just above my signature," answered Russo. "Only reason I Hancocked that shit."

Kevin Edward nodded to the bus operator and turned to walk down the vehicle steps.

"Hey now," yelled Russo. Edward stopped. "We still have some loose fatties and we ain't stayin' on this ride until that bus driver, and your medical *whatevers* sittin' there in the back smoke 'em up. Better to have *cannabis* than a *Canni bus.*"

"Sir, I can't have our personnel . . . "

"Mr. Edward," interrupted Dr. Papperello-Venito, eyes closed in her seat, "they need to smoke 'em up. Mr. Russo is extraordinarily persuasive."

The sunrise formed a glow around the mountains as the last of the marijuana was smoked on the bus. Rob's hand was being treated in the rear by a freshly baked paramedic team.

"Caroline, what made you realize that cannabis might inhibit the infected state?" asked V. Anderson.

"These tunnel people, Don Russo's people, they smoke a ton of weed. That was the only real variable that I could see from others in those tunnels; others who had flipped. I knew it wasn't the physicality of the tunnels or the depth. Made no sense. Each day I watched the sunlight trickle down upon us. With the sun surely came the virus. Then there was Teresa . . . "

Her voice trailed off.

"Who is Teresa?" asked Dr. Papperello-Venito.

"My best friend. One night we all smoked; all but T. She then became one of those things and . . . well, there were other instances as well. I stopped smoking weed. Rob and the others kept on. Then I was the one who flipped. It seemed that there were lots of stories of cops flipping, train operators, pilots. Maybe people who were procedurally drug tested and couldn't smoke if they wanted to. Just seemed like a thing to me."

"You're a smart young lady," smiled V.

"But," interrupted her boss, "there will need to be sufficient testing . . . "

"Oh, come on," replied V. "You saw what happened in there, Dr. P."

"Dr. P?" replied the White House big shot.

"I am not going to say that forty-syllable hyphenated name with every sentence. Sorry. Plus those perms went down in a heap when the pot flowed in."

"So did we all. That could have just been smoke inhalation."

"Then, why the fuck were your lips all over that fatty ten minutes ago?"

"Better safe than canni."

"You know how cannabis can be effective against Epilepsy, Dravet Syndrome, muscle spasm . . . "

"Of course. If this is comparable, we will need to formulate an injection or an oral product . . . "

"Fuckin' brownies. Already invented," offered Russo, eyes closed.

Dr. Papperello-Venito continued. "We can't have four-year-olds going around smoking this shit."

John G laughed loudly, smiling at the attractive but older doctor. "You are so pretty," he said.

"Well, thank you, young man."

"For what it's worth, this dude just got sight like a few days ago," added Russo, eyes still closed. "He says that to every chick he sees. I once walked in on him petting a fucking sewer rat. He thought it was a cat."

DANIEL O'CONNOR

Virginia

Endgame. That was the title of the book; a strategy guide for advanced chess players. It was dog-eared and yellow, adorned with the brown stain of some coffee mug from years past. It sat on a small table right beside the office chair upon which, minutes before, sat Joe Isley.

Now though, he stood in an interrogation room. A single light hung from above, dangling in the thick heat. Eileen O'Dowd, the American traitor and brilliant scientist, was secured in a hard-backed chair. Her mouth was untethered and she was free to speak.

"When you left our country on your journey into evil, you abandoned your three children, am I correct?"

No reply.

"Well, you left them with your sister. I'll give you that. Wasn't like they lived on the streets or nothin'. No fucked up homeless shelter for them shiny white kids of yours, Dr. O'Dowd. Fluffy blonde hair and all."

The doctor remained still save for her eyes, which followed Isley at all times.

"So," he continued, "I got no idea how you actually feel about those kids. I mean, you are a mom, and there is supposed to be that special bond. Yet, you and your monkey-ass friends went and poisoned our country, including your own fucking kids. Now, what the hell is that? More ironic shit includes the fact that I could flip to canni right now and tear your ass up. Now, that wouldn't really help either of us, but hey, you infected me, and what will be, will be."

He walked over to a long window, clouded and dark, and gave it a firm knock. The lights behind the window came on. There stood, not bound in any way, three young adults: two male, one female. All blonde.

Eileen O'Dowd stared, her eyes no longer following Isley.

"Don't worry," said Isley. "They don't even know you are here. Grown up all nice and pretty, haven't they? Your sister did a wonderful job, Eileen O'Dowd. Oh, we gave them a huge, fancy breakfast. More styles of pancakes than motherfuckin' IHOP, swear to Jesus. Syrup straight from Vermont. I might let you see them and even talk. They can't hear you through that glass though, so don't bother yourself just yet."

She continued to peer at her grown sons and daughter, all late teens through early twenties. They seemed to share jokes with each other yet stood where they'd been told. They appeared relaxed. Dr. O'Dowd showed no emotion.

Isley went on. "Sometimes in games, like chess maybe, we are left with options, and at first they all seem shitty. We wonder how we painted ourselves into such a corner. Sometimes there is just no way out. Checkmate, and all that shit. But sometimes taking the least of the fucked up ways out is the way to go.

Get out of that mess and take up the fight a little down the road. Give up that bishop, you still have the other one, and maybe a queen too. Know what I'm saying?"

Nothing.

"Dr. Eileen O'Dowd, you know that Boy George's name is O'Dowd? Any relation? Never mind. So, you have three choices right now. Not tomorrow, not in ten minutes, only right now."

He walked to the far end of the long window. "*Do you really want to hurt me?*" he sang under his breath. O'Dowd's eyes did not follow.

"Choice number one," he said loudly, "you answer each and every question I have for as long as it takes and until I say it's over. I know that sounds just terrible to you, so don't answer until you hear the other choices, okay?"

A single bead of sweat appeared on her forehead.

"Choice number two: under your chair, right now, is the biggest, sharpest, and ugliest knife I ever did see. It's taped right under your ass, doctor, on the Jersey side of the seat. I will remove your restraints right now so you can get at it. You'll probably try to kill me with it, but please don't. You'll fail, and you might get injured in the mayhem. The true purpose of that ugly knife is that you will use it to murder one of your children. You can choose which one, and I will bring them in here so as you can finish them off."

The sweat beads were multiplying.

"Choice number three is my least favorite, if I may say so. It's also the default choice, should you ignore me. That would be where I bring all three of your children in one by one and I kill them all, right on your lap. After that, I start removing body parts from you, and I am a terrible surgeon. I'll give you a few seconds to make your decision. Not sure how many seconds, though."

Then he stood, arms to his side, looking through the glass at O'Dowd's children. Whatever they'd been told, they remained standing, though not at attention. They still conversed with each other while trying to look straight ahead. The young girl tended to her golden locks in what was to her an expansive but smudged and sullied mirror.

"The girl," Isley said quietly. "Dana is her name, right? She had the chocolate chip pancakes."

O'Dowd's eyes met Isley's for just an instant when he uttered her daughter's name.

"Okay, time's up," he said. "What have you decided?"

The doctor's lips parted, opened a bit wider, before closing again. She said nothing.

"You sure?"

Silence.

Isley marched over to O'Dowd, leaned over, reached down, and pulled. She heard the tape tearing away from the chair's underside. He came up holding the longest, blackest, double-serrated blade that she had ever seen. It wasn't new, either.

"This here has been inside more people than Wilt Chamberlain," he said. "I'm gonna bring Dana in first. Maybe you should talk to her about the pancakes or somethin'. It'll make it just a little easier for the girl."

He pulled the last strap of tape from the knife and let it float to the floor. He strode toward the door and opened it. The outstretched arm of an underling greeted him, phone in hand.

"I was on the way in, sir. POTUS on the line."

Isley let the door close behind him so that O'Dowd could not hear.

"Hello, Mr. President."

Isley listened, his company man standing in shadow beside him.

"As you wish, Mr. President. I will await further instructions, sir."

He disconnected the call and handed his knife, still sticky with tape residue, to his subordinate.

"Put that in my bag. Have the three young guests returned to their hotel. Same blackout van they came in. Obviously, they can't be permitted to know this location. Put someone at their hotel door."

"Yes, sir."

Isley and his man walked in separate directions, with Joe returning to his chair. He sat down, lifted his ragged chess book from the table and opened it. His bookmark was an expired Arby's coupon. As he turned the page, he half-sang to himself.

"*Karma karma karma karma karma chameleon . . .*"

CANNI

Washington, D.C.

President Collins was still staring at his secure phone. He'd called Isley moments after hearing the news of a potential cure. He hadn't told him that, but he asked him to cease any interrogation that might be taking place; at least until more was learned. The commander-in-chief didn't want to know the particulars of the janitor's methods, he just wanted results, and an immediate cure for the monstrosity unleashed on the people who elected him.

The president's mind raced as he returned the receiver to its hook. Yes, it was a wired phone, mounted on the wall. In this case, the bathroom wall of his White House residence. George Edward Bernard Collins had taken the most important call of his life while sitting on the toilet. He'd immediately phoned Isley from the same location. His bathroom trips had become more frequent of late, with his intestines in stressful sheepshank for most of each day. It was there on that cold, hard seat, with the Wall Street Journal folded upon his lap and *Chess For Beginners* on the white tile at his feet, where his brain took off.

Fucking marijuana? This was possibly the great cure? His first thoughts went to airline pilots and train operators. Was our only option now to have folks like them ply their trades in a diminished capacity? Would this be any better than the current situation? Would the government force parents to force children to force edible cannabis down their throats?

Well, everyone enjoys cookies. But what of pregnant women?

How to protect citizens from those who will refuse to avail themselves of the potential cure? Some genius will slap a softer moniker on internment camps, if it comes to that, so that any new housing areas for the segments of opposition will be distanced from the stigmas of history. Other chronicled stains of our past include, all relative to intelligence, the fear of being in the presence of victims of leprosy or rubbing elbows with the HIV positive. Enlightening the naïve was always a priority, but now, those afflicted, those with whom our sympathies must remain, will on occasion cherish nothing more than to tear into the warm blood of the nearest neck.

Some sort of guarded colonization of the refusers might be the only option.

And what of those with an allergy to cannabis? Runny noses are one thing, but what of anaphylactic shock? Where will the line be drawn between those who *can't* take the drug, and those who *won't?*

Would doses be administered in the school nurse's office? President Collins knew those decisions would be best left to the doctors. He wondered if some type of card could be mailed, much the way stimulus checks had been, to virtually every household on file with the government, with such cards to be used to purchase official cannabis. Of course, this would be of no use to people living

244

in boxes, under bridges, or even in tunnels. There was much to be done, and no time for partisan bickering in the House or Senate. This was Threat Level RED, DEFCON 1, the Doomsday Clock, and everything else all rolled into a big fat joint.

But the immediate future included the president's fiancée, Madison, coming to the White House, where Collins would insist they smoke their first fatty together. He hadn't lit one since Princeton, and this particular herb was going to be provided by the medical staff.

The President of the United States of America then flushed the toilet.

Over the next week, all of the well-worn quotes about slow government, red tape, and the wheels of justice took one to the chops. It seems that when the children of elected officials are eating one another, shit moves at a rapid pace. The potential cure was tested and retested with encouraging results. Case studies weren't flipping, for the most part. It appeared to be over ninety-five percent effective. For those stuck in Canniland—a.k.a. the perms—the results were less effective, but still over seventy-five percent. The downside meant that roughly one quarter of perms would have to be housed and controlled somewhere. Another set of renamed internment camps? Then, if no progress presented itself down the road, would come the discussions about euthanasia.

The ingredients of the cure would continually be fine-tuned, always searching for improved performance, and the optimal dosage for both symptom relief and the ability to think clearly, but there was no time to await perfection. It was being shipped already—first to those responsible for our infrastructure, those with whom the new normalcy would have the greatest and most far-reaching effect on the general population.

Exodus.

That's what they called it, and who could really argue? Growing enough to feed a nation was a concern. Some cornfields were actually converted to cannabis and there was a whole new spin on the word "farmer". There were grow houses larger than Amazon fulfillment centers. There were going to be random check points for officials to test if citizens *had* taken their cure. If they had not, they could either voluntarily take it right there, or be taken to a detention center.

There was an immediate spike in the sales of snack foods and Pink Floyd albums.

More students enrolled in the arts.

CANNI

Las Vegas

The wheels of governmental action blazed as if on the Autobahn, though when it came to Cash, Rob, and the Las Vegas tunnel people, those same wheels clacked as if dragged by horse wagon across the desert plains.

They'd heard nothing from Washington D.C. during that first week, but acknowledging the priorities involved in saving the country, not one complaint was uttered, other than the fact that Don Russo wanted his reefer reimbursement from the president.

The fact was, Russo's folks had donated their stash in the rescue at Area 51 and things had been dryer than before pot was legal, never mind required. They'd been able to scare up a bit here and there, but the street supply was thinner than a blade of grass, the licensed shops were empty and there was now more weed at Sunday school than in the tunnels of Las Vegas. In fact, Quinn had flipped while on bucket detail, climbed a wall, and darted blindly into traffic, only to be struck by an unmarked government van on a high school cannabis delivery route. He was uninjured.

The Jean Conservation Camp sounds like a place where one might go to study butterflies, but it is actually a women's prison, twenty minutes from Vegas. It is minimum security and they only have about a dozen correctional officers, but one of those guards became friendly with Phaedra during her short stint there, and that guard happened to be involved in the new cannabis delivery chain for the prison. In exchange for some close personal time with Phaedra the officer smuggled her just enough edibles for the group to have a little party—and hopefully prevent them from killing each other.

They sure looked like regular chocolate chip cookies; tasted good, too.

"Funky President (People It's Bad)" was the James Brown anthem that blasted through the speakers via Don Russo's iPod Classic.

"Funky president gotta get me my weed," grunted Russo. "I like to smoke my stuff up. What am I, seven years old, with these Keebler shits?"

"Has Paul heard anything from that Dr. Anderson?" asked Phaedra as she handed Russo another cookie while looking at Rob.

"No," answered Cash.

They all sat in a loose circle within Russo's lair, surrounded by his Raiders curtains, some damaged from the flood. Paul was absent, but almost everyone else took part. There hadn't been much communication from the government of late, either directly to the tunnel people or to the nation as a whole. The president almost seemed to have vanished. There was a lengthy broadcast that featured the White House Press Secretary and messages from the Secretary of Health and Human Services, along with the Surgeon General. They were unsure if Exodus was a cure or merely a treatment for symptoms, and they relayed that to the citizens, along with a directive that it must be taken or relocation was inevitable.

Further televised confusion featured, on successive days a Fox News commentator who had refused to consume cannabis—without his station's knowledge—literally flipping to canni during a live broadcast, and being fatally shot on-air after attacking his interviewee, the Administrator for the Agency of Toxic Substances and Disease Registry. The network immediately took viewers to an ad for a battery-powered lantern. Then, the host of an MSNBC discussion appeared to fall asleep at her desk, generating a few chuckles, which quickly subsided after learning that she was actually in a coma. She'd sprinkled her own additives into her ration of Exodus. MSNBC quickly cut to their montage of Barack Obama's greatest speeches. Finally, there was the CNN reporter, who was terminated after his plan to fake a canni episode in the White House briefing room was exposed, with recorded evidence, by an anonymous source.

"It must be mayhem at the White House. We can't think that our little group is high on their priority list," offered Rob, his three-fingered hand taking another cookie.

"Back in the day, it took long for the government to agree on getting blocks of cheese to the hungry, so imagine the fuss over shipping weed to feed *everyone*," added Hoffman.

"Yet," said Cash, "they did it."

"Not everyone," answered Russo, eyes glazed. "Here we all are. We saved the world, but we have to scrounge for our weed. We gave up our stash in that government spook house."

"We saved lives—*you* saved lives, Mr. Russo—up at Area 51. You saved *our* lives," said Cash. "You're a hero."

"There was another hero," said John G. "That professor; he died there for us."

"Daniele, right?" asked Rob.

"Yes. Christopher Daniele."

Cash's eyes, already red, welled up. "So that was his full name. Christopher Daniele."

John, savoring the power of a sense he'd never had, studied her face as her cognition drifted. Her blank stare told even his novice eyes that she had gone to the past—or perhaps even the future.

"He loved Bruce Springsteen," said John.

"Not cool of that Dr. Anderson to blow off Paul, though," said Russo.

Still gazing at Cash, John replied, "Doc Anderson was a pretty one, though."

Everyone laughed, even though it was true, because John had said it. Everyone but Cash, who was still on her mind's journey.

"We're just returning to our natural form," said Hoffman.

"Huh?" asked Russo.

"Hunters and gatherers. The strong survive. That's this."

"Why don't you go and *gather* us up some snacks then? These here cookies are just making me hungrier. Man, like have y'all ever gone to the movies—like one of them multiplexes—and they always got that second candy counter, like deep down the halls, and that fucker is *never* open? All dark. Not an employee to be found. That's bullshit, man."

"Wait," said Rob, staring at the stark-naked leader, "*you* go to the movies?"

"Not lately," laughed Russo. "Because of those fuckin' barren candy counters."

"I've never been to a movie theater," said John.

"Let's go tomorrow," said Rob. "Or, you come back to New York with me and Cash and we'll go to the nicest ones in Manhattan."

"I just might if the airlines ever resume flying."

"They will, buddy, with pilots baked out of their asses. And I still believe that President Collins will get us on a flight."

Quinn and Yurman came running in.

"There's a van outside," said Yurman, catching his breath. "Same kind that ran Quinn over. The driver is asking for Don Russo."

Most of the group hurried toward a particular tunnel entrance; the one where they dumped the buckets. Russo led the way, hoping his weed had arrived. They could see the sunlight before them, a single figure awaited, three large boxes on the concrete beside him. His pants were tightly fitted from the knee down, but unnervingly baggy above that, all the way to the waist.

Midway between them and the mouth of the tunnel, they spotted an elderly woman; clothes ragged. She kneeled, head almost touching the ground. Most of the group initially thought she might be in prayer, but as they passed, her actions became clearer; she was drinking from a large puddle of water. The plash contained several of the same crayfish once fed by Polish Joe. The creatures brushed by her withered tongue as it dipped for a sop.

"Anyone recognize her?" asked Russo.

"Not one of ours," replied Yurman.

"Lady!" hollered Russo. "We have water. Food too. No need for that, ma'am." No response. She never even looked his way.

"Maybe she's deaf," offered John G. He broke from the group, walked to her, and touched her shoulder. He noticed that her skin was pale and cracked. She just kept slurping.

"We'll catch her on the rebound," said Russo. "Let's see if this dude has my reefer."

Steeping out into the sun, Russo's first words were, "Sweet pants, brother. Tell me that you've got packages for me."

"Jodhpurs," answered the visitor.

"Okay, Mr. Jodhpurs," replied Russo, "where do I sign?"

"The pants are called *jodhpurs*," was the emotionless response, as the man studied the bare-skinned, hairy physique of Don Russo. "I'll need to see some ID."

Russo stared at the visitor. He then began patting his naked chest and buttocks, as if searching for a wallet. Rob glanced over at the white concrete wall. There it was, gray with dark crossbars. Surely it was a different lizard than the one he'd seen weeks before while he sat wondering where Cash had gone, but here it sat, in almost the exact spot. Being there among the buckets and seeing the lizard brought back the torment of Cash's kiss with Paul. He still wondered if there was more to it. Despite burning that ice cream truck to the ground, the haunting lingered.

"I can't deliver this without seeing identification."

"This," said Russo, "is from the President of the United States, addressed to me."

"It is from the government. Nowhere on my paperwork does it mention the president. Now Mr. Russo, it is apparent that you are a bit muddled, as are your friends, due to consumption of some kind of another. I admit that I have never delivered to the homeless before . . . "

"Hey brotha," interrupted Russo, "we are not homeless." He pointed to the dark tunnel opening. "That is our home."

Yurman moved toward the boxes. "I have an ID and I will sign for this," he said, reaching down for the first package.

The deliveryman calmly grabbed Yurman's wrist. He seemed to hold it for an eternity before he bent it backwards, snapping it. Yurman howled as his hand dangled from his freshly cracked radius. Before anyone could react, the jodhpur-wearing visitor tore into his victim's neck, blood erupting like an errant firehose. At first, the group didn't know whether to run or fight. Some just screamed.

It was Rob who acted first. While the canni chewed on Yurman's throat, Rob grabbed a well-worn five-gallon bucket—part of the Home Depot logo was still visible on the faded orange container—and slid it down over the attacker's head, separating his teeth from Yurman's flesh. It had been the nearest bucket to Rob and the fact that it was still loaded with human waste mattered not.

Urine and feces coated the canni as if it were pig's blood in prom night. He let go of his prey and thrashed about, unsure of how to simply lift the bucket from his head. It was ready to fall off on its own by the time Russo got his claws on an old steel fence post that had come loose months before.

He slammed it across the canni's knees, then again and again. It went down right beside the bleeding Yurman, who was being pulled away by Quinn, Hoffman, and others. The bucket fell off the attacker's head, which remained bathed in shit and piss. Its legs apparently broken, Russo went hard on its arms. They could be heard shattering under the power of the fence post.

Rob put a hand on Russo. "You can stop," he said. "He's immobilized. He won't do any more damage."

Russo kept pounding.

"Mr. Russo, this is a human being. He'll probably return to normal in minutes. He's going to wake up in unimaginable pain. Stop it!"

"I got no ID!" growled Russo, still swinging, "But, I got plenty of fucking id."

He struck him several more times, breathlessly exclaiming, "This condescending piece of shit should have taken his Exodus. It wasn't his choice. Authentic motherfuckers like Yurman have to suffer because of *his* personal beliefs?"

Rob moved between Russo and the incapacitated canni. He questioned his decision immediately as Russo hoisted his weapon high, as if he hadn't noticed, or hadn't cared to notice, Rob's presence. In that fraction of a second, Russo seemed to grow in size. Rob's thoughts, possibly aggrandized by the cannabis, flashed back to a snowy night in Brooklyn when he and Cash had been watching *An Officer and a Gentleman* on TV. She'd fallen asleep, so he switched over to a documentary about Insular Gigantism; a true phenomenon whereby the size of an animal isolated on an island can increase dramatically compared to its mainland relatives. He convinced himself that Don Russo had acquired this trait, with the tunnels being his "island", and that it was instantaneous rather than evolutionary.

It was then that Phaedra stepped between the men, and Cash, behind Russo, grabbed onto the pipe and hung from it as Russo held it high. His strength was imposing. Cash thought about how Quinn, in the cannibal state, had been hit by a truck and sustained not a scratch, yet Don Russo had just likely shattered a dozen rigid canni bones with a length of pipe.

Rob, sensing that he was probably not going to be bludgeoned by the steel post, reflected on how Russo could swing from empathy to enmity without notice. It would be wise to always cradle the notion that this was, above all, an exceedingly dangerous man.

Russo let go of the pipe, leaving it in the hands of Cash, who was taken by its heft. He ignored Rob and turned to Hoffman and the others, who were tending to the bleeding Yurman. The bite victim was sweaty, pale, and babbling on between coughs.

"That . . . worthless . . . delivery . . . cunt," he gasped, as Quinn mopped his brow. "Wait . . . I don't want . . . my final uttered word . . . to be . . . *cunt*. Fuck me . . . it still . . . is . . . *cunt*."

Russo glanced down at Yurman, then out past the fencing and beyond the tunnels, to the street.

"We got these three boxes of Kush right here," he said, the waste-covered canni writhing and biting on the ground beside him, "and suddenly, we got what just might be an entire truckload sitting right outside, waiting to be claimed. All for us. I don't care if they're for smokin' or eating. They belong to me now. Let's get to unloading, boys."

Rob knew better than to intervene. He'd set his mind to calling an ambulance for the delivery man, once he could distance himself from the others. He knew he was stoned, but his sense of purpose remained. He looked over at the wall, searching for his unshakable lizard friend.

It was gone.

Yurman's last word was *cunt*.

CANNI

Virginia

The three terrorists, less some toes and a bit of bravado, were still housed in the North Wing deep below Dr. Robert's barn. Some of their children and other loved ones remained safely at their hotels, guarded and supervised. They had varying levels of suspicion as to why they were taken to the outskirts of Washington D.C., but they were never told the truth. The hotels were upscale, the food exceptional, and the Exodus was primo.

Joe Isley, in his janitorial attire, was having lunch alone in his makeshift office when the president walked in.

"Mr. President?" was all he could muster as he scrambled to his feet, dropping his hefty sandwich.

"Hello, Joe. Sorry to interrupt lunch. I didn't know."

"Please, sir, never a problem, of course. I wish I knew you'd be here, but . . . "

"Last minute decision. I have to keep these visits on the down low, you know. Avoid the press and what have you. We didn't even drive over in "The Beast". Came in a van that is made to look like a plumber's. My guys are outside the door. They don't even know why I'm here or anything about you, of course. It helps that they're high."

"I know that van, sir. It's really time for something new. I wouldn't trust it as cover anymore."

"You know of it? Really?"

"Yes, sir. Just my opinion."

"But it's fitted with all the trappings; bulletproof, all the tech stuff . . . "

"You can use the same van. Just repaint it. Maybe change a thing or two about the exterior. Ding it up a bit. Give it a new identity. No more plumber."

"I will pass that along to the Secret Service, Joe."

"Tell them you thought of it. I'm just a janitor."

"Done. Sit down, Joe, I'd like to talk with you."

"Of course. I haven't touched that half of sandwich if you would like it. I ate two others already. The munchies, I guess. Boar's Head bologna, fresh American cheese."

President Collins sat directly across from Isley.

"Thank you, but the team has to be aware of anything that I might choose to eat."

"I understand, sir."

"Mayo?"

"Miracle Whip."

"Give it here."

As President Collins took his first bite, he continued. "You're right about the munchies. I downed a bag of Cheetos in the van. Look here, evidence."

He held his fingers out, complete with orange coating.

"Would you like a napkin, sir?"

"Nah. Fuck it. Anyway, Joe, here's the deal: straight up, I've been a little bitch."

"Sir? You mean with your non-violent positions prior to this attack?"

"No, not that, per se. What brand of cheese is this?"

"Kraft singles."

"Delicious. What I mean is that I sat in the White House, letting you do what needed to be done: the ugliness of interrogation, and I turned a blind eye. I wanted results, but I sheltered myself from the storm. It was like that *Don't Ask, Don't Tell* bullshit, in a way. I'm supposed to be commander-in-chief, but I task you with the horrific duties."

"Not a problem."

"I have to face my responsibilities, Joe. It isn't fair to you."

"I like doing it."

"I want you to tell me what we've done and where we stand. I know you've made a bit of progress with the North Korean. Though we may have a treatment for the initial stage of canni, we are faced with other problems. These scientists have tested this process all the way through, deep underground in their home countries, and sadly, using their own people as guinea pigs. We only know that because of you, my friend."

"YoMomma'sFatTitties!" screamed Joe Isley. Collins jumped.

The door opened. The helmeted head of an agent peered in. The president waved him off, and he closed the door. Outside the room, a second agent asked of the first, "What's going on in there?"

"He appears to be eating sandwiches with a janitor."

Inside the room, Isley spoke. "I am so sorry, sir. I had been doing much better with my affliction."

"I've noticed that. Don't you worry. So, I'd like for you to tell me what methods you have used thus far on our prisoners."

"I took all ten toes and nine fingers from the Iranian but he told me nothing. Not so far, anyway. The American traitor—the woman—I threatened to execute her children in front of her."

"And?"

"Your phone call halted the interrogation."

"These are some tough bastards. You made a bit more progress with the Korean; I'm afraid to ask how."

"He watched his dog starve."

"His *dog?*"

"Correct. I had it leashed in his room where he could see it. I gave it water, but no food."

"The poor animal."

"It's alive, sir. It has been fed. A reward for what he has told us thus far, but the Korean knows the starving can resume at any time, based only upon your orders, of course."

President Collins stared at the final bite of his sandwich, as it sat on the table before him.

"A North Korean who loves his pet dog?" he asked, rhetorically.

"He only got the animal when he was in Iran."

"I thought they frowned upon dogs there too."

"Not if you're creating a virus to kill Americans."

Collins dropped the remaining morsel into his mouth.

"Joe," he asked, "why did you only take nine fingers from the Iranian?"

"I'm not an evil man, Mr. President. People get itchy."

"Joe, my friend," responded Collins as he stood, "I would shake your hand, but the Cheetos dust, ya know? I thank you for telling me everything, and I want to know each detail from now on—before you do it."

"Absolutely, sir. Would you like to visit with any of the prisoners?"

POTUS stood there, rubbing his orange fingertips together and considering his options.

"Can I go see the dog?"

Ten minutes later, the president and his three helmeted agents emerged from the secure North Wing doorway into the research area of the facility. They headed not for the exit elevators but proceeded further into the testing area, unannounced. Some employees responded with audible gasps. Almost none of them had ever seen their big boss in person.

The White House contingent opened the door to one of the labs. The few employees within were studying—through a large, thick window—four perms who were strapped to tables. Music was playing in the room on the safe side of the glass.

It was Radiohead.

"Good afternoon, doctors," said the president.

They all turned: Doctors V. Anderson and Martinez along with the visiting Papperello-Venito. Surprise was the prevailing reaction.

"So, what are we working on today?" he asked with a smile.

Dr. Papperello-Venito responded as the ranking official. "Mr. President, the doctors were showing me how they are trying to find some dosage of Exodus, or some mixture that might restore the resistant subjects to normalcy. We don't want to leave anyone behind."

He approached the window. Dr. Anderson walked toward the single speaker that provided the music. "Jessica, mute," she commanded, and the device went silent.

"You didn't have to do that," said Collins.

"Oh, I just like commanding Jessica," smiled V. "Honestly, it's so convenient, but I like two speakers, better sound, and I can do without the wireless craze."

DANIEL O'CONNOR

"Still on that trip?" asked Dr. Papperello-Venito.

President George Collins ignored the exchange as he stepped up to observe the perms. He observed two young women, he guessed mid-twenties, an older man, and a boy no more than nine years of age. They were all growling and snapping like monsters. He suddenly felt less guilty about Joe Isley's methods. The commander-in-chief said nothing for several minutes. He just watched. Mostly, the boy. He was African-American. Collins recalled that he, at that age, was primarily concerned about hitting the newsstand with his allowance and grabbing the latest issues of his favorite comic books. *Fantastic Four* was his first choice, but he enjoyed most any superhero series; *Daredevil* and *The Flash* were cool, and he loved seeing the occasional black hero, like *Luke Cage*, *Falcon*, and *Black Panther*. He'd often fantasized about growing up to be such a warrior, but despite all of his accomplishments he could never see himself that way.

That was Joe Isley.

But as a nine-year-old, comics were little George Collins' life.

He stared at the boy on the table, squirming and drooling, eyes wide, redder than the ink that flushed The Flash's crime-fighting costume.

This was the life of the boy on the table.

"I am confident that you exceptional doctors will be able to help these folks," said the president.

"We won't stop trying," answered V.

"What is that little boy's name?" he asked.

"Umm . . . that's number P21—let me see . . . " stammered V, as Dr. Martinez took to a laptop.

"Jamal Davidson," said Dr. Martinez.

"Can one of you take a photo of him?"

"Yes, sir."

As Dr. Martinez headed for the room on the other side of the glass, President Collins turned to the others. He put his hand on V's shoulder, the one that had been bitten by a prior canni encounter.

"We will have the official photographs and plaque shortly," he said softly.

"Sir?"

"I thought Dr. Papperello-Venito had told you. This research facility will be officially named."

He looked over at Papperello-Venito, and she revealed the name to V.

"The Anderson-Daniele Research Center," she said.

"For your brother and that professor from Nevada. True American heroes," added Collins.

V was stunned. Fighting to keep her composure, she glanced over at the can of Diet Mountain Dew on her desk. A drop of condensation slid down to join the small circle of water at its base.

"Of course," sighed Collins, "this is a top-secret location, so the dedication will be private, and few will ever know, but I hope you understand that it is no less important because of that. There are no greater heroes than those represented only by stars carved on the CIA Memorial Wall, most of their names unknown to the world. The confidentiality bears no relation to the momentousness."

V. Anderson, never at a loss for words, now found herself struggling to reply.

"It's okay," offered the president as he gave her a warm hug. He may not have thought of himself as a superhero, but he felt like one from the inside of his embrace.

Dr. Martinez returned and handed her phone to the president. On the screen was an image of young Jamal Davidson. He was scowling at the camera, drooling. His singular thought centered on his desire to kill the photographer.

As Collins studied the picture, he spoke. "I first thought that our enemies just wanted us to all kill each other. Then, when diseases began to vanish, I wondered if their true goal was simply overpopulation. Maybe we'd all live too long. Then I considered the fact that maybe that aspect was just a surprise to them as well as us. Now, it looks like we may face other problems. Where will this lead us? What is in store for Jamal Davidson?"

"Sir, it's not my place," said V, "but if our military can just somehow capture one of the architects of this disease . . . "

Her statement reminded him that this side of the facility had no clue what was going on in the North Wing.

"You're right, doctor," was his reply.

"Hey, we only need one," she smiled.

He stood silently, then turned to Dr. Martinez. "Do you mind if I forward this photograph to someone?"

"Of course not, sir."

Collins tapped some numbers into the phone, waited, press more buttons, and handed it back to the doctor.

"Dr. P-V," he said, addressing Papperello-Venito, "do you need a lift back to the White House?"

"Okey-dokey, sir. I have never been in the presidential limousine!"

"You still won't be, doc."

With a puzzled look she gathered her belongings.

"Dr. P-V?" said V. "That's neat. Can I call you that?"

"No."

Collins shook hands with Drs. Anderson and Martinez, and then he led the way out alongside Dr. P-V with the security team behind. The doctor was struggling to hold all of her work accessories, so V. Anderson took some of them from her and, with her Diet Dew in one hand, walked out the first door with them.

"I know that you big, strong gentlemen are prohibited from carrying unnecessary items," she whispered to the agents.

They strolled through the corridor toward the elevators that would take them up to the barn, Collins smiling and waving at a handful of star-struck employees. As they neared the secure entrance to the North Wing, its heavy door opened. Out came Joe Isley, still in maintenance garb and actually wheeling a trash can. He made no eye contact with the President of the United States, and that fact was not lost on V. Anderson. Who *wouldn't* be impressed by this giant among men being mere feet from them?

Isley did, however, lock eyes with Dr. Anderson. They gave each other a slight but cordial nod.

She took a final sip of her Mountain Dew and dropped the empty can into Joe Isley's wheeled receptacle.

CANNI

Washington, D.C.

The following morning, President Collins needed a few moments for himself. He sat alone in the Oval Office, eating his Exodus cookie. His eyes studied the bust of Dr. Martin Luther King Jr. Whenever he took the time to enjoy that work of art, his body would initially weaken as he would recall that the man himself had been within this very office on more than one occasion. But then he would become robust with strength because he hoped that Dr. King would have been proud of his accomplishments. Weakness followed by power. It happened every time.

With his next bite, he looked over at the bust of Sir Winston Churchill. He thought about how America's friends in the four countries of the United Kingdom, and a host of others, had lists of volunteers willing and able to cross the shores and provide any help requested, despite the looming probability of infection, and no guarantee that they could ever return to their homeland.

We shall fight on the beaches, we shall fight on the landing grounds, we shall fight in the fields and in the streets, we shall fight in the hills; we shall never surrender.

President Collins knew that portion of Churchill's speech quite well. It was a favorite of his late friend, Vice President Montgomery.

He turned back to the cast of Dr. King's face.

DANIEL O'CONNOR

Virginia

The face filled Joe Isley's phone screen. He studied it as he ate his cannabis cookie.

Jamal Davidson.

CANNI

Washington, D.C.

The speech was originally going to come from the state floor of the White House residence, but George Edward Bernard Collins had a late change of heart; it was going take place in the chamber of Martin and Winston, the Oval Office.

He sat at the Resolute Desk, flanked by the Stars and Stripes and the Flag of the President of the United States. This desk, a gift in 1880 from Victoria, Queen of the United Kingdom, was brought into this office by President John F. Kennedy in 1961. Though used by many distinguished presidents since, it is the image of an almost three-year-old JFK Jr. playing under and within the desk that most often flashed through Collins' brain. Though there were indeed Secret Service agents and two dogs in the room in addition to the production crew, all that the viewers saw was their president at that desk. Mid-speech, he took his first sip of water.

"So yes, my fellow Americans, I am under the influence of cannabis, as are all of us in government. We continue to work toward a strain that will minimize any undue effects on our thought processes while being most effective against this disease that has afflicted the great majority of us."

DANIEL O'CONNOR

Virginia

A small television was on within the Virginia interrogation room that held the toeless Iranian scientist. His feet were bandaged, as were his hands, save for his one remaining finger. The bound terrorist, with Joe Isley sitting across from him, watched President Collins' address.

"I ask you all to trust me," continued Collins. "We need to take our Exodus; all of us who can physically deal with it. If you cannot, you are obligated to contact your local police so that we can make arrangements for you. It is for the greater good."

This brought forth a laugh from the terrorist. Isley stood and left the room. In a minute, he returned with an icy can of Coke in hand. He popped it, inserted a straw, and presented it to his captive. The scientist wrapped his parched lips around the straw and sucked deeply.

"This will pass," said Collins. "We are too great of a nation to allow this to defeat us. We will not. Think of all the great American men and women who have lived; we will each have our own list of favorites. Would they shrink from this challenge? Not a chance."

The Iranian drank half of the can in one continuous act of suction. He then lifted his head and belched while still listening to the speech. Joe Isley placed the can down and took out his phone. One touch produced the image of the constrained and agonized Jamal Davison. As President Collins went on, Isley held the phone screen in front of the Iranian and whispered in his ear. His manner was non-threatening, even humble.

"I have come to realize just how far our allies will go to support us," said Collins. "They are the best of humanity. It is also evident that some groups, no matter our course, will despise us. I, and previous administrations, have tried every approach imaginable. We have been stern, we have been diplomatic, we have been proactive. None of it has had any effect on the hostility from those who despise our freedoms, and it never will. Our women will always be the equals of men. Our gay community will share in all of the rights that every American enjoys."

Isley had finished his whisper. He held his phone screen at the scientist's eye level. He even managed a slight smile as his other hand brought the Coke back up to his prisoner's lips. The Iranian took another sip, eyes darting between images of President Collins and Jamal Davidson.

"There is one new problem for those who would do us harm, and I am no doctor, but I am your commander-in-chief," continued the president. "And I know they desired to create monsters."

The Iranian turned his eyes to Joe Isley, who held the soda can and the phone. His Middle Eastern cheeks puffed with Coca-Cola, he spat his mouthful onto Isley's phone, causing the young boy's image to fizzle away. Isley silently wiped the cell on his shirt, placed it in his pocket, put down the soda can, and unlatched every strap that had bound the scientist to his chair.

Joe Isley then walked out the main door. As the Iranian struggled to stand on his bandaged feet, the president continued on television.

"They have made me into a monster," said George Collins. "Not because I might experience a seizure, foam at the mouth, and hunger for a meat never before desired. No, we now have ways to combat those effects, thanks to some young folks from the streets of Brooklyn, along with their friends from *under* the streets of Las Vegas. I am not a monster from the disease. I am a monster because I have been pushed past the limit, and sadly for those who would do us harm, I and my advisors, are quite literally Snoop Dogg stoned all of the time. So, with apologies to all who might be offended, I say to our adversaries: from this day forward, if you bring violence toward an American citizen, be it home or abroad, we will stone cold fuck you up."

Joe Isley watched his prisoner through the window. He pressed a button, much like the ones on his damaged phone. The side door to the interrogation room opened. The Iranian terrorist stood beside the TV that still projected the image of the President of the United States. He stared at the newly exposed exit. His first thought was that for some reason he was being released from his incarceration. Had they given up trying to break him?

In effect, they had.

But that exit was more accurately an entrance, and in walked the spitting, growling, starving P21. Jamal Davidson was in the room.

The scientist picked up the small television, squeezing it between his bandaged, one- fingered hands. It would be the only barrier between him and the perm that he created. Jamal spotted him, shot across the room as if he were The Flash, bit off the one finger that protruded from the terrorist's cotton gauze wrap, and got his arms around him. Though half the height of the Iranian, it was over in seconds.

Jamal dragged his victim's body across the room, the television line entangled in the dead man's legs. The TV cord turned taut, and the plug was yanked from the wall socket. The broadcast went dead as President Collins said, " . . . and God Bless Ameri . . . "

DANIEL O'CONNOR

Las Vegas

"Hey brother, wake up," said John G.

Rob turned over and opened his eyes. The Vegas sun was filtering through the tunnels as it did every morning. "What time is it?" he asked.

"Not sure, but it is time to get up," smiled John.

"Man, I had a dream that the president mentioned us on TV."

"Well, that actually did happen, it seems."

"Huh?"

"Yeah, not by name, but he mentioned young people from Brooklyn and Vegas during a televised address yesterday."

"No shit?"

"All true, bro. Man, you look out of it. Not much sleep last night?"

"Maybe not . . . "

"You still staying awake to guard your girlfriend while she sleeps?"

"Not to guard her. Hell, I don't know. It's a crazy world, John."

Rob, clearing the webs from his brain, began to notice that the tunnels sounded different. Sure, there was the rumbling of traffic above, but nothing else. No chatter. No music.

"Where is everyone? Is Cash here?" he asked, eyes growing wider.

"Here, have your cookie." John handed him some Exodus.

"Where is she, John?"

"I'm not entirely sure. Now, stay calm, but it seems she went somewhere with Paul. They aren't answering the phone."

Rob sighed. "Oh, man."

"I'm sure it's not what you think."

"I don't know what to think, Johnny. Where is everyone else, though?"

"That's a separate issue. Russo has been arrested."

"What?"

"Yeah, the feds got him. Probably for what he did to that deliveryman. Some of the group fled, while others went over to wherever the local FBI office is, to try and help Russo."

"I am one heavy sleeper. Lord Jesus."

"Hoffman is here, though."

"Why?"

"He has a car today. Don't ask. He has an idea where Cash and Paul might be. He said he'll drive us before he heads to the federal building."

Hoffman's head leaned in from behind a curtain. "Sorry about your girl. We will get her. No worries."

The car was a ten-year-old Beetle, barely worth any time that police might waste searching for it. The ignition had been popped. Hoffman drove while eating his cookie with Rob beside him and John squeezed into the back seat. They had been to three locations already without any apparent connection; a lumber yard, a car wash, and the Tropicana hotel. At each stop, Hoffman would exit the vehicle, go inside for ten minutes, and return without Cash or any pertinent information.

"Why are we stopping at these random places?" asked Rob.

"You will see."

"Do people at these locations know Paul or something?"

"Some."

Hoffman's phone, or whoever's phone he was using, signaled an incoming text. He looked at it.

"Shit," he said.

"What is it?" asked Rob.

"They are taking Don Russo in front of a federal judge. We have to go there to support before we continue. I'm sorry. It is my duty to him."

"Let me see that phone," demanded Rob. Hoffman handed it over and he read the text.

Russo being brought to fed court now. Plz come.

This is some serious shit, thought Rob as he saw the police vehicles surrounding the downtown building. Hoffman had parked several blocks away as captaining a stolen vehicle into a nest of cops was too brazen, even for him. He had also given Rob the phone so that he could try to call Paul and Cash as much as he wished. Still no answer, but he kept at it. A woman in a pricey business suit took them through the metal detectors after Hoffman told her they were here to support Russo. They were then scanned by an electronic wand, frisked, and sniffed by an enormous dog.

They made it to an elevator and soon emerged in the presence of yet more police.

Don Russo smoked a little black market dope in an underground tunnel and he is treated like fucking El Chapo, was Rob's initial thought.

A door opened and he, John, and Hoffman suddenly saw Russo. Not naked. He wore a pair of sweats and a Raiders tee. He was plopped on one of the many courthouse benches. No handcuffs. Beside him sat Phaedra. There was Skunk, Quinn, and the others. They smiled. Rob turned to look for the judge's bench. It was hidden from view by a flowered trellis, beneath which stood a feminine figure, clothed in the white wedding gown that Phaedra would often wear while silver mining. The veil was down, but he knew it was Cash. She clutched a stunning, cascading bouquet of pink and burgundy orchids. The thought crossed Rob's mind that she might be marrying Paul, until the latter approached and shook his hand with a smile. Rob turned to see John and Hoffman, the accomplices, grinning.

He had questions, but Cash was at the front of the room in a freaking wedding gown, so he just went right for her.

Her face was only partially hidden by the veil, but he couldn't resist. "I really hope that is you under there, babe."

The kick to his shin reassured him.

"You really weren't supposed to see me yet, I guess," she said, "but maybe it still counts if you don't see my face clearly."

"Right," he smiled, not knowing what to do with his hands. "I think I'm supposed to be the one standing here waiting for *your* entrance."

"Logistics," she replied.

"You look so beautiful," he said, "but I'm wearing an old tee with a 1968 Buick Skylark on it."

"We have a suit for you," said John from behind. "Obviously we couldn't dress you earlier because of the surprise. There's a room through there for you to change."

"But . . . what about a marriage license? How can we . . . ?"

"It's in the room, with the suit. Come on."

John led Rob toward the side door, opened it, and they saw the new suit dangling from a wooden hanger.

The hanger was being held high in the left hand of the President of the United States.

He extended his right, "George Collins. Congratulations, Rob. It's an honor to meet you."

Jaw drop. After a moment, Rob took note of the several helmeted guards and sundry other people hovering around the president. All of the cops he'd seen, and the extreme security measures, suddenly made more sense.

Rob clutched POTUS' hand, mumbled something or other, and turned to look through the open door at Cash. Her silk-covered head just nodded. Still squeezing Collins' hand, Rob then turned his eyes to John G.

"Errr," offered the president, "do you want the suit?"

"Oh, yes. Sir," stammered Rob. "I'm just . . . with her in that gown . . . and now you . . . it is a lot, Mr. President."

He took the suit. Collins patted his back and added, "I've brought some of the crew with me. I know you've already met." He pointed to the far side of the room, just behind some of the security team; there stood Doctors Anderson and Papperello-Venito. Rob smiled.

"All right," said the president. "Our groom here needs a place to change, so let's all maybe head into the main room."

As they all filed out, Rob received quick hugs from the two doctors. He watched everyone leave, yet he couldn't help but focus on Cash standing out there in the main room. She appeared to be so alone. He waved her in. She shook her head. He waved more forcefully, and she came to him. He closed the door behind her. They were alone.

"Put the flowers down," he said softly. She placed them on a table beside his plastic-wrapped suit and his chosen Fleetwood Mac compact disc. He lifted her veil. She made a short motion to stop him but changed her mind. He placed a finger under her chin.

"How did all of this happen?" he asked.

"Well, I'm not exactly sure. Paul and his mom—she's here, too, by the way—were in contact with the White House doctors, and it seems that Don Russo . . . "

"Don Russo?"

"Yeah. He is extraordinarily persuasive."

"I've heard," smiled Rob. "What I need to know is . . . "

There was a hasty knock on the door, but Paul and John G rushed in without awaiting an answer. Paul held an electronic tablet.

"We got it," he said to Cash.

"Oh," she responded, as if she'd forgotten. Paul handed the device to her. On the screen, waving, were her Aunt Margie and cousins Laura and Jen.

"Carrie! Hi! Oh my God, a wedding gown! We knew it! Where is Rob?"

"He's right here," she smiled, as Rob popped into frame, waving.

"What the heck are you wearing, young man?" asked Aunt Margie.

"Long story," he answered.

"Well, you can't get married in that thing!"

"I promise I won't," he said.

"Where is Uncle Reg?" asked Cash.

"Oh, Caroline, wait till you see," replied her aunt. "He is much improved! Well, he was really great last week, but he's still lots better than when you guys left. Praise God!"

Laura repositioned the camera so that her dad came into view.

"A wedding without me?" he smiled. His cheeks were full and flushed, his eyes clear and vibrant.

"Uncle Reg," was all that Cash could say before her throat tightened. The tears were building, and that wouldn't be optimal since she was wearing much more eye makeup than she normally would.

"Hi, sweetheart," he said. "Is that my favorite mechanic there with you?"

"I hope it is," laughed Rob.

"You look like you almost have your old tan back," said Cash, fighting her emotions.

"Really? Nice! They've been letting me out in the courtyard some. The weather's been good. Not summer, but decent!"

"That is amazing! You know, I have a feeling that we might just be coming home very soon."

"No kidding? As man and wife, too!" he smiled.

"You know I'm bringing you those brownies and cold milk, first thing."

"Caroline, you should only know the kind of brownies I'm eating these days."

"She knows, Dad," said Laura, laughing. "We're all eating the same stuff."

Still battling tears that she didn't want her family to see, Cash had an idea. "We are going to take care of a few things, then we'll get you back on video chat. Don't go anywhere, guys. We love you."

She gave Paul a nod, telling him to disconnect. As her family said their goodbyes, Uncle Reg had one final comment, before the feed was lost. "The happy couple," he said to his daughters, "Rob and *Cash*."

Silence.

"I told you," whispered Rob, the gentle white bridal veil brushing against his lips.

"He called me *Cash*?"

"Yep."

She looked down at her bouquet.

"Hey guys," said Rob to Paul and John, "can we have a minute, please?"

As Paul and John emerged from the side room to the main, they saw that the White House doctors were seated on a bench with Dr. Anita Chuang. Standing by the trellis was the smartly-dressed woman who had ushered John, Rob, and Hoffman through security. She was addressing the assembled guests.

"I am Colleen Ipalook. I know that President Collins had the great pleasure of meeting with all of you earlier . . . "

Collins stood off to the side, in conversation with another man behind a helmeted security team.

Russo, seated with Phaedra on one of the benches, leaned in and asked her, "Who do you think is carrying that nuclear football?"

Ms. Ipalook continued, "Before our bride and groom enter, and as we await the honorable Judge Ruvnick, who will preside, I want to go over some of the nuts and bolts of our package. A sort of *thank you* to your wonderful community for your patriotic service regarding the recent challenges facing our great nation. There is a newly refurbished community residence on Flamingo Road, not far from your current . . . *dwelling* . . . that has just received brand new beds and appliances. It is for your use, and your use only. There will be counselors on hand with regard to job training and placement, medical treatment, any possible addiction issues, and the like. Of course there will be no cost to you. We had intended a debit card issuance for the purpose of purchasing clothing, essentials, and what have you, but due to time constraints and difficulties with regard to harvesting proper identification, we do have packages—one per person—containing a generous cash stipend to help you all with your transition."

Applause.

"Now you're talking my language," yelled Russo, fist in the air.

"Mr. Russo, we will talk later about your particular circumstance."

"Whoa, now. What does that mean, lady?"

"In a moment, sir."

"You can tell me now. I got no secrets from my people."

Ms. Ipalook glanced over at the president, who nodded. She trained her eyes on Russo.

"Mr. Russo, there was a government employee delivering Exodus at your location. He sustained serious injuries during the performance of his duties. While, due to extenuating circumstances, no charges will likely be sought in the case, that gentleman has a family and will need to be compensated in some way. I'm sure you would agree that your intended stipend would be a good start toward that."

"Hmmm," replied Russo, "sucks to be me, but when you're right, you're right."

"Naturally, you are still entitled to all of the benefits at the new Flamingo Center," she said.

"Yeah."

As John and Paul looked on from the side of the room, a large fellow accompanied by an attractive young lady walked up to them. The big man was grinning.

"Hello," said Paul. John G smiled and gave a polite nod, before turning his attention elsewhere.

"That's it? A nod? You don't recognize me with those new eyes, Daredevil?"

John was stunned. Even President Collins looked over when he heard the name of one of his comic book heroes invoked.

"Willie?" asked John, already knowing the answer.

"Damn right. Be real now, am I better looking than you expected?"

The men embraced.

"This is my sister, Michele—even prettier than me," he said.

"A pleasure to meet you," responded John, extending his hand. "You are stunning, and your brother literally saved my life."

"I know," she smiled. "Super Willie has a knack for that."

"Whoa, you're the dude from John's bus ride to hell?" asked Paul

"That's me. Hey, get this: no bus ride back. They set us up with a limo, and said we get to meet President Collins today!"

"He's right over there, you know," said John, pointing.

"Hot damn," exclaimed Willie, spotting POTUS. "Sniff me."

"Huh?" said John.

"I sweat a lot."

"You're fine."

President Collins waved them over. Willie took his sister's hand, and they went.

Rob and Cash were alone in the side room. The suit and bouquet were still on the table, along with the disc that contained the wedding songs. Her hand was nestled in his.

"Do you like me in a suit?" he smiled.

"I do."

"Should I put that one on?"

She looked down at it, searching for the right words.

"Teresa always said I could never find a better man than you."

"Teresa is our angel, and I love her, but she's not the one in the wedding gown."

"I . . . I . . . all of the people from the tunnels said that if we got married before we went back home . . . I just . . . You and I could be completely different in five years. People change. But you should know that the *me* who is here with you now, the *Cash* that you love, will always be yours, no matter what the future holds. We might change, but our history never will."

"I understand."

"I mean, holy shit—the President of the United States has come to see us get married, Rob."

"Well, you might have just saved the world . . . " he smiled, caressing her hand.

"Yeah, so why are the Secret Service guys still wearing those helmets?"

"I guess they can't be sure who really ate their cookies."

"I really need another cookie, Rob. Getting married in a world like this . . . "

"One thing I do know is that I would rather be with you in this vile world than be without you in a proper one. However, you can't marry me out of obligation. Please don't."

She put her other hand on his. It was shaking.

"All good," he said, holding up his bandaged left hand. "I don't even have a ring finger anymore."

Eyeliner raced mascara down her cheek. She swallowed hard, managed a smile, and said, "Wanna start a band?"

He dabbed the streak of makeup from her face and replied, "What would we call it?"

She rested her head on his shoulder. The veil tickled his face, so he gently removed it.

"Tomorrow Never Knows," she said.

He kissed the top of her head, "That's a cool name."

Fifteen minutes later, the assembled guests mumbled as Rob and Cash entered the main room, he in his Buick shirt, she in her Mets tee. President Collins, having already been briefed, stood before the flowered trellis with some words for the group.

"Well, folks, I could never hit a curveball," he said. "Or even a fastball, for that matter. But we've sort of had one tossed at us today. But it was actually the rest of us, not Caroline or Rob, who called for the strikeout pitch. I think we got a bit ahead of ourselves. They are young with a boundless future before them. One day, when they're ready, and *if* they are ready, I suspect there might be a beautiful wedding back in New York. But that day is not today. Nor should it be. There were some words that were going to be read today; words from Caroline's best friend, Teresa."

He unfolded a small note.

"And they shall be read. Teresa once said, 'Love colors all things bright. Love transforms the drab, the uninteresting, the routine. Love makes all things new'. Now, I am not the youngest sumbitch, and we have Judge Ruvnick twiddling his honorable thumbs here, and my fiancée Madison and I have been planning a wedding anyway, and maybe it's those cookies talking, but . . . "

The crowd began clapping and yelling.

"Who needs a fancy wedding, packed with stuffed shirts, right?" asked the president.

More cheers.

"Where is that kid who told me he is trying to blow up his YouTube channel?"

Paul's eyes widened. His mother motioned to him to raise his hand. He did.

"What is your name again?" asked the president.

"Bhong. Paul Bhong."

"You got your phone?"

"Yes, sir."

"Paul Bhong, you are the official, and only, White House cameraman for this event. An

American president has not been married in office since 1915. When we add *interracial* wedding to the mix, that takes it up a notch, and when we drop *gay* on top of all that, well, Mr. Bhong, you are about to own YouTube."

President Collins held out his hand, which was taken by his fiancée, Madison, a petite gentleman with milky-smooth skin and flowing blonde hair that would do Thor proud. Paul fumbled to get the video rolling as the guests cheered. The judge took his place, Cash's hand was snug within Rob's, and the future First Couple of the United States of America turned to face the magistrate who would marry them.

No rice was thrown but many bubbles were blown, and the country had a First Gentleman. A covey of heavily guarded limousines and SUVs formed a line outside the courthouse.

"Air Force One?" smiled Paul. "You bitches are going home in style!"

"I guess if I'm gonna get on a plane, Air Force One and some Exodus is as good as it's gonna get," said Cash.

"Yeah, and the flight crew are as baked as you are. Fuckin' Stoned Temple Pilots," he laughed. "Damn, with no commercial flights, McCarran and JFK will be open only for you!"

Most of the tunnel-dwellers had said their goodbyes and loaded into the cars that would take them to their new housing, but Russo and Phaedra remained. Don held a large box.

"The Magnificent Seven!" he said, looking at Rob, Cash, Paul, John, and Doctors Chuang, Anderson, and Papperello-Venito.

"That's been done," said Rob. "Maybe the *Magnanimous Seven*?"

"The Magnanimous Seven," repeated Russo.

"Phaedra, can you take a pic?" asked Paul, handing her his phone.

"Of course."

Everyone in the photo was smiling. Paul had his tongue out.

Don Russo stepped up to Rob with the box in his arms.

"This was supposed to be like a wedding gift, but y'all fucked that up, so I guess it's a little going away present. I didn't wrap it or nothin', so just take the lid off."

As Rob took the package, there was an audible rattling around within. He placed it on the ground and lifted the lid.

His 8-tracks. His father's 8-tracks.

There they were; Emerson, Lake & Palmer, Rush, Black Sabbath, Pink Floyd, all of them.

"What?" was all he could muster.

"I really tried to get your car back for you, bro. I was too late. This was the best I could do."

Rob wrapped his arms around the Don of the underground.

"Thank you."

Russo and Phaedra said their goodbyes and walked toward the cars. They had a brief but animated discussion. They then entered separate SUVs.

Cash was filling her palms with Purell hand sanitizer. Rob hadn't seen her do that in quite some time.

Paul, with his arm around his smiling mom, said to the other five, "Well, I guess Air Force One awaits you lucky bitches."

"Yes, we'll need to get a move on," replied Dr. Papperello-Venito.

As the group took their first steps toward the vehicles, John G took Rob and Cash aside.

"I . . . I don't think I'll be going to New York with you guys," he said.

"What?" replied Rob, holding his box of tapes.

"Yeah, I'm gonna catch a ride with Willie and his sister back to California."

"Come on, we are gonna have a blast back home," said Rob. "We're going to see Scarlett Johansson on the big screen, Johnny!"

"Yeah," he responded. "The thing is, I might be blind again by the time we get to the theater."

"What are you saying?"

"My vision is deteriorating. Quickly, too."

"Oh, John," said Cash, grasping his arm.

"The White House doctors!" said Rob. "Maybe they can help. They must know the best ophthalmologists. You know President Collins will help. Who gets a chance like that?"

"Rob, it's the cookies."

"Huh?"

"The Exodus."

"It's making you blind?"

"No, it's minimizing the effects of the canni virus. *All* of the effects."

Cash could feel the germs crawling up her arms. "I know what he means," she said.

"It's okay, though," said John. "That's what it's supposed to do. Bring us back to who we really are. Only more fried."

"Even so, you can still come to Brooklyn," said Rob.

"That's the problem," answered John. "I don't know if I want to go back to who I was."

"No, buddy. You can't stop taking the cookies."

"I don't know . . . "

"But your friend Willie?"

"No, jackass," said John, "I'm still on Exodus. I'd never endanger anyone else. But, when I get home, I'm going to decide if I should check into one of those dissident camps."

"For the refusers? No! You'll be caged all alone in a cell. You'll flip. What if you become a perm, John?"

"But Rob, I'll be able to *see*."

The embrace was long. It included three people. Then, John G was off to Willie's limo. Rob and Cash hurried to catch up to the Washington D.C. doctors, who were being ushered into their own luxury ride. As they walked, Cash had a realization.

"Rob, what about Uncle Reg? He was so much better."

"I know, babe. How about we visit him first thing?"

They reached the limousine. The driver, holding the door, reached for Rob's box of tapes but he held it tightly and brought it in with him.

As the door closed, Cash said, "I can't believe that the President of the United States would have Air Force One stop at JFK, just for us, on his way back to Washington."

"Caroline," said Dr. Papperello-Venito, "he just got married, and you're going to New York City for Christ's sake; I'm not sure there'd be a stopover if you guys lived in Owatonna, Minnesota."

The army of vehicles, with police escorts—despite the fact that the

DANIEL O'CONNOR

Presidential Limousine and its immediate entourage had already departed for McCarran Airport—rolled out onto the streets of Downtown Las Vegas, along with a singular civilian motorcycle, atop which sat a fellow who was gaining YouTube subscribers by the thousands. He was wrapped in the arms of a mother who loved him.

As Air Force One lifted off the runway, the car transporting John, Willie, and Michele had stopped at Alien Fresh Jerky, just off I-15 in Baker, CA. The big football player stocked up on barbeque jerky, his sister bought some mints, and John couldn't resist purchasing a typical tourist tee. Willie had read its inscription aloud for his friend.

I Survived Area 51.

In Las Vegas, several SUVs unloaded the former tunnel dwellers into the bright and clean Flamingo Center; Hoffman, Skunk, Quinn, and Phaedra included.

A few miles away, Don Russo, still in his Raiders shirt and sweats, trudged alone toward the darkness of a tunnel opening; the same one where he'd beaten the jodhpur-wearing deliveryman.

He stopped walking, removed his clothing, dropped the garments to the ground, and disappeared, naked, into the dark of the tunnels, his elongated shadow following him in. The clothes remained there, still, the only movements being the breeze, and the appearance of a gray, long-tailed lizard on the far concrete wall.

After a moment, Russo reappeared, picked up the Raiders shirt, left the pants, and returned to his tunnel.

The lizard scurried about on the wall, searching for a spot where it might feel most comfortable. Once it found it, it stayed. There they sat, the motionless reptile and the unwanted sweatpants. The tunnel entrance remained static for eleven minutes. Then she came out, slowly crawling from the dark, hands and knees shredded.

The old woman who had been drinking from the crayfish puddle.

She dragged herself along, maybe searching for water. At one point, she attempted to stand, but could not. The concrete being bone dry, she eventually writhed her way back to the black of the tunnel.

CANNI

Virginia

Below Dr. Robert's barn, a television showed amateur video of the Presidential nuptials.

Courtesy of YouTube channel, Bhong Rider.

Under the wall-mounted television, beside a soda machine, in the cafeteria of the Anderson-Daniele Research Center, a chess instructional was taking place.

"So," asked the lovely Dr. Martinez, "a knight can move two squares horizontally and one square vertically, or two squares vertically and one square horizontally?"

"That makes it seem harder," smiled the janitor. "Two up, one over. One up, two over."

"Right," she laughed. "Now, don't let me win."

"I'd never do that, cocksucker. Sorry, again."

DANIEL O'CONNOR

Air Force One

The president's jet soared above the clouds, crossing a country that still faced its greatest challenge. A new version of life had been birthed below them; a nation whose people were either consuming regular cannabis or locked away for the greater good.

In Minnesota and elsewhere, the wood frogs were coming to life. Winter had perished in the arms of spring. Seeds grew roots and unleashed their shoots up through the earth. They would not stay buried, much like fossils or time capsules.

Far below Air Force One, from the seaports and surf shops of San Diego to the body shops and barbershops of Brooklyn, much like the frogs and the seeds, there was an emergence.

The fortunate ones, like Teresa, had been cremated. But for the rest, it had begun.

The clatter of the caskets. The stirring of the slabs. The graveyard gait.

They had no agenda. No hunger for flesh. They craved nothing but water. The only harm they would do us is to dare lumber and crawl among the living. While rotting.

The hearts of the human race can be cold, like canni, or they can be brought to life, like the wood frogs, or the living dead.

In their spacious private quarters, just behind the nose and directly below the cockpit of Air Force One, as Rob, Cash, and the doctors enjoyed a lavish meal in the center of the plane, President Collins held hands with his new husband, yet his mind kept returning to the mantra repeated by the Iranian scientist.

You die as canni, no?

FOR A HEART DRAINED OF BLOOD, ONLY LOVE REMAINS

Acknowledgements

Daniel would like to thank everyone who has taken the time to read anything he has written, and especially those who've shared his work with others. Special thanks to Blood Bound Books for their hard work and dedication, and to Tell-Tale Press for valuable editing contributions.

ABOUT THE AUTHOR

Daniel O'Connor was orphaned at age six. He is a retired New York police officer. His first novel, *Sons of the Pope*, was praised by several NY Times best-selling authors and has a near five-star rating on both Amazon and Goodreads. Daniel's short stories have appeared in several anthologies and his writings on Canni.blog have been read by millions of people in over 200 countries. He lives near Las Vegas with his wife, Joanne, and daughters, Kelly and Jennifer.

Daniel dislikes the devaluation of music and the unnecessary use of shaky-cam.

Blog: Canni.blog
Twitter: @DanOVegas
Facebook.com/DanielOConnorAuthor/
Email: AuthorDanO@Gmail.com

"Please keep your inner canni in check, as will I."—Dan

Made in the USA
Middletown, DE
24 August 2019